AURAS
OF THE
FALLEN
STARS

MARA VAN NACHT

Auras of the Fallen Stars

This is a work of fiction. Names, characters, places, and incidents either are the product of the author's imagination or are used fictitiously. Any resemblance to actual persons, living or dead, events, or locales is entirely coincidental.

Cover designed by MiblArt
About the Author Photo Captured by Miss Cara Photography
Map illustrated by Dewi Hargreaves
Interior formatting illustrated and designed by The INKfluence

Hardcover ISBN 979-8-9931536-3-6
Paperback ISBN 979-8-9931536-6-7

www.authormaravannacht.com

*To anyone who's still working to build a life
your inner child would be proud of…*

*To anyone who's healing era began at the
formation of your frontal lobe…*

*To anyone who found themselves again the day
they picked up a book about fairies or magic
after a decade without reading…*

YOU'RE SAFE HERE

TRIGGER WARNINGS

Please consider the following list of potential triggering
topics before reading:

PTSD

SELF-HARM

OPEN DOOR EXPLICIT CONTENT

DROWNING

BURNS

BUILDING FIRES/ARSON

NONCONSENSUAL SLEEPING POWDER INGESTION

KIDNAPPING

GASLIGHTING

DEATH

EMOTIONAL MANIPULATION

THE GREAT FOREST
EVERGROOT MOUNTAINS
Thessarlan
Noctheris
LEONDELL
AMARION
LUNERIS LAGOON
THE IVORY HILLS
AURALIAN MOUNTAINS
Liravel
Lunnera
AURALIA
CURATIA
THE LOST DESERT
Aurevyn
Quinthold
ESHRADOR
Map of
CELESTERA
LIRAVEL SEA
N

Part One

NEBULA

The Convergence of Aeons is a week away. The winds tell me that a profound story prepares itself for our arrival at the temple; thus, I've prepared my finest scrolls and quills. The six have conversed about our unified demands and are prepared to confront the others about their transgressions. Celestera treats us all too well to bring genocide to its soils.

—An excerpt from Fallen Reginald's Journal

Year 36 A.L.

The sun's warmth chased away the lingering frost on the fields of Leondell as Reginald awoke before dawn on the 17th of May. He reveled in the sound of the distant caws and roars of the many beasts of his lands filling the morning air, and his room was warm from the crackling fire that his wife, Loree, had started in the corner fireplace. The flames cast dancing shadows on the walls and filled the space with a comforting warmth and the scent of burning oak.

He snuck out of the sheets and up behind his wife as she finished rubbing in her hand cream by the window, the hydrangea scent hanging in the air, and wrapped his arms around her waist. His hands wandered, and his lips graced her neck and shoulders as he gently pulled her back to the bed. "You didn't think I'd leave without properly saying goodbye, did you?" he whispered in her ear.

Today, he would join his fellow Fallen of the twelve provinces of Celestera at the Second Annual Convergence of Aeons, led by their Sovereign Fallen, Linea. He had anticipated this day for months with both unease and excitement—a day to address both the successes of their lands, and the morality of their decisions.

He was the first to arrive at the temple, the imposing stone steps rising before him to the odeum where the day's events would unfold. At least that is what he jotted in his leather-bound notebook, clean and ready for the transcripts of their day—he took his role as secretary during their gatherings very seriously.

A sharp gust of green wind nearly threw him off-balance, but Gabriel caught his arm and pulled him into a reassuring embrace. His friend full-body laughed with the enjoyment of nearly knocking him over with his entrance. "How are you supposed to capture every detail if you're on the ground, brother?" Then Gabriel raised his palm—and with it, the ground below Reginald's feet. Only a few inches, but enough to annoy.

Reginald shook his head, failing to hide his amusement at his friend's wielding of the lands, before stepping off the small raised patch of land Gabriel had created. "How you keep a wife is beyond me, but it's great to see you too."

Within an hour, thirteen of the original Fallen Stars had arrived at the temple.

"Reginald, it is lovely to see you. How is the family?" Linea's high-pitched and airy voice floated from behind him, and he turned to see her arms open wide for their embrace. A wave of mint came over him from her scented oils, but there was something off about her today. Her smile didn't meet her eyes, which darted between each of the Fallen as if she was monitoring their every move.

"Loree is taking the kids—" But Linea was already walking away before he could respond to her question.

He scanned the room for Niall, whom he found already seated on one of the stone pews facing the dais at the back of the temple. Niall could sense an aura. Niall could help.

Joining him on the bench, Reginald leaned in and asked, "Does she seem different today?"

His gaze fixated on Linea as she moved from Fallen to Fallen, Niall narrowed his eyes, assessing her energy before Reginald even sat down. "I can't sense her at all. I've never felt blocked like this." He pursed his lips, a line forming between his brows as he tried, unsuccessfully, to read Linea's intentions.

Reginald turned from his friend back to his notebook to jot down the worrisome phenomenon, and soon the entire roomful of people had joined them on the pews, ready to begin. Gabriel sat on Niall's other side, giving him a rough pat on the back in greeting.

Linea walked up the steps of the dais and turned when she approached the podium to address her gathering. Her long golden hair fell to her waist, and her flowing silver dress shimmered in the early-afternoon light. "Shall we?" she began, still wearing an expression that didn't match the welcoming tone of her voice. But then a look of sheer terror flashed across her face, and a ripple of apprehension spread through the room as all eyes turned to the temple's entrance.

A tall woman stood in the entrance, the intricate archway framing her form, which was silhouetted by the sun. She wore a flowing tan dress and had a face that commanded their attention. When she moved, it was with a preternatural smoothness that made Reginald realize she was not like the rest of them—fallen from the skies and still young for these lands.

"It's over, Linea." The woman's quiet words echoed through the temple, and their quorum looked amongst themselves for answers, but none came. Confusion hung heavy in the air.

Linea raised her hands to fight, but her usual powerful wisps of milky white magic didn't emit from her fingertips, and her eyes didn't glow. He watched as their Sovereign's facial features turned from fear to agony to defeat. The others' cries sounded around him, but he was in too much shock over what was occurring to consider a response, his calculating scholar's mind trying to take in every detail so he could record it correctly.

A large firm, hand gripped his bicep, calling his attention. "Reg!" Gabriel's eyes were wide with fear, and Reginald looked down to see a thin fog covering the ground. Their ankles were stuck within the haze that was holding them in place as if they were cemented in stone.

Linea walked backward until her back was against one of the limestone pillars of the temple. Another woman—no taller than

Reginald's chest and with a full head of luscious red curls—appeared out of thin air. She linked one arm through Linea's, and the two were gone.

The first woman, unfazed by the reactions of the Fallen, turned her umber-colored eyes on him. "Reginald, please join me. We have much to do."

She introduced herself as Titania, and then, to Reginald's dismay, told him why she was there. He wept as she unfolded for him the transgressions of the Fallen throughout the recent decades. His gift of truth confirmed each statement as she made it, some carving deeper wounds than others, and while he currently held many more questions than answers, there was one thing he knew for certain—the Fallen's time in Celestera was over.

TEN YEARS AGO. 8629 A.L.

"You're spending all your time across the river. Can you save some time for me soon?" Nova Whittley whines, her feet dangling off the edge of my bed where she sits.

"You sound pathetic. It's only four days a week, and someday I'm going to serve the most delicious food this city has ever tasted. Maybe I'll even serve the Fallen!" I call over my shoulder as I struggle to find enough light to pack my bag for my day in Quinthold. Nova made the bag for me out of dragon hide, claiming that, as destructible as my plans could be, I needed a bag that was indestructible to make it through. She equipped the bag with hidden pockets, locking buckles, and a waterproof and slash-proof exterior. And when I told her how I wanted to become a chef, she added a built-in blade sharpener. The bag now proves very useful for transporting several chef knives at a time.

Today, I'm meeting with a restaurateur who specializes in large kitchens and catering, Celesteran-renowned chef Vincenzo Cuoco. By day, he manages a local pub called The Goblet and has agreed to take me on as an apprentice. He's even letting me stay the night at the connecting inn a few evenings a week to help with the travel time across the river.

"Dream big, August, dream big…" Nova's voice trails off as she walks to my bedroom window to peer out at the skies. Her raven-black curls sit tucked behind her pointed ears, and taupe eyes frown back at her in the glass. "Be careful today, the waves on the river are crashing. Even the sun has hidden from this storm rolling in."

I join her at the window to assess the conditions. She's right—I can smell the imminent rain in the air, and the sky is a murky shade of gray. I point to a row of buildings across the river, only an outline from this far away. "See that port? See the buildings lined up behind it? I'll be right there. You can just look out the window and see me. I'll do the same. We can even wave. Each day when the sun reaches its peak in the sky? It'll give me something to look forward to between courses. And don't worry, I'll bring you along on my ride to fortune and fame. You can be my assistant, my right hand, the general to my army of servants," I say, extending my arm out toward her. Nova accepts the embrace, wrapping both her arms around me and squeezing tightly.

She has always had enough confidence for the both of us. When I had a crush in school, she was the one to sneak compliments about me when they were nearby. If I need an outfit for any occasion, it's Nova sewing me a custom bag to match. She taught me how to line my eyes with kohl, how to wear my hair so it's not a frizzy mess after a day in the kitchen. But most importantly, she's taught me what it means to love.

Sometimes I wonder if, for once, she's jealous of me—of the fact that I am making a name for myself in the big city, while she stays here sewing and building in her family's store.

"Promise?"

"Promise," I reply, just standing there hugging my best friend. She's stood by me since before I can even remember. Nova and her family provided shelter, physically and emotionally, when I needed it most. We even introduce each other as sisters when people ask. I owe them everything for who I am today. Four days apart at a time is the longest we've ever gone without seeing each other, so I can't blame her for pushing back.

She turns back to the window. "I wasn't kidding about that storm, though. Please be careful."

"I will, okay," I say, drawing out the second syllable. "I really have to go now or the ferry will leave without me."

"Wait!" she yells at me when I'm two steps out the door. I turn to see what I've forgotten, but she just adds, "May the Celestial Mother bless your ventures." A small smile lifts the corners of her lips as she hints at our favorite childhood fable.

"You as well, my sister," I respond, hand over my heart, before taking off running for the ferry.

The Liravel River that runs through the center of Quinthold is a beautiful sight, but it makes traveling from one side of the city to the other a lengthy task. Today, though, it takes twice as long to cross. My teeth chatter, and my fingers, tinged blue from cold, shake as I hold on to the boat's railing—wind and rain threatening to tip us before we can make it to shore. And just when I think my hands may freeze to the side of the boat, we make it to the dock. I wobble as take my first few steps on land, my body and stomach still rocking viciously back and forth from the motion of the waves.

The port station is open, so I take a moment to rest there and dry off before walking into town. Several patrons have the same idea; they all huddle inside, as far from the door that keeps swinging open with the wind as possible. Once I clear the water from my eyes, I see a bench toward the back of the room—mostly empty besides a man sitting to one side, hunched over and staring at the ground from under his hood. The bench is large enough for me to fit on the other side of him.

Please let him be human, or friendly. Preferably both, I think to myself as I make my way toward him, my shoes squeaking and water sloshing out the sides with each step.

He looks up when I'm a few feet away, and *Fallen,* do I wish I had chosen a different bench.

Are all men from the city this attractive?

"Is it okay if I sit here?" I ask, voice cracking through the broken words coming through my chattering teeth.

He nods, moving to the very end of the bench, gesturing to the open space, as he says, "Of course. I can move if that would make you more comfortable. My sea training got canceled, so I'm waiting out the storm too." He looks out the window to his left, frowning at the dark skies.

I collapse onto the bench, sitting on my hands in an attempt to will warmth back into my numb fingers. "No, no need to move. I'm August, by the way," I choke out, too cold for embarrassment over my broken sentences to sink in.

"Blaine. What brings beauty like yours to this side of the river?" He looks at me through a half cringe, half grin, and I just know he's holding back a laugh at the wet, shaking mess that I am. "Here, please take this before you catch a cold," he offers, stretching out the arm holding his Advisory jacket. First rank—I can tell from the stripe on the sleeve. That explains the sea training.

"Th-thank-k you," I say, shrugging the Advisory jacket on over my shoulders, moving my hands to hug myself beneath it. His warmth lingering in the fibers instantly soothes my numb core. I wouldn't normally borrow a stranger's jacket, but I also never thought I would be this cold. My eyes close instinctively, and I focus on pretending I'm sitting next to a fire on a warm summer night.

I hadn't realized he had been watching me the entire time, but he clears his throat as he angles himself in my direction. His boyish smile and high cheekbones instantly warm any gaps in my middle that the jacket might have missed. I attempt to meet his gaze, but somehow I can't pull my eyes from his biceps, which are on display under his tight wetsuit.

Maybe I should just become a chef for the Advisory? I muse.

He is waiting, August, use your words, an internal voice of reason reminds me.

My eyes snap up, along with my lower jaw, as I blink twice, calling reality back into focus. "Um, sorry, what did you ask me?"

"I was asking what brought you to this side of the river?" he repeats, slower this time, as if the speed at which he originally asked was what distracted me.

"Oh." I huff a laugh at the simple question that previously stalled my brain. "Work. I'm going to be a chef, or, hopefully. I'm training."

He gives me another flash of that heart-stopping smile and scoots about two inches closer, his brows raised. "Maybe you can show me sometime?"

I nod but turn my face to stare at my lap. I have never before considered potential hypothermia to be a good thing, but currently I'm clinging to it as the excuse for how red I know my cheeks are.

I have to change the subject.

"So the Advisory, huh? What made you choose that?"

"Girls dig men with power." He wiggles his eyebrows and gives me an animated, sly grin, showing that he knows how cheesy that line was, but wanted to try it anyway. I burst into laughter at his ridiculous face.

"Try again," I get out between biting my lip to keep a straight face.

"Okay, fine, but I tried the one way, so you asked for it." He clears his throat again, and this time he's the one who stares at a spot on the floor between his feet, hand reaching up to rub the back of his neck. "I know how ridiculous I sound saying this—and you probably wouldn't want to share a bench with a man who feels this way—but it's the most glory a human can achieve. I just want to be known for something, you know."

I do.

But I don't get the chance to answer.

A flash of blinding light erupts through the windows, the roar that follows shaking the ground beneath us. People throughout the room cover their heads as glass shatters, spraying the room with shards. Water bursts through every broken window and door until there's nowhere to go—until there's no air left in the room. I'm completely submerged, and we're both thrown against the wall behind us in the undertow. My head and ears ring with the impact.

I look to my right where light comes through the now missing port wall, streaming inside in jagged rays as the light outside refracts through the water. A few others swim their way toward the opening, but Blaine reaches for me. I reach back, my arms struggling to escape the Advisory jacket, heavy in the water, but something pulls me back. My bag is weighing me down. No—not weighing me down, stuck. My bag is stuck on the bench where we were just sitting, its strap caught on a broken piece of the wood.

I can't leave it. It's my piece of Nova. It has my knives. Everything that I am is within that bag. I turn from Blaine to the bag, then back to Blaine—my decision made. I dive down against the pressure, accidentally kicking him as I try to propel myself. Despite the blow, Blaine is faster. He wraps his arms around me, tugging us backward and forcing us to the surface. I point at my bag, thrashing against his hold, darkness threatening to take over, the ringing in my ears growing louder with each second. My chest aching for breath, I refuse to leave the bag.

"AUGUST, AUGUST, CAN YOU HEAR ME? AUGUST!"

I lurch at the sound of my name, gasping for air but only finding water.

This is how it will end—drowning in front of an attractive man.

My gasps turn to choking as I lean to the side and empty my stomach of salt water and, apparently, a small piece of seaweed. My ribs are sore. I grab my middle, wincing. It hurts to breathe, each rise and fall of my chest causing me to wince. He must have done compressions to save me.

Blaine crouches in front of me, panting for breath, soaking wet from head to toe. Just like me, just like everyone else—the panic, still rampant around us, is unsettling.

"My bag!" I scramble to my knees as I remember what I was last doing, looking for my belongings. Faster than I should in my condition, but I don't care.

"Here, here—it came to the surface behind us. I grabbed it for you."

How could I have forgotten?

Nova made the bag to always float, no matter its contents. She wouldn't explain her method, but she's always been a gifted inventor, which is why her family business needs her back home. I smile, remembering how clever my friend is. Grabbing the bag from Blaine's outstretched hand, I give him a simple, "Thanks. Looks like someone upset Beryl today, huh." The Sovereign Descendant of Galevarr has been known to cause catastrophic storms in reaction to the smallest inconveniences.

"You could say that." Blaine's tone is full of despair, and he's staring out at the water with a grim look on his face—so at odds with the smile he used on me earlier.

I stand, gaining my bearings, and realize the thunderstorm may be over, but I'm witnessing something far greater. Following Blaine's gaze, I peer across the water to where I should be able to see my street, where Nova is, waiting to wave to me.

Only it's gone. Water is all that remains. My half of Quinthold is just…gone. I drop back to my knees, wrap my arms around myself, and weep.

DECENDANTS WITH THE POWERS OF STRENGTH AND WAR WILL DISPLAY THEIR CAPABILITIES EARLY AND OFTEN. THOSE WITH POWERS OF THE MIND, HOWEVER, WILL NEED A STRATEGIC PLAN TO DISENGAGE.

CONFIDENTIAL: REGULATORY CODES OF THE ADVISORY, ARTICLE 17, SECTION 3, TACTICS IN DEFENSE

Present Day

"I'm headed to the market and then The Goblet. Are you coming?" Our apartment isn't large, a studio above a bookstore with a view of the Liravel Sea. One of six units upstairs in a large building in the business district of Quinthold, the capital of the province of Eshrador. But Blaine is in the bathing room, so I raise my voice a bit for him to hear me through the door. "I need to stock up on sharpening stones and leathers before the ball."

I've been invited to cater the Advisory Ball in a week, to be held at a prestigious seaside estate. The event will be the largest and most high profile of my career, and I intend for every detail to land flawlessly. Blaine told me for years that he would help me land the gig, but I never wanted his help. I want my food to speak for itself. He, of course, will attend as a guest, and if I have my way, I'll be able to sneak a dance or two. It all depends on the competence level of my staff for the evening.

Blaine exits the bathroom in silence, finding anywhere to look but at me as he walks over to join me by the kitchen worktop where I sip my coffee from my favorite mug. Blaine had it made for me during Quinthold's Celebration of Colors Festival. The handle looks like a knife and makes me feel dangerous, like I'm breaking a rule by holding the blade.

Today's coffee beans are sourced from the Ivory Hills, the province northwest of Eshrador, and grown on a field shared with papayas and surrounded by banana trees for natural shade. The sweetness of the fruits comes through in each sip—whether or not Blaine agrees. I don't dare add any milk to this brew so that I can savor it, though a sprinkle of cinnamon contrasts nicely. I pretend I'm in those fields now, closing my eyes to ignore what Blaine will say next.

"I would love to pick out sharpening tools with you, sweetie." He presses in from behind me, one hand next to mine on the worktop and the other lightly grasping my hip, and lays a chaste kiss on the top of my head. Per usual, he's focused on the part of my request that has nothing to do with Vincenzo, The Goblet, or ultimately the Resistance.

I turn to see him leaning against the front door, head cocked just slightly to the side. His dark curls, cropped close to his head, are still slightly damp from getting ready, and he wears one of his off-duty casual leather jackets.

"Shall we?" The grin on his face is the same as the one that made me fall for him over ten years ago in the port station after Beryl's attack, an event we now refer to as the Break, but it's forced now. "Unless you want to turn back around and continue leaning on the counter, the view is magnificent from over here."

I suppose he's still trying to win me over. The difference now is he's not trying to get me to love him, he's trying to get me to leave the Resistance. I can't stand to be the reason that smile fades, fake or not, so I simply take one last sip of my coffee, grab my dragon-hide bag Nova made me, along with his hand, and follow him out the front door. He'll bring it up on his own at some point, and we can commence fighting once more when that happens.

We head down the stairs and Blaine waves to the bookstore owner behind the counter through the store window as we turn the corner onto the busy street. The store is great for my reading habit, but awful for my reclusive personality. The owner always wants to talk so much.

Nicola? Natalia? Something like that.

She sees Blaine and her eyes light up, widening in excitement, while she holds up a finger, prompting us to stop and wait. The bubbly blonde skips out of the store, and I crane my neck to see if I can count how many people are walking toward the market—so much for getting there before the rush. Pushing my shoulder into Blaine's bicep, I give him a look that lets him know I'm annoyed.

"I was kind of in a hurry," I whisper to him while we wait on the sidewalk outside the entrance to the store. He narrows his eyes in annoyance right back at me. I hate how friendly he is sometimes. The bell jingles when the door opens, snapping our attention back to the shop owner.

"August! I was hoping I would see you soon. Wherever did you get your coffee beans from? I can smell them from my store, and I just have to try some for myself." She leans in the doorway of her store, wearing an adorable, anticipatory grin, her brows high on her face.

"I imported them for some events I'm catering soon; they're from the Ivory Hills."

"We'll bring you a jar when we return this evening," Blaine interjects, showing her the smile that I prefer only be directed at me.

"Oh, thank you!" she squeals as she jumps from the doorway to wrap her arms around Blaine and me at the same time. "That is so nice of you!"

"Okay. Okay," I say, tapping her back with what little mobility my outer arm has. I try again: "We need to go now; we have a busy day." Anything to encourage her to loosen her clutch on us. We were already behind schedule to get to The Goblet on time, and this stop has not only cost us minutes, but now my precious coffee beans as well.

Goodbye banana notes in my daily vice.

"Of course, see you later!" She releases us, a wide grin on her face, before turning back into the store. I frown at her retreating form.

She almost makes it hard to be mad about the coffee beans.

When we're out of range of being seen through the store windows, I playfully slap at Blaine's arm. "And what if I don't want to share my coffee beans, hmm?"

"Yeah, August, well, sometimes you have to consider those around you. Sometimes making sacrifices is the right thing to do." He pauses, turning to face me. Passersby give us a wide berth, sensing his change in mood, hearing his rising voice.

I lean in closer and place a hand on his arm, meeting his gaze. "Okay. I hear you. Can we not do this here? Just forget the coffee beans, please?" I've lowered my voice, so hopefully only he can hear me. I don't give a shit what anyone else in this town thinks of me or us, but I really don't want to fight with Blaine right now. We haven't gone more than two nights recently without yelling at each other, and I really don't want to be at odds going into the ball.

Gently, I tug on his arm to keep us moving. He relinquishes his firm stance and follows me on the second tug, but I'm close to losing him, I can tell. The market is only two more blocks away. "Should I make a fresh spring salad, or roasted potatoes and carrots for the ball?" If I can direct our conversation back to normalcy, I may be able to get him back. Looping my arm through his, I look up at him, awaiting his response.

"Salad. You shouldn't do potatoes if you're planning to make your lasagna," he responds, tone flat.

I knew that, of course, but I had to ask him something. "What would I do without you?"

Knowing it's rhetorical, he takes the opportunity to ignore me. He is too much of a gentleman to overtly shake off my hold on his arm, but his strides pick up length and pace, making it hard for me to keep up. But I do. And I don't let go, as if I can hold off our fighting with my grip on his arm. We walk in silence for another moment and finally turn the corner to enter the market.

"I'll meet you back here at the entrance." Blaine pulls from my clutch, and I'm staring down his form fading into the crowds before I can even respond.

Have fun. I'll miss you too, I say silently to myself.

Stalls draped in colorful fabrics stretch as far as I can see down the wide stone alley, and flags of the twelve provinces of Celestera hang on lines strewn from wall to wall. There is only one way into and out of the market, and tall stone buildings stand on both sides, turning that path into a bottleneck of people entering and exiting the chaos.

One would think that years in busy kitchens would have accustomed me to crowded environments like the market, but if anything, they have done the opposite. Crowds mean people, and in my thirty-one years alive, I have only met a handful of those that have shown they're worth my time.

Unfortunately for me, though, my taste in high-quality blades requires me to come to the market, where I can gain access to vendors with magic capable of sourcing fine metals and materials. It's not that humans can't create a knife of equal caliber, it just takes much longer. And crowds aside, the alley smells like piss once you get past the food stalls.

"Anything good today?" I call as I approach my first stop. The human couple who runs the stall began a sourcing trade for fine materials after the Break, hoping they could glean information from along the coastlines during their travels. Here, I can usually find quality materials to sew new aprons, caps, table linens—they even have a scrap bin, which is a real gem for me because they provide me with free rags for cleaning the kitchen.

I don't need any linens today, and don't have any messages to share with them from the Resistance, but I never miss a chance to say hello. After the Break, I knew nothing about sewing—Nova had always created or made anything I needed—but they didn't hesitate to teach me how to do it myself.

"I've got a lovely silk from Auralia!" she squeals, clapping her hands in excitement. Grabbing a bin from behind her, she shuffles through until she pulls out a thin bolt of black silk—the fabric falling off the roll like liquid.

My urge to touch the material takes me back to being a child, needing to touch anything that shone, sparkled, or had a different texture than surrounding items. I sometimes still have to tell my adult self that it's okay to touch the pretty materials, no one is going to pull my arm away or slap my wrist, so I let myself run my fingers through the delicate fabric. Even sitting in the sun, it's cool to the touch.

"Magnificent," I say under my breath, wondering what it would feel like to wear a gown of this material.

"Authentic Auralian silk," she states, staring at the material and wearing a full smile, as proud of her offering as I am in awe of its beauty. "It's rare. I haven't been able to confirm, but I've heard it can—"

She's cut off by the sound of a tent collapsing nearby, the crates underneath crashing as they fall to the ground. Three men are cornering the tent owner, but I'm too far away to hear what they're saying. Marketgoers avoid the area, squeezing through the tents on the other side of the walkway to avoid the aisle, and I take the air of panic as my sign to leave.

"It was good to see you, but I've gotta run. See you next month!" I call, already ambling away.

The fights are breaking out early this month.

Quinthold is one of the larger integrated communities, meaning humans and descendants live and work here alike, and because of its prime location on the sea, sellers come from far and wide each month to have the chance to set up their tents in this market. Those with greater strength usually win the competition for new spots. It's why Advisory members stand on patrol at the entrance, as well as post up at various points throughout the market—not that it's helped deter anyone.

I don't slow down till I'm at my next stop—the metals tent. The owner is busy interacting with another patron, so I start at the bin of sharpening stones. The man who runs this tent was visiting Quinthold on the day of the Break and found himself trapped here forever, just like me. Lucky for him, he essentially guaranteed himself a monopoly on the local steel market.

My small hands lead me to prefer the smaller stones that are often ignored by others, and I make myself busy studying them until he finishes with the other customer. Though I don't miss his frequent, quick glances in my direction to ensure I'm not stealing his precious goods.

Fallen forbid a descendant to trust that a human isn't going to rob them.

I suppose I don't blame them for thinking this way. Humans only exist because evil overcame good in our familial lines, but I think the curse of mortality and lack of any magical powers for the rest of our bloodline should stand as punishment enough. Any Descendant that voices an actual concern over human existence usually complains about our preferential treatment. They somehow believe that our getting to simply exist in this world is too much.

I think this man's problem, though, is that he's just an ass.

"Oy, what do you want?" He finally turns my way completely, the other patron having vacated their spot. On some level, I respect that this male has sold to me several times before and still treats me the same as he did the first day I approached his booth. We don't bother to learn each other's names, and in that way we understand each other—this is transactional only.

I dig out my final few red diamonds from my bag, the favored currency of his home province of Molvaria and place them for review on the table alongside the three sharpening stones I've chosen from the bin. I have been holding on to these diamonds for over a year, making do with old and borrowed sharpening tools as needed.

For the Advisory Ball, though, I'm sacrificing the last of my Molvarian currency. I'll have to figure out a plan to replenish my stores soon. I enjoy knowing that I have currency available to purchase anything I may need at any moment—should the worst occur. Nova made the pouch I carry it all in: fourteen pockets, one for each currency of the twelve provinces of Celestera, as well as silver and gold—many of the pockets are empty at the moment.

"I will also need a good leather," I add as he stares down at my offering.

He looks at the table, up at me, then back at the table. His knuckles flex once on the grip he has on the edge before he pushes himself off and crosses his arms, staring me down with beady red eyes. "I'll need more than this if you want a leather too."

My eyes flare in annoyance. "This exact amount has gotten me more than this in the past. I'm making a fair trade here," I say as confidently as I can, standing my ground. These may be the most words the male and I have ever exchanged. I've never needed to barter with him in the past, and something tells me he wouldn't push this if I had Blaine next to me—like I normally do.

"Quality metal is becoming more and more rare. I can't produce as many blades as I used to." He stands firm, though the edge in his voice lessens slightly as his chin dips and he looks at the table again.

He's struggling.

Molvaria was one of the six provinces lost to the Break, so he certainly hasn't been sourcing his steel from there for the past decade. Wherever he found a supply near here must be running out.

I clench my teeth and look around, wishing again Blaine was with me. He might have some diamonds on him I wasn't aware of. "This is all I have."

Fallen, I hope that didn't sound like pleading.

"Two gold coins, and I can sell you the leather. Final offer." He turns to pick up the leather from the table behind him, and even from several feet away, I can tell the leather is soft and worn—used.

"Two gold coins for a *used* leather? Have you lost your mind?" My hands smack the table in front of me. Screw composure. This male has gone insane if he thinks he can ask that price for used goods.

"Have a good day, then." He collects the stones and pushes the diamonds back my direction.

Pride or not, I will not serve inferior cuisine next week at the ball.

"Wait, fine, fine, here." I grab the two gold coins from my bag and chuck them onto the table so hard they bounce. What does he even need Molvarian currency for, anyway? It's not like he can run home and use it.

He doesn't react to my display, simply says, "Until next time, then."

Fuck. Him.

I stuff the stones and worn leather into my bag and make my way to my final booth, hoping to get to The Goblet as quickly as I can to down an ale and drown the anger ringing in my ears. My feet drag, and I almost trip on a rock stuck in the grooves of the stone street. A couple of women stare as I audibly grunt my frustration at the ground, but I don't care anymore.

Fucking descendants.

My final stop is a nondescript stall between two of the busiest booths of the market, which sell custom jewelry and spice blends. Bland spices, if you ask me, but it's not my cooking being subjected to their use. The woman working the booth doesn't look up from the book she's reading to pass the time until I am directly in front of her.

"River, whatcha looking for today?" she asks in her singsong voice, using my Resistance alias.

We use code names in our communications to avoid exposure if captured. Vincenzo gave me the name River years ago due to surviving the Break and not drowning in the Liravel River, now the Liravel Sea. Vincenzo, Blaine, and Vincenzo's partner, Norris, are the only ones that know both of my identities.

"How are the eggs this time around, Ruby?" I ask, my frustration subsiding at knowing I'm finally participating in the Resistance agenda—my favorite part of any day. Ruby raises chickens a little ways from here, and even though I couldn't care less about eggs today, her produce is usually quite high quality.

"Fresh as always. The usual?"

"That would be great, thank you."

She grabs two cartons of eggs from the crate and, to anyone watching, I hand her two silver coins in exchange. Though when our hands meet, I push a scroll up the sleeve of her tunic with my thumb. She raises that arm to adjust her red hair, which I assume is the source of her alias, and allows the scroll to fall completely into her billowy sleeve. Nodding her head once, she sits back down and opens up her book to where she had paused—as ready to move on with her day as I am mine.

Finished with everything I needed to accomplish, I weave my way back into the crowds and head to the front of the market, hoping to find Blaine waiting. Once there, I look around but don't see him. Leaning against the stone wall of one of the adjacent buildings, I wait for him, hoping it's not long, hoping he's let off some steam since we parted ways only a bit ago. Thankfully, The Goblet is only a few doors down, though I don't want to go on ahead since Blaine specifically said he'd meet me here.

I jump from my spot on the wall when a man shoves past me at a jog. Even from here, I can hear a commotion breaking out deep in the market. I step back out into the street to assess the source, happy to be out of that crowd myself. This fight sounds bigger than the one from earlier. People closer to the entrance yell, and more and more begin to frantically exit the market in waves. Whatever is happening must be bad if people are giving up their market time altogether.

A sound, almost like an explosion, echoes through the alley, and smoke billows from the back. The armed Advisory members take this as their cue to investigate, and they make their way against the crowds toward the chaos.

"Ma'am, I'm going to need you to leave the area." A booming voice breaks through my trance as I stand on my toes, trying to see over the people escaping, hoping I can find Blaine.

I turn to see a member of the Advisory. "Blaine Woodson is in there. Tell him I went to The Goblet." Blaine is high enough up in Advisory rank now that any local member would know his name.

He nods once, and that's all the confirmation I need before I turn and make my way to my next stop. Blaine is probably playing hero and trying to help with the fights, even on his day off.

I make it all of four steps before I stop, frozen in place. Flames engulf The Goblet.

You will learn to respect the kitchen above the food, the craft, or the customer, or risk your environment dictating your results. A clean, organized, and well cared for kitchen is your most valuable ingredient in any dish you create.

—Vincenzo Cuoco to August Monroe on
day one of her apprenticeship

Anyone exiting the market needs only one quick glance in this direction to see the smoke billowing from the roof and upper windows of The Goblet, alerting them to choose an alternative route to safety. My mind doesn't give me that option or advice, though, as I watch the pub I've spent time in at least five days a week for the past decade go up in flames.

A chunk of the burning roof falls into the building, and embers spray off the debris in all directions as if sending warning flares to anyone in the vicinity. I turn to look back toward the market, at the smoke billowing out of the alley, and a sinking feeling settles in my core.

I can either wait for Blaine, possibly trapped in the market, or sprint to The Goblet, where Vincenzo might be in trouble. My boyfriend, a combat and defense expert, leads the Advisory's aerial wing and trains fire-breathing dragons, but he's without his mount, Teliquis, today and unarmed.

Vincenzo is the safest chef I know: his kitchen is always clean, he never forgets to put out a flame, and a pail of water sits in the corner. But the Resistance operates from the basement of The Goblet, and the escape plan if compromised is to light the place on fire and flee.

And neither of them are fireproof.

Everyone around me blurs in my peripheral vision, and I feel dizzy—the screams are coming from every direction. I fall forward a step when a woman, dragging along her young, scared child, bumps my shoulder to pass by me. The child and I stare at each other for a long moment, both trapped in time.

Move August, you have to move, a voice separate from mine tells me, catching up to my thoughts.

I don't remember deciding, but my body takes off at a sprint toward The Goblet.

The front door to the establishment already hangs on its hinges— heat rolls off it, like from the openings to my ovens. I hold my palm in front of the wood, trying to find a spot that isn't too hot to touch, burning the tips of my fingers the moment I try.

Fuck.

I sprint to the side of the building, jumping to peer through a window, but all I can see is smoke and an orange-red haze pulsing through the flames.

My bag.

I hurry back to the front door. Nova made my bag fireproof, so I slide my arms through the straps and hold it to my front, using it to help push the burning wood to the side so I can peek in. Smoke escapes the pub as soon as I give it an opening. The onslaught of smoke blinds me, and I throw my arm across my face trying to block as much as I can, waiting till I can open my eyes again.

I turn my neck to take one last deep breath of clean air before pushing all the way inside. "Vinny? Norris? Hello?" I use my held breath to shout the pleas for existence toward the rear of the building. A high-backed chair, which normally sits at the front window overlooking the street, cracks as it crumbles at my side, and I gasp—breaking out in a fit of coughing as ash fills my lungs.

Think, August, think.

I squat to the ground and spare thirty seconds to grab a rag from my bag to tie around my face to breathe through. It's not perfect, but it will give me a few more minutes alive inside to find them.

I clench my fists to avoid placing my palms directly on the hot floor and crawl toward the back. The longer I can stay close to it, the better the air quality will be. Blaine taught me that.

A shard of glass beneath my arm slices through my sensitive skin, making me hiss through my teeth. I wore pants today, which now protect my legs, but I'm certain my forearms will be shredded and burned if I make it out of here. This linen rag already feels as if it's melting onto my face.

A ceiling beam cracks above me, and I look toward the sound just in time to roll to the side and cover my head as it comes crashing down. My bag strapped to my back has limited my range, and it only allows me to roll to my side. I barely make it far enough away. The charred beam still glows red internally in spots, as if it has a heartbeat all its own, the embers sparking only inches from my face.

There are only three ways in and out of The Goblet. The first is through the front door where I came in. The second is through the side door that connects it to a small inn, frequently used by travelers coming through for the market—where I lived for a year after the Break. Only members of the Resistance are privy to the third, located under a floor panel behind the bar.

A decade's worth of intel is in the basement of this pub, and it would incriminate dozens of people here in Quinthold and hundreds across the remaining half of Celestera if found. Also via the hidden basement door is an escape tunnel that connects to Norris's pub, Quinthold's Fare, a few doors down. The flames dancing through the service window tell me the fire started in the kitchen, though, so I cling to the thought that this wasn't a bust.

"Vinny!" I risk raising my face from the floor to call again to the fiery void—begging a Fallen I've conspired against since the Break for a response.

Continuing to crawl, I take small filtered gasps through my makeshift mask, my lungs burning with each one. Ten more feet is all that stands between me and the doorway to the kitchen, and I have to pass the bar to get there.

My heart beats a little harder, pounding against my ash-filled lungs as I approach, and I close my eyes, preparing myself for what I may see. I pause before turning to look, needing a moment, but when I finally do, the dark runner still covers the hidden door.

When Blaine's Advisory partner died after a tragic fall from their dragon during a training exercise, he told me that seeing the macabre scene was the hardest part. He said his dreams showed his friend screaming and falling helplessly from the sky, while he remained too far away to assist. The echoing sound of his partner's body hitting the mountain haunted him for months. He told me he watched the life drain from his friend's eyes as he bled out on that cliffside. He told me he wished he had never known his friend—because you can't be haunted by memories you don't have.

And I told him he was wrong.

I spent so much time reminding Blaine that his partner was lucky to have such a brave friend like him by his side.

I know now, though. I was wrong.

I know this with full certainty as I peer into the kitchen, and a single pair of legs are all I can see from behind the large worktop in the center of the room.

I scramble across the floor, half running, half crawling the final several feet to where the body lies. Every part of me that touched the floor tingles in pain, numb from the burns. I round the corner, and my tunnel vision takes over. It's Vincenzo, unconscious.

NO. No, no, no, this can't be happening.

A sound, somewhere between a sob and a scream, escapes me as I fall to my knees. Two fingers on his neck, checking for a pulse. While present, it's slow. I have to get him out of here. I have to do something, anything. As I attempt to lift him, my shoe slips and my knee slams to the floor. I won't be able to lift him on my own, but I cannot leave him. I will not leave him.

"Wake up, please wake up," I plead, grasping his shoulders and lightly shaking him, but he doesn't move.

I try again, moving my arms farther underneath him to grip his sides, only to fall backward when I try to stand, my ass hitting the floor when my feet slide from underneath me. My skin stretches and stings where it catches on his shirt, as if it might rip with the friction, and I clench my teeth through the pain. Tears stream and sizzle on my cheeks before they can even fall. Sweat beads down the back of my neck, off the ends of my braid, and spreads across my palms.

I look around me, at the kitchen I learned to cook in—from the man lying next to me—to the doorway to the bar and dining room. It can't just go up in flames. My world doesn't get to just vanish in front of my eyes—not again.

A cabinet, only a few feet away, crashes to the ground as the flames surrounding it swell, sending a barrage of ash in our direction.

"Tell me what to do!" I scream at him through the rag still covering my face.

I summon every ounce of strength left in me to try once more, this time trying to secure him to me using the straps from Nova's bag. Kneeling next to him, I raise his torso into a seated position and place my bag on his back while passing his limp arms through the straps. Then I spread his legs slightly and turn my back to him, squatting in the space I just created between them. I loop my arms through the same straps, pulling Vincenzo's front flush to my back. His head lolls to my shoulder, and I tug the straps firmly up my arms before reaching around the outsides of his upper thighs and grasping my hands underneath.

I grunt through the pain, but I find the strength to stand. Vincenzo's slack weight on my back threatens to make my knees buckle at any moment.

"Don't you dare give up, Vinny," I whisper to myself as I take my first slow step, hunched over to hold his body in place. I feel my mask slipping down my face, but I can't fix it, and I watch as it falls to the floor. My face sears from the sweat that coated my cheeks under the mask. I can hear my skin singeing from the smoke, but I keep going. My muscle memory will have to take over to find our way out.

I don't see the raised floorboard a few steps out of the kitchen, and I catch it with the front of my shoe. There's nothing I can do to stop the momentum of us tumbling forward. My sore knees hit the floor first, and instinctively, my palms splay to catch the rest of my fall, but I'm crushed under the weight of Vincenzo on my back. My chin cracks against the hardwood planks as I bite through my tongue, blood filling my mouth. Any air that was left in my lungs is expelled, and my body acts to replenish it. The resulting gasp, as shallow as it is, burns.

The bag straps bind us tightly together. I can't breathe or see with him lying on top of me. The room spins, the edges of my vision litter with stars. Never have I felt so hopeless.

I lose my hearing first, a faint ringing in my ears rising until it's all I hear. Even my last attempt at calling for help is absent to my hearing. Next is touch. The pads of my fingers, then my arms, then my torso start to feel fuzzy and numb. Then comes sight. It turns from black to hazy, with spots of white. I bury my face in the floorboard and succumb to the fumes.

You can trust healers.

They may be the only light remaining in our dim world.

—An excerpt from the journal of Vincenzo Cuoco

Waking up in the healer's center feels like waking up in a children's classroom. Every wall and surface is a different color, and paintings of suns shining, rainbows, and beautiful creatures line the walls. Different-colored glass makes up the windows, casting a unique hue in each room. I'm in a turquoise room today.

The colors represent the healers' vow to rehabilitate all citizens from all provinces. Curatia, the home of healing magic, is the only province where descendants can cross borders freely without declaring themselves for this reason. I remember learning in school that there isn't a single documented healer known to have refused the vow, or to have broken it.

But why am I here?

My heavy eyelids feel like sandpaper, and I flinch when I try to raise my arm to wipe at my dry eyes.

Burns.

I recognize the feeling well from the countless encounters with hot liquids and wood-fired ovens in the kitchen I've worked in. Moving any part of my body, even an inch, hurts, like my skin has been pulled as tight as it goes, as if it will crack if I stretch it farther. My breathing comes in short, audible gasps, each breath a struggle to reach my lungs, a sensation like rocks are grinding down my throat.

I lay in the bed a few moments, attempting to recollect my last memories, but my breath catches on the need to let out a hoarse cough, and the pain that answers has me curling onto my side, wrapping my arms around my ribs, ignoring the stretching skin—crinkling at my joints—to condense my internal organs. I find a cool section of the sheets where I haven't spent an unknown amount of time resting and nuzzle into the soft fabric as silent tears stream down my face.

"You're awake." Blaine rushes over from somewhere else in the room, crouching to eye level by my side.

He's alive.

The sight of him jolts my memory, and I remember the last time I saw him at the entrance to the market. His brows knit together as he looks at me with a mix of relief and remorse, but also like I might fade away in front of his eyes.

"Hi." The singular word comes out barely above a whisper, but it's all I can offer.

He reaches out to embrace my hands, clenched and tightly wrapped around my middle, and I flinch at the touch. "Let me get help." His voice and features are soft as he stands and hurries to the door.

An older woman wearing the traditional healer's magenta jumpsuit comes into the room. It's the last thing I remember before sleep takes me once more.

I turn my stiff neck to the side to look toward the window. Blaine sleeps on a couch against the wall under the window. Good. The moment he wakes up, he'll tell me what I already know. For now, I pretend that the world is the same—that it didn't all fall apart around me. Vincenzo is alive. The Resistance is intact. Blaine and I are okay.

I'm alive. I repeat these affirmations to myself a few times, watching Blaine sleep.

His hair is oily and tangled, like he's spent several moments with his fingers knotted through his locks. I haven't seen circles that dark under his eyes since he went on a five-day trip to rescue Advisory members from a mission in the Curatian Desert. I estimate I've been here for at least three days, given his state.

I flex my fingers and toes, ensuring I have feeling in my extremities. The healer must have been able to repair my skin while I slept, but then I attempt a deep breath through my nose and finally break. My breath catches, and a fit of coughs echoes in response, as if my lungs are still full of the ash from the fire. I don't fold in on myself this time, though my rib cage digs into my core, reverberating to my spine, the pain bearable if I clench my teeth.

At least there is air to breathe, I tell myself.

The bed shifts, and a slight chill settles on my sensitive skin as Blaine lifts the plush purple blanket to slide under it. He rolls to his side to face me and leaves just an inch of space between us, careful not to touch, wary of my state, laying his arm across me on top of the blanket. He uses enough care that I'm not in pain, though my fragile skin tingles momentarily while it adjusts to the warmth and pressure.

I go to open my mouth to say something, but nothing comes. What is there to say?

"Not yet. Just this," he says, nuzzling into the pillow beside me. *He's alive.*

I shift to lay my hand on his above the blanket, turning my head toward him to breathe in his scent. Truthfully, he smells awful, just like he looks, as if he hasn't bathed in days. But past that is the scent of *him,* and I close my eyes, thankful for anything I can get. *We're both alive.*

I'm not sure how long we lie here like this, if sleep comes during the moments I close my eyes or not, if the flames I picture are a bad dream or a vivid memory. I'm vaguely aware of the healer entering the room a few times. She draws the blinds to give us a calm space, and I can sense her healing the more painful spots on my skin with her magenta tendrils of power. The burns I earned crawling through fire, still not doing enough to save my friend, now turn to scabs under her touch.

Blaine brushes a lock of my hair behind my ear that had fallen over my face during rest. "How do you feel?" His voice is hoarse, as if he's just waking up as well. His eyes roam down my body, not sexually, but as if checking that I'm still there—in one piece. "Is it okay to touch you?"

"I'd feel better if you did." My chapped lips crack, wobbling with emotion, while I force a smile for him. I've nursed him through countless injuries from his Advisory duties in the past, but outside of my kitchen scars, he's never needed to care for a physically broken version of me.

The thought takes me briefly back to the beach on the Liravel River, realizing that half the continent of Celestera was gone. I cried every night while I slept on the couch at Blaine's apartment and spent every day learning under Vincenzo, until I admitted to myself that I was never going home and turned my focus over to the kitchen, my anger to the Resistance, and my emotions to Blaine.

Blaine closes the final inch between us, burying his face in my neck, still holding back from more than light touches to spare me additional pain, and then the clear sensation of tears slide down my shoulder and onto my chest.

"I'm okay," I whisper into his ear, and I stretch my arm around him to run my hand down his back. I gently draw waves across it with my nails for several moments.

The healer clears her throat from the doorway, and I raise my neck just enough to see her peeking her head in, glancing our way. "Are you up to visitors, my dear? There's a gentleman here to see you." The green light hits her ebony skin, casting an ironically cheery shimmer across her face and arms.

I nod once and attempt to shift to a seated position, but Blaine playfully tightens his hold on me. I think we would stay like this for the rest of time if he had his way. One dig of my nails into his arm has him releasing me, but I follow it with a brush of my lips on his forehead as we shift. The door swings open, and the healer gestures to whoever stands in the hallway to enter my room.

Norris is a shell of the man I know. His smile is strained, and his pale skin and wrinkled, stained shirt—worn for days, it seems—give me an external image of the pain peering at me through his hollow eyes. He is defeat embodied. For a moment, we stare into each other, conveying our silent condolences before he has to admit them out loud.

The healer follows him in as well, coming over to help prop me up to a seated position, placing a couple of pillows behind me and pulling a cup of water closer to me on the side table. Before she leaves, she hovers her hand above my forehead, and a cooling sensation runs through my veins, remedying internal burns I couldn't feel through my grief.

Blaine stands and walks to Norris, reaching out a hand to shake. Norris ignores it and wraps his arms around Blaine instead. The healer takes our silence in her presence as the cue for privacy it is, gently closing the door on her way out.

"If you ever put yourself in danger to save one of us again, I will kill you myself. Do you understand me?" Norris's voice cracks on his last question, and he's visibly shaking by the time he finishes, lower lip sticking out, quivering.

Norris isn't a small man. Where Vincenzo is of average height with a slim build, Norris has spent years eating everything that Vincenzo tests in the kitchen, washing it down with pints of cold ale. He's tall and spends a fair amount of time in the water catching fresh seafood to burn most of it off, but he still gives huggable teddy-bear vibes when you meet him. So seeing Norris shaking, pale, tired—I know I could never make that promise to him. I would run straight through flames again. I would make the same choice every time.

"No."

His cheeks puff as he blows out a laugh, a hint of a smirk blooming on his lips, and I heal a bit more knowing that I put it there.

"I would have brought the healer right back in here if you had answered any differently," he responds, roughly plopping himself down on the couch under the window.

It could have been minutes or it could have been days that Norris and Blaine spend filling me in about the fires in the market and The Goblet. Blaine tries to stop Norris several times from telling me, but we all know it has to happen—the inevitability of the conversation will hang over us until spoken aloud. I pass the time focusing on a blank spot on the wall to help me avoid eye contact with them during the stories. My nails dig into my palms to feel pain that matches the conversation, my burns not being painful enough—a trick I used as a child when I needed physical proof of my internal pain.

I listen to them tell me how the fire started, that an angry patron from Molvaria decimated The Goblet during a bar fight. Fellow Resistance members snuck in to clear the basement of any evidence, and Norris has secured the intel at his pub. That the fights at the market actually involved friends of the arsonist, fellow fire wielders, though the two events were coincidentally simultaneous and not believed to be premeditated. It seems that group of friends all had idiocy and self-absorption in common.

And finally, they tell me that Vincenzo is gone.

I vaguely sense the healer coming to my side, then she lifts my clenched fist and forces my tight knuckles to open, showing the blood my nails have drawn. Little crescent-shaped holes now speckle my palms. With a wave of her hand, the blood vanishes, and she grabs a wrap and salve to gently care for my skin.

It doesn't matter; it wasn't enough, anyway. The pain I feel inside is beyond any physical scar I could ever have.

I don't know when Norris leaves, or how long I lie there, but at some point the world moves again as Blaine scoops me up and carries me to the front of the building, where, as if to mock my misery, the sun shines bright in the sky. I blink long enough to ride in a medical carriage back to our apartment, and then I let Blaine carry me up the stairs to our bed.

Witches are made by the light of the moon.
Therefore, it is by her light that they shall worship.

—The Tales of the Obsidian Witches by Tresta McVey

Not four days later, skin still stained red from burns that no longer sting, I stand in the kitchen provided to me for the Advisory Ball. "If I don't get those tomatoes in thirty seconds, a head will be on my cutting board instead." I might as well be yelling at a wall for all the response I'm getting from the excuse for a staff I have to work with tonight.

Why is good help so hard to find?

Vincenzo's passing quickly became public knowledge across town. Regulars of The Goblet set out candles in remembrance, their actual grievance being having to find a new place to imbibe, sobriety apparently clouding their ability to see the irony in their gesture. Why should they care if the remains of the pub burn down—again? Unfortunately for me, it's also public knowledge that I was Vincenzo's protégé. The sorrowful glances, as quick as they might be, are constant reminders tonight that my staff thinks I'm weak. I almost threw a ball of mozzarella at a poor server earlier for simply asking how I was doing.

Blaine, Norris, and I held a small funeral for Vincenzo last night, denying another human life the formal ceremony granted to a descendant's death—as if there could be an evil bone in Vincenzo's body. No, rather than the descendant ritual of a vessel sent to sea, carrying the soul and body of the lost life back to the aether, alight in flames the color of their magical heritage, we buried Vincenzo in a field outside of town. His physical form from these lands will rest under a large tree he admired for its unique purple leaves, forevermore. Norris slept on our couch afterward, unwilling to go back to his and Vincenzo's home.

And this morning, as if time never stopped, I woke up, gathered my knives and aprons, and started prepping stations for the Advisory Ball. Blaine stood by my side until he couldn't anymore, being needed inside the ballroom itself. He asked countless times if I was still sure I could handle this, but he knows I would never abandon my career obligations, and standing in this kitchen, knowing that I'm delivering the lessons learned from Vincenzo's legacy, provides me a small sense of pride and purpose.

The red splotches that scatter among my freckles and over my forearms serve as the sole proof of my attempt to save Vincenzo. That will change tonight, though. I raise my fingertips to my closed lips and give them a kiss, then pass the kiss to Nova's bag sitting on the corner of the countertop to my left. I turn back to the worktop to taste a bite of the ricotta I'm prepping for my signature lasagna, acutely aware that I still don't have the tomatoes I need for my next step.

Damn, that's good.

"Your tomatoes, Chef Monroe," a junior staff member says, setting the vegetables down carefully, as if they might explode if not handled with care. Fallen forbid that tomatoes get to me in a timely manner. It's not like they're a key ingredient in the lasagna dish I'm known for. He just stares at me, as if waiting for direction. He probably is.

"Go home if you need to be told what to do every step of the way. You're wasting my breath by needing direction, and I have dinner to focus on." It isn't a suggestion, and he knows it. He scuttles out of the kitchen faster than I can finish a pint of ale—a fifteen-second task I'm known for around here, or at least was known for at The Goblet. I grin at the fear I invoke, one of the things I love about being in charge.

Vincenzo scared the shit out of me when I was starting out.

Speaking of a drink, I look back down to my worktop, continue chopping, and yell out, "Someone bring me wine!" Then I dip my finger into the sauce I've started prepping—it needs salt. "And salt!" These tomatoes aren't as fresh as I need them to be. The texture isn't the problem. I can get that right in the saucing process, but I'm struggling to get my spice blend to come through the acidity of the fruit effectively.

Or maybe it's just that all of my senses have been dull for days.

Wine isn't going to help that, another voice of mine reminds me.

An audible voice comes from behind me again: "Miss?"

"What?" The word comes out sharper and louder than it should, but I can't control my nerves anymore. I've hit my social limit, and now my emotional limit.

"A server mentioned you required wine?" I don't know the man, but I'll take the drink regardless of who offers it at this point.

I return to my worktop and stay quiet for the rest of dinner, dessert included. The staff eventually gets the message, miraculously completing their assigned tasks on their own, despite the salad going out five minutes late.

When I finally send out dessert and can no longer stand this kitchen, I find the first staff member I see and let them know I'm impressed with their service, congratulating them by letting them clean up the mess. I then grab my bag and a bottle of liquor I previously commandeered from behind the bar to head into the ballroom for my dance.

Advisory leadership, wealthy socialites, and members of each of the six Provincial Courts this side of the Break, including the Sovereign Descendants themselves, comprise tonight's guest list. The ballroom, illuminated solely by candles, provides an escape for those who neither deserve nor need it. I would burn this place to the ground with no remorse if it would prove my point.

And if fire wasn't already haunting my dreams at night.

Perhaps I've chosen this life on some level. A life pretending none of this was real could have been mine had I moved to a human-only city. But I fell in love, joined a rebellion, and became too good at what I do, both undercover and in the kitchen.

Occasionally I let my mind drift to easier times for us, in some small human town farther inland. Blaine could learn a craft, and I could grow my own garden to use in the town's restaurant. We wouldn't have to worry about fire wielders getting too angry, or mind wielders playing games with our heads just for being human. We would just live.

But as I watch Blaine mingle throughout the room, genuine laughter escaping him when a peer tells him a joke, I know that kind of life could never have been for us. Blaine has been serving in the Advisory for eleven years now, earning himself the rank of vice general for the Southern Aerial Wing—a feat few other humans can claim. I just finished catering the finest event of my career. He and I were both made for more.

As if sensing my presence, his face turns in my direction, and our eyes lock. I wiggle my fingers in greeting, giving him a wink before spinning in a circle to let him see the gown I snuck into just moments before. The boat neck covers most of my burns—save for my arms—and the floor-length flowing orange velvet will keep me warm when I head outside later.

He holds up one finger, a smile stretching across his clean-shaven face, which shows off his sharp jawline and tan skin. He may need a minute before he can dance, but it doesn't stop me from swaying my hips while I slowly walk away, gazing over my shoulder at him while I let him see what he's missing until then.

The bar is against the back wall, a few tall cocktail tables grouped around it, so I grab a fresh glass of merlot and wait by one of the empty ones. The music, a romantic tune, drifts through the room, as if carried by the wind. A couple I hadn't noticed entwined in the shadowed corner behind me skips past, making their way out to the dance floor. The man pulls the giggly woman behind him while she playfully tries to say she doesn't want to.

I think back to the early days of my and Blaine's relationship, finding the shadowy corners, and with them, the excuses for our hands to roam. The past couple of days have been the closest we've been to those early days in several years. He took this week off work to spend with me, no discussion of the Resistance, no Advisory sessions, just pretending nothing but the two of us existed outside of the four walls of our apartment. We'll go back to normal soon—whatever normal is.

"Is this spot taken?" A man's voice pulls me out of my thoughts, and I jump slightly at seeing him standing next to me.

I look across the room to where Blaine still stands, in conversation with someone, then back to the man awaiting my response. "Actually, I was just leaving. The table is yours," I offer, giving him a polite smile.

"The dinner was lovely, by the way," he says before I make it two steps away.

I pause. There is something about the way he says the words that makes them sound like more than a statement—hidden in the uptick of his tone, or his casual pacing. Not sultry or flirtatious, nor a quick nod to the chef before she can hurry off.

"Thank you for the kind words—" As I wait for his name, I gaze into narrowed eyes that look me up and down, and at a coy grin paired with furrowed brows, two states fighting for his demeanor at once.

He huffs a single laugh, scratching his chin while he gazes at the floor. "Names are not a game I'm hoping to play tonight, Miss August, but I would enjoy some company and a drink." He offers me a second glass I hadn't seen him carrying as he takes a step in my direction—so close I can smell the cedar and mint oils he wears in excess.

I lean back, taking one step to add a few inches between us. "Well, as you can see, I don't need another drink, but my guess is that there are more than a couple of women here who wouldn't mind keeping you *company*." I emphasize the last word for what it is—an invitation—and hold up my glass of wine to show him I'm already taken care of. "I was just heading out to find my boyfriend. Enjoy your evening."

He reaches out, lightly, though still obtusely, and grabs my upper arm. I peer down at his tan hand wrapped around it, only inches below a thick scar about two inches long on my shoulder, and then back at him. "Please don't touch me," I comment, softly, though still confidently, and then shake him off—walking away with a bit more purpose this time. But he speaks up again.

"Did your mother teach you how to cook like that?"

I take an extra moment to turn this time, composure coming slower after a long week. I plan to ask how he knows who I am, plan to fire whoever pointed me out to him, but when I finally face him—he's walking away. The man is already in the doorway, headed to the outdoor lounge space.

A firm hand slides onto the small of my back, and I spin so fast out of the touch that I spill my wine all down the front of Blaine's suit.

Fuck.

"August!" He hops backward, as if he could jump out of the wine's trajectory, brows furrowed as he wipes at the drops of wine rolling down the wool coat. "What in the Fallen was that?"

"I don't know, I—" My sight swivels from him to the door and back. "There was someone—I'm sorry."

He gives me a look that tells me how sorry he still feels for me before wrapping his arm around me, leaning in, and whispering, "I know how you can make it up to me." He tugs me onto the dance floor, where we float into a familiar routine.

"You look good tonight, General."

"So do you, Chef."

With his hand on my waist, we twirl and sidestep our way across the dance floor to the tunes of the orchestra, occasionally nodding to a peer of Blaine's as we pass them. He takes his new title seriously, and I love seeing him wear it so well.

"You're distracted," he says, looking down at me as we slow our motions for a ballad.

"It's just been a long day."

He looks around the room over my head for a moment, then leans in again. "I've known you for over ten years, August. Did you push yourself too far today? We can go home, I don't—"

I want to shake him, tell him that of course I'm distracted, that of course today was too much after the past week, that at any moment I don't know if I'm going to cry or yell or flee Quinthold altogether. I want to tell him that all I want is to pour myself into reviving the Resistance to distract me from my reality, but I can't do that because he doesn't support me.

He would go beat the shit out of that strange man from earlier, and spend all night listening to me vent about my incompetent staff, but none of that would matter if he continues to look at me as if I might shatter into a million pieces before him at any moment. Every second that he holds my stare, I'm one step closer to exactly that.

So instead, I say, "No! I'm fine. We can't leave early from your first ball as a general. I just need a coffee."

He nods, albeit hesitantly, and when the song ends, he takes my hand to lead us back off the dance floor. Thankfully, we're intercepted by a junior member of his wing. The young flier looks so excited to finally speak to the new general.

And who am I to take that away?

"Blaine, you stay. I'm just going to go find that coffee and head home."

"I'll walk you."

"No, I'm fine, really. Stay." I give him a look that says I'll be more offended if he leaves than if he escorts me, and he concedes.

"See you at home," he says as he leans in and kisses my cheek.

6

Select your blades carefully. Not all blades are suited for all purposes. A well-prepared chef has one for cleaning, one for preparing, one for practice, and one for death.

I take a minor detour before heading home. There's a variety of outdoor seating options on the large balcony that hangs over the Liravel Sea, where a more peaceful arrangement of couches awaits, and a single violinist plays for the guests this evening. I turn the corner to a secluded section under the shade of a large tree, where I see two benches with comfortable-looking cushions. I choose the bench where I can see anyone heading this direction and swipe my hand across the cushion to brush away any loose leaves or debris that have fallen there.

The relief in my tired joints when I sit down is

immediate, and I take a moment to knead the sore muscles in my shoulders. Blaine would assist if I let him. For years, his muscular arms have eased the knots formed in my muscles from long days in the kitchen, but this is something I need to do alone. In fact, I should hurry if I don't want him to come looking for me. I already hope he doesn't beat me home.

I focus on my breathing as I roll my neck and shoulders, before moving to my knees and ankles. The sounds of the various animals in the area keep me company in a way a human never could, as if each chirp or squeak is meant to be a sound of support.

After several minutes of soaking in the moonlight, I return to my task. Reaching into my bag, I grab one of my favorite blades, a dagger Blaine gifted me when I graduated from my apprenticeship with Vincenzo. It was such a thoughtful gift—the blade of the finest craftsmanship, and the detailing on the hilt intricate. If you look closely, you can see vines of various produce stemming up the handle, imitating the tomatoes I have learned to work with so well for my lasagna.

And despite the grief weighing on my soul, I grin at the memory as it surfaces. This blade is on me at all times, though I, of course, don't use it in the kitchen. That night was the night I taught Blaine that daggers, which have sharp edges on both sides, are for battle, while kitchen blades only have one sharp edge, the other being flat, for balance.

I remove the sheath slowly—made of a thick brown leather with the letter "A" stamped in the middle. I run my fingers over the embellishment and admire the glint of the blade against the one ray of moonlight that finds its way through the branches of the tree overhead.

One more deep breath. You got this, August, my other voice assures me, one much more steady than my own.

Occasionally, my inner monologue sounds in a voice that's not my own, and I contemplate whether it doesn't belong to me at all. Sometimes I wonder if it's the spirit of the mother I never knew, attempting to guide me during the life she abandoned me to. Though I doubt the mother who chose to abandon me would pop back in just to encourage me on my hard days—nor does she deserve to. I can pretend it belongs to Nova, that she's with me still, but the voice doesn't match hers, a vibrant tone I could never forget.

Maybe it's simply a part of me that still has hope. A part of me that stays buried deep inside, that I've subconsciously protected all these years from reality, a piece of my inner child that refused to grow bitter alongside the rest of me. It's this final explanation that I favor, particularly on days when I have to accept that I'm the only person I can rely on to protect myself from this life I've chosen.

Staring at the dagger for a few moments, I give my respects to the tool in my hands. Most people think of blades as weapons, used to hurt, maul, kill. But as a chef, I would be remiss not to honor its ability to create, to provide, and to protect.

I draw the sharpening stones and worn leather from my bag. I sharpened the dagger at home, as I do nightly when caring for my blades, but I give it a few ceremonious strikes against the stones, and a few swipes of the leather strap to detail the edges.

When finished, I place the dagger carefully on the bench next to me while I pour myself a small amount of the liquor I brought from inside. I then place the dagger back in my upturned palm and angle my whole body so that I can raise my face to the moon.

"Celestial Mother, I offer you this piece of me in grateful exchange for a place in your orbit for my late Vincenzo. Tonight, I wear my grief with pride. His soul is worthy of your finest rankings. May the aether celebrate his return home as powerfully as I honor his life." Then I close my eyes and allow the sharpened blade a moment to continue to absorb the moon's rays.

It's a funeral prayer from a fable about women who called themselves witches—a tale I fell in love with as a child. Vincenzo would laugh at my use of the prayer, but as a human, it's all I have.

A lump forms in my throat, which I swallow whole, needing a steady hand for what comes next. As I down the clear liquor, it burns away any emotions fighting to surface. I then take out a clean scrap of linen, soak it in a bit more of the liquid, and wipe down both sides of the dagger before dabbing the rag at a spot on my left arm, just below my shoulder, just below a raised scar about two inches long that I've worn for about ten years.

I put the used linen in the cup as I retrieve flint and a throwing knife from my bag and then stand, turning to grab a few fallen leaves and sticks from the surrounding trees. However, I notice a small pile of twigs a foot from my seat on the bench that I must have missed when I cleaned it off—the perfect tinder for my fire.

I gather the twigs, bundle them together, and cross them over one another inside the cup, then strike the steel against the flint several times until embers shine on the dried pieces of wood. I circle my hands behind the cup and gently blow on the sparks until they glow a little brighter, and smoke swirls toward the moonlit sky, disappearing when the wind catches it.

I let the tinder absorb the flames begging to grow. Building a fire by hand wouldn't impress a fire wielder, but it's the closest to magic being a human allows me to come.

The flames double when they meet the liquor-soaked rag in the bottom of the cup, and I take advantage of the quick burst to run the dagger through the fire, allowing both sides to heat. I place the leather sideways between my lips, so both sides stick out of the corners of my mouth, bite down, and press the blade into my arm, about an inch below my original scar.

The metal stings, and I fight the urge to scream through the leather protecting my clenched teeth. I try to tune out the hiss of my skin sizzling, but the sound feels like crawling through The Goblet again.

I freeze—hand stalled in midair. As hard as I try, I cannot breathe in any of the cool night air. The dagger falls from my grip, and I watch it tumble to the ground as time seems to slow. My heart races, and it quickly becomes the only sound I can hear above the ringing in my ears. I'm back in The Goblet, about to burn alive. My vision is hazy, but I swear the flames have grown.

I need to move, I need to put it out before I light the estate on fire too.

You need to breathe, my other voice reminds me.

But I just stare at my bleeding arm, unable to move, unable to disconnect my panic from the reality of the moment, the growing flames heating my face.

I need air.

Then the fire is gone, and the heat vanishes while the cool embrace of the night air envelops me once more. My lungs fill as I gasp for breath, panting and waiting for my heart to slow. My hands—I look at my hands and see no burns. I take a deep breath through my nose—it doesn't sting.

The distinct sound of someone clearing their throat interrupts my thoughts. Another woman sits directly across from me, and one of the linen napkins from the event covers the cup where I'd built the fire. She simply grins and says, "Hi, August. I was hoping I'd be able to find you."

The woman has her long, sleek black hair pinned to one side. Her hair matches the dress she wore for the evening. In fact, everything on this female is black, down to the shade she chose for her full lips. Her necklace is quite stunning—a gold chain with an obsidian charm. It looks familiar, though I can't quite place where I've seen something similar before. She has a deep olive skin tone, the kind that looks effortlessly beautiful in any color clothing or during any time of year.

A viscous red clings to the inside of her glass as she swirls it in midair, and a hint of pride blooms within me knowing that she opted for my wine pairings with the evening's meal. Nova would have immediately tried to befriend her, just to have access to her wardrobe and beauty secrets.

She must see my look of confusion, because she says, "How rude of me, I'm Zalya. You're welcome for putting that fire out, by the way. You looked panicked." She smooths her dress as she says it before taking a casual sip of the wine.

Can she not tell I don't want to be bothered?

Maybe you should speak if you want her to know...anything, my other voice points out for me.

"Thank you for your help with the fire, though I had it under control." I glance at my arm and note the open wound. Beads of blood trickle down my arm like condensation on an icebox, connecting my freckles like a chain. I retrieve another clean rag to staunch the bleeding while I add, "But if you don't mind, I'd prefer to be alone this evening."

She pauses, humming to herself, never breaking eye contact—for effect or response, I'm not sure. She eventually sets down her wine and shifts to her own bag, perusing it for something.

I take the free moment to gather my own bag and the now empty bottle of liquor, waiting to hear her point, not caring if I do. If she won't leave me alone, I'll just find another place to be. I had planned this evening for mourning, not—whatever this is. After the strange man earlier, I've had enough.

"I'm here on behalf of a client. He was in attendance this evening for the ball, and loved your food, particularly the lasagna. I believe he actually used the term 'ravishing.'" Zalya waves her hand to the side, as if showing the description on a platter. Those nails would never suit that woman for kitchen work. They'd snap off when she picked up the first heavy dish.

What I want to say is, "My secret for the lasagna? The way I prepare my ricotta. Such an underrated cheese."

Instead, I say, "Thank you for the feedback. Please write if you'd like to book my services for your future events." I stand and sling my bag across my good shoulder, careful not to move my arm much until the blood clots. I have a long-sleeve shirt in my bag ready to cover myself before I see Blaine again.

"Oh, we will. However, my client would like to inquire about a bit more commitment than a single event. You see, he's looking for an in-house chef, starting next week, and he'd like it to be you."

My lips part in question. "Why?"

"Did the ravishing compliment not give it away? He devoured your meal. Honestly, you'll have to teach me that soup recipe."

Zalya leans back, crosses one leg over the other, and tucks a stray hair behind her ear while she stares out at the water. "You know, I quite prefer the view here as a sea instead of a river. I can imagine that there's a better world out there somewhere, instead of just knowing it's a continuation of this one."

Though I'm actually interested in the latter conversation, I need to remain focused. "You haven't told me a thing about the role—who the employer is, where this job is located, what it pays. If he needs someone in less than a week, why are you just now making an offer, and to someone you just found this evening?"

She looks up at me with knowing eyes, like she expected these questions. "Let's just say that my client has his reasons for how he operates. I'm simply the messenger. I can tell you that you'll be generously compensated and provided with room and board on-site. To help entice you, he wanted me to give you this." She holds out the long rectangular box that she retrieved from her bag a moment ago, immaculately wrapped in thick gold parchment and tied with a delicate indigo velvet bow. The gold of the parchment shimmers in the moonlight.

I hesitate to take the box, my gaze shifting between it and her. Then I finally reach out and grab it with my good arm. It's heavier than it looks, and I stare down at the package, confused.

"I'll send a messenger in a few days to collect your answer," she says as she stands, collecting her bag and wine. She pauses after only a step, turning her neck so I can only see the profile of her face. "Oh, and please say yes. I could use a friend."

"But how will you know where I am?" I look back up to see her already heading back into the estate.

Friend?

"Descendants have their ways." Zalya waves over her shoulder as her voice trails off with her exit, leaving me alone once more.

7

It is my belief that magic, itself, is not a source of energy, but rather a product of energy expenditure.

—An excerpt from Vincenzo Cuoco's journal,
recovered from The Goblet

The following evening, despite several pleas from Blaine otherwise, I'm back to my nightly routine of Resistance work. We are looking at a map of the original lands of Celestera, kept flat with one of my knives in each corner holding it to the table. A disgrace to the fine steel blades, but it's the best we can do in the makeshift meeting space. The mask I wear across my face to hide my features feels suffocatingly close to the rag I used when I tried to save Vincenzo from the fire.

I didn't tell Blaine about my visit from Zalya and the mystery job. I would never take a role working for a descendant anyway. The voice in the back of my head hinted that I should consider it, if only to work the Resistance from the inside, but it would mean relocating Blaine, and that would never happen with his recent promotion in the Advisory.

Instead, I spent today reviewing old Resistance correspondence recovered from The Goblet, but all I've gained is a sore neck from leaning over the kitchen table reading the documents and correspondence all day.

I'm lost in so many ways without Vincenzo. My role in the Resistance is to coordinate incoming and outgoing messages to other units across Celestera. Blaine's role was to bring in intel from the Advisory. Norris handled recruitment and *relieving members of their duties*. Each member is to be an expert in his or her specific role, and to know as little as possible of what others know or do. This principle ensures our safety and the movement's security in the event of our capture. We use aliases for the same reason.

Except Vincenzo. Vincenzo was our expert on the descendants, their history, their laws, their culture, but most importantly—their magic. *Our fearless leader.* I guess he never considered what would happen if he was gone.

Now Norris's grief prevents him from stepping up, and Blaine is on strike from participating in Resistance work in an attempt to convince me to give up the movement. Vincenzo's death was a direct example of why we formed this unit. Descendants' powers need to be checked.

For now, I've set up a temporary space in the attic of Norris's pub. It's not secure like our previous location, so we need to speak in hushed voices, but we can pretend we're planning a casual trip to the mountains if anyone were to walk in. It's warm in here, or maybe my mask is too tight. Every once in a while, I have to feign a sneeze just to have an excuse to turn to the side and pull down my mask for a moment to breathe.

"Tell me again. Why exactly haven't we been able to get in touch with Ash?" I ask the lone fellow member with me tonight.

The female at my side chose Mel for her alias. She's been around for about a year, which is the longest of anyone I've worked with directly for the Resistance here in Quinthold. Working closely with our field leader, Eclipse, she creates and updates our maps and locations. She left a message at Norris's pub calling a meeting, so here I am. She told me she wanted to update our records on the latest temple search mission. Mel is clearly as annoyed with me for continuously asking the same questions as I am with her lack of answers. So, I think that makes us even.

She takes a deep breath, visible in the rise and fall of her shoulders, before repeating, "I told you, we lost our latest temple search unit. The Advisory caught them headed north past the Selcairn Volcano." She takes a quill and marks a circle where their assumed last location was on the map. "However, if you see these three circles close to each other, we can assume there is a reason that the Advisory is heavily patrolling this area." She takes three pins from a pocket of a leather pouch she wears around her waist, places them in the center of each circle and then winds a piece of red string around the pins to wrap them together, creating a triangle of marked area on the map.

I pinch the bridge of my nose in concentration, digging my nails into my eye sockets a little, and begin slowly, talking out loud to myself more than asking her the questions. "So we can assume that Linea's temple is somewhere within this triangle of The Ivory Hills? Who have we shared this information with? Any of the other provinces aware of the latest loss?"

"We've spread the news to our neighbors in Curatia and Auralia; they're working to disseminate it from there. This triangle of space is still very large. I'd like to send a unit in from the north this time to see if we can narrow the space down further. We're learning with each unit that goes in about how and where they attack. Aerial attacks hit the survivors from the first two units, and both reported hearing dragons within an hour before the attack. We need to learn where the dragons patrol from, and when, and then we'll have another leg up." Mel chews the inside of her lip, glaring at the map as if hoping it'll come alive and tell us the answers we're looking for. "I just wish we had a contact in the Advisory."

Everything in me wants to tell her we do, but I can't expose Blaine. Not to mention, I asked him about the patrols. He's as in the dark as we are about any activity or stations in this area.

I stare at another sketch of Linea's temple we've pinned on the wall, mumbling to the Sovereign Fallen herself, "Why couldn't you just write down how to find your temple? Aren't we fighting the same fight?" In school, we learned Linea yearned to start a land of peace after escaping a Celestial War herself. She entombed her fellow Fallen within the stone of her temple to prevent inevitable war. It's how and why the Advisory was born, to protect and defend those, whether descendant or human, across all of Celestera—a defending presence not of provincial borders, but for peace *despite* borders. According to history, only Linea's direct descendants can call on her from the temple, and only in times of dire need. The Resistance believes that half of Celestera's disappearance constitutes a dire need.

The problem is that we haven't been able to find any historical records that can trace Linea's descendants. Or if we have, they likely died last week in the decimation of The Goblet. Currently, the Resistance is just searching for the temple, hoping we can gain more answers once we have its location. Hoping that we might locate it without magic, even if we can't access it right away.

Essentially, the Resistance is currently surviving on hope, and it's running pretty low after ten years of barely any answers. The only thing I can say I've accomplished is helping to spread information across the lands by reporting back information from Blaine's Advisory intel to our messengers, and I can't even do that anymore.

Mel reaches over and grabs my clenched fist. "River, we're going to find it. We get closer with each unit that we send out." Her voice is soft, not full of the usual pointed strategy with which she holds herself. She tucks a strand of blonde hair behind her ear with her free hand and clears her throat before continuing, "Maybe we should take a break. We can talk about anything besides this—just pretend we're normal for a few hours."

"No."

Not her too.

"It's just that I know you and the leader were close, so if you need to take a break—"

With a hand gesture, I silence her. I'm close to firing her. She's gotten too soft if she thinks I'm going to abandon our rules about fraternization at this point. "Please, just focus. Vincenzo put anti-fraternization rules in place for a reason."

But neither of us gets the chance to continue before the door at the bottom of the stairs to our meeting space bursts open, light flooding the room from below.

Mel and I are both on our feet, chairs thrown behind us, prepared to light the oiled fuse that will set the entire room on fire and all the documents and evidence of any resistance with it. It's the escape plan: light the room on fire and run. Kill those in your path if you're found out. Sacrifice yourself, if need be. We all took an oath and vowed to follow the plan. Setting up the fire trap was the first step I took before agreeing to use Norris's pub for the Resistance meetings. I had Norris check it ten times before I let go of the worry of accidentally setting it off—if I'm going to die in a fire, it will be one I entered on purpose, not one accidentally lit.

I grab two of my blades from the map, ready to throw, when I hear Blaine's voice through the mask he wears. "August, they're on their way. You've gotta go!"

Mel turns to look my direction, eyes wide. "August?"

"There's no time now, Mel. Run!" I rip the map we were working on from the table and into my bag, preparing to light the room on fire in my exit. Blaine comes barreling up the narrow, rickety set of stairs.

Blaine grabs Mel and pushes her to the stairs behind him now. "Run! You were never here. There's a bag with a change of clothes ready for you at the bottom of the stairs—change as soon as you can find an alcove, and remember, you were never here." He turns and tries to push me toward Mel, who is now paralyzed in shock, staring at me from the exit.

"Blaine, I swear to Linea herself that if you get in my way, you're going to be incinerated along with this room." I draw my blade, hoping the physical threat gets through to him. "If you care about me, get her out of here, I'll be right behind you."

His eyes narrow, the only sign I can see above his mask that he's taken in what I just said. He turns to Mel, tosses her over his shoulder, and barrels back down the stairs the way he came. Her loud protests are incoherent through the haze of my panic.

Frantically gathering the last of the documents, I can't bring myself to ignite the fuse that will set the pub ablaze, yet. For too long, I stare at the oil-soaked rope, convincing myself it's the plan, wasting precious moments I don't have. My hand shakes as I extend a candle toward the catalyst, hot wax dripping into my palms where it mixes with my sweat, and finally light the fuse.

And before I know it, I'm out the back door and racing down the cobblestone alley behind the pub as fast as I can go. A few blocks away, I reach another pub's back door and make a quick change of my clothes before dipping into their establishment. Out of breath, I sit down with the friendly bartender, let him know I'm lost, and take the time to grab a cold pint and gain directions back to my side of town.

The friendly bartender, a fellow Resistance member named Arrow, of course knows who I am. He's also aware of the message I'm relaying by asking for directions back to my apartment. It's how I know that my departure will trigger a coded message to surrounding province Resistance units, warning them of our compromise and halting communications until further notice.

An older woman comes and sits down next to me, up in arms about another fire at a pub a few doors down. Arrow quickly scuttles out the back, claiming to want to see for himself. I take the chance to finish my pint and excuse myself to watch Norris's pub join The Goblet in the afterlife, and with it the Quinthold Resistance.

But I have just one more stop before I force myself to confront what will be waiting for me at home. There's only one female in this town that I can talk to about this.

The edge of the Old Forest, where it meets the Liravel Sea, is tranquil at night. Blaine and I used to come here often to get lost in each other under the stars, back when we both thought the other could do no wrong. I distracted myself from tonight's events by watching my shadow on the ground as I walked, accompanied by what felt like thousands of neon flies lighting my way.

Blaine's accomplishments are impressive, but his dragon has been the greatest reward. I think I adore Teliquis more than I have ever adored another human. We don't know where she came from. Her egg popped up among others at the Advisory's hatching grounds around the time Blaine started working for them, slightly smaller and a different color than the rest. When she hatched, she stumbled out of her shell and rolled straight onto her back, huffing a small relieved stream of steam from her floppy nostrils, her jelly limbs tossed to the side. And I knew—she was the one. She and I were the same at that moment, just exasperated with being alive. It helped that she was adorable, with her bright white underbelly sparkling in the sun. Blaine agreed to train with her, and I agreed to be her friend.

I wait a few moments before calling for her. Teliquis knows I'm here, though. The beautiful beast always tries to sneak up behind me while I'm busy watching the waves calmly flow onto the shore, but she hasn't learned yet that stealth will never be on her side as long as she's ten feet tall and has a tail longer than the rest of her body.

I let her get close enough that I don't need to raise my voice before telling her she's failed to catch me by surprise, beckoning her over by patting the sand next to me. She lets out a frustrated snort, annoyed that she hasn't managed to scare me once again. But she plops herself down next to me, shaking a few coconuts off the trees behind her from the impact. The knocking sounds as they hit the tree trunks and other fruits on the way down remind me of horses' hooves on stone streets.

Blaine's dragon is the only female I speak to outside of brief conversations with fellow women Resistance members, and I don't even know their names. Blaine knows I come out to see her from time to time, but he probably doesn't understand quite how often, or why. I don't speak for a while, soaking in the quiet air and her company, but I lean to the side and she nuzzles my cheek with her warm snout. Her unconditional compassion is something I won't get from Blaine when I return home, but it's what I need right now. We can fight tomorrow. Right now, I need this.

"Everything has fallen apart, and I don't know what to do," I finally murmur through the imminent tears welling in my eyes. "What am I supposed to do?"

She huffs a warm, slow breath as she nods her head, showing her understanding. It's all the validation I need to let the sobs finally release. I cried this past week, tears leaking out that I could catch before they fell, but I held back the visceral sobs of loss and pain, so sure I had everything under control still.

We lie there in the sand until the sun peeks back up over the horizon, both falling asleep at one point, her snout a warm, heavy blanket across my lap. But soon enough, it's time for me to face the reality of my situation.

✦

August is becoming dependent on Blaine, is refusing to socialize outside of The Goblet. I am having Norris work to recruit more young women for her to make friends with. We worry about her.

—AN EXCERPT FROM VINCENZO CUOCO'S JOURNAL, RECOVERED FROM THE GOBLET

"You're welcome for saving your ass." Blaine leans against the worktop in the kitchen, a casual stance, bringing levity into a situation I'm not ready to unpack.

When did I get inside?

I look at him, then back at the front door, indeed closed and locked behind me. "Blaine, I'm not in a great place right now. See, I just lost my mentor last week. I am still exhausted from the biggest night of my career. Oh, and last night, my rebel unit got busted, which I've been leading alone since losing Vincenzo." Before continuing, I remove my leather jacket, wincing as it pulls at the bandages on my arm when I attempt to shrug my shoulder through the sleeve. "I escaped, delivered the message as planned, and I'm fine, by the way. I need to clean the throbbing wound on my arm, but otherwise, I'm fine."

To drive my point home, I whip my gaze back in his direction to add, "Oh, and not to mention, my boyfriend is being a real pain in my ass about something important to me. So please excuse me if thanking you isn't the priority on my list of things to do right now."

"Where in the celestial aether were you? I've been up all night." He asks more calmly than before, but I can tell he's holding back. Silent for a moment, he stares at the ground. He's always been more thoughtful with his words than I have been. It pisses me off. I want so badly for him to fuck up so I can rip into him. I can feel the emotions of this past week sitting in my gut, festering, waiting to be released—last night's sobs were just the beginning.

"I went to see Teliquis. I fell asleep." I glance down at the bandages on my arm, now visible thanks to the sleeveless linen tunic I adorn. A spot of red peeks through the wrappings, but I don't think it's actively bleeding. Hopefully, I have a little extra salve from the healer's center.

"Choose me." His words are a whisper now, the last burning embers of a fire that's slowly been dwindling for him over the past several months. His eyes are now glued to the bandage he wasn't aware of until now.

"What's on the kitchen table?" I nod toward it as I move past him into the kitchen to grab a bottle of wine. A handful of items, varying in size, sit there: a box wrapped in butcher paper, a small worn-looking envelope, the gift from the strange woman who offered me the new job. And then there is a thin leather briefcase that has seen many better days.

"Can't you see now that the Resistance is going nowhere, that it's more dangerous than it's worth?" He won't look at me as he lets it out, pacing the kitchen, his hands conducting the conversation, his voice rising with a renewed strength. "If I hadn't been on a walk last night, I would never have seen the unit headed to Norris's. I wouldn't have been able to warn you."

Reaching into the cabinet, I grab a glass, fill it to the top with wine, ignoring custom, and take a small sip to check the quality. Hints of wildflowers from Galevarr peek through the aroma as I hold the glass to a candle to inspect its color, which is odd since Galevarr has been missing since the Break. The erratic flora that grew in Galevarr from their weather magic always produce the strongest undertones, but the bottle offers no descriptive notes regarding the wine's origin or production. The irony of weather magic being catastrophic enough to cause the Break, yet nurturing enough to produce the finest wines, isn't lost on me.

Strength shows up in many forms.

Blaine accidentally smacks me in the back of the head as he paces the kitchen, his arm movements expanding alongside his emotions.

"Ow." I glare at him for a moment before adding, "Have I seen that briefcase before?" I nod again to the case, letting the wine breathe before taking another sip. There is something about the case that looks strikingly familiar. I gaze at it from across the room, willing the memory to make the connection in my head.

"You could have died tonight—you almost did die last week! Not to mention if the Advisory catches you, then I'm murdered for treason as well." Blaine now stands on the opposite side of the worktop from me, gripping the counter with a strength that turns his knuckles white, tears beginning to well in his eyes.

I swirl the bright white in my glass, slightly underchilled, but coating my nerves all the same. "Come." I round the corner and grab Blaine's clenched hand from where it still holds the counter like a vise. One by one, I unlatch his knuckles from the edge of the counter and, carefully, lead him to the kitchen table, pulling a chair out for him before sitting myself.

"August, please talk to me." I can hear the unshed tears in the back of his throat, threatening to break free at any moment. His head hangs as he stares at our feet, his hands interlocked behind his neck.

This night, this week, hasn't been easy for either of us. I recognize that I'm not the only one grieving. But I cannot have this conversation with Blaine right now.

I will break if he makes me face reality.

I stare at the packages on the table, now in front of us, running my hand over the top of the thin leather briefcase. There are knicks and scuffs in the leather, even a long rip down the side. The leather is a deep sandy color, like the inside bark of a young tree.

Where have I seen this before?

"They're bereavement gifts for you, dropped off from the estate lawyer."

My attention snaps back to Blaine. "It was Vinny's?"

"I wanted you to choose us. But instead you chose Nova and Vincenzo, and a fight that is going nowhere. Tonight proves that.

I have risked my job, our lives, our futures for this rebellion for ten years alongside you. I'm asking you to finally choose me."

I lean over and lay a small kiss on the top of his hung head, needing to respond in some way, but keep my attention focused on the briefcase. I try the clasps on the case—locked. I don't see a key lying anywhere nearby, though I also don't see a keyway anywhere near the clasps. "Did this come with a key?" I ask in one more futile attempt to change the conversation.

Blaine slams his fist down on the table with what I have to imagine is any physical strength remaining in his tired bones. I jump slightly in my seat and stare at the spot where his hand made contact. A small crack remains in the weathered wood from the impact, and though my glass still stands, a small amount of the wine has splashed over the rim and onto one of the packages. The liquid now flows across the butcher paper–wrapped package in a slow wave. I stare at it for a moment, watching the wine spread without restraint.

"You need to calm down or the neighbors are going to hear you," I say, still staring at the crack in the table, and the spilled wine. I can't have this conversation again. I won't make it through it again.

"In case you haven't noticed, I don't give a flying fuck about anyone else, August. This town, this apartment, the pier, all the establishments you have ever worked in could all crumble to the fucking ground if it meant you and I could finally just settle down, live our lives, and put this Resistance work behind us." He bites out the words, his face reddening with the restraint he's using to not scream them.

"What have I worked for over the past ten years if I simply give up now, Blaine?" I taste blood. I hadn't noticed how hard I'd been chewing on the inside of my cheek. Tears are already making their way down my cheeks.

"Us." He's directly in front of me, but I can't bring myself to raise my eyes to meet his. Giving in to Blaine is to give up on what I believe in. To give up on finding Nova and getting revenge for Vincenzo. He goes to gently grip my shoulders, but pulls away when I flinch at the contact with my fresh wound.

"All I want is for the descendants and humans to live peacefully together, to be held to the same checks and balances, just as Linea herself set forth to do when colonizing Celestera. Those with the strongest powers in our realm shouldn't be able to cleave the lands in half and get away with it. Beryl is out there still, and who's to say he won't attack again? Linea's descendants can call upon her again. She'll be able to fix it, just like she did in the beginning. She'll be able to bring them back."

"Please, August—" His voice cracks as he tilts my face up toward him, his hands braced along my jawline, repeating, "Please."

My lips wobble as I stare at the love of my life.

I told him I couldn't have this conversation again.

"I have to do something for me, Blaine. Don't you get it, everything in my life has happened *to* me. Fighting for the Resistance is my way to be the change. I've lost too many people, too many *years* to stop now."

"Is that how you see our past decade together? As lost?"

Fallen damn.

He looks at me, on the brink of his own tears now, fists clenched in frustrated sorrow.

What's one more blow when the gash is already bleeding?

"I'm moving away in a few days. I've accepted a new job. It's best if you don't know where I go." Not that I'd be able to tell him where or what my new job is.

The chair falls to the ground with the speed at which he clambers away from me, like he can't put enough distance between us, and I feel my heart crack. He's across the room by the time I look up. The gaze he gives me is one I wouldn't wish on my worst enemy, like he doesn't even know me. Honestly, I'm wondering if I even know myself. And I want nothing more than to run to him, to take it back, but I know I can't. We won't ever be able to get past this.

"Bye, August." And with a few long strides, he's gone. I've never seen him move so fast.

I sit at the kitchen table the rest of the evening and into the night. Only when I lose feeling in my bottom do I move to my armchair in the living space, grabbing a fresh bottle of wine en route. Still, I never take my eyes off the door. I sit there under a blanket, hugging my knees to my chest, waiting. I'm not sure which muscle *feels* emotion, but I'm fairly certain I lose feeling in it too. There is no longer a line between the physical and emotional reality of my world. My body can't decide if it is angry, or sad, or nauseous—so it rotates through all three. And I let it.

I'm in and out of sleep for a few hours, fighting against the dreams that force me to relive the past week over and over again— sometimes seeing flames, other times Blaine's face. A few times, my eyes snap open to my mind imagining the sounds of a door opening and closing, hoping it's him returning home. A kiss of chill autumn air touches my warm, throbbing arm, finally waking me up from my restless night, and I peer out the window I don't remember opening, the sun shining through—morning. I likely opened it to wave to Nova last night after my sixth glass of wine, and I briefly remember that secondary voice in my head telling me to get some rest.

Maybe the voice does belong to Nova.

If this were any other day, I would tell Blaine about my dreams while I prepare us both coffee. His shirtless form would mosey to the worktop to join me, and I would take the normalcy for granted. My eyes now wander around my studio apartment—massive without Blaine. If he were here, he would beg me to get ready, say we were missing precious time in the daylight. I would respond by trying to tug him back into bed.

What did I do?

I lean my forehead to my knees, wrapping my arms around myself once more. Blaine can't be gone. Yet he is. It was the wine speaking, or my frustration from the evening. A sane version of myself would never have decided in less than a second to end my relationship of ten years. But if he were here, if I hadn't said the words, would he still be asking me to leave the Resistance? Would anything have ever changed?

An odd scratching sound comes from behind me, and I turn to see a squirrel on my windowsill, its cheek stretched to the size of a small lemon. One by one, it slowly pulls a variety of nuts from its mouth, setting them gently at its own feet. I don't have enough energy to shoo it away, so I just watch it unload its next meal onto the sill. After the squirrel lines up six slightly wet nuts, it nods once at me, turns, and climbs back the way it came.

I should really close that, I think to myself, not even bothered by a squirrel leaving half-eaten nuts in my apartment. It seems like the least of my problems currently.

"Okay, August, you need to get up. You can't take this job if you never actually formally accept it. Not to mention, your entire existence here in Quinthold imploded last night," I tell myself as I pick at the remnants of sleep caught in the corners of my eyes. And as if the Fallen themselves hear me, a knock sounds at my door.

My head spins from how fast I throw myself out of my chair and sprint to the door, blanket strewn in my path. But when I throw it open, he's not there. In fact, no one is. My peripheral vision starts to fade to black, and I cling to the doorframe and hang my head to gain my bearings, catching my breath. I moved far too quickly, and am running on far too little food and far too much wine.

That's when I notice a large box lies there on the ground, wrapped in the same gold parchment as the gift from Zalya the other evening. The gift I never opened, but that now sits among the other untouched packages on the kitchen table.

Well, looks like they know.

When the stairwell stops spinning, I reach down to pick up the box with one hand, the other still clinging to the doorframe for support. Clutching it to my chest, I stand in the door for a few more hopeful moments, as if it might produce a beacon to Blaine that I'm ready for his return.

The box isn't heavy, so I don't think it contains any kitchen tools. I suppose it's possible that it could be a uniform, or maybe they've sent over a contract and it just looks like a gift. I bring it to the coffee table and set it down gently. My feet shuffle in my heavy steps back and forth to bring the other packages from the kitchen table over to the sitting area. My desire to burrow in my blanket outweighs my need for enough space to examine my deliveries.

I start with the smallest package. A box wrapped in parchment paper, only a few inches wide and tall. The wine I spilled on it yesterday stains the outside, and the image of it spreading across the table while Blaine fights for me flashes through my eyes. The package is sealed with a brown wax that smells oddly familiar. Notes of something rich and fruity drift through the gaps in the paper.

A candle and a small piece of parchment fall out as I rip through the wrapping.

August,

I heard about your friend. I know you loved him very much. I made you this candle with the coffee beans you and Blaine shared with me. I hope it brings you joy in the darkness. Feel free to come downstairs if you need company – Navaya

I stare at the small gift. Now, not only am I out of my favorite coffee beans, but if I want to smell them, I'll have to be reminded of Vincenzo's death. Considering today cannot get any worse, I light the small candle before continuing to the rest of the packages.

But damn if I can't smell the banana leaves in the smoke.

I move on to an envelope. The paper is soft, likely from being crumpled and uncrumpled several times over before its ultimate use as this envelope. Rather than using a wax seal, the sender folded the paper in on itself, making it rather easy to open.

Something about an inch long, solid metal, with an orange ribbon tied to the end, falls to my lap, along with a note. I would recognize it anywhere—Vincenzo's key to The Goblet. It's a sentimental gift. The key has no purpose any longer since The Goblet has burned down. I only notice I'm crying again when I look down and see my tears on the parchment. Not just any parchment, but the first menu written for The Goblet when it opened. Vincenzo kept it on his desk in the pub's office. He always told me that he needed it to remind him of where he started.

My Dear August,

Vincenzo would have wanted you to have these. We love you.

- The original key to The Goblet
- The original menu from The Goblet's grand opening
- His briefcase

Love, Norris

I pull the blanket from my chair tighter around me, imitating the squeeze of a hug from Blaine. A feeling I'll never sense again. I already know the briefcase won't open, so there's no reason to waste the minimal physical energy I have on that. Just like the answer to the question of how I found myself here, I may never know what Vincenzo kept in it.

All that remains are the two gifts from an employer that I assume somehow knows I accepted their offer. The first is about nine inches long and a few inches wide. The second one is larger. They are both clearly wrapped by someone with an attention to detail. Not one paper edge shows through; instead, the bottoms of the packages have intricate layered angles tucked in one over the other, as if kept sealed by a paper zipper. The indigo velvet bows are soft and thin, yet keep their shape on the tops of the boxes.

Something put together this way doesn't deserve to keep the same space as me. So I rip through the wrappings over and over until there are shreds and ribbons of thick golden paper littered all around me.

Better.

In the smaller rectangular box, I find a kitchen knife. I can't quite place the material of its construction. It could be steel, but I've never seen steel this dark. The metal seems to almost absorb light rather than reflect it, and it gives off an almost matte black hue. I hold it up toward the light shining through the window and still can't detect any shine. I wonder if I could take it to the market and have the Molvarian assess it.

There's a card on the top of the second package.

August Monroe,

I am looking forward to your arrival next week. As you join our family, please consider this gown a welcome gift. May its elegance match your unbound radiance.

Cliff will arrive to transport you and your belongings to my grounds. I do hope that our carriage will be comfortable enough for your travels. Your rooms are ready, and I believe they will be up to your standards.

Love and Regards,
- R

The letter reads as if "R" already knows me. Assuming an assistant wrote it, I set the card aside, making a mental note of the moving details, and watch a gorgeous indigo floor-length gown pour out of the box like liquid silk when I lift the lid. I've never felt or seen anything like it.

Where the hell am I going to wear this?

The letter gives no details, but if they expect me to dress like this every day, they'd better be prepared to buy me a whole new wardrobe. At that thought, the first laugh escapes me since possibly before Vincenzo's death. Although it feels like emotional betrayal, the reaction is cathartic.

"Well, I wanted a new start. I guess the new me wears gowns," I mumble to myself as I let the fabric run through my fingertips like water. But that's exactly who I will be when I leave Quinthold. A new me.

A new August may just be what the lands need right now, my other voice encourages me.

I put on the dress, and of course, it fits like a glove. It moves with me, almost guiding me. I spin a few times and marvel at the near-silent swishing sound and the carousel of movement I catch in my hall mirror. For the first time in a long time, I feel beautiful. I assume that's why I can breathe without pain in my chest for the first time since Blaine left.

Another knock sounds against my door, and I spin my way to it, unable to let go of the giddy feeling I have in this dress. A tall man in an indigo guard uniform stands on my step.

"August Monroe?"

I look behind me, out into the hall, then down at myself. "I guess so," I finally respond. "And you are?"

"You can call me Greyshan. Do you accept the job offered to you by Zalya Tunverein?"

"Do I have to give the gifts back if I say no?"

He stares at me. Sarcasm clearly isn't his primary language, but I spend the silence taking in his purple eyes—striking, yet kind.

"I'm here to help escort you."

I give him a look that I'm hoping clearly displays that I think he's insane. "Well, as you can see, I haven't packed, and quite frankly"—I pause while I stick my nose into the crook of my shoulder, smelling what I've become—"I need a bath."

He steps into the apartment uninvited, looking around the room. "That's not an issue. Feel free to bathe. Is it okay if I wait at your table until you're ready?" He stands tall, with his hands at his sides, awaiting my reply.

"I mean you're underdressed"—I gesture down at myself—"but sure." I watch as he walks to the table and pulls out a chair for himself. "Want some coffee? Oh, and didn't the letter say someone named Cliff was coming to get me?"

His face lights up at my offer. "Cliff is waiting in the carriage. He's not one for small talk. But coffee would be great."

At least he's normal enough to want coffee.

I brew and pour him a cup before heading to my bathing room to wash off. It's the last thing I remember from Quinthold.

Part Two
PROTOSTAR

It is a strange phenomenon to begin a life with expectations and predispositions to morality already formed. Most souls carve their own opinions and values from their first breath. I must live with the knowledge of our past. I must pray I'm still allowed a resting place amongst the constellations when my Celesteran journey ends.

With a wave of her hand, the woman who called herself Titania silenced his fellow Fallen. Reginald stared at the wide, scared eyes of his confidants Niall and Gabriel, at the anger radiating in Horus's glare. Eleven of the Fallen sat awaiting their judgment, awaiting their fate, as he prepared himself for the task in front of him.

His hand shook as he gripped the quill that would

write the official history of the creation of Celestera—or at least the pieces that he could share without damning them all. He used an albino turkey feather today, finding the bird's beauty against the snowy peaks of the Evergroot Mountains to be breathtaking. He hoped it would bring honor to his note-taking at this second Convergence. Instead, he now stood before the podium on the steps of the dais in Linea's temple, preparing to write a full history of the Fallen, or else have his blood and that of his fellow colleagues on his hands.

Her instruction was simple—write their history with enough detail to warn against following in their footsteps, but not so much that it decimates their legacies. Reginald recognized it for it was—pity. She was taking pity on them for blindly following Linea here from the skies, unaware of her ultimate plans. Though, looking back, the signs were there.

He recalled the day Linea had invited him to join her in her next world. Her face lit up at the mention of peaceful lands and unbound power waiting to be harnessed. He never asked how she had found this world, or the loophole they would use to bypass official soul assignment to enter the world. He never asked how they would be able to fall through its atmosphere, wise and aware, rather than as the birth of something new. He was too eager, blinded by the beauty of the possibility. "Ask the right questions" was the mantra of the scholars, and Reginald cursed himself now for never having asked while he had the chance.

Tears fell, not in steady streams, but at odd intervals, dripping onto the parchment before him, ruining the premier scrolls he had prepared for today. He cannot, will not, lie or deceive—an offense not only to his gifts of truth but also to his line's integrity. Truth was but the umbrella that protected any deity beneath it. It was to Truth that he prayed, that he sent his vows of loyalty, and he would not betray her.

Titania's instruction was clear, but she never said he couldn't strategically place clues throughout the texts, that he couldn't give his children, and their children to come, a chance to find the whole truth for themselves.

How do you prepare yourself for the end, when you woke up thinking today was the beginning?

With a deep breath, he gathered his resolve, addressed the challenge before him, and recalled the day that the Fallen fell to Celestera.

"Linea, a streak of incandescent light, cut through the velvet night, a fleeting brilliance against a backdrop of swirling galaxies. Time was running out, and Reginald was still missing. She had one last stop amongst the Celestial Preserves to search for him—Reginald's favorite haunt—where he was likely absorbed in helping to write another historic event amongst the constellations. Unbeknownst to him, it was hers. Souls everywhere would eventually know this constellation by name, and they would call it Linevolence. Reginald was always hopelessly romanticizing the truth.

Linea's time on Cimturnine was over. The others had waited patiently for her assignment to end, avoiding their own potential placements until they could go together as a group. They had all survived the latest black hole, the recurring wars of the constellations, and their own deadly worlds for centuries—now was their time for peace.

The others trailed behind her. Her lover, Micah, soared at her side. They were but a fleeting caravan journeying through the night, thirteen stars diving and climbing through the night skies. At least that's what any other star would assume. Just reborn souls venturing to their next assignment, a celebratory meteor shower in flight. Most of the atmosphere would not yet have heard about the tragedy of Cimturnine yet, and she didn't intend to still be moonside when they did.

She held that thought close as she slowed her group enough to limit suspicion and glided into the preserves. Spotting Reginald, she called out a coded sound—the signal. His head spun around, and she didn't wait longer than the time it took to see his confirming nod. He would catch up, they had to go.

An asteroid spiraled from the left, and she veered her crew right, narrowly missing the attack—the Sun Council knew. Avoiding battle zones and narrowly escaping her search parties, she led her followers to the edge of their new world and up to an atmospheric line that, once they crossed, would propel them to their freedom.

Centuries ago, when she told her followers of this new world, she described the lands as powerful—yet barren, and ripe for them to finally live a life of peace. She described to them lands they could grow with, lands worthy of their auras and their bloodlines. She had spent centuries searching for a world like this. One by one, she pushed her followers across the line and through to their new world before passing through the barrier, finally, herself.

Mountains and valleys formed with their impact as they crashed to the ground. They could see it as they fell—lush green lands, and white sand deserts. Linea radiated with energy from the moment she joined her fellow fallen stars on the ground, seemingly glowing from the inside out.

She called their new world Celestera."

ADVISORY MEMBERS ARE NOT TO CROSS BORDERS INTO SOVEREIGN TERRITORY UNLESS EXPLICITLY INVITED OR ORDERED BY A LEADER IN THEIR LINE OF COMMAND. CAPITAL CITIES ARE CONTROLLED AND DEFENDED BY THE SOVEREIGN GUARD FOR THAT PROVINCE.

CONFIDENTIAL: REGULATORY CODES OF THE ADVISORY, ARTICLE 12, SECTION 8, CONDUCT IN REGARD TO TRESPASSING INTO SOVEREIGN TERRITORY

My heart sounds in my ear against my pillow like the tapping of a conductor's wand. Tap. Tap. Tap. Each tap calling me to wake up. I ignore it as long as I can, nuzzling farther into the abundant silk bedding engulfing me.

Eventually, I roll onto my back, but the onslaught

of the sun's rays on my eyes has me rolling right back to my stomach and hiding in the pillow. Turning my neck just enough to see through one eye, I try again, but the sun reflects so brightly against the gold-foiled ceilings that I have to shield my eyes with one of my hands. Something about this isn't right. I sit up, covering myself with the sheet, and look around.

I don't have gold-foiled ceilings. Or silk sheets. Or a four-poster bed. Where the fuck am I? The last thing I remember is fawning over the silk indigo dress sent to me by my new employer, and I was definitely in my apartment in Quinthold.

Well, there was the stranger you invited in and offered coffee, my other voice intrudes

I really don't have time for you right now, I respond, shutting out the imposition.

Okay, don't freak out, I tell myself. There has to be an explanation for why I am waking up in a room that's not my own, in a new bed I've never seen, and unable to remember how I got here. I'm alone at least—unharmed as far as I can tell. I check my limbs just to make sure—all freckly and just as limber as always.

Ivory tiles cover the floors, speckled with gold and indigo, reflecting light onto every surface from the floor-to-ceiling windows that span the entire exterior wall. The slightest hint of citrus and mint floats through the air, not overwhelming but enough to feel refreshing. Judging by the sun, I assume it's morning. The room isn't large, or possibly feels small in the presence of the enormous bed and vanity, both made of solid oak, or maybe pine from the north in Leondell.

A knock sounds twice against the door. I look around, as if there must be someone around to handle it, but it seems I am truly alone. I raise the silk bedding to further cover myself, tucking the sheet under my arms, before responding. My voice cracks from lack of use when I try to speak, so I clear my throat and eventually get out, "Hello?"

The door opens slowly, just enough for the visitor to stick her head through, and a familiar woman looks at me from the doorframe. "Hi, August, I came to see how you're doing."

I look around again, thinking she must be talking to someone else, but she welcomes herself in and starts flitting across the room to where trunks line the perimeter, unloading their contents as she goes.

An older version of me would have immediately attacked the woman, asking her to explain where I am and why. But today, I think my brain has decided the headache is more important than answers. I press the palm of my hand into the front of my forehead, where the pounding is the worst, and let the woman go through my possessions while I consider where I know her from.

"I'm so excited another human woman is around now! It's just been me for the past ten years, and dealing with all the descendants can be such a drag with no one to gossip to," she calls from the corner as she unloads a few of my cosmetics onto the vanity from a trunk, inspecting and—did she just test my red lip oil?

"Who are you?" I finally ask, annoyed mostly at the volume of her voice, mildly at her touching my things, and a little at myself for putting me in this situation.

"Zalya, remember! You're not great with names, are you? I get it—you just woke up. I can't think straight in the mornings either." She recites this in a singsong voice, bobbing her head to the side in a childish imitation of not being able to think straight. Her tone this entire time has felt so friendly that she's reminding me of the woman from the bookstore back in Quinthold. Though there's something about the way her eyes linger on each item of mine that she pulls from the trunks. Like she's checking its value, or judging its purpose. "I was so happy when I heard you had accepted our offer—" She pauses, jumping from the trunk she's hunched over. "Praise Descent, I haven't offered you any food or drink. You must be ravenous." And just like that, she skips out of the room.

By the Fallen, please let her be grabbing coffee.

Good, new August is already adjusting well, my other voice comments in response.

As I get out of bed, I marvel at the cool silk moving against my skin—again, a familiar feeling that I cannot quite place. My stiff bones reverberate up my limbs when my feet hit the floor, the shock reminding me I'm not twenty anymore. I bend at the ankles and knees as my stiff joints pop away the extended sleep.

The rug under the bed is plush, with intricate shades of blue and purple that wind across a muted beige yarn, creating a distracting design that I get lost in for a moment, my eyes going in and out of focus as they follow it.

Or maybe that's another indicator that I need food.

I pad to the first door and find a bathing chamber just as large as the primary space. A tub big enough for two, shelves lined with bathing oils, soaps, and salts—anything I could want, or imagine ever wanting. The marble flooring from the main room continues not only across the floor but also up the walls of the chamber, and soft rugs of the same purple-and-blue design lead from the tub to the door. A thick robe hangs near the salts and oils, and enchanted lights flicker on when I open the door.

Anyone wealthy enough to live in a place as grand as this could hire those from other provinces to come in and help enchant the decor. The lights are clearly an addition from the home of light and shadow magic, The Runda Isle.

My breath catches when I open the second door. More enchanted lights illuminate a wardrobe nearly half the size of the bedroom and filled with more clothing than I've ever seen. On display on the far wall is the indigo dress, hung like a piece of art, calling to me to don it again. The wardrobe doesn't just have gowns, though. There are riding leathers, nightgowns, chef's robes, aprons, even casual sweaters. I allow my fingers to graze over the various fabrics and pieces as I peruse the racks. If my employer expects me to pay for all this, I'll be in debt for a long time. I'd intended to grow my wardrobe slowly, but this—

"Gorgeous, isn't it?" Zalya's voice startles me.

Sneaking up on me when I'm hungry is a dangerous thing to do, but she's holding a silver tray full of food, and the sight is intoxicating. I stare blankly at the tray, half wondering if it's poisoned, half not caring if it is. "You're the woman who offered me the job here," I finally speak, the memory coming back to me.

She smiles, waving her hand in a gesture back toward the room— all the answer I need. I follow her through the third door, which opens up to a landing. To the left are stairs down to where I'm assuming the rest of the rooms are. However, straight across from my door leads into a living space, twice as large as the bedroom and just as luxurious. Floor-to-ceiling windows must extend across the entire exterior of the building, as they run down the length of this room as well. I wonder if hidden curtains exist for privacy.

There's a small dining table in the room, built-in shelves filled with books—all of mine, alongside several new ones displayed in the center—and a cozy sitting area by a large fireplace. Whoever unloaded my books even organized them by topic, which I admire as I run my finger down the spine of *The Tales of the Obsidian Witches* that Nova bound for me when we were young—its black leather is cracking in places. I'll need to find some oils soon to condition it.

A breeze kisses the back of my neck, and I turn to notice a large balcony that extends the length of my two rooms. Zalya had opened two doors earlier to allow in fresh air while she set the table. The crisp autumn air now drifts in, and with it the scents of drying leaves and—cinnamon, maybe? The dining table sits perfectly in the path of the breeze, as if whoever designed this room planned everything meticulously. It's the type of purposeful design I would ask for in my dining rooms.

I venture onto the balcony to take in the view and see an entire community spreading out below, past the edge of this property. The grounds are dry, but various palm trees and cacti line the perimeter, surrounded by decorative rock, and a stream flows from the large gate at the entrance and continues beyond the palace.

A palace—that's what this is. If I'm counting correctly, I'm on the fourth or fifth floor. Floor-to-ceiling windowed walls indeed mark each level, with thick limestone slabs between them.

"Ready? I wouldn't want you to have to endure cold soup," Zalya calls from inside.

I spend the meal mostly in silence while she goes through a clearly rehearsed monologue of apologies and explanations. The food is mediocre. I've already made a mental list of improvements for the salad dressing, the under seasoned potatoes, and the dry rolls—along with firing whoever decided dill goes into a squash soup.

When I've finished and pushed my plate to the side, I ask, "So, let me see if I've got this right. My employer's name is Rivian, this is his palace, and these are my rooms. Rivian sent his lifelong friend and right hand, Cliff, to retrieve me. Cliff gave me a sleeping powder, while one of his guards sped up time, packed my apartment, and teleported me here. Now I'm supposed to believe that Rivian did not know and wants to apologize over breakfast tomorrow morning, and that you're here to break the ice before then?"

"Yes," she says definitively, nodding at the statement between sips of coffee. "And please go into breakfast with an open mind. Rivian would *never* have allowed Cliff to do such a thing knowingly. Between you and me, Cliff and I don't see eye to eye on many things." Her nose wrinkles ever so slightly at the mention of Cliff, which I'll ask more about later.

"Why is this place so secretive?"

"I wouldn't say it's *secretive*." Her eyes widen when she emphasizes "secretive," as if she herself is wondering what the right word would be if not that. "But you should really let Rivian explain all that in the morning." She must see my eyes narrow in suspicion because she quickly adds, "Rivian really cares about everyone here." She eyes me for a moment through her thick lashes while I continue to look around and take in my new space. "Want some wine to wash down your first meal? We have an incredible vineyard on-site."

I haven't had any female friends since Beryl's storm took Nova from me, but this—this feels like it could be what that's like. At least, this is what friends do in the books I read. Zalya also seems to play a key role in whatever the operations are here. She could be a valuable source of information regarding the lives and circles I've just joined of the elite descendants. "Actually, yes," I say, giving her a small smile, "but would it be rude if I asked to drink it alone? I'd like some time to rest before meeting Rivian tomorrow."

She waves her hand dismissively. "Of course, of course. I don't know what I was thinking. I need to check on Rivian, anyway. I'll have a staff member bring some up."

The wine arrives shortly after Zalya leaves. The staff clears the plates in silence, which I'm grateful for, leaving me alone to ponder my next move. Once everyone is gone, which I confirm by checking behind all the doors, I track down my knives, which are in the wardrobe near my chef aprons and dragon-hide bag, and spend the rest of the day sharpening them while sitting on my new balcony.

10

I woke up several times throughout the night, each time my mind hoping for a familiar view, each time telling myself that I chose to come here. Now that the sun is up, I remind myself that have the chance to start fresh, on my own terms, to manage the Resistance from the inside. I pay attention to my breathing, trying to settle my nerves—the citrus and mint essences in the air clear my mind. Today, I'll meet my new employer, see my kitchen, and most importantly, find out how the palace imports their ingredients.

"August?" Zalya's voice calls from the doorway, though I missed the knock. "I thought you might want a friendly face around before breakfast. You okay?" Her voice sounds different today, possibly concerned, though I can't quite place the tone. On the night of the ball, she was rough-edged, a little bitchy—conceited. Yesterday she was fake, perky, and overly apologetic. If I was just meeting her for the first time, this version of her would feel genuine, but I don't know her well enough to know which version is real.

"I'm fine," I reply, not even looking at her as I get out of bed. "In the future, you could knock."

My other voice calls me out on my pre-coffee attitude. *So much for polite, new August.*

I ignore it and head straight for the bathing chamber, where the fresh lemon bath oil and salts are calling my name.

Citrus has a powerful energizing complex. I love to sneak citrus fruits and juices into desserts to rejuvenate guests after the grandiose meals they have usually just consumed—particularly at balls and parties that go late into the evening. Throw in some coffee and you have renewed excitement among your festivity-goers.

Fallen, please let there be coffee at breakfast, I say to myself as I draw the bath, thinking about Zalya probably still waiting on the other side of the door.

Getting dressed feels a little overwhelming. All the options in my new wardrobe combined with wanting to make a good impression today make me nervous, but I end up choosing loose beige pants and a white tank, plus a dark brown cardigan with gold embellishments that catch the sunlight beautifully in the brightness of this room. I plait my hair, weaving a yellow ribbon through my chestnut waves. The bright morning sun catches the hints of red in my strands, which in turn makes my freckles pop. While abundant, they're one of the unique characteristics of mine that I enjoy—a built-in accessory always on my skin. I swear they move throughout time, taking different shapes and hues to always keep me guessing.

As I'm walking out of the wardrobe, a gold chain with an obsidian stone charm catches my eye from where it sits on a velvet tray. I rarely wear jewelry in the kitchen, but the stone reminds me of something I can't place, and it goes perfectly with the gold details on the sweater. It pulls the outfit together nicely. Not to mention, I want to look good for meeting my new boss.

"You're wearing the necklace I picked out!" Zalya squeals when she sees me walk in, jumping from her chair, instantly making me feel guilty for snapping at her this morning.

"I guess I am. I couldn't resist the obsidian with the gold," I comment, fingering the stone. "Did you pick out my entire wardrobe?"

"Most of it." She nods, a humble grin hinting at the corners of her lips. "I loved that necklace so much that I bought myself one too. We'll match sometime. Come." She waves for me to follow her down the stairs.

"You'll have to show me where you sourced everything. I could have never built a wardrobe that size back in Quinthold."

"I'd like that. I'll show you the shops in town when you're ready."

The same color scheme as the one in my room flows throughout the entire castle, from the gold-and-indigo-speckled ivory stone to the windowed exterior walls and gold-foiled ceilings. Even the purple-and-blue rugs make appearances as runners down the long hallways.

A few workers shuffle by in uniforms of pressed indigo linen. Occasionally, guards are stationed in doorways, their uniforms displaying a vaguely familiar sigil, all sporting a different weapon of choice. Each gives an almost imperceptible nod as we walk past. I notice a rather attractive guard wearing a thick leather vest with at least a dozen daggers sheathed across it, and I wonder if I could convince him to throw knives with me sometime.

"How many guards are on staff?" I ask through the corner of my mouth to Zalya while I continue looking around, feeling almost uncomfortable with the silence of the palace.

"Hundreds, but only the most senior or rooks are stationed here in the palace."

"Hundreds?" I ask back, louder than intended. I check my shock before continuing. "Why?"

"It's common for someone in Rivian's position to ensure his grounds—and city—are secure," she replies nonchalantly.

I want to ask what she means by "city," but I'm taken aback when we turn a corner and the ceiling disappears. This wing of the castle is one story, stretching the height of the rest of the structure. The windowed walls to the left reveal a courtyard in the castle's center, and the wall to the right reveals two sets of double doors, each at least two stories high.

"The north and south wings of the palace don't have upper levels like the eastern and western wings. The premise is an exact square, so you'll catch on quickly. On this side are the library and ballroom, and on the north side is the entry atrium," she says, and even though she speaks quietly, her voice still echoes from wall to wall for several seconds.

We slow down in front of the first pair of intricate double doors, and I watch as they open on a phantom wind. Zalya leads the way into a grand room with mahogany bookshelves lining one wall and tables with cushioned chairs and couches along the other wall, which of course are both windowed and five stories high. It's a library. Not just any library—the largest I've ever seen.

I crane my neck to ogle how high the shelves stretch and the ladders that run down the wall. There is only one gap in the shelving; it seems to be an entry to the back area, probably containing more stacks of bookshelves.

"I'm going to leave you here. Let me know if you need anything," I hear Zalya say. Then I hear her footsteps retreating as well.

We passed a quiet librarian on our walk in, stationed at her desk right inside the entry. She looks about my age, and I consider if she might help recommend me books about Linea and the Fallen.

"Do you enjoy reading?" a male voice asks from behind me.

I jump, turning toward him. "Fuck, you scared me." I hold my hand to my chest, blinking the obvious shock off my face—wishing I could start this day over.

Did I just greet this man by cursing toward him? I ask myself in horror.

Smooth, my other voice interjects.

He's well-dressed—casual yet polished, wearing an argyle sweater vest over a cream shirt and tailored black slacks. His hair is a tousled mess, but the kind I know he spent time perfecting. He's thin, but not lanky. I can tell he's fit under the fall layers he's sporting. I have to look up at him, though he's not as tall as Blaine. I'm guessing he's around six feet, possibly just under, but it's his eyes that catch me the most: deep indigo like the ocean depths. Damn if I don't want to dive right into those.

You're drooling, my other voice points out.

I quickly turn back to the shelves, shaking my head free of the thoughts of the attractive man I just violated with my eyes. "Um, sorry. Yes, I very much enjoy reading," I mumble, feeling my cheeks warm with embarrassment and attempting to hide my inner turmoil from my face

"The library is yours to enjoy," he says, taking a step to my side so we stand shoulder to shoulder. He scans the same shelves I do, arms crossed behind his back. "I can't claim it myself. Brennan helped me collect most of these. I just keep them safe. I'm Rivian, by the way. Welcome to Liravel." He turns and holds out a hand to me. His broad smile above a chiseled jawline reminds me briefly of Blaine, but that's about the extent of their similarities. Rivian's features are more striking than Blaine's, whose face naturally has a softness to it.

Liravel—the capital of Auralia? That can't be right. I would have needed a Sovereign permit to cross the border from Eshrador. But I don't spend time considering that. I reach out to shake his hand, only making eye contact for as long as necessary before breaking our touch—praying he doesn't feel how sweaty my palms have gotten.

"Thank you. Your grounds are lovely," I manage, still feeling a bit thrown off.

"I like your bag, by the way. Dragon?" He nods at the bag across my shoulder.

"Thank you, and yes, good eye. It was a gift from an old friend. I try never to be without it."

He doesn't respond directly to that, but clears his throat and says, "Care for some breakfast?"

His hand finds the small of my back as he guides me to one of the sitting areas. My nerves sing in response, nearly squealing with the shock, and I take a few large steps to shake him off. What is wrong with me today? I have never felt this way about a man before.

Yes, you have, eleven years ago, soaking wet in a port station, my other voice responds—and I hate that it's right.

Staff members enter with trays of pastries, porridge, fruit, and—thank the Fallen—coffee. The first sip is bold, yet bitter. They are clearly sourcing a weak bean and using double the grounds to mask the flavor profile. I make a mental note of the flaws in their service etiquette to address with the staff.

My staff.

Rivian sits on a muted mauve love seat, indicating with a gesture for me to join him. I ignore him, choosing to go with the oversized emerald armchair with a high back across the low oak table, hoping I can regain a bit of dignity if I place some distance between us. The food spans the table between us beautifully, and I make a note of this positive placement from the staff.

"I want to apologize for the manner in which you arrived here," Rivian begins, his words blatantly rehearsed for the confidence with which they're recited. "It was unprofessional, and on behalf of the palace and my staff, I want to ensure you feel welcomed and cared for."

I take another sip of coffee, thinking about my response. I'm not angry. Sure, someone drugged me and teleported me here, but I still achieved the outcome I asked for. Right? I need him to trust me, believe that I'm a happy member of his staff, if I'm going to get anywhere with finding intel for the Resistance. "Okay."

Rivian stares at the floor, smiling a contagious boyish smile that warms my core. I'm sure my face betrays the fact that I find him attractive—extremely attractive. There is an energy emanating from this man that I'm intrigued by. He's not just physically attractive. There is something else here that I can't quite put my finger on, something deeper, and I think he feels it too. I do my best to push the thoughts to the side for at least today, pocketing how I can use this attraction to my advantage.

"So tell me about what you are looking for in your menus?" I ask, changing the subject, also needing to do a good job in the kitchen.

He follows my lead, spending the rest of breakfast answering my questions about the job and fellow staff here in the palace. When the conversation slows, he takes me on a tour of the library and ballrooms, and when we're finished, asks, "Care to see your kitchen and prepare for this evening's gathering?"

Select ingredients for every meal with honor and pride. For others will trust you only as far as they can trust your cuisine, and even the most undetectable poisons fail to subdue if the target cannot trust your company long enough to dine.

—A note to August Monroe inside a recipe book from Vincenzo Cuoco

The other multistory double doors in the atrium lead to an ornate ballroom, which connects on one side to the kitchen. The other side of the kitchen connects to a more formal, intimate dining space with enough seating for no greater than ten at a time. The kitchen sits in the palace corner, and through the windowed walls I can see a vast vineyard stretching across the grounds below to the south, and mountains spanning the western skyline. The midafternoon sun sits above the mountain peaks, casting a glow across the vineyard like I've never experienced. I can't wait to see it in the moonlight.

Rivian stands silently in the doorway, leaning against the doorframe with his arms crossed in front of him, while I take everything in. He asked the few staff members already here to vacate momentarily so I could peruse the kitchen of my own volition, though I can't shake the idea that he simply wants a bit more time alone with me. Even now, I feel his eyes following me as I make my way around the room.

A long island-style worktop runs the length of the room, three separate ovens span one wall, and there's an icebox that is easily the size of the tub in my new bathing chamber. If filled, I expect I could feed the palace and town for at least a week on the amount of meat it could hold.

"Is everything up to your standards? I'm happy to upgrade any tools to your liking."

"No, I—" Rivian's voice sounds behind me while I am halfway in the oven, checking its size—causing my head to hit the top of the opening. "Everything is lovely."

I turn my back against the stovepipe to keep from brushing him as I sidestep out of his reach. Fallen, he is making it hard to remain professional.

"Well, I'll leave you be, then. Send word if you need me, love," he says, turning on his heel to head back out the door to the ballroom.

Well, your boss just called you "love," my other voice confirms.

"Dinner, August. Focus on dinner," I instruct myself out loud. Then, nodding, I affirm my directive and turn to scan the room for my next move. The first thing I do is open the icebox, hoping a wave of cold air will bring with it the sanity I have obviously abandoned the past few days. It helps. I close my eyes and soak in the chill, letting the lid lie against my back while my top half reflects on the past several hours, wondering how I can recover. But then a rare meat catches my eye, its silver veins glinting even in the darkness of the box.

"Is that—is that catoblepas?" I mumble to myself, half in disbelief, half in awe of seeing a cut of the animal I've never had the chance to work with. Catoblepas is a rare and gamey meat found in the deserts of Curatia. In fact, most descendants of Curatia won't touch it, claiming the animals are sacred.

"It is," a clipped, nasally voice affirms from behind me.

My head hits the lid of the icebox.

How many staff members are going to see you hurt yourself today while half inside kitchen equipment? my other voice asks, a question I'm afraid to know the answer to.

Once out, I turn to see a tall, spindly man with slicked-back fire-red hair standing a few feet away. It's possible he has more freckles than I do, from what I can see of those across his face alone, a feat I've never found someone capable of. He wears an expression that says, "I've assumed you're worthless until you prove me otherwise." Respectable.

He wears the same indigo linens as the staff I saw earlier, but his tunic is higher quality, collared, and with decorative stitching—the same sigil the guards wore is embroidered onto his chest pocket. He sports a pressed apron around his waist, with a leather belt on top, holding a couple of quills, a fresh linen napkin, and a small spoon, which slides through a small loop sewn to the side of it. To top off the look, with an embellishment I'm sure he added himself, there is a silver silk neckcloth tied around his neck.

I have to admit, while I take kitchen and staff dress codes seriously, he pulls off the custom accessory well. I finish sizing him up while he continues to hold that look of disdain on his face, staring down his sharp-angled nose at me.

"You must be my new assistant." I introduce myself while straightening to my full height and extending my hand in greeting.

He hums as he takes my hand by only the tips of my fingers, as if he's afraid of what he may catch from the brush of my skin, still looking down his prominent angled nose. "We'll get to that. Why are you here?" His chin rises ever so slightly, now to a point where I can see straight up his nostrils from my angle—lovely.

Adjusting my unhinged jaw, and relaxing my brows, I try again. "I'm August, the new chef. You can call me Chef or Chef Monroe. I arrived yesterday, and someone should have informed you I was coming. And you are?" I fold my hands in front of me, but keep my stance tall and firm to show him I'm not intimidated by his demeanor. My first goal here is earning and maintaining the respect of my staff, and this man is making it quite the task.

"Rowan," he drawls, pausing briefly before continuing. "The previous chef was here for fifty-seven years before he died ever so unexpectedly. Did you kill him?"

I wonder if he has to think about making his voice sound that way before speaking, as if it's an accessory of his personality that he puts on for others, or if his voice really is that judgmental as its baseline. Also, why in the aether would he assume I wanted this job so badly that I would kill to get it?

This cat-and-mouse game with staff? I've played it before, and I can do it again. "I assure you I am innocent of murder. Further, I assure you I'm qualified to be here, though I'll skip the detailed list of my qualifications. I will be the new head chef of this kitchen, and we can either work well together, or you can leave and I'll find another willing participant to assist me."

His indigo eyes shimmer in the bright light coming through the windows as he scans me up and down, but he must finally decide on his analysis of me as his new boss, He slackens a bit from his tense stature and responds, "Fine. I take it you were informed about the dinner planned for this evening?"

Rowan and I spend the next couple of hours taking inventory of the food and tools in the kitchen. I have him note a couple of requests, which he lets me know will go through Zalya. I tuck that information away in Zalya's profile in my mind, along with the information of when delivery day is for produce—my opportunity to communicate with the Resistance.

First, I find and inspect the knives. They won't do, so I send a staff member to my rooms to gather my own, while I shrug off my cardigan and change into an apron. When my knives arrive, I spend the time they deserve to polish and sharpen them before getting to work.

Since Rivian didn't give me direction on the type of meal he wanted, I decide on a simple, yet elegant, menu—quail on toast, served with a seasonal tomato-and-onion salad and a hearty bean soup. It's a meal that will show both class and skill without being too extravagant for the guests.

It helps that Rowan lets me know Rivian loves quail. Food and drink have their own unique ways of loosening inhibitions. Tips like this will go a long way toward getting in with the key contacts in the palace, and when the quail doesn't work, some of my backup recipes from my books upstairs will do the trick.

Finally, down a set of rickety steps from inside the pantry, through a cold and musty stone corridor with only torches for light, there is a large wine cellar with hundreds of bottles of wine available to choose from—most of which were crafted on-site, affirming the vineyard I saw through the windows earlier. I choose a light-bodied red to pair with the evening's meal. Time to do what I do best.

Meal preparations are smoother than I expect them to be for a first day with a new staff. Rowan takes my needs, many of which he predicts before I announce them, and handles them by directing and communicating with the staff. The staff clearly respects Rowan, making me want to sit down with him and learn his backstory here in the castle. I have a feeling he knows where the secrets are, and I start his profile in my head too.

Once the main course enters the oven, I go through my nonnegotiables in plating and serving etiquette with Rowan. He takes the time to train the others on those while I slip out of the kitchen to monitor the place settings in the dining room.

Three long tables form a U shape in the center of the room. The exterior wall faces west, and the golden glow of the early-evening sun shimmers through the large golden chandelier above the table. Spots of golden rays reflect off the gold-foil ceilings in all directions, like a shower of light. The effect is mesmerizing, almost distracting enough to make me lose track of my time as I run my finger down the wood grain of the table, checking for dust, admiring the elaborate setup.

There is an indigo runner with enchanted candles hovering above grapevines pulled from the vineyard for decor. Plush golden chairs slide under the table, ready for the guests. Each setting holds golden chargers for the warm plates, fresh indigo linens, and water and wine goblets waiting to be filled. Whoever handles design here has quite an eye for sophistication.

Well, the staff passes this part of the test, I think to myself as I head back to check on the quail, reentering the kitchen just in time to hear the end of Rowan's training for the evening. This is the most important part of the test—to see if they can handle the attention to detail that I expect with the food. I'll demand new staff without hesitation if they fail.

Really? New August is going to fire an entire staff on day one? my other voice asks.

Maybe just the incompetent ones, I think back.

Guests begin arriving in the ballroom, and a wave of anticipation comes over me, first as a prickling behind my neck, then a shakiness in my hands. I roll my neck in circles, trying to release the energy as I go to pull the final tray out of the oven and switch into a clean apron. Then Rivian walks into the kitchen. He looks—well, the well-tailored, all-white ensemble he's wearing leaves very little to the imagination. The top of his collared shirt stretches to cover his wide shoulders, and the top button remains undone, showing taut skin across his chest. The faintest layer of facial hair graces the lower half of his face, emphasizing the shadow in the dimple of his chin, and, if possible, his purposefully tousled hairstyle is even more mussed yet even more alluring.

"Chef?" One of my staff members snaps me out of my daze with a tap on my shoulder.

Put down the tray, August, my other voice pleads, somewhere more distant in my mind than normal.

Rivian strides toward me, concern written in the lines of his forehead as he quickly closes the distance between us. "August, what are you doing?" He reaches to take the tray from my hands and tosses it onto the countertop nearby. "You've burned yourself! How did you not feel that? Are you okay?" He carefully grasps my forearm right above my wrist, assessing the damage with narrowed eyes.

"Oh, um, years in the kitchen. I guess I don't even feel it anymore." I toss my braid over my shoulder and move to grab the fresh apron I was searching for earlier.

"Are you sure? You need a salve. Let me get a healer—"

"I'm fine, really," I insist, giving him a look that says I mean it. He hesitates but finally concedes.

"What are you doing?" he asks again, making me look back at my hands to ensure I didn't pick up another scalding tray.

"I'm freshening up before dinner service," I reply, feeling only slightly annoyed, possibly more out of habit than at his inflection. Normally, all these questions would exasperate me, but Rowan's ability to predict my needs have made this the easiest first day in a kitchen I've ever experienced. Even so, something about Rivian is throwing me off.

He shakes his head. "No, I mean, why are you putting on an apron? Dinner is ready, right?" Rivian asks, hands in his pockets now, rocking back on his heels as he scans the kitchen with those piercing eyes. Those beautiful, deep indigo eyes.

"Yes, it's fully prepared. I just prefer a fresh apron before mingling with the guests and introducing the courses." I assumed he wanted me to introduce the courses, but maybe he prefers me to stay in the kitchen? "Is there something else you'd prefer me to wear?"

"On it!" As if on cue, Zalya appears out of nowhere, grabbing me by the elbow and whisking me away before Rivian or I can respond. "You, my dear will be dining with us."

There's that annoyance setting all the way in, quickly followed by a sinking feeling of dread in my stomach. Zalya wears an indigo strapless gown with lace detailing. A simple gold clip holds her hair swept to the side, and a hint of kohl accents her long, dark lashes. For such a nuisance, she looks stunning. Meanwhile, I probably look—and smell—like I've bathed in the bean soup I prepared for the first course.

"Who's going to manage the kitchen?" I ask, still being hauled off by my arm, head pivoting between the kitchen and the direction we're walking.

"Have you not prepared your staff?" Zalya asks, her tone curious but with a hint of something else—as if she's hoping I'm not confident in my work, as if she's hoping I'll fail.

"Yes, but I'm used to monitoring during dinner service, and this is my first meal here," I admit as we make our way back to my rooms, feeling like we got here faster than it took to get to the kitchen this morning. "Did we take a different route?"

"Nope, the castle is a square. You took the long way earlier by starting at the library; go this way straight to the kitchen and it's much quicker." Her tone suggests I should have known that, and I'm about to respond when she continues, her quick pace saving her from my opinion. "It can take a while to get your bearings around here. You'll figure it out soon enough."

She heads straight for my wardrobe and pulls out the indigo dress Rivian gifted me. "How about this one?" She holds the dress out at arm's length and smiles. The version I receive of her tonight is somewhere between the fake perky and genuine ones I've seen so far.

"Is it just me, or is everything indigo here? Is Rivian related to the Sovereign Family somehow?" I ask tentatively, wondering if royalty could be the source of all the money here. Accepting a job in a palace connected to the Sovereign would be a sure way to gain access to intel to help the Resistance, but there's no chance I got that lucky.

She waves her hand, then pushes the dress into my arms. "Rivian loves Auralia, that's for sure. This dress suits you. Wear it!"

"Did you pick it out?" I take it with me into the bathing chamber, where I make do by washing myself quickly with a rag, just enough not to smell like the kitchen for the evening. Not perfect, but the best I can manage.

After all, revenge doesn't wait for vanity.

"Not that one," she responds when I return from my quick wipe down. She shows me the vanity, stocked with various creams, plus kohl and rouge. I'm able to let out my braid and clip my waves halfway up. I swipe some peach-colored gloss across my lips and add a light line of kohl to my lashes. I keep the gold-and-obsidian necklace from this morning on. Zalya isn't wearing hers, so I don't need to worry about matching in that regard tonight.

The silk of the dress soothes my nervous, warm skin, its flowing nature contrasting nicely with a long day of stiff aprons. The same subtle sense of calm it had the day I tried it on in Quinthold seems to radiate from the silk threads into my skin. "Who exactly will be here?"

"Just various peers of Rivian. Don't worry, you look amazing," she responds, gesturing back toward the exit. I guess it's time to meet some socialites.

She stops at the double-door entrance to the dining room, both opening slowly on their own, and gestures for me to go ahead. "Go in without me. I just need to visit my room for a moment. I'll be right in. Mingle." She's gone again without another word. While I frown at her retreating form, I still can't shake the feeling that she doesn't actually hope I'll be all right.

Descendants' eyes glow. Descendants' eyes glow. Always check descendants' eyes, especially when they glow.

Ten to fifteen people flit about the ballroom, mingling with one another, all dressed in bold and vibrant colors. I get the sense that this group has worked together for a long time as I watch a woman in a forest green cocktail dress lean toward a male in turquoise, whispering something behind her hand and nodding toward another couple grabbing a drink at the bar. I can't help but wonder what my place will be in this room.

My eyes catch on Rivian in his bright white, like a beacon in a technicolor sky calling my attention. He's speaking with a tall gentleman in purple robes. The deep timbre of the man's laugh echoes through the room like warmth given sound.

I've catered countless events like this, but have only actually attended as a guest a handful of times. Those have all been Advisory celebrations with Blaine, where I was nothing more than the girl on the general's arm.

Nope, not going there tonight, I tell myself as my eyes wander the room and I wonder where I'm supposed to be. Where to put my hands.

I've managed to keep my mind off Blaine for the past twenty-four hours, and I'm not sure which surprises me more—that my thoughts haven't wandered to Blaine, or that I haven't even needed to stop myself. I pull my shoulders back, taking in a deep breath.

I don't have to actually have confidence to appear as if I do, and I won't hear anything I can use from this far away.

As if sensing that I'm ready to join the group, Rivian's head turns my direction. He meets me halfway in a few long strides, taking my hand and leading me back to the gentleman in purple. He gives my palm a light squeeze before releasing it, a move Blaine would use when he didn't want to let go.

New August is caving fast for the boss. My other voice tells me what I already know, always stating the obvious.

It's a Resistance tactic, I counter.

"Where did Zalya go?" Rivian's voice pulls me from my thoughts.

"She needed to stop by her rooms. I didn't catch why." My voice comes out quieter than I expected. "You omitted mentioning that the guests tonight would be so well-dressed." A beautiful woman in a backless maroon jumpsuit stands maybe ten feet away, speaking to another male in a matching suit. She wears her black hair shaved close to her scalp, and the jumpsuit shows off the expanse of her back, which features detailed wings tattooed in shimmering onyx. The wings are subtle yet stunning against her golden brown skin, which itself shimmers as if the sun radiates from within her. The tattoo reminds me of fairy wings from tales I would read as a child.

"Tonight is more formal than most of my gatherings. We had a business meeting earlier today, a Convergence, as we call it. Tradition calls to bid everyone farewell in style." An answer, albeit vague—that seems to be a standard operation here.

He doesn't pause long enough for me to ask him to clarify before turning to the gentleman before us. "Vellas, I'd like you to meet my new chef, August. She prepared the most outstanding lasagna I've ever tasted at the Advisory Ball, and considering our previous chef's—unfortunate—death, I snatched her up."

Vellas. Where have I heard that name before? I scan my mind, coming up blank for the unique name that I'm sure I know from somewhere.

"Was that you?" Vellas's deep voice resonates like the vibration of a drum. "My, my. I was dreaming of the cake you served for dessert for days. I'll have to borrow you for a celebration sometime in Amarion." His deep brown skin shines against the moonlight coming in through the windows, and the shades of purple from his robes match his eyes.

"If Rivian is okay with me taking leave, I would be delighted to share my dishes with you and yours," I respond, not chancing offending a peer of Rivian's. Amarion borders Auralia, but depending on where he lives within the province, that is quite the distance to travel for a simple business meeting.

"Good." Vellas bounces on his toes in genuine or imitated

excitement, I can't tell. But the less than subtle grin across his face would suggest genuine, so I smile back.

I look toward the door to the kitchen where Rowan stands, giving me a nod that tells me the meal is ready when the room is. "Rivian, it looks like the kitchen is ready when you are."

"Well, then, shall we?" he asks Vellas, swinging his one arm out toward the dining table for me to lead the way.

His hand finds that spot on my lower back again, and his fingers graze my bare skin, on display from the low cut of my dress. A shiver radiates up my spine from where his fingers splay, a reaction that has nothing to do with the temperature in the ballroom. In this dress, I don't have the same range of movement to skirt the touch that I did earlier in the library, and suddenly I'd give anything for one of those pantsuits the other woman is wearing.

I hold my composure while he leads me to a seat in the center of one side of the table. When he pulls out a chair for me, the flame on the hovering candle in front of my place setting changes from its fiery hue to indigo, glowing brighter as I sit down. He leans down as he pushes my chair in, and I feel his breath before the brush of his lips on my ear. "The images I had in my mind of you in that dress do nothing to compare to the beauty you radiate this evening, love," he whispers, the words spreading the nerves from my lower back across every last inch of skin. I don't look, but I'm certain every hair on my body is standing.

I turn on a sharp intake of breath and think I catch him winking as he pulls away. Okay, I'll just have to figure out how to gain intel from him *while* sleeping with him. That's the new plan.

Sellout. My other voice again states the obvious.

The custom flames of the candles are likely a simple enchantment, but as a human, magic has always mesmerized me. I never knew my mother—though, according to my father, she was also human. My father would tell me it didn't matter when and where magic died in my ancestral lines, I didn't deserve to bear magical gifts anyway if I was related to her. The accusations never stopped me from wondering what I could have been if my ancestors hadn't angered the Fallen along the way. Or rather, what atrocity my ancestors could have committed in order to anger them enough to curse the remaining lines to a mortal human life.

Zalya's voice sounds behind me, acting like a splash of cold water to the flame building within my body from Rivian's touch, and for the first time since arriving in Liravel, I'm thankful to hear it.

I turn to see her hanging on Rivian, running one long black fingernail down the front of his vest, the other hand clasped behind his neck, fingers lightly drawing circles beneath his hairline. She has a fresh coat of red gloss spread across her lips, which she pouts out as far as she can without appearing posed, and I believe her breasts sit ever so slightly higher on her chest than when I saw her last.

"Sweetie, that's my seat," Zalya coos into Rivian's ear, nodding her head in my direction. "August, you don't mind, do you?"

"Oh, of course not." Embarrassment creeps in as I consider the image before me.

Are they together?

I stare at the table to hide my reaction while I slide one seat over, contemplating how I mistook his interactions today as flirting. Red splotches bloom across my chest, and I cringe at how impossible it is for my skin to hide my emotions.

Without my peripheral vision to assist, I bump into something—someone. I feel it, then I hear it, then I smell it. I've knocked a man's whiskey out of his hands, and by the aromatic scent now wafting from the rug, it was an aged varietal. The smell makes me think I'd be furious if someone knocked my drink over. I jump out of my chair to apologize and help clean up, but now my face stares straight into the broad chest of a man at least a foot taller than me. I take a small step back, putting as much distance as our chairs and the table will allow between us, and crane my neck to look up at him. A muscle ticks near his jaw, visible even through his thick beard.

I open my mouth to form words, but there are none—my mouth might as well be frozen agape. This is what it feels like to die of embarrassment. It has to be.

You need to calm down if you're going to make it through this dinner. My other voice attempts to calm me, calling my attention to my racing heart and shaking hands.

"I thought August could sit here for her first dinner," Rivian grits out through clenched teeth toward Zalya as he removes her hand, still gripped behind his neck like a vise. "And Cliff, get over it." Rivian's gaze snaps to the man in front of me, eyes narrowed in a look I would not want aimed at me.

My neck swivels from the angry male to Rivian and back again, as if Rivian might jump in with a solution that takes all attention away from me. By the time I turn to look at Rivian a second time, Zalya's hand has moved back to his bicep, like a leech stuck to his shirt. He again pulls her hand away, dropping it once it's disconnected from his shirt, and waves over one of my servers for Cliff. Then he gives me that core-melting smile before adding, "First-night jitters, hmm?"

Zalya looks toward me, raising her brows in inquisition, silently asking whether I'm going to move back to where I was or let her have her desired place at the table. That's when it hits me. Did Rivian say "Cliff"?

I spin back to see the man I assume now to be Cliff glaring in my direction. When I do, my dress catches the very tip of a knife placed too close to the table's edge—the flowing fabric betraying my need to stay low profile.

Instinctively, I reach out to grab the falling knife. Cliff does the same. We both watch as I grasp the hilt at the same time that Cliff catches the blade. I felt it happen in slow motion, an image forever seared into my memory. Now, not only have I spilled this man's whiskey, but his palm is dripping blood onto the rug below. The crimson blood seeps into the beige yarns, giving tangible proof to my social crimes of the evening.

The wound doesn't appear to hurt him as much as it looks like it should—that is, if I'm interpreting his narrow eyes burning holes into my skin correctly. I turn back to Rivian, back to Cliff, back to Rivian.

Why is my mouth open? Why can't I find words? Why am I sweating from places I didn't know I could feel? Why does Rivian suddenly look so exhausted? Why me?

I go to grab a cloth from the table for Cliff's palm, but before I can, the woman in maroon I saw earlier comes over and has him healed with a simple touch. Her eyes radiate the same color as her outfit, shining with her power. She hovers a hand over the spots that have hit the carpet, and those too vanish before my eyes.

I have never witnessed a healer strong enough to heal that effectively, that quickly. It's incredible. But I don't have time to ponder it long. I begin to apologize to Cliff, but he has his back turned to me, thanking the healer.

Rivian shakes off Zalya completely, who was somehow able to sidle up close enough to loop her pinky finger around his open palm, and he pulls out another chair. "Here, take this seat, and I'll sit between you two," he suggests tightly to her.

She obliges him, though I don't miss the quick look in my direction before she does so. Rivian places himself in the chair I just vacated, and hesitantly, because apparently anything I touch can break, I pull out my chair once more and take a seat. With shaking hands, I reach for my goblet of water, take a sip, and smooth my dress.

It can only go up from here, I think as I pay attention to the cool water making its way down my throat, calming my racing heart.

Hold on to that spirit, my other voice tells me, and I wonder if it knows something that I don't.

Cliff sits back down to my left. I don't chance looking his way, but I feel him lean in, and in a gruff whisper he asks, "Ready?"

I take the opening to look his direction. His thick beard contains a variety of shades of brown, ranging from the light hue of the sands of the Molvarian dunes to the deep brown of ground coffee, while the thick hair on his head balances them out with a warm mahogany. He's just as tall as Rivian, probably taller. Though I wouldn't describe Cliff as trim. No, Cliff is a brute. He obviously spends his fair share of time training, and I wonder if he's ever seen battle. Zalya told me he captains the guard, so I add that to his mental profile. If he's anything like Blaine, he'll be hard to crack under pressure.

"Not sure. Is the food going to put me to sleep?" I ask, looking up at him through batting, inquisitive eyes. I may have just put a gash on this man's hand, but he drugged me a few days ago, and I don't forget things like that.

There I am. A proud grin blooms on my face, returning a bit of confidence with it that I had lost.

"You can travel with me awake once you prove yourself. Shame that you knocked yourself down a peg with the spilled whiskey." He states the second part in an airy tone, scratching his beard, as if he had actually decided we were on good terms before the events of the past twenty minutes.

Honestly, I think I'm going to like Cliff. Outside of the comment just then—from which I can't tell if he means I have to prove myself as a human, or if everyone has to prove themselves—he gives off the same no-nonsense energy that I immediately saw in Rowan.

Rivian stands, clinking a utensil against his glass, to address the room. Could it be the candlelight emphasizing his pale skin? The sun has set by now, so maybe the lighting is just playing tricks on me, but his skin at this point almost blends straight into his white shirt.

"Welcome, Sovereign Descendants of Celestera, to the province of Auralia—"

Instant regret.

I choke on the sip of water I've just taken, spewing a couple of drops onto my place setting before covering my mouth with my napkin.

Did he just say Sovereign Descendants of Celestera?

You caught that too? my other voice confirms.

"You okay there, human?" Cliff whispers, leaning into my space so only I can hear him.

I don't respond, choosing to stare at my plate while I carefully wait for Rivian's words to prove I misheard him.

"—As the current standing Sovereign Descendant of Auralia, representing our Fallen Niall, I appreciate the efforts from each of you to continue to uphold the laws and values set forth for us by our Sovereign Fallen, Linea. It is tradition in the presence of the standing Sovereign of Leondell to call upon him for a prayer before our meal. Brennan, would you do us the honors?"

Celestial Mother, bring me strength, he did say it. I send a prayer to the same mythical moon goddess of the witches I asked to save Vincenzo. I'm out of real deities to call out to.

This wasn't just a business meeting—this was a Convergence of the Sovereigns. Why didn't I catch Rivian's unique word choice earlier? I didn't just take a job for a rich descendant, I took a job in a palace of one of their leaders. If I wanted access to intel, I just fell straight into the belly of the source. These are peers of Beryl, the Sovereign responsible for the Break after his weather magic cleaved Celestera in half during a fit of rage—or at least they were, ten years ago.

And they have no idea who just entered their kitchen, my other voice adds.

Zalya's eyes meet mine, and she gives me a questioning look, as if to ask, "What's wrong?" But she knows exactly why I choked on my water, and I won't believe she didn't expect my reaction.

I turn to see who I presume to be Brennan, standing toward the end of the table on the opposite side. I pictured Reginald's heir as thin and wispy, the product of years on end spent hunched over books and desks. I imagined him to wear oversized glasses and appear malnourished. However, Brennan more closely embodies Cliff, the epitome of strength, only this brute wears glasses, oversized still, but classic.

With a deep breath, he begins. "Fallen Linea, this evening we offer ourselves to your loving purpose—"

It's the Sacred Prayer, used in formal settings only so as not to diminish its weight with overuse. I had to memorize it when I was a young girl at school, as if humans could gain any small amount of redemption with the words. Our teachers would have us sing portions of it to various tunes to help it stick in our minds. I gaze around the table to see the reactions of the others—some bow their heads, others close their eyes with their chins slightly raised toward the ceiling. Zalya twists a strand of her long black hair around her finger. My mind wanders in and out of the words of the prayer.

"—to restore peace to the lands you so bravely fought for—" Brennan's voice carries so naturally through the space. Where Vellas's voice overshadows the room, Brennan's pulls you in. I see how his gift for storytelling could shine, even after only hearing a few words.

Nothing stands out as new or eye-opening information that I can send off to local Resistance units hoping to solve any mysteries. I scan my mind to remember Niall's gifts, humming the tune internally of the memorization song for the twelve Fallen. *Callie took to the forests, thriving in nature, opening her lands for all living creatures. Alloria showed all her emotions with rain, only those brave enough for the weather's elements could survive her reign.*

"—All Praise Linea." Brennan finishes, and the room echoes his chant.

Cliff clears his throat, loud enough for all to hear. Brennan shoots a glare in his direction, raising his brows in a look of contempt, unbeknownst to or ignored by Cliff. The server somehow interprets his gruff request—the poor girl rushes over to top off Cliff's glass. He now stares out the window toward the starry sky.

I don't know the dynamics here yet, but Cliff seems to not give a fuck what others think. Another quality trait.

Brennan seems content with the length of his unreturned stare at Cliff and proceeds to sit back down in his chair.

This must be Rivian's cue to resume speaking, as he stands once more from the chair to my right. I stare down at my lap, knowing that everyone in the room is now looking in this direction, and clench my fists till my nails dig into my palms, giving me something to focus on.

"Thank you all again for a productive day today. Please enjoy the farewell meal this evening, prepared by my new chef, August."

He lightly grasps my shoulder blade, and I close my eyes to avoid making eye contact with anyone in the room, focusing on how long I need to wait until I can shrug off his hand. I need to get back to my rooms, I need a new plan, one that doesn't involve getting in bed with the Sovereign Descendant of Auralia. But then it hits me. *Niall knew who you were before even a word, your aura shines bright, even when blurred.*

Rivian has the gift of Quintessence. He can read my aura. The only question that remains is, does the Resistance make me a bad person? Would he have hired someone with a negative aura?

By the end of the meal, the room swims before my eyes, a pleasant haze settling over me I could easily attribute to the plentiful wine. Or perhaps I'm in shock—a feeling akin to my response upon hearing of Vincenzo's death in the healer's center. The numb fog in my head certainly fails to focus on anything but my breathing for a period of time.

However, after I learned who Rivian was, the energy filling my veins felt more like lust. An emotional, heady hunger that I have never experienced settled in my stomach—in my veins. The solution? The only thing that will satiate my need?

Control.

I excuse myself at the earliest polite moment to check on the kitchen before returning to my rooms. After all, it has been a long first day, and I need all my energy to focus on continuing to deliver quality culinary services. Not to mention, I still need to sharpen my knives.

According to Piatt, the recovered journals all had a few striking similarities. Sourcing easily explained some, like their size and materials. Yet others, such as frequently used symbols and commentary, were harder to explain.

—An excerpt from Chapter Six of *Recovered Journals of the Fallen*

The coffee maker in the kitchen is enchanted to precisely measure the grounds, heat the water, and even flavor your brew if you load the tray with sauces or spices—and yesterday's batch still came out wrong. I will need to teach the staff a lesson on proper coffee preparation techniques, because today's batch, brewed by me, tastes exquisite. I'm on my third cup, sitting on the worktop and staring out at the vineyard, still covered in its morning dew. There isn't a cloud in the sky, and I watch as a few horses gallop through the crest in the mountains in the distance. I have never been so content.

I estimate I got around two hours of actual sleep last night. I tossed and turned, playing out scenarios in my head for how my time in Liravel will go—most of which end with me dying, but that may be a fate I have to accept. I came here to accomplish something, and now I have to decide what that is going to be. It's not as if I have anywhere to go if I decide I'm too scared now. I made sure of that my final night with Blaine.

The priority is to get a message out to local units, letting them know where I am, that I'm no longer in Quinthold. I'll need to figure out Rivian's weaknesses, how to make the most of where I'm at. Using sex as manipulation no longer feels safe considering how powerful he is, both in royal status and magical strength. He did love my quail last night, though, so regardless of my string of embarrassing actions yesterday, I consider dinner a success.

I hear Rowan's footsteps stamping down the corridor before he ever opens the door. I listen as they get closer, trying to catch how loud they are right before the door opens—possibly useful information for later. When he does reach the door, he's not three steps into the kitchen before he stops in his path and yells, "NO!"

"No? No, what? I haven't asked you anything." I jump down from the counter to see what could possibly have gotten into him.

He saunters over to me, his red hair curling at the ends today, running his eyes up and down my frame, analyzing me. "No, not today. Your energy feels all agitated, and I will not work in an agitated kitchen."

"It's good to see you too, Rowan," I say as I reach into my bag on the worktop to pull out my roll of knives. I also gather a quill and parchment to come up with a menu.

"Fine, stay, but I need a minute to find my amethyst. Your mood will not take me down with it." He raises a finger in the air, turning on his heel and heading back into the pantry.

I shake my head in his direction, unsure whether what I'm feeling is annoyance or entertainment. "The Amari currency? What do you need that for?"

While Rowan does whatever Rowan does, I pour myself another cup of coffee. At this point, it's just being proactive for what I'll need to handle Rowan for a few hours.

He exits the pantry wearing an amethyst necklace, if you can call it a necklace. The crystals are all of varying shapes, and rather than connecting by a chain, they seem to be held by three metal rods, welded together to make a triangle that fits around his neck. The monstrosity doesn't look like it would be comfortable at all.

"What are you wearing?" I'm doing my best to hide my opinion, but he's making it so hard, standing with his chin in the air, blatantly proud of his design.

"Negative energy finds me, so *this* protects me." The look he gives me as he says it suggests that I am the negative energy he refers to. It's taking far more than my normal allotment of patience to not just kick him out of the kitchen and find a new assistant.

"Okay," I say definitively, hoping to end this conversation, and turn back to my menu. However, new August is curious today, so I look back up and ask, "What?"

"Amethyst. It wards off evil. Everyone knows that."

Fallen help me. I can feel my good mood from this morning

dwindling with each statement he makes.

Not sure even the Fallen could claim this one, my other voice chimes in, validating the feelings as annoyance.

Of all the provinces I could have ended up in, why Auralia, why with the aura experts? Why couldn't it have been with the healers in Curatia or the time travelers in Amarion?

"Well, since you're wearing that"—I gesture toward the necklace—"I don't need to worry about how bitchy this next statement sounds. Watch your tone with me, Rowan."

"I'd make you one too, but I'm sure you would just drain the powers too quickly with your *aura*."

"Well, thank you for what sounded like a polite offer, but since you're shielded from my *energy* now, can we move on to creating menus for the next couple of days?" But then I realize that Rowan just gave me an opportunity to see myself through Rivian's eyes. "Rowan, since I'm a human and all, care to tell me what exactly you see when you analyze my aura?"

He looks at me with an exasperated face, as if this question is too much work for him to answer, but finally responds, "Your *aura* is bland, the color of honey. It's your energy that's on edge today. A calm person's aura floats around them like a summer breeze. Yours is spraying outward like glass shattering, the shards trying to escape your atmosphere altogether. You really need to find some excitement in your life before you die, with cooking for other people being the only thing you're known for. And probably some meditation."

Well, that was mildly depressing, I think to myself as I take in his comment. At least he didn't tell me my aura calls me out as evil. I want to ask more, but don't want to test my luck too much in one day.

He moves to where I'm still leaning over the worktop, working on the menu, and lets out a couple of judgmental hums as he peruses what I have so far. "Fine."

"Fine? Would you care to elaborate?" I glare up at him.

"Does my chef need additional praise this morning? Would you prefer I kneel to kiss the floor at your feet to show my agreement with your decisions?"

Oh, he's a gem this morning.

I hang my head, considering my next words. "Please save your sass for another day?"

"No, you'll have to get used to it. *My* aura is approximately eighty-three percent *sass*, as you call it. But I will try to stifle it today. I'm hoping to get out early."

"Fine." I echo his original response. "And good, I also want to get out early."

"What could you need to run off to? A hot date? Looking for a good time? I'd be happy to show you a couple places in town that would turn that energy of yours right around in no time." His mischievous grin gives me the sense that he's right.

I momentarily let myself remember those days in Quinthold, staying out until the sun came up, accepting any drink or *substance* offered from a stranger. I'll never know how Blaine always made sure we got home safe, or at least to The Goblet.

Don't plague yourself with thoughts of them today, my other voice says, trying to protect me from myself.

I turn back to Rowan. "For the love of the Fallen, can we please talk about this menu?"

"Yes, Chef." He mocks me by standing straight and crossing his right arm diagonally across his chest, the symbol of salute in the Advisory. "And don't think I didn't notice your failure to decline my offer."

"You know, if you were working with a previous version of me, I would have fired you by now. Also, my ex is an Advisory general, and you wouldn't last a day in their training."

"Ex? So he's available?"

"ROWAN."

He seems to get my urgency, either by my tone or the whites of my knuckles as they clench on the worktop. "Fine." He relaxes after another mock of what seems to be the word of the day. Leaning down to examine the menu closer, he marks a few ingredients with a small X using the quill from his apron. "You'll need to place an order for these. If we push these options to two days from now, we can get the delivery order in today and have them by tomorrow afternoon for prep."

"There's a delivery tomorrow?" I ask more abruptly than I probably should. I calm myself a touch before continuing, attempting to sound nonchalant. "You know, as the new chef, I think it would be smart to send correspondence to the local farms and distributors introducing myself. If I wrote a letter, would you be able to make sure it made it to the delivery courier?"

14

It is this scholar's opinion that Leondite Scholars tend to hold too much admiration for their libraries—tend to idolize their existence. I believe the continent would be better suited to store the tomes in libraries across the lands, accessible by all, before the books come together and create their own truth.

—An excerpt from *Celestera: The Beginning*

After several hours, and many debates with Rowan on which wines, breads, and cheeses paired well with each entrée, we get the kitchen to a place where I can leave for the afternoon.

The smell of aged paper, leather, and that signature citrus-and-mint scent hits me like a wave as I enter through the double doors of the library. I nod to the librarian stationed at the front, who gives me a kind smile in return, and head toward a section of chairs near the back windows.

"August, I was wondering if I would see you today. If you're looking for coffee, I had a pot brought in a bit ago—" The last couple of words trail off as Brennan catches sight of me. He sits in an oversized burgundy armchair, coffee mug in one hand, one leg crossed over the other, with an unopened book in his lap.

"Hey, Brennan, like what you see?" I wiggle my brows suggestively in his direction and spin in a circle, letting him see the full disaster that I am this afternoon. I may have gotten a bit of the food prep splashed on me in my hurried state this morning.

I was able to spend a few moments with Brennan last night before I hurried off to my rooms. I haven't gauged whether I can trust him yet, but there is something about him that feels comfortable, so I humor this brief distraction. At best, I glean information I can use. At worst, I have a stop for coffee.

"The water systems connect to your rooms, yes?" he asks tentatively, skirting around what he actually means—that I look like shit. He grins at his wit, the smile hidden in his beard but visible where it meets his eyes. I assume I smell as bad as I look, just unaware of it after spending all morning with myself.

I give him a teasing glare, scrunching my nose and squinting my eyes as if they could send rays of my annoyance in his direction. Then I ask, "Are all of you still here?"

"Assuming you mean the other Sovereign Descendants you met last night? No, they all went home. Rivian and I are close, we have been our whole lives, so I try to stay a few days when I come to visit. Cliff needs an authoritative figure around now and then too."

"How long have you known Cliff?"

"Since the little shit came out ass-first into the world, unfortunately," he tells me matter-of-factly between sips from his mug.

"I should have known you two brutes were brothers." Another note I add to their profiles in my head.

"What happened to you?" I hear from behind me, only a moment before the signature shuffle-stomps that echo through the high ceilings, telling me it's Cliff.

"Kitchen things. The scone batter had a mind of its own this morning," I say with a shrug, picking out a chunk of dried batter from the tip of my braid. I believe there's an element of life in the ingredients I use in my cooking—that it's all about finding harmony in the combinations. I once introduced a citrus juice to some butternut squash, and it proceeded to rot right in front of my eyes.

Cliff looks good this morning. The plain brown sweater he wears brings out his blue-green eyes, which I didn't notice last night, particularly with the bright sun shining through the windowed walls of the library.

"That doesn't explain the cheese in your hair." He reaches my side and frowns at the top of my head. I reach up and run my hand through the strands. Sure enough, there are a couple chunks of cheese stuck there.

"Ah, I think that may be from some friendly hazing among my staff," I muse as I untangle a piece near my ear. Esmerelda and Rowan seem to think kitchen jokes are funny.

They're right, but I can't tell them that.

My all-black outfit today has a white powder outline, made from loose flour, across my chest and just above my knees, showing where the apron covered me from the chaos. I haven't looked in the mirror, but my guess is that cheese in my hair is just the beginning. The obsidian necklace made it through clean, though. I finger the charm momentarily, admiring the design, resenting who picked it out, and wishing I didn't feel conflicted about wearing it because of that.

I flick the piece of cheese I pulled out of my hair onto a mug saucer on the lower table in front of Brennan, and swing my braid over my shoulder as I join the cluster of couches he's chosen for today. Cliff takes my offering of a fresh mug for himself before I pour my own.

"This is not up to standard." I wrinkle my nose as I look down into my mug to examine the color. It's weak; I can see halfway through the glass. Then I smell it, bringing it to my nose—bitter. "Who brewed this batch?"

I wonder to myself if I can source the same beans I had in Quinthold and bring them here to Auralia. But I shake my head of the thought before I can dwell too long—thinking of Quinthold will lead to Blaine. Thinking of Blaine will lead to Vincenzo.

Stop doing this to yourself, August.

The cushions of the couch shift when Cliff sits next to me, pouring the inadequate pale brown coffee into his own mug. After a long pause among the three of us, he clears his throat and pats a quick, calloused hand on my shoulder. "I think it tastes great, A."

Still frowning at the coffee, I mumble back, "Thanks."

I look back up at Brennan, who gives Cliff a contemplative gaze. He blinks his eyes a few extra times than seems necessary before turning back to me. "Would you like any assistance finding books for your research today?"

"Research?" I ask unambiguously, wondering if Brennan knows my intentions. "Oh, you mean for the poisons that I can easily sneak into Cliff's snacks?" I cross one leg over the other and lean back farther into the plush couch as I continue to sip the inferior coffee.

Brennan stares at me for a moment, scratching his jawline and tilting his head to the side before saying, "You know, August, you may be peculiar enough to finally crack my brother's shell—but please don't kill him. Our mother would smite me from the aether."

I wave a hand, dismissing the request. "I'm only learning how to incorporate the poisons for now. Amounts, ratios, temperatures— that way, I'm prepared for when the time presents itself." I turn to face Cliff this time, whose forehead now rests in the palms of his hands, his eyes closed, elbows propped on his wide-set knees. He blatantly wants this conversation to end as quickly as possible, and in return I just give him those batting eyes he's going to grow to love.

This is fun.

"Well, I won't help with that, but I was referring to your intended research on the descendant culture and history of Celestera." Brennan moves straight back to the point.

"Why would I be researching Celestera?" I ask, growing cautious. I don't recall discussing my intentions for the library with Brennan.

"You had quite a shock from the dinner. Cliff let me know you weren't aware of Rivian's position prior to my prayer." He nods toward his still-silent brother. "As well as his *questionable* method of escorting you here. No one would blame you for taking advantage of the library of resources I personally helped curate."

I don't miss the humble nod to himself at the end, nor the gleam in his eye as he says it. "Are you able to handle your alcohol? I would just love to pick your brain over a bottle of whiskey." I throw it out, half joking, half serious, and without waiting for an answer to my rhetorical question, I add, "I kid. I know Cliff's the fun drunk." Cliff's silence makes this even more fun. "So it's not some fancy ability you have to read my mind?"

"No, I cannot read your mind or the minds of others. Neither can Cliff, for that matter." He is so articulate compared to his brother—hard to believe they're of the same bloodline. Which reminds me that Cliff shares the same gift of knowledge as Brennan. Another tidbit I add to his profile.

I consider simply asking Brennan to give me a full rundown of the Fallen, but I'm not sure I trust him enough to answer me without getting suspicious. After all, he was already smart enough to deduce my reason for being in the library. I could ask him which books to consult, and I still plan to, but I think I'll best use my time with him by getting answers unavailable in books.

"How does your power work? Can you recite any book in this library in full? Do you know personal truths as well?"

"Which question is it, August, that you would like the answer to?" His glowing turquoise eyes stare back at me, bright enough to hurt my own eyes if I stare too long.

Show off.

"The first one."

Brennan's eyes would shine bright, being a Sovereign Descendant. The further removed you are from the Fallen of your bloodline, the weaker your strengths. You can always tell the strength of one's power by the intensity of the glow in their eyes. I'm so far removed from whatever magic my familial lines held at one point that my eyes aren't even a color of one of the magical energies of the lands. I don't mind the silver, though—better than brown. If my eyes were brown, I'd have to question if they were just an extension of the millions of freckles that scatter my body.

Brennan switches his crossed leg and sets down his mug before indulging me. "I can't sense the truth until I hear the question spoken. That's why asking the correct questions always yields the greatest results. As well, the definition of truth is less clear than you may believe. Depending on how firmly you believe you contain the actual truth, the harder it can be for me to decipher. Even for myself, the truth isn't black-and-white. Beyond knowing and holding the truth, Fallen Reginald's lines expertly keep records and tell stories. I am quite proud of storytelling—stories tell the accounts of those who lived the events, after all."

So, not true omniscience, then. "If I ask you a question, do you have to tell me the truth?"

His lips purse while he contemplates his response. It reminds me of Blaine, the way he calculates his words before spewing them out. "While I know the truth, and can sense it in others, there is no requirement that I relay that truth to any other parties. However, I see little gain in telling falsehoods. A lie can act as a brutal weapon when wielded with intent, and too many make my stomach hurt."

I let that last statement process before I continue. There is something about the thought of deceiving this man that makes me uncomfortable. Like I would regret hurting him, though I can't quite place why yet. "Can I trust you?"

"The real question is why would you trust any of these books when you have access to the standing Sovereign Descendant of Reginald's line?" Before I can respond with another question, he picks up a few rather worn-looking leather books from the table to his side and places them in front of me. "I got you a welcome gift. I don't promise answers in these, but it could help pass the time."

Celestera: The Beginning now sits before me on the table. "Not a very creative title, but I suppose not a lot of creativity goes into history."

"You'd be surprised," Brennan says, as he monitors my perusal of the books from across the table.

"I didn't realize I'd said that out loud."

"You mumble to yourself a lot, actually. I'd enjoy hearing the other side of the conversation sometime. Clifford, are you ready?" he asks, turning to his brother.

"Please, she smells like curdled cream," Cliff grumbles to the ground.

I turn to glare wide-eyed at Cliff, but notice the same childish grin I've seen on Brennan today—the one that hides in his beard but meets his eyes—and I realize he's joking. I'd love to make a suggestive joke toward him, but instead of spooking Cliff into returning to his grumpy self, I turn back to the moment. "Ready? What are you two doing today?"

"That's an odd note of appreciation," Brennan says, ignoring my question as he stands.

"Thank you, Brennan," I add in a mockingly sweet voice, the kind a child would use to get their way with an adult, one I'm not sure I could imitate again if I wanted.

"One last tip, August. Always ask the right questions. It's a saying of the scholars from my province, Leondell," Brennan says before giving me a wink, turning on his heel, and heading toward the main doors, Cliff up now and at his side. I watch them walk away and can now see the similarities between the two, blinding as day.

Brennan left four books for me. Other than *Celestera: The Beginning,*

I also find *Recovered Journals of the Fallen, Regulatory Codes of the Advisory,* and a smaller blank leather-bound book that looks like a journal itself.

Its soft tan cover shows what looks to be years of scratches and lines. I take my time running my fingers over a few of the deeper ones. A black string around the middle stretches slightly to hold it together when not in use, and I carefully slip it up and over the cover to look inside.

It's blank. The paper is soft, though it doesn't threaten to tear at my touch. The material is one I've never seen before. It feels like something between paper and linen. I flip through the pages a few times before confirming—it's definitely blank.

Try writing in it, my other voice encourages me.

"I was getting there," I mumble back before digging into my bag for a quill and ink.

The quill glides across the page with ease. I assumed I would need to be gentle with the material, that its age would make it vulnerable to ripping under the quill's point. I write my name at the top of the first page, with a curvy underline—like Nova and I would do when we passed notes in school—then use the first page to jot down a few details about who I've met so far, translating their personality traits into ingredients and the ways to take advantage of them as the directions on their recipe cards.

"Hey, how ya feeling?" I knock over the pot of ink at the sound of Zalya's voice over my shoulder, which makes me jump. What is with people sneaking up on me?

I quickly close the journal and pick up the quill, dripping another ink spot onto the couch as I do.

At least I didn't spill blood this time. I think to myself, staring at the splotch of black ink on the thick beige rug.

"Reading," I say, already moving my books into my bag.

"I've been looking for you." She gives me a nervous smile, tucking a familiar-looking leather book under her arm as she moves to the chair across from me. "I'm worried I was rude about where you sat last night at dinner. I don't know what got into me." She looks uncomfortable saying the words, her shoulders hunched a bit, making her smaller. "You don't have to respond," she quickly interjects, looking down at her fidgeting hands. "I just wanted you to know that I know." A long pause sits between us before she moves on. "So? How are you doing?"

I tuck a loose hair behind my ear. "Physically, I feel fine. Mentally—" I pause, considering my next words. "I'm not sure. Confused, maybe?" I say, gazing at the ceiling, as if the answer could be there.

She nods to herself, and I get the sense that there is something she wants to tell me, but can't decide whether or not to share.

Gesturing broadly, I say, "I actually came to the library today hoping to learn as much as I could about Rivian's world—this world." Then it hits me. Zalya is another human here. "How long did you say you've been here?"

"Around ten years."

"Ten years. So around the time that Beryl caused the Break?"

"Exactly at the time that Beryl struck. I was alone, had no money, and ran into Rivian at a pub. I didn't realize who he was, but he said I could come here, that he had a job working in his vineyard. So I took it. Well, turns out that I couldn't grow a grape, but he let me stay and help with planning functions, managing some of the staff, and whatever else he may need." She said the last line suggestively. I am fairly positive I know what she means by that. Her pouty lips no longer look as nervous. "Want to come into town with me? I'll show you one of the better pubs and you can see the rest of Liravel?"

15

"Witches use their gifts to empower the land beneath them, restore what has been taken, and heal what has been harmed," Ceress reminded Nessa during their final training session. Nessa peered up at Ceress as she cast her first spell, allowing the moon's rays to power her soul. Ceress nodded at Nessa. She was ready.

—*The Tales of the Obsidian Witches* by Tresta McVey

Zalya doesn't leave me alone to my books until I agree to go with her, though I do convince her that we need to stop by my rooms before leaving the palace. It's one thing when everyone around knows that you're the chef; it's another when strangers have to question why there's cheese in your hair.

By the time we make it out the grand front doors, down the entry steps, and reach the cobblestone walking path that leads to the village, the sun is behind the palace. The silhouette of its frame shadows the town in an early-evening hue, and with it has come a slight chill to the air. Zalya hasn't talked much during our walk. Even only knowing her for a handful of interactions, it seems odd, so I try to open her up. "Does it get lonely? Being the only human here? Until now, I suppose."

"Rivian found me alone. I may not have magical gifts like those I'm surrounded by now, but I'm not alone. Not really." Her voice fades as she responds, as if the last part was to assure herself more than me.

There's the return of that authenticity I've only seen peek through a couple of times, like when she made the profound statement about the Liravel River the night of the Advisory Ball.

I sense she wants to change the subject when she quickly adds, "So, what were those books you were looking at in the library?"

"Oh—" I quickly run through in my mind what to tell her and what to keep to myself. If she's in bed with Rivian, I can't risk letting her know what I'm doing here. "—just some books Brennan suggested to learn more about the descendants. Didn't *you* have a book in the library too?" I ask, noting that the leather-bound volume she was carrying then is nowhere to be seen. Though I'm quickly distracted by the massive iron gate that swings open for us as we reach the edge of the property.

"It's enchanted to allow any of us in and out at our will," Zalya lets me know when she sees my eyes widen at the phantom movement. Apparently, the gates work just like the doors here.

Buildings have mostly consumed the town of Liravel, and I can't help but miss the green lawns we just left behind. People, like animals, need room to run. I know that the dry conditions of this province don't allow for many faunas to thrive, but the land could use some trees, for the birds if for nothing else.

The streets are quiet, though a few people are off on their evening strolls—not as many people as I would see out in Quinthold, but close. Passing brightly lit storefronts, I catch sight of exquisite silks displayed in one window—the same luxurious material as my indigo dress, shimmering under the sunlight, a cool, smooth memory against my skin.

Unlike Quinthold, though, the streets aren't littered with trash or people living in the alleys and trying to take advantage of rich travelers docking for the night. The streets seem clean, as if they're washed regularly. The streets in Quinthold often had sewage running through them, particularly when storms would come through and flood the grates. I get the sense that everyone here comes from money. Or the more likely answer as to why this city is better taken care of is that it's a provincial capital, and therefore a protected descendant territory. Humans can only be here while working or through marriage.

Zalya leads me to a pub on the town square, discreet enough that you might pass it on the street and not even notice. The old stone building could use a wash, assuming the brown used to be a deep shade of red. In contrast to the well-maintained buildings on either side, the pub cultivates an aged appearance. I can't help but think that at least stone doesn't go up in flames, like what happened to The Goblet. The wooden door seems ready to crack at any moment, and I cringe watching someone slam it behind them as they stumble out—clearly starting their evening ales early today.

A sign above the door reads "Connor's." I appreciate establishment names that don't try too hard. Vincenzo always emphasized that culinary craft should speak for itself. However, the scent of garlic and spilled whiskey clears out my sinuses the moment we walk in. Too much garlic—I'll keep that in mind when reading the menu.

Zalya waves to the bartender while signaling for two ales. She's so short that her head and neck barely show above the counter, but it's her shoulder-length dark curls that stop me in my tracks. Even just seeing her hair, it could be Nova, let alone her stature—the way she moves. I don't realize how long I stare before Zalya clears her throat.

I shake my head. "Sorry, I—that bartender just looks like someone."

"Someone close to you? I lost you there."

"Yeah, but it's not her. I'm fine." If I can't be in the library today, at least I can try to glean any information I can from Zalya—or at least find out who she really is.

She leads me to a small high-top table toward the far wall of the room. The room isn't large by any means. Thirty or so people might fit in here, including the seating available at the bar top. The low ceilings don't do the space any favors, instead creating a sense of captivity. Our table is much sturdier than it appears, and thankfully, there is a fireplace in the corner that keeps the room warm enough to actually want a cold ale. I look down at the tabletop, running my fingers through two letters carved into the wood, most likely with a sharp blade—A+B.

August and Blaine.

"August?" Zalya snaps her fingers in front of my face, staring wide-eyed at me. "Sure you don't need to talk about anything?"

"I'm sorry. Maybe I'm just tired. It's just—that bartender looks so much like my best friend, who I lost in the Break." A lump forms in my throat as I try to appear calm.

"Tell me about her," she asks softly, leaning in a bit closer.

I consider her question, taking a deep breath as I do. Talking about that time, about Nova, doesn't feel like something I should get into right now. "I'd rather not. Why don't you tell me more about what you do for the palace?"

"Oh, that's boring." She waves her hand in the air, brushing off the question. "I mostly just wait around until Rivian needs something. Occasionally he'll send me here, into town, for an errand or to deliver a message. I handle logistics for large events, assigning staff to their various tasks. Except for the guards, who are under Cliff's command, and of course, the kitchen, which is now yours." Her long, straight hair drifts over her face as she examines it for split ends.

The bartender shuffles by quickly, dropping off our ales on her way to clean another table. The mugs are chilled, and I revel in the ice-cold liquid as it burns its way down my throat. "It looks like we'll work together a bit, then, considering I'll be planning the menus for any of the gatherings or events?"

"Absolutely. That was one reason I was excited to hear you took the job. The previous chef was fine, but he was old and cranky, and Rowan is a piece of work." She rolls her eyes as she lifts her mug to her full lips to take a sip.

I grin at the comment about Rowan. "Rowan is a character, all right."

"I wish I could have told you more, by the way, the night I made the offer. Rivian swore me to secrecy. I don't know why, but I've never questioned his ways."

I consider that for a moment, wondering what Zalya really thought about offering me the role. Was she actually happy I took the job if it meant removing responsibility from her? "Why weren't you in indigo that night?" By now I've realized the purpose behind the abundant use of the accent hue. It's the royal color. I was so blinded by Rivian's flirtatious personality and addictive smile to consider the color of his eyes—or rather what the color of his eyes could tell me.

Hormones win again.

You should really get those under control. And at that refute, I block out my other voice.

"We don't have to wear indigo unless we're specifically at a Sovereign event. And if you can't tell, I gravitate toward the color black." She tucks a strand of her sleek black hair behind an ear with one of her jet-black painted nails, using her other hand to gesture down the length of her body. The conversation is feeling easier, like one I could have had with Nova when we were young.

"Really, why black?"

She bites her lip, staring down into her mug for a moment before answering. "Promise not to mock me, but you know the children's story about the Obsidian Witches?"

I nod my head, very aware of the tale. It was one of my favorites as a child, featuring women who called themselves witches. There were five witches in the Obsidian Coven, and all who came into their path feared them. According to the fable, in order to join, one would wait until a full moon, then pledge allegiance while performing a sacred ritual. Nova and I would dress up and pretend to cast spells and charms on each other like the witches did in the stories. The witches were supposedly more powerful than the Sovereign Descendants and got their power from the light of the moon.

She looks nervous as she continues, as if I might make fun of her for her adult obsession over childish tales, but she doesn't know I too escaped to the world of witches as a child. "Well, I was so obsessed with it as a kid. Along the way, I guess I made it part of my personality. My mother eventually stopped making me clothes that weren't black, and once I was old enough, I started painting my nails black whenever I could afford the paints at the market. Maybe it has something to do with my black hair? Regardless, it stuck."

She turns back to her ale, drawing a circle with her finger around the rim, until I ask, "Ever try to re-create the Initiation Ritual during a full moon?"

Her menacing grin says enough, but she adds, "Far more often than you can imagine."

We're interrupted by the bartender sidestepping around another table to check on us. She's so small that she's able to make the tight spaces work. "Anything else I can get you two?" Her voice is airy, yet genuine, not dripping with vapidness like Zalya's was last night at dinner. Her eyes go wide when she spies my dragon-hide bag slung across the back of my chair. "Tell me where you got your bag!" she squeals, reaching out to hold it in her hands.

"An old friend made it for me." I get a better look at her up close, and even her ears remind me of Nova, slightly pointed at the top—as if they were pinched that way during birth—along with the dark raven eyes and high-pitched voice. If she feels my curious stare taking in her features, she doesn't let on, continuing to run her hands down the hide and hidden seams of the bag.

"My uncles on my mother's side make bags like this. It's a family business, but I've never seen another like the ones they're able to create. Is that a blade sharpener?" She narrows her eyes on the detailing down the side. The design incorporates a sharpener into the outer sheath, automatically sharpening the blade with each use. I keep the dagger Blaine gave me in there, as I can't see me ever needing to get a kitchen knife out with the same urgency as a dagger.

I'm about to show her the inside pocket that can fit far more than it should when Zalya clears her throat, causing us both to redirect our attention back to her. She lightly grasps her throat with one hand before continuing. "Oh, sorry, I might be catching a cold. August, this is Bianca. Bianca, meet August, who was just hired to work in our kitchen."

I stare at Zalya for a moment, thinking about my response. The urge to call her a bitch and throw my drink on her is high, but I don't want to scare Bianca with my personality just yet. "I prefer 'Chef,' but yes, technically, I primarily do that work in a kitchen." I grind out the words through my clenched teeth, so as not to raise my voice, trying to keep a pleasant look on my face.

Bianca's dark eyes perk up at the mention. "My roommate works up at the castle too. You'll have to meet her. She's new to Liravel as well. But, Chef? Wow! Do you have a signature dish?"

"My lasagna." A momentary feeling of pride fills me from hearing my favorite question about my career that I can get. "Who is your roommate? Maybe I can add her favorite foods to the menu."

Zalya reaches over and sets her hand in front of me on the table. "Oh, and August, don't let me forget to go over the notes Rivian gave me about last night's dinner. Nothing crazy. You did fine considering it was your first night."

I'm certain my jaw has unhinged.

Yeah, you might consider closing it a bit, my other voice confirms, getting through my block.

"Um, I think I hear someone calling me from over there," Bianca says, pointing to the opposite side of the room and weaving back through the tables a bit more quickly than she came.

I straighten in my chair, turning myself so that I face Zalya completely. "I would appreciate bringing professional concerns up in private in the future."

"Why? From what Rowan told me, you already walk around like you own the place." She says the whole thing so nonchalantly, back to examining her split ends.

Maybe it's the beer. Maybe it's the poor sleep. Maybe it's the chunk of my heart that hasn't beat since losing Blaine and Vincenzo, but everything I haven't let myself feel since the night Blaine left hits me like a blow to the stomach. "I was under the impression that Rowan and I worked well together on my first day. If I appeared authoritative, it was simply to step into my new role on a good foot. In the future, can you ask members of my staff to come to me with their concerns directly?" My voice already wavers with my impending emotions.

Her eyes pop up from her perfectly manicured nails, her face softening when they meet mine. "Oh, August, I didn't mean, I just—"

I take a deep breath in through my nose and blow it out through my mouth. I lift my eyes to the ceiling. I will myself to think of anything that will stop the flow of anxious sorrow threatening to pour out of me, but it's becoming harder to breathe past the lump in my throat. The walls start to feel like they're closing in, inch by inch.

"—forget I said anything. Please." Her voice turns to pleading as she reaches her hand across the table again.

I don't respond yet, afraid of what will come out if I open my mouth. I examine my palms resting in my lap. Crescent moons litter them from my nails digging into my clenched fists. A single tear slowly releases from my welling eyes, and I wipe it away as quickly as I can on another deep breath in. Nova always told me it's impossible to cry if I'm taking deep breaths—a lie, but it helped when I would show up emotionally bruised in the middle of the night to her bedroom.

Zalya makes a gesture toward Bianca, but I ignore her. Instead, I pick up the rest of my mug of ale and finish it in one go. By the time I set it down, Bianca has returned with two small glasses, each with about an ounce of amber liquid. I think I hear her say it's on the house, but it doesn't matter. I take them both, one in each hand, and knock them back.

"August?" Zalya asks tentatively, wearing a face of worry. As if she's cornered a spooked animal she can't predict—wondering if I'll flee or attack.

Zalya may be erratic, but remember that you still have to live and work in the same building as her, my other voice reminds me.

Taking the internal advice, I unclench my fists and run my sore palms down the tops of my thighs. I'm about to suggest a different topic when the bar door is flung open. It cracks down the center from its impact against the brick wall, like I predicted it soon would. Spots fill my vision from my quick whirl toward the sound, and I sway in my seat, the effect of the liquor catching up to me.

Rivian's deep indigo eyes meet mine. The boyish twinkle I saw in those eyes yesterday is gone. I hold his gaze while his long, quick strides quickly close the distance between us, and I've never felt as safe.

"Grab your bag. Let's go." His stern voice isn't a suggestion.

I grab my bag to leave, and he takes my hand to lead me. We make it three steps before he turns to Zalya and adds, "Get a fucking hobby."

16

In the beginning there was Linea?

—An excerpt from the journal of Fallen Niall

Rivian is silent the whole walk back, but I watch his fingers twitch in his pockets and his brows furrow, as if he's holding back the words he wants to say. Occasionally his gaze wanders off toward the Auralian Mountains spanning the horizon. But mostly he stares at the ground.

The silence is deafening. I don't know if he's mad, and if he is, whether it's directed at Zalya or me. Is he going to fire me? It only occurred to me once we were halfway back to the palace that we left Zalya back at Connor's alone. Would he do that if he loved her?

The route feels twice the distance it was just a couple of hours ago—twice the time to think about how my conversation with Zalya turned so bad so quickly and what it means that Rivian walked straight to me in that pub.

By the time we reach the front doors, my embarrassment has festered into a pain in my stomach. Or maybe it's the whiskey. I do know the feeling is so uncomfortable I could scratch right through my skin. None of this was supposed to be this way. I threw away everything I knew—to what? Make enemies and cry in bars? I pick up my pace to escape to my rooms, stalling when I hear his voice.

"Where are you going?"

"To my room, I—"

"Follow me." His words are soft, more like a plea than a question, as he holds out his hand in invitation. And when I hesitate, he takes a step closer and says, "There's something I want to show you."

I open my mouth to decline. I *should* go to bed. But something about this moment makes want to follow him. Maybe it's the hope that shines in his eyes, or the need in his tone, but something in his demeanor pulls me in like a moth to a flame. The tension under my skin subsides when I take his hand, and while I can't define why, I feel safe. The same feeling I had when he crashed through the door of the bar sinks in—like as long as I'm with him, it will be okay.

Everything in me says to go to bed, but I get the sense I would follow him anywhere. So I do. His large hands warm mine, still sore from the anxious clench I forced them to hold back at the bar.

The leaves from the trees in the courtyard that fills the open center of the palace have fallen, and the yellows, oranges and browns that speckle the ground crunch under our feet as we make our way across the stones and toward a grand fountain in the center. The fountain features statues of a string quartet mid-performance, shoots of water flowing from the ends of the bows of their instruments. Each stream of water sounds a distinct note as it hits the water, filling the space with symphonic sound. I pause at its edge and close my eyes, allowing the splashes of water to cool my still-tingling skin. When I open my eyes, I see Rivian's gaze fixated on the sky above.

"I come here to think," he says, not taking his eyes off the sky.

Then he tugs on my hand, and I follow him down another stone path toward a bed fashioned from bales of straw in a back corner. A shimmering, sheer canopy of delicate and gauzy fabric graces the sides of the four-post frame, which has vines of ivy twisting around it.

He momentarily stares, narrow-eyed, at the structure before releasing my hand. "Hold on." He jogs off purposefully, making me laugh at how normal this interaction feels, and how quickly the mood has lifted. A short moment later, he is back, placing two pillows at the top of the bed, then spreading out a large, soft blanket and lighting a small fire in a fire pit off to the side that I hadn't noticed. "Care to join me?" he asks while gracing me with the boyish grin I fell for during our first meeting in the library.

"Getting me into bed on my second day on the job? I don't know how professional that makes me look." And because I don't know how to ask what I really need to know, I add, "Or how your girlfriend would take that?" I sit on the edge of the bed, eyeing him innocently, but hoping he'll indulge me with the details of his relationship with Zalya.

Rivian leans casually against the corner post at the foot of the bed frame, his arms crossed. Though he looks down, I don't miss the smirk that spreads even farther across his face, warming me with its sight. "August, love, I have yet to be with a woman who could handle a permanent space in my life."

I guess I'll add confidence to his list of talents.

"But as for your professionalism? Tonight, I wish only for your company."

Thank the Celestial Mother for that. I don't trust myself to say no if it got to that. And with the thought, it occurs to me—I *can* sleep with Rivian.

He grabs the post he leans against and spins himself around. In one swift motion, he goes from standing at the corner of the bed to lying down next to me, raising his arms to place his hands under his head on the pillow. I follow suit, but fold my hands across my center instead.

"When I need to think, or just be by myself, I come here." He pauses before continuing. "And I get the sense that you could use a space to think too."

"How did you find me?" When he came into Connor's earlier, it wasn't by mistake. He knew I was there, and he knew I was upset, but I don't know how he did it. It's the only explanation for his purpose in entering the pub.

"Brennan told me you went out with Zalya." He keeps his gaze toward the sky, where stars are just shining through the fading rays of the remaining sun. The moon already hosts the other side of the sky, preparing to take over for the evening. The fire he lit mixes with the cooling air to drift rivaling breezes across us.

"I mean, how did you find me for this job? Did you really enjoy the meal at the ball so much that you were ready to make me an offer on the spot?" If he won't disclose his motivations for tonight, maybe he'll make sense of the Advisory Ball.

He points to a star that would be hard to miss. Its indigo glow is visible even before the haze of the sunset has left the sky. "See that star there? We call these our ancestral beacons. It represents the location that my Fallen Niall ripped away from the wars of the constellations to find peace and safety here in Celestera. My ancestors have lived and died to protect a genuine sense of self for others. It's a blessing and a curse to see not only their emotional burdens but also what those emotions do to their souls, the unseen scars, like tattoos on the heart. Souls aren't born good or evil, and when they return to the aether, I believe they return to that neutral state—though others have their own beliefs on that matter. Get Vellas drunk and ask him about his opinions on the topic."

"I'll keep that in mind." When I was little I would play a game with myself as I tried to fall asleep: find all the colored stars in the sky. But I never knew what they were—that they were called beacons.

"I can sense when an individual's current emotional burden clashes with their soul's aura—like dissonant notes played together on an organ. There is nothing I can do to influence one's soul. Each living being in these lands holds their own responsibility for how they allow tragedy to shape them. Certain traumas stick around longer than others, and certain souls hold on to the pain."

I move my neck just enough to peer over at him watching the stars like they may spell out the answers to all our needs, like they may fall from the sky to save us again. It's the same look I use when I gaze across the Liravel Sea, praying to deities I don't believe in to bring back Nova. He's not telling me about his gifts—he's telling me he's seen my soul.

"Your aura called to me the night of the Advisory Ball. Even through your wonderful meal, it was all that I could focus on. It took every ounce of restraint I possessed to sit through that dinner without coming to find you, to resist coming to you, to hold you, protect you. And when I saw how beautiful you were—" He cuts off, his throat bobbing with a swallow, as if the confident man who just told me no woman could handle him now struggles to tell me about the night he first saw me.

Rivian is the Sovereign Descendant blessed with Quintessence. In our lands, he possesses the strongest power to sense a soul's aura, and he just confirmed mine is as broken as I feel. I don't know if that makes me feel validated or weak. Probably both. If he can assume where my internal pain came from, that I ever worked for a Resistance unit—

I roll onto my side, reaching out my hand to graze my fingers down his shoulder. "Tell me about your family," I ask, letting my fingers find the base of his neck, lightly running my nails over the edge of his hairline. I watch as his eyes close in a haze of comfort. Blaine used to get the same look at my touch—before he quit trusting me, and before I quit caring. Rivian leans ever so slightly into my palm, the movement not visible to the eye, but I feel the warmth of his scalp against my skin.

"My father was the ninth Sovereign from my Fallen Niall's most recent Descent. My parents always told me that once they had fulfilled their duty of providing the province with an heir, and saw how perfect I was, that they knew their family was complete. I suspected that my mother couldn't bear another, but I never asked." The timbre of his voice vibrates through his throat and into my hand as I continue drawing circles and swirls across his skin. He releasees a barely audible hum as I drag my nails across the spot where his spine meets his hairline.

Nova used to do this when I showed up at her door crying, usually after another fight with my father. She would talk about anything and everything, tell me stories about the Obsidian Witches, or even just hum a made-up tune—all while drawing lines from one grouping of freckles to the next on my back. I didn't grow up with many examples of how to love, but I know I felt loved when she did this. Nova could have gotten me to do anything for her after a few hours of the comforting touch, and that is exactly what I'm hoping for here with Rivian.

A thick indent between his brows is the only indication that this topic is difficult for him, but he continues. "About fifty years ago, my father passed, his inner star finally burning out. My mother followed soon thereafter from the heartbreak." He pauses, taking a deep breath in through his nose, eyes closed now as he talks. "And then one day, years later, I woke up and realized I was alone. I would walk the halls and still hear their voices, see them in the shadows. So I hired Cliff to come serve as my hand and captain my guard, and then I rebuilt the castle. A new home for a new era."

"That makes you the final Sovereign in your bloodline before Niall's next Descent."

He slowly lifts himself up on one elbow, turning toward me. He gently grasps my hand, which now lies on his pillow, outstretched and cold from the lack of his warmth, and pulls it against his lips in a ghost of a kiss. "That is correct. If I ever find that woman who could stand to complete a lifetime with me," he answers, his eyes locked on mine. They shimmer against the starlight, the color of the night sky, and I gaze into them like forever exists in their depths. The act is so sweet, so vulnerable. It's been a long time since anyone has looked at me like Rivian looks at me right now, since anyone has held my hand with care—not as if I might break, or from pity, but like I deserve it, like I'm special.

It's okay to be attracted to someone you're seducing…for your own rebellion…which happens to be against their culture, right? My other voice actually scoffs at my internal question, and I can't help but think it's correct in scoffing at me. I have lost my mind.

Footsteps against the crunch of leaves break our silence. I raise myself up on my elbows, pulling my hand and gaze from his chokehold, the hairs on my arms standing for reasons that have nothing to do with the chill in the air. Rivian grips my bicep and pulls me back down as he falls back to the bed too. A squeal escapes my lips at the surprise, and he holds a finger to his, a playful look in his eyes, telling me to be quiet. I scan his face, trying to figure out what he's doing, and he must notice because he whispers, "It's Cliff. Ignore him and maybe he'll go away."

"Can you sense his arrival?" I ask, curious if this might be a form of his gift.

"Yes, but only because the man walks with the impact of a beast," he says, raising his voice now that Cliff is near enough to hear. I grin at the levity. "Clifford, what do we owe you for the honor?"

"I poured us a round in your office, but it looks more like I'm interrupting a wake." Cliff frowns as he looks from me to Rivian, like we're a couple of children being caught after creating a mess with their toys. His voice may be gruff, but the way Rivian speaks about Cliff makes me believe there's a soft side to him somewhere.

A part of the deeper side I got to see last night at the dinner. The side of him that actually went out of his way to comfort a blindsided human, simply because he was there.

I pop back up onto my elbows before adding, "It could be your wake if you slip me sleeping powder again." I give him a wink before lying back down. If I'm not mistaken, I feel the shake of a held-back laugh from the other side of the bed.

Rivian stands, comes to my side, and offers me his hand, ever the gentleman. "Care for a nightcap?"

"I think it's time for me to go to my own bed—of my own accord." I emphasize the last part to Cliff. "But thank you." And I tell myself my entire walk back that the giddy flutters in my stomach are a byproduct of my calculated efforts to get Rivian to fall in love with me, not me falling for him.

PART THREE
NUCLEAR FUSION

The caves of the mountains to the north of Thessarlan are dark and damp, often crumbling at their entrances or closed off from the greater network by rocky debris. However, they offer a system of spaces with clearance to move and capacity to utilize. From my brief journey into the cavernous tunnels, I have not sensed dangers that could not be defeated by blade or healing. Further exploration is needed to confirm the extent of the opportunity before us.

—An excerpt from Fallen Reginald's journal

A sudden streak of light, a brilliant silver slashing through the deepening twilight, snagged Reginald's attention, making him jump.

Thoughts of captors far less merciful than Titania flashed through his mind, along with questions that he would never have answers for. Were they discovered? Had the Sun King finally found their hiding place in his galaxy? Was his real crime following Linea to begin with, or ignoring her pursuits?

Linea had told them all that when her soul's current assignment reached an end, she had already found a new barren world for them to retreat to next, together. Thirteen stars hid among the galaxies, avoiding placement and awaiting her return. And when she found them, on the day the asteroids showered the skies in angered revolt, they followed her and her dream of freedom. No longer would they answer to the Sun King, no longer would their fates be controlled—they would live on forever, with the magic of immortality that Linea would grant them.

Reginald stared at the path the comet had just stained across the night sky and remembered that day. But these memories wouldn't change their dire predicament—wouldn't stall the grim fate that awaited them. He knows better than anyone that the truth always revealed itself.

The beautiful woman who had walked into their temple only hours before stood stoically behind him, watching the comets soaring in and out of her atmosphere. She was giving him all the time he needed to complete his task at hand, but her patience only emphasized the weight of his guilt pressing in on him from every side. Their actions didn't deserve her kindness, but surely his compassion, extending to so many, partially eclipsed the weight of those he couldn't save. He clung to this hope.

So Reginald pressed on, documenting his own history for the generations to come.

"Linea, now in a body of the lands of Celestera, with sun-warmed skin and eyes that shimmered with the power of the stars, blessed her followers with beauty, strength, and opportunity in abundance. She tilted her face toward the sun, converting its rays to energy and reveling in her own freedom.

She withdrew gifts from the lands, pressing her hand to the ground and holding its essence in her palms, palpable power a vibrant thrum beneath her fingertips.

To Callie, Linea gifted the bright orange powers of the beasts—their forms and words to be an accessible army at her beckoning call. Horus accepted the gifts of time and space, eyes glowing purple as he accessed his own well of energy. Quincy took control of the surrounding air with the tangible wisp of red that Linea pulled from beneath their feet.

One by one, she imbued each of her twelve Fallen with these powers to match their colorful auras, offering her hands to the next in line and passing the gifts they each embodied, and the air crackled with newly awakened spirit as she taught them to command it.

Along with their newfound gifts came land and the opportunity to create a namespace for their lines. With provinces to lead and skills to master, she urged them onward, while she remained where she fell, to build Aetherion, her capital. Drunk with their appreciation and ready to prove their worthiness to their leader, they took no time for questions, moving to their new homes and building communities across their new territories.

As her Fallen settled and built their vibrant communities, the comforting warmth of Micah's presence beside her eased the lingering ache in her bones from the long celestial journey and the chilling memory of astral warfare. Linea was filled with pride watching the provinces of Celestera grow and thrive, their burgeoning communities a testament to their resilience. Within decades, there were hundreds of descendants of the Fallen Stars inhabiting the lands.

Yet, inevitably, powerless beings emerged from the Fallen, for even the most powerful lands weren't immune to corruption. Unremarkable in both appearance and presence, those who craved power for selfish gain bore offspring devoid of magic, cursed with the fragility of mortality. She called these beings humans.

Sovereign Fallen Linea yearned to govern from a place of peace, but the winds carried news of tribulations. She established the Convergence of Aeons, an annual gathering held within her grand stone temple in Aetherion, as a forum for celebration and reflection. She sensed betrayal as chilling greed and lust for power. Her Fallen coveted more power than they possessed, their desires a looming shadow on the colorful expanse of her lands.

Linea, her heart heavy with foreboding, devised a plan, a silent counter-strategy. She knew her followers existed solely because of her grace, their power a gift given from her discovery of Celestera, a world shimmering with untold potential, and its bountiful energy was her gift to them. Their prosperity reflected her power, and any threat, would be swiftly and decisively eliminated."

ANY INHABITANT OF CELESTERA EXHIBITING MAGICAL ABILITIES OUTSIDE OF THE DOCUMENTED CAPABILITIES OF THE TWELVE FALLEN STARS, AS GIFTED TO THEM BY THEIR SOVEREIGN, LINEA, SHOULD BE REPORTED TO THE GRAND GENERAL IMMEDIATELY. FAILURE TO DO SO WILL RESULT IN CHARGES OF TREASON, AND THEY WILL BE PUNISHED ACCORDINGLY.

CONFIDENTIAL: REGULATORY CODES OF THE ADVISORY, ARTICLE 28, SECTION 18, POTENTIAL MAGICAL ENCOUNTERS IN ACTION

A week later, I finally get to spend my first full day in the library. My staff needed more help than I anticipated learning my expected techniques. We lost two staff members to lack of competence altogether, and another to a moment where I probably should have poured myself another cup of coffee instead of taking out my frustration on others—not that I would admit that to him.

Last night, while I was sharpening my knives, I rehearsed how I'm going to ask the librarian for help today. It's not that I'm nervous or anything, but I want to come off friendly, and I don't have a lot of practice doing so. Usually, when I interact with others, I don't give a shit if they feel like I was abrasive—they're usually right—but I need this girl to trust me.

Ignoring the guard who stands at the bottom of my stairwell, I take the corner out of my rooms at a brisk pace, but then I pause, turning slowly back to the guard. The suggestive wiggle of his left brow is repulsive, but I can play along for now.

"What's a guy like Cliff doing working for a Sovereign Descendant?"

"Cliff and Rivian have known each other their entire lives, would be my guess." His tone is hesitant, and I notice as he watches the hall past me while he responds, like someone might come around the corner and hear him speaking with me.

Not so confident when the human starts asking questions about your boss, are we?

I can't let him run off and tell Rivian or Cliff I'm asking strange questions, so I briefly consider how I can make this conversation feel casual. A ray of sun glints off one of his daggers, and I find my excuse. "Hmm, makes sense," I murmur to myself, pretending to ponder that possibility. "Gorgeous blades, by the way. Know of anywhere to target practice around here?" I motion toward the three daggers sheathed down his thigh, each one with the signature smooth patch on the hilt where his thumb slides off while throwing it in a spinning motion. All of my retired kitchen blades become target-practice blades, and they all match the ones at his side.

He looks both ways down the hall this time, while I follow his gaze and flutter my eyelids a few times, attempting to appear as innocent as possible. I finger my obsidian necklace and take a step closer to him. "What? Is there some sort of rule that if we work here, we don't get to have fun?" I ask, using a saccharine tone, moving closer until we're only inches away from each other.

He clears his throat, shifting in place while straightening his shoulders, dipping his chin to whisper, "I could show you a spot, miss. Meet me here at sundown sometime when I'm at this station." His hushed tone hints he wants to be discreet, but I launch myself onto him in a hug, feeling his spine stiffen further under my touch. His cheeks are an adorable shade of red when I let go.

"Sounds like a date!" I call over my shoulder as I skip off.

Now I can play with knives and ask questions at the same time.

That should end well, my other voice mocks.

I distract myself during the walk by peering out the windows toward town, watching the streets fill with patrons and merchants for the day, when I hit a wall, bouncing back a couple steps. Well, Cliff is *basically* a wall. He stares at me momentarily through glazed eyes, and I can't help but think he looks like he just woke up.

"Cliff. Have a good night last night?" I say, biting my lip so I don't laugh. His hair looks as if he finger combed it after handling something sticky, and the dark under his eyes suggests an intense lack of sleep. "You know, I know a guy that can get you something to put you right to sleep if you're having trouble."

Cliff, the male of few words, just stares at me while he lets out a grunt that is something between an affirmation and a growl.

"Okay, then, well, you let me know," I sidestep to continue my walk to the library, when he extends his arm, blocking my way.

"Wait."

"Yes, Cliffy?" I look up at him through my lashes.

He closes his eyes and rubs his brows between his thumb and forefinger before emitting a throaty growl that I interpret as his form of contemplation.

Okay, unless I'm going crazy, that was an *actual* grunt. "Could you try that one again? I'm having a hard time understanding your version of our language."

He lowers his arm, takes two steps away, and pauses, with his back still turned. "Sorry."

I beam toward his still-turned back. "Aww, does this make us friends?"

I take his tacit silence as a yes. I also think I'm starting to speak Cliff, which I'll count as another win for the day. Rivian must have asked him to apologize to me, which I note for later consideration, along with figuring out if Cliff knows enough words to have a full conversation with me about his role here in the castle. I've picked up enough from this brief encounter that asking him questions right now would lead nowhere—except maybe more interpretable grunts. That's a game I'll play another time.

The library's enchanted doors are great in theory, but the wind created by the size of the grand doors when they open is enough to blow over a small child. I hold my still-drying hair behind my head so it doesn't tangle in the gusts from the swinging doors before walking up to the librarian's desk.

I grin when I see the librarian at her desk. The light reflects off her shiny hair, and she has a steaming cup of coffee next to her as she reads a book. If I painted a portrait of this moment, and added some freckles, she could be me. I cannot believe I convinced myself it would be hard to relate to her, as if it hadn't even crossed my mind to bring up books—to a librarian.

"*Lust Amongst the Wings* is one of my favorite romance books too. Have you gotten to the scene where there's only one bed at the inn?" I ask, hoping I did okay breaking the ice. The book is an adult version of the fairy tales I read as a child. If fairies actually existed, and were anything like the male fairies in this book, I have a feeling I would do just about anything to woo one into being mine. Back in Quinthold, I would beg Blaine to reenact the steamy scenes—and while he pretended to be annoyed, a man can't fake that kind of pleasure.

Nope. No more thoughts of Blaine today.

Thanks for the reminder, I think back to my other voice in gratitude for redirecting my wandering mind.

Wondering how many people I can make blush today, I watch as her cheeks turn a rosy hue. To save her from admitting to reading the scene in question, I go another direction, choosing to also take a seat so I'm no longer standing above her—a trick I use with shy attendees at my dinners when I introduce myself. "Is there more than one copy in the library? I would love to reread it."

She clears her throat, closing the book and nodding before responding meekly, "Would you like me to grab it for you?"

"Whenever you get a chance. I'm actually looking for something different today, but if you ever want to chat about books like that—" I gesture toward the now pushed-to-the-side novel. "I'd be happy to make us a soufflé, just like the one Max makes for Seralynn in the cottage, and steal some wine from Rivian's cellar."

That wasn't weird? That's a normal thing to do with friends? I ask the voice in my head, drowning in internal embarrassment that I hope the librarian can't see, as if the voice in my head is somehow better at being social than me.

As normal as you can be, it comments back.

"I'm August, by the way, the new chef."

Her eyes flash in recognition, and the warmth that bloomed on her cheeks subsides a bit. "I'm Hazel." Her voice is soft. I can finally see her eyes now that she's committed to eye contact, and they have that same blue green that I see in Cliff's and Brennan's eyes. Unlike theirs, she has a few speckles of burgundy and amber—works of art in the light of this library. She must have a few types of magic in her ancestral lines. Her long sandy hair, also the same color as Cliff's, makes her irises pop. "And a soufflé and wine sound nice."

Look at you, making friends. I ignore the patronizing jab from my other voice.

"Do you think you could help me find some books on the history of Celestera, or maybe even the Fallen?"

"I can, but that's a big topic. Anything specific, or just looking to start with something general?" She looks around the library as if seeing the tomes she is already thinking of through the wood of the tall shelves. The turquoise in her eyes pulses with a vibrant glow when she thinks.

I can't lie to Hazel, she would know. So, I have to approach my conversations with her carefully. "Nothing specific, just feeling a little lost living in a Sovereign's palace and not knowing a thing about him."

"Give me a minute." She hurries off into the main atrium of the library, straight toward one of the long ladders attached to the walls.

Once she's on the ladder, it glides to the spot she must want, and a book wiggles itself to the edge of its shelf. This must be her indication that it's the book she's looking for, as she climbs to the spot where it waits and tucks it into her arm before the ladder glides to the next spot. I watch her do this three times before she climbs all the way down and heads back my way.

"You can move ladders?" I half ask, half exclaim when she's within hearing distance, feeling as if I just watched a cake rise in an oven for the first time again—how a few different ingredients could make a liquid grow into a solid always fascinated me.

Her grin widens as she hands me the books, responding, "While the ladder is enchanted, it's the books that make the call. They answer to me as the librarian and as a Leondite Scholar."

"I have so much to learn," I mumble while shaking my head internally, staring at the shelves she just rode the ladder to. I thank Hazel for her help and head to claim a spot for the day.

I wonder what I could accomplish if I could control or call to something, like Hazel with books. Thoughts of ripe tomatoes picking themselves off vines, and spices collecting in reasonable proportions for my stews play through my mind as I settle into a small pod of chairs, laying the options Hazel picked out for me on the table in the center.

The Powers of the Lands is by far the thickest book in front of me. The book doesn't look old in appearance, but smells aged, like it's sat through many decades locked on a shelf without sunlight, probably avoided by most due to its size. I carefully open the cover, the stiff leather of the spine cracking as I do.

But before I can turn past the title page, a thump sounds from somewhere in the back section of the library—the sound akin to a door being slammed. I look, but no one else is around to hear it. Even Hazel must have run off somewhere; her desk at the front of the library is now empty.

I don't know if I'm being nosy or simply curious by walking toward it, but I leave my belongings where they are and venture that direction. Natural light doesn't reach this far back in the library, but there are torches enchanted to light when I pass that make it easier to see. Each one has a bright turquoise flame, creating hazy shadows on the shelves that make me feel like I'm underwater. It takes me back to the Break, and I search my mind for something different to focus on—a thought that doesn't feel like drowning.

The shelves back here aren't straight, nor are they arranged in rows. Rather, some are curved, and some lean against each other. Some books are placed on shelves carved directly into the walls, and others are stacked on top of each other on the floor. I even pass a large circular area, where books somehow stay on shelves that curve over the top, creating a dome of books. I'm not sure how they stay, but I still don't risk walking through, worried the books could fall from their homes at any point. The stone flooring and walls back here make me think this must be a section of the old castle.

I pause when I see a portrait of a beautiful woman made from pages of books. The scriptures get bolder and darker on certain pages to emphasize her features, and someone burned a few of the page edges to create brownish tints on the parchment, thus adding depth. A small card under the portrait displays the name "Bella," but nothing else. A shadow flickers against the back wall, reminding me of how Nova and I used to make shadow images on the walls of her bedroom with our hands on stormy nights using candles.

I turn a corner, and another torch casts light on a new shelf of books, the last shelf against the back wall. A thick leather spine the color of onyx catches my eye, almost so black that it shimmers—a book titled *The Ones We Left Behind*. It contrasts with the faded books on either side of it. When I reach out to pick it up off the shelf, an orange flash of light emits from my hand.

I pull it back, shaking it as if to dry it off after washing, assuming the shock came from my dry hands. I'll have to ask for some cream to use on my parched skin now that I'm living in Auralia. The air in Eshrador is much more humid since the winds bring in moisture from the adjacent sea, and my skin isn't used to the arid air of the Auralian Mountains yet. At least, this is what I tell myself.

I reach for the book again, when another book falls—no, not falls, *dives* off the top shelf and into my outstretched hand. I glare at the book as it lies on the ground, pivoting my neck to look back to its place on its shelf. Having seen Hazel gracefully retrieve her books, I shouldn't be surprised, but I'm not Hazel, and I didn't summon this book. I bend to reach down and pick it up, but it won't move. I try both hands, hold my breath, pull with all my might—it will not budge.

Maybe I need to start having more than coffee for breakfast.

"Fine." I stick my tongue out at the book, feigning defeat and turning my head as if scanning for other books—ever the curious human. Then I launch my attack. Pouncing on the book as fast as I can, I tug at it, even throw in a grunt, but it still sticks.

Well, it remains stuck for about two more seconds before releasing itself. Bested by a book, I fall for the trick and can't catch myself before my hands pull back too quickly from the change in resistance. The book slams into my left eye, causing me to fall on my ass and drop it. The book scurries back under the stack, and I watch it through the throbbing of my eye, which is slowly swelling more and more.

Did I just get a black eye from a book?

For a moment, I sit there, rubbing my eye. Checking my hand and seeing no blood, I think I'll be all right. Once I can get my books back to my room, I'll track down some ice from the kitchen. No more random books for me today, but I'll ask Brennan how to get on their good side.

I retrace my steps back toward the library atrium, taking a different route than before, no longer caring about the mysterious sound, when the pages of a book a few shelves down starts to glow, inching itself toward the lip of the shelf just like the books Hazel picked out for me, until it reaches the edge.

Did I say no more random books? I meant to say, just one more random book.

I approach the glowing book, slowly. After all, the last book I tried to pick up gave me a black eye. There is no title on the spine of this one, simply a small letter "G" embossed on the top of the tan leather spine in green ink. The book would be easy to miss when perusing the stacks, possibly misplaced from the rest of a collection since none of the others nearby seem to match.

I can't explain the feeling that courses through me, but I know that I need to open that book, a realization I accepted when my hand was already halfway to reaching it. The cover opens wide in my hands. Its pages continue to glow as they turn on a ghostly wind, flying back and forth as though they are reveling in the fresh air against their parchment. The breeze it creates soothes my sore eye, though dust scatters in its path, and I sneeze at the onslaught. All at once the pages stop, the glow dissipates, and the vibrating halts.

"I take it I should read this part?" I ask the book, open to talking to inanimate objects at this point. Taking it as affirmation when its glow pulses once more, I sit down on the floor to read.

"It is my belief that while Linea and her selected few work endlessly to eliminate threats, we may cause undo harm to the lands. She claims she wasn't aware of the natives and now considers it her duty to alleviate the interference, so we can build our communities. Reginald works diligently to code the truth. We are calling these accounts The Auras of the Fallen Stars.*"*

My head snaps up when I hear what sounds like a door closing nearby again, the same sound I heard earlier. "Hello?" I call out from the floor while I read.

Please don't tell me another book took a dive?

18

"August? You there?" I can tell from the voice—and the skip in my heartbeat when he says my name—it's Rivian.

"Over here!"

"I've been looking for you everywhere," he calls as he rounds the corner, halting at the sight of me on the ground. "What are you doing down there?" He reaches to help me up, eyes wide. "What happened to you? Did someone here hurt you? Was it one of the guards?" His head pivots, looking for the attacker. I hate to admit it, but it turns me on to see him jump into savior mode like this.

"Um, not *who*. What."

"What?" He gazes down at with an expression somewhere between confusion and concern. "How hard did you hit your head, love?" He speaks softer now, reaching out to cup my face, allowing his thumb to graze across the tender skin below my eye. His narrowed eyes scan me for signs of delusion or pain, and my own flutter closed at his touch—which I then remember is a strange and inappropriate reaction to your boss assessing your black eye.

I snap them open, then slowly take his hands and guide them away from my face, clearing my throat and taking a step back. "There was a light coming from—" I point to the floor where the book should be, but it's gone. "Where did it go? I swear there was a book, and light—"

His face is a picture of amusement while I stammer through my thoughts. "Let's get you to a healer for that head," he says as he puts his arm around my waist, his hand gripping the curve above my hip bone, and steers me in the right direction out of the stacks.

Hazel gives my swollen eye a worried glance, but says nothing further as Rivian and I head out the doors of the library and down the corridor. I wave to her on our walk out, hoping the half smile I make conveys that I'm all right.

"Well, I intended to simply let you know that planning for the Annual Constellation Ball—" Rivian cuts off mid-statement, looking toward me hesitantly as we head out the large double doors of the library.

It's the same look Blaine continuously gave me after the fire at The Goblet. The look that says, *I'm not sure you can handle an event like this right now.* Instead, he continues. "But if you need a few days to continue settling in—"

I spin out of his outstretched arm, exclaiming, "No, no, I'm fine, I'm fine. See!" I'm not sure what he's supposed to gather from seeing me standing there with my arms outstretched, other than I'm unscathed, minus the eye. Then I flinch, raising my hand to the tender spot where my smile reaches my cheekbone.

Rivian gives an obvious cough, biting the inside of his cheek— clearly trying to hide his laughter at my display. "What, exactly, am I supposed to be seeing?"

I drop my shoulders with an audible *humph* in defeat.

"I don't know. Maybe I did hit my head."

"Come on, love, let's keep walking." He wraps his arm around me once more. The embrace feels so warm after spending the past week in a bed alone, but I haven't changed my mind about Rivian. Flirting or not, I can't let myself get involved romantically with him.

He pauses in front of a stairwell, gesturing for me to precede him down the stairs that will take us to the underground level. Once we're in the stairwell, I continue where he left off, refusing to let something as minor as a book attack stand between me and my job. "So, Constellation Ball?" My question echoes off the walls, and I let the cool air of the underground soothe my sore eye. The winding staircase is slightly dizzying with only one good eye, so I grip the railing like the lifeline it is.

Just like in the stacks, torches light up as we reach them coming down the stairs, though these flames are in the house indigo hue. I think the enchanted flames may be why the fires haven't brought me back to The Goblet, like the small fire I made the night of the Advisory Ball to sterilize my blade. The indigo is calming; the purples and blues flicker against my black shirt—and Rivian's hair. The way the colors dance in the layers of his mussed strands. The way they sit slightly on his chin, emphasizing the small dimple there.

What is wrong with me?

Someone's in love—nope, mental wall thrown between me and my other voice because *that* wasn't helpful.

"Yes, our annual celebration of the constellations that formed us, held on the eve of each New Year. It's Auralia's year to host. It's actually the event that gave me the idea to hire you. You have a couple of months to plan the spread, but tell Zalya whatever you need and she'll ensure it's taken care of. Maybe you can wear that dress you wore to the council dinner last week, or if you'd like, I can have a new one made?"

Shameless, my other voice comments, sounding more impressed than anything else.

I need to keep the line drawn until I get what I need from him. I need him to trust me first, I think back before deciding I need to get better about that mental wall I thought I just threw up between my other voice and me. Its distractions are getting distracting.

"How is Zalya?" I ask, wondering if he's heard her side of last week's story, wondering how she might play it off to sound like the victim, which is exactly how I picture her response. I've seen her in passing since that day, but haven't stopped to talk to her.

"Fine, I assume. Haven't seen her since I picked you up from the pub, but I'll see her later today to address plans for the ball with her as well. I believe she is favoring a masquerade theme this year."

I'm not sure if knowing that neither Rivian nor I have spoken with her since that day makes me feel better or worse. Has she had anyone to talk to? But before I can ask if he knows who else she spends time with, Cliff turns the corner ahead of us.

"Cliffy! You got my bag!" I pick up my pace to reach Cliff, his arm outstretched to hand over my dragon-hide bag, which I left in the library just now. I completely forgot about it when I saw Rivian, or rather couldn't remember with his arm wrapped around me.

"What in the Fallen happened to you?" Cliff looks at me as if I'm a walking accident waiting to happen. I don't blame him when so far he has seen me wine-drunk, full of nerves, covered in food, or now—wounded.

"Books." I shrug.

Rivian mutters, just loud enough for me to hear, "Well, you two seem to have patched things up." He flashes a grin in Cliff's direction that I can't quite decipher, but there's something almost playful in his eyes. And though he thinks I don't notice, or that I can't see through my one good eye, he mouths to Cliff, "*Cliffy?*"

Cliff throws him a look that I interpret as, *Don't repeat that.*

Yep, I am definitely learning to speak Cliff.

"Thank you." I give him a faint smile, knowing a full one will hurt my face. He doesn't respond, but his eyes soften at my acknowledgment.

Rivian steps closer, draping his arm around me again. "I was just escorting August to the healer," he says smoothly, as that wave of nervous energy flutters through me. "I'll meet you in my office." He doesn't wait for a response before giving my shoulder a slight squeeze and guiding us once more down the hall.

I enjoy the silence for the last stretch of our walk until we reach the healer's room, and Rivian releases his hold to knock on the door. I take a step away from him, putting enough space between us to cool down from his warmth and look at the surrounding walls.

The walls are solid stone and older than the rest of the palace, if the erratic watermarks and chips across them tell me anything. Paintings of various former Sovereign Descendants hang on the walls, each a different size, but their subjects all clearly of the same lineage. I walk over to one that is the spitting image of Rivian, except with long, flowing black hair past the length of the portrait. "How far are you removed from Francis?" I ask, noting his ancestor's name scrawled across the bottom of the painting.

Rivian looks my direction, then to the painting, with his head slightly cocked to the side and one eye narrowed, as if my question confused him. After a moment, though, his face lights up in recognition as he walks up behind me, close enough that my back ends up flush with his front. "I believe Francis was the third in my line for this Descent."

Six generations of separation, and still, the two could be twins. *Strong genes run in Rivian's line*, I think to myself, quickly stepping away again to peruse more of the portraits farther down the wall.

There are no rugs on this floor, likely to avoid mold in the case of flooding, and I can feel the cool floors through the bottoms of my shoes. I remember that the wine cellar is also down here, making me wonder which other rooms are on this floor of the original castle.

But what strikes me the most is the deep maroon of the healer's door, bringing color to the otherwise dreary underground level. The rusted hinges and handle show the age of the door, which no longer sits flush with the frame. Even though it's closed, I can still see light shining through the top right corner of the door, and the bottom right has scraped itself smooth from opening and closing across the stone floor many times.

Rivian must pick up on my wandering thoughts or eyes. "The healers have always had their own style."

A female with short, chin-length platinum hair answers the door. She's a couple of inches taller than me, with a lithe build. If she were human, I would guess her to be about my age, but it's nearly impossible to tell with descendants, whose lifespans are much longer. Her ebony skin seems to have an almost shimmer to it, and her magenta jumpsuit flows from her waist through the wide-leg design down to her black ballet flats.

"August, this is Mia. Mia, please meet my new chef, August. August got into a fight with a...book." I can see him in my peripheral vision slowly turning his head in my direction as he says the last word, a smirk on his face, as if giving me to opportunity to change my story. I raise my chin, keeping my eyes on Mia.

She gives me a kind nod and then turns to Rivian and asks, "Now tell me the real story. What did you do to her?"

Color drains from his face at the accusation, and I can't help my smirk as I watch his almond eyes form wide circles in shock. His temples spasm as if his brain is flipping over in his head thinking about how to respond—poor Rivian. His flustered reaction is cute.

Her eyebrows shift in a proud gaze toward him before she turns back to me. She did that on purpose, and even though I don't know her yet, I love her for it. It may be the first time since being here that, in his presence, I feel like the more grounded party emotionally.

"Well, I hope the book is wearing its own battle wounds. Fallen knows they deserve a good fight back now and then," she says, reaching out and cupping my face with her palms. Her magenta eyes narrow as she strokes light circles around my affected eye with her thumb, the same way Rivian did in the library.

Maybe it's not just Rivian's touch I'm attracted to; maybe it's just the gentle touch of someone who cares, I think to myself as I allow her healing touch to soak into my sore eye.

"I'd say I came out on top," I suggest as she drags her thumb across the most painful spot, where I assume the corner of the tome struck the padded area between my eye and cheekbone.

"Good," she declares with another of those kind nods. Everything she says and does has such an assured, yet empathetic, tone behind it, and I can't help but think that healing was more of a fate for her than simply a gift passed through lineage. "Now let's get that eye sorted. Then we can have a celebratory drink. I'd love to add a few requests to your upcoming menus, though yesterday's muffins were to die for." She opens her door farther, gesturing to a chair against the back wall.

Rivian looks between the two of us, shaking his head, and I just know that he did not expect the conversation that just occurred between me and Mia. I leave him alone with his thoughts in the hallway, taking my spot in Mia's chair, and watch as she wiggles her fingers in a goodbye motion before gently swinging the door shut on Rivian. The last thing I see is Rivian's eyes widening as the door shuts him out.

19

The door comes off subtle compared to the bright designs inside the healer's room. Four different colors—red, blue, green, and yellow—cover each of the walls. There is a magenta rug spanning the length of much of the floor, and I take my seat in a large turquoise armchair. I'm wishing I had more than one eye to take it all in.

Mia flits about, gathering a couple of white rags from inside an orange cabinet, an amber bowl of hazy purple liquid, and an apple before pulling up a small stool in front of me. "What's the apple for?" I wasn't aware of apples having healing properties, and I've had my fair share of cuts and bruises from the kitchen.

She shrugs her shoulders as she takes a large bite out of the ruby-red fruit, its juices spraying out the edges of her bite with its crunch. "I'm hungry," she states through her full mouth. The angle accentuates her slightly sharper than normal canine teeth and her pearly white smile. She brings the bowl and rags over to within reaching distance of our chairs and joins me. "Want to tell me the real reason your eye looks like this? I just moved here myself, but I've been looking for a reason to fight a man."

"I miss that feeling," I relate out loud, staring off toward the wall, wondering where that part of me has been since coming here. She dabs at my skin with the liquid and rags, and cooling tonic soaks into my bruise, taking away any pain in its path. "But it really was a book."

She hums in contemplation under her breath, continuing to dab at my eye. Her magenta eyes glow as she works, and I must stare too long because she pauses, grinning, her hand stalling in midair. "Cool trick, isn't it? Though I prefer the light, if I'm being honest."

She holds out her palm to the side, and on top, a hovering ball of light appears. She winks once, emphasizing her irises' transition to yellow, and closes her fist as all the light leaves the room in a swirl of shadow. It lasts only for a second before the room is once again bathed in the same multicolored torchlight as before. Frowning, she looks around the space. "I can't do that one for long. My light magic is much weaker than my healing. My mother told me it was my great-great-great-grandpa who possessed the light. Though I might be missing a 'great.'"

"I wish I could do any magic, even for a second. I spent most of my time in Quinthold hating magic. Well, not the magic itself, but the concept of magic holding supreme power." Pausing, I watch her eyes scan my face. "Shit. I'm sorry, I shouldn't have said that. Please, just forget about it. I mean, this is the most beautiful healer room I've ever been in."

Why did I just say all that?

"Oh, don't worry. I don't give a shit about any of that. I don't blame you." She scoffs as she gathers the used supplies. "I was just impressed you said it in front of me. That takes grit."

Attempting to switch the subject, I turn to the first thing I can think of—the books. "Ever heard of *The Auras of the Fallen Stars?*"

"Can't say I have. What is it?"

"A book, I think. Another book I was reading in the library mentioned it." I stop rambling to watch Mia while she cleans up the tonic and rags. I can tell she's passionate about her space as a healer—she picks up the clutter with the same care that I use to tend to my kitchen, carefully making sure every item is placed back in its spot.

Back in Quinthold, with cooking, I knew everything. What spices complement each other, what temperature to serve wine, what season to serve different courses or cuisines, which knives will cut into various meats with ease, and how to sharpen those knives to a lethal point. I spent every hour of every day honing my craft, and I split the few remaining hours between the Resistance and Blaine. Here, I am lost.

"Want to grab that drink and tell me more? Maybe I can help you find it," Mia asks, breaking through my trance, but I don't get the chance to respond before a series of loud knocks sounds against the door.

"August, if you are in there, answer this door—I'm coming in either way." I roll my eyes at the demand. It's Rowan. I could never mistake that voice.

"Can I fight this one, or are you going to make me open the door in peace?" Mia asks, already stretching out her forearms and rolling her neck while staring down the door as if she can see through it.

I think Mia and I are going to be good friends.

I get up to open the door, afraid Mia may actually follow through with her threat. "Rowan could use a good fight, but we can let him slide this time."

The door creaks, and the bottom corner scrapes across the stone as I open it to see Rowan standing in the doorway with his hands on his hips—a rolled-up piece of parchment crumpled in one of his fists. He lifts that hand to wave it in my face. "I am not a courier. If you are going to flirt with the distributors, be there to receive their love notes yourself!" He emphasizes the last word before pushing the parchment into my chest, turning on his heel, and stomping away.

"I miss you too," I call mockingly toward his retreating back.

I peer over my shoulder to see where Mia is before stuffing the note down my shirt, sneaking the parchment between my breasts where it won't show through my sweater. Thankfully, the basement is cool enough that I'm not worried about sweating too much in that area. Although, the body heat did come in handy the time I needed to use this process to soften butter. I felt particularly resourceful that day.

I go back to my chair, planning to grab my bag and head out, when a high-pitched caw sounds at the same time that something sprints up the side of the chair and across my lap before proceeding to sprint in a circle around the room. Seemingly released from its confines for the day, the most adorable filaminx pup I have ever seen now spins in circles before me. She runs in place momentarily on the rug, trying to catch up to my stationary form, and I watch as her claws gather the material under her, the movements out of sync with the traction of her paws.

"August, meet Snitch. She couldn't stand knowing that there was a new friend here and not being able to meet her," Mia announces from the doorframe that she now leans in, watching the interaction. I hadn't noticed the door on the far side of the room earlier, through my one good eye.

"Aww. Hello, friend!" I call to the pup in my high-pitched voice reserved for babies and animals. "It's nice to meet you, Miss Snitch."

Snitch must have burned off her first burst of energy; she now controls herself enough to pad slowly toward where I sit, as if needing to meet me for the first time with caution, and her green eyes dilate as I reach out my hand for an introductory sniff. Her paws seem too big for her growing body, and she hasn't lost all of her baby fur yet. Her hair and feathers poke in different directions where she has probably lain in the same spot every time she sleeps. Even the dim torchlight catches on her fiery orange coat and reflects a soft shine. She's the smallest pup I've ever seen, making me wish I had a pet for companionship, one like this who could just fit in my bag for all my adventures.

I sit patiently while she sniffs my hand—waiting for her sign of approval. After all, being deemed honorable by an animal really is the highest praise one can receive. I wish I could judge another just by sniffing their hand, though I suppose that's kind of how Rivian's gifts work—examining someone's aura with a hidden magical talent.

Snitch tentatively continues sniffing, and a puff of steam emits from her nose when her warm breath meets the cool air. After pulling back and giving me another once-over with those big green eyes, signaling approval, she sits back onto her hind legs and lowers her beak to her front paws.

"What are you doing?" Mia calls to the pup, giving her a curious look from across the room. Snitch doesn't look up, despite being called.

"Is this odd for her?"

"Yes. She is crazy to begin with, let alone when meeting a new friend. I think she likes you, though," Mia adds, walking over and sitting next to Snitch on the floor, giving her some scratches behind her ears.

"Well, I could use a calm friend, so thank you, Snitch." The pup finally looks up at me—her green eyes shimmering in the light.

A pang of emotion hits me, thinking of Teliquis back in Quinthold. I hate that I didn't tell her goodbye—that I don't have her now to talk to. And I wonder if she misses me too, if she would forgive me if she knew where I had gone and why—if I would forgive me.

"The fire catches on your orange eyes brilliantly, you know," Mia says, pulling me back into the room.

"My eyes are silver," I rebut, looking wide-eyed right at Mia so she can see and reveling in the relief across my face with the movement—all thanks to her. "But I have heard that they reflect colors well, so I'm not surprised."

She squints, as if trying to see me better, before shaking her head. "I guess I just saw a reflection in the torchlight. Okay, still want to grab that drink?" She claps her hands as she pops up from the ground.

"Actually, I just remembered that I have something I need to do, and it's kind of urgent. Why don't you come by my rooms this weekend? I can snag some wine from the cellar and snacks from the kitchen. Meet there around sundown?"

I sprint, climbing the stairs two at a time, twice almost taking out a guard as I turn a corner too quickly—the piece of parchment between my breasts burning a hole into me in anticipation—a feeling of vitality running through me for the first time since coming to Liravel.

The first coded message I ever sent for the Resistance, Vincenzo helped me write it. Well, "help" is a strong word for the assistance he actually provided me. Rather, he sat next to me, repeating the same response every time I asked a question. I can still hear his voice echoing through my memories: "If you write this directive in my words, you'll never become who you could be. They will follow my voice, not yours." This was not far off from how he handled mentorship in the kitchen, but learning to soufflé didn't hold quite the life-or-death weight that passing information for the Resistance did.

The next several times, I worked with Blaine to make sure I was getting all my details right. It was technically against Resistance policy to share my messaging with Blaine, but if Vincenzo assumed Blaine and I didn't speak about the Resistance in private, that was on Vincenzo. Eventually, though, Blaine's advice didn't match how I envisioned my voice—from the format to the code words. I had truly created my own language.

By year two in the Resistance, I was confident enough to handle messaging on my own, though I still leaned on Norris for the smaller details, like which wax colors to use to seal the parchment or which strings to hold the scrolls together. Norris was always who I went to when I wanted validation or needed help talking to Vincenzo.

Red wax or string stood for death, blue indicated a discovery, green represented Advisory intel, gold was miscellaneous, and black meant a unit was compromised. We drank wine with blue, green, and gold, and we drank whiskey with black or red—incoming or outgoing, we always celebrated or mourned.

Today's incoming message has dark green wax and a gold string. A unique way of indicating that there are multiple topics awaiting me. I stare at the message for quite some time before opening it. I'm not opening this scroll with my only responsibility being to report up and respond. I'm reading this message as a leader. How I respond to its contents could lead to salvation or death—and I am so tired of death. But I'm also ready to do something, be something—so I carefully slip off the string, peel back the wax seal, and read.

River.

The moon was high over Quinthold when we last saw you. The farms of the Auralian Mountains were worried to hear that this year's crops weren't favorable. That Quinthold could no longer contribute crops to the trade system. I've shared your new location through the network.

Do you have any farm hands in your new location assisting you?

P.S. The council is using resources to search for you. I've spread the update, but you may also send a note to Veil.

- Delphy

Blaine is looking for me.

A pain in my chest spreads through my veins like water rushing through street grates after a pouring rain. I stare at the sheet of paper, focusing and unfocusing my eyes, hoping the words will change. It's Blaine's alias, chosen for how much he needed to hide his face from the movement or risk being charged with treason by the Advisory—Veil.

Blaine is looking for me.

I haven't once considered that I left without him knowing when or where I was going. I've been so absorbed in processing my own changes, in establishing Resistance motions here, that I forgot about the half of my heart I left behind. My skin tingles where it touches the cooling silk of the comforters I sit on, where my skin heats from my racing heart. My hands shake. I drop the parchment to wipe my palms against the silk, but it doesn't help.

Who have I become? How selfish have I been to forget who held me together the past ten years?

I scramble across the bed to grab a piece of parchment from my bag, jumping down so fast that I trip on the corner of the rug and have to skip a couple times on one leg to catch myself. Blaine's continued search for me jeopardizes everyone, and the Advisory can't allocate resources to me unnecessarily—I'm fine.

Am I fine?

It doesn't look like it.

"Not now!" I yell out loud to my other voice.

Throwing myself back onto the bed, I fumble with the clip to open my bag, shaking with the thought of Blaine out there using the Advisory to find me. At least that's what I tell myself—that his risk of trial for treason is why I'm so upset.

Or maybe the breakup is finally setting in. My other voice says the words I'm too scared to admit.

I don't have the time to grieve, I respond. *Or for you.*

Why am I not breaking down? How am I not curled in a ball underneath the covers right now, like I was for hours after Blaine left our apartment? Sure, I'm shaking, nervous, *near* tears. But as I sit here, a lump lodged in my throat, fingers trembling, heart racing, stomach sinking, I expect the tears to come—and they don't.

I really am broken.

Maybe it's because you made the right decision coming here, my other voice offers, sounding more like a question than a statement.

I can be in the right place, and give Blaine the mourning and respect he deserves, I counter.

I take a deep breath and finally open the clasp to the bag to tear through the contents. I don't know why it matters how quickly I get to the parchment, as if Blaine will receive the message as soon as my trembling hands can move the quill, but I dump the entire bag onto the bed in my pursuit.

There's the journal Brennan gave me, but I don't want to rip a page from the perfect leather-bound notebook just yet. I find my quill first, but it's what's under the quill that catches my eye. A rectangular black box—that I don't remember putting there—with about ten rolled-up, blank pieces of parchment sitting inside.

I don't remember putting them there, or where they came from, but the thickness of the parchment is impressive, and I admire the way the quill glides across its surface. I lay a couple of knives across the one I choose, one on top and one on bottom to keep it flat above the journal, which I use as a hard surface to write on.

At least I don't need to code this message.

Blaine,

I'm sorry I didn't write sooner. I wish our last day could have been different, but everything moved so quickly once I accepted my new job.

It's going well. I'm a head chef, in a palace of all places.

Please don't look for me, this is something I need to do.

I'll never forget you, and if we find each other at the end of this, I hope we can pick up where we left off. But if we never see each other again, I hope you find your calling too.

August

Fuck.

A wave of emotion hits me as I stand to grab a string to wrap around the message, and I barely make it to my bathing chamber in time to release the contents of what little I ate that day.

20

After having spent several years researching through the archives of Leondell, conversing with countless peers, leaders, and citizens of the lands, and having traveled far and wide both solo and in company—it is this scholar's opinion that Celesterans may need to consider the theory that Linea's temple and Micah's descendants may never be found.

—An excerpt from *Celestera: The Beginning*

I've spent any spare hour of the last few days outside of the kitchen in front of the fireplace in my room and huddled over books. I still haven't had an actual conversation with Zalya since that day in the pub, though she has popped into the kitchen a couple of times to mention meals she enjoyed—a nicety, if nothing else. I considered finding her and inviting her over tonight to join Mia and me. After all, I've had my fair share of bad first impressions on others, and I know the feeling of shame that lingers when you're aware of your own shortcomings.

Tonight, I sit on my couch, same as the previous nights, though I keep the balcony door open to bring in a breeze. When the warm fire and cool air meet, I imagine I'm gliding through the air on the back of Teliquis again—a nostalgic feeling that reminds me there's more to this mortal lifespan than fighting for answers. I might miss Teliquis the most right now.

Answers, however, have been scarce. My journal officially has pages of questions that I've scribbled down while reading the ancient tomes I've hoarded in my rooms. Brennan told me the first night that I met him that asking the correct questions was more important than finding the right answers, and now I stare at my list and can't help but think that these questions aren't helping me at all. I do find joy in using my new quill, though.

Rivian has left me a small gift on my bed the past two days, the first being this quill, and the second a framed map of Auralia. Both wrapped in the same meticulous style as the gifts I received back in Quinthold. It's as if he can sense my thoughts: both gifts have arrived while I studied the history of Celestera in my rooms. I hung the map above the fireplace and look at it now as I contemplate the books in front of me.

I don't even know what I wrote at the bottom of that page, I think to myself as I stare at my sleepy script angling off the page.

A knock sounds at my door, and I call out that I'm coming as I finish the page about the Fallen's journals that I'm referencing—an intriguing story I can't seem to pull myself away from. Apparently, a Leondite Scholar named Piatt collected all fourteen of the Fallen's journals after their entombment in Linea's temple in his pursuit of accurately documenting the event for the scholars' historical records. It took him decades to find them all, traveling across the entirety of Celestera and often having to pay for them in currency greater than gold or gems. After all that time and effort, he began cross-referencing them to check for accuracy and to create a timeline of events. He secluded himself in an unknown location, a fortress of solitude, to dedicate himself to what he knew would be one of the greatest historical events of his life. However, he was never seen or heard from again. The scholar who wrote the tome I'm reading believes the key to harnessing the full extent of descendant powers likely lives within those journals—just another section of research that brings more questions than answers.

I jot the words "full extent of powers?" down with my new quill, slam the book shut, and stuff it into my bag before jogging off to open the door.

"Celestial Mother!" I exclaim. "Bianca told me her roommate worked here. How did I not put this together?" It makes so much sense. I was so focused on the strange books, it didn't even cross my mind when I met Mia the other day that she was Bianca's roommate.

"I hope it's okay that we came together, Ceress." Mia winks at me as she uses the playful nickname and passes me to head into the living area, as if she's been here dozens of times. Her address is a nod to my use of the phrase "Celestial Mother"—another learned from my beloved tales of the Obsidian Witches, a callout to the mother moon in the sky responsible for watching over the witches. She must know the tales since she responded to me using "Ceress," the term blessed to the head of the Coven.

"I brought bread!" Bianca stands in the doorway, holding a paper bag out to the side showing off her contributions for our evening, much like a sailor would display his prized catch of the day, with a large grin shining across her face. I've never seen anyone light up this much over bread, but it's the exact level of seriousness I am striving for this evening.

"Oh, good! We can grab some of my fresh herbed olive butter when we pick out a wine." I grab the bread from her hands, welcoming her in as well. I sneak my nose into the bag to take a whiff of the fresh loaf—a sourdough, and a good one at that.

Mia is scanning my bookshelves, occasionally grabbing one off the shelf to leaf through its pages before replacing it. "Where did you find this many books?" Mia asks me while browsing one of my cookbooks.

"I lived above a bookstore back in Quinthold, though that one I found at the market one weekend—a sailor's grandmother left it behind, and he had no use for it without a kitchen on his boat." I learned a great lamb seasoning from it, or at least a seasoning that can effectively cover the use of belladonna. I don't often think about those early days of the Resistance anymore.

Bianca already made herself at home on the couch, fitting completely under the small blanket that barely covers me from feet to waist, but she looks up when I mention the market, her brows jumping high. "You had a market?"

"Well, Quinthold did. I went there to gather supplies for my kitchen—usually fresh blades or sharpening stones. Sometimes rags, or spices, though many restaurateurs have a pretty good relationship with the farming trade route for most food product. Why do you ask?" It's not necessarily an odd question, but no one has ever seemed excited by the thought of the Quinthold market before—it's not necessarily a glamorous environment. But even as I say it, I remember the scent of the Terrlyssian cinnamon that I could find at the back corner stall.

"I grew up going to the markets in my hometown. My extended family always sold their goods there. I loved seeing all the people coming through. Each purchase meant another fresh meal that night. Many purchases meant a happy evening, maybe even a cake for dessert…" She trails off, looking out the open balcony door. A reminiscent twinkle in her eyes matches what she didn't say out loud—that the markets were in the past. It's how I sound when I talk about Nova.

"I know the feeling. It's why I became a chef."

"For cake?" she asks curiously, unsure where I was going with my comment.

"So I could always make sure, at least for that evening, that everyone could leave the dinner table full and at peace."

I don't have happy memories from dinner growing up, but I'm saved from having to delve into that further by Mia speaking up from the bookshelves again. She's standing on a stool to reach the top shelf.

"Come on, Ceress, where's the good stuff?" Her voice is strained as she stretches her arm as far as she can to reach the top shelf, rising up on the tips of her toes.

"You're going to fall! What are you looking for?"

"You just mentioned the witches. I know you have the tales here somewhere." She cranes her neck, trying to read the spine of every book. The sight makes me wonder if Hazel could call to my books as well, like she did in the library.

"Oh. Well—" I scan my shelves, looking for the special bound edition of *The Tales of the Obsidian Witches* that Nova made for me on my twelfth birthday. The night that my father told me I was lazy for living vicariously through books about women who didn't exist, Nova hand sewed their existence into fresh leather. And as if the gift couldn't be more Nova, she somehow waterproofed the parchment. She couldn't tell me how she did it, but it didn't matter. It remains the most special gift I've ever received. "I don't see it, but let's go grab the wine. We can ask the guard on our way out if he's seen it." I remember back to my first day here, seeing the book on the shelf and being thankful it made the trip, so I know it's here.

We head back down the stairs, stopping at the bottom, where my guard stands a few feet outside the door. "I wanted to see if you could help me find something, but it occurs to me I don't know your name," I stammer to the same guard I've had all week, the one I asked to throw knives with me. The cute one, who now stares at Bianca even while responding to me.

"Morgan, ma'am, the name is Morgan."

"Hi, I'm Bianca," she calls from my side, holding out her hand to introduce herself. Her voice has the same airiness as always, but there's something in her tone now that differs from before— something I can't quite place. I turn to look at Mia, who now gives Bianca a look similar to the one she gave Snitch in her office, like she's developed an alternate personality. The same face I would make toward anyone new in my kitchen, causing Vincenzo to pinch the back of my arm until I remembered to be pleasant.

Morgan doesn't hesitate to take Bianca's hand, lightly grasping her fingers in midair. I give them about thirty seconds before the already strange encounter becomes near comical, and to avoid standing here watching these two hold hands all night, I cut them off with, "And this is Mia." Mia doesn't take her eyes from Bianca, now squinting at her roommate on my other side. Morgan looks at Mia but doesn't drop Bianca's hand, and I stand in the middle feeling as if I've interrupted a reunion of some sort. "And now that everyone knows each other"—I physically lower Bianca's arm back to her side—"I was wondering if you've seen a large black leather-bound book. It would have been with all my others, but I don't see it upstairs."

"I have not, but I'm happy to ask around."

"Thank you, that would be great. Are we still on for knives soon?" I ask, already walking backward to get to the wine as soon as we can, pulling Bianca with me as I leave.

"If you insist, Miss August." He waves to us, gaze stuck on Bianca. The moonlight catches his amber eyes—twinkling with a childish crush.

Piatt examined several of the journals before he had the completed set. Friends of his often worried that he would go several weeks at a time with little food or rest, and often questioned his ability to complete his project with sound mind. One of his notable tells from long weeks spent researching was that he would swear new entries would appear in the journals, despite them being in his ownership.

—An excerpt from *Recovered Journals of the Fallen*

With wine, butter, and some cheesecake bars I whipped up the night before, we set up the spread on the low table between the couch and fireplace. Mia and Bianca sit on the couch together, one on each end, and I curl up in the oversized armchair.

"So, how did you end up here in Liravel?" I ask them, realizing both have hinted at being new to the capital of Auralia—and that I have no idea how to start a conversation. I already knew Bianca was here first, and that Mia found her when searching for a room.

Mia speaks up first. "Rivian needed a healer, I needed a job, nothing special." She waves her hand dismissively while opening the gallon of wine by holding the lip to the fire until the cork pops out. "Honestly, I was looking for a reason to move. The war is taxing, and as a healer, I have felt a duty to help for a long time. This job felt like a step away from the battlefields—a chance to feel insignificant." She stares at the flames crackling in the fire, and I wonder if she's back in a battle now, the same way I return to the flames of the fire at The Goblet when I think about it. Mia comes off so strong that it's odd to see something akin to pain in her eyes. She has no idea that I led the Resistance in Quinthold, about my alias, River.

Would she hate me if she knew?

"What about you? If you're from Quinthold, why do you have the Auralian map on your mantel?" Bianca asks, her eyes admiring the framed map from Rivian.

I follow her stare for a moment, debating how to answer. "Rivian needed a chef, I needed a change," I answer, using Mia's phrasing. Not a lie, but not a conversational topic I want to leave open, so I offer another idea. "Anyone want to play a drinking game?"

"Yes!" Mia exclaims, as Bianca simultaneously asks, "What?"

I explain the rules of our game for the evening. We'll take turns asking the others if they have done a certain thing in their past. If they haven't, they are safe. If they have, they have to drink—once if they'll tell us the story, twice if they refuse.

Within an hour, we've moved from our spots on the couches to the floor, creating a bed of pillows. Crumbs from the crusts of the bread scatter across our blankets, and there is now a dark stain on one of the silk pillowcases from the butter. Between the warmth of the fire and the burn of the wine, our cheeks are all a matching shade of pink, similar to the wine we chose for the evening, a varietal made by halving the time the grape skins remain in the barrel.

The questions start off basic. Bianca shares that she stole a purse at the market as a child. Mia confides she cheated on a school exam while growing up in Curatia. I even tell the others about how one time I cooked an old piece of meat for a rude customer in one of my first restaurants.

By the time we were finishing our second bottle of wine, the questions became a little more personal. It turns out Bianca once made love on the back of a dragon. I choked on my wine when that story came out. Though Mia's story of reattaching a soldier's severed groin in a training accident still shocked me more. I was feeling comfortable enough by that point to share about the time I had hives across my body for weeks from sneaking into the woods behind my home to meet up with my teenage love. Never again would I take my clothes off in random shrubbery.

"To new friends," Mia proclaims, holding her entire bottle of wine in front of her to cheer us. We all abandoned glasses after the fourth or fifth time one of us spilled. The poor maid assigned to my rooms tomorrow is going to have quite the mess.

"To new friends." Bianca and I clink our own personal bottles to hers.

"My turn!" I squeal, unsure of if it actually is or not. "Beeyanca," I ask, emphasizing the first syllable of her name while my brain processes the rest of what I want to say. "What was that with Morgan earlier?"

Her eyes go wide, and she presses her lips together. "Thath's not how this game works." A lisp that wasn't there before the wine is now apparent in her words.

"No, but this is my room, so your answers are coming to my questshun," I respond, staring at the ceiling, wondering if that made sense—but her narrowed eyes tell me she knows what I mean.

"He's cute." She shrugs, taking a long pull from her bottle of wine. "And I need to get laid."

I knew it.

"What happened to the dragon boy?" I ask, sympathizing with her plight.

"He's back in Amarion." She sighs, a reminiscent edge in her voice. "I kindoth of ended up here in Liravel by mistake." She lifts herself back up, her finger now running circles around the rim of her bottle.

"Continue." Mia's inquisition is more of a command than a question, and though Bianca gives her a look of disdain, she tells us her story.

"Neb and I were hiking through the Auralian Mountains with no idea how close we were to the capital. I was bored, so I decided to scare him." She takes a deep inhale through her nose, her cheeks puffing out on the exhale, before continuing. "Something you probably don't know is that I'm descended from the Fallen Horus on my mother's side."

"Sorry, dumb human here. What powers did Horus possess?"

Her expression turns to an almost grimace, but she finally says, "The ability to move through and alter time and space."

"Like Vellas, then, right? So you can—time travel?" I try to hide my fascination, but can't help feeling like I'm doing a horrible job.

She huffs a laugh at that. "I forget how little humans know about us. No, I can't time travel per se. But I can slow down or speed up time, and, of course, teleport."

Fucking teleporting, I think to myself while she continues, remembering how I got here.

"As I was saying, I was on a hike, but apparently we were actually hiking through the boundaries of Liravel. Neb was walking ahead of me and I came across a snake in our path. I got the idea to pick it up and scare him. It wasn't venomous or anything, I just wanted to have some fun." She bites down on her lip, telling me that what comes next isn't her favorite memory to recall. "I picked up the snake and attempted to teleport directly in front of Neb, to shove it in his face. However, I must have teleported into Liravel, because the next thing I knew, I was standing here in town. Facing Connor's. With a snake in my hands. Neb nowhere to be found. And the worst part was, I was so afraid of getting in trouble that I never told anyone."

If Bianca can teleport, why wouldn't she just go back to Neb?

I reach for my bag to grab my notebook, wanting to add my question to it so I can remember in the morning—forgetting that I wouldn't want Mia and Bianca to see it.

My brain on wine is so fucking slow.

Mia doesn't have a meek bone in her body, and she calls out in a teasing tone, "Are we so boring that you need to pull out your diary while we're still here, hmm?"

I stick my tongue out at her while I scramble to stuff the journal back into my bag. "Noooo. It's just my notes about descendants."

A truth I can give her. "I don't want to look dumb working for Rivivan." Just like my letter to Blaine, it feels good being able to share even small truths with these girls.

She doesn't respond, crawling over the pillows like an animal released from a cage, scurrying to my bag before my wine-hazed mind can realize what she's doing. She knocks over Bianca's bottle in her pursuit, spilling more precious liquid happiness across the silk pillows and blankets. Within a moment, she has the journal in her hands and scoots back to her spot so I can't rip it away from her. She reads through the partial words and sentences I've snuck onto the paper, between notes about chapters read and meals prepped, and though she won't find anything incriminating, it really feels like a piece of me is being laid bare for these girls to see.

The last thing I need is for Mia to see how ignorant I am.

Even in the kitchen, you started somewhere. My other voice puts a loose bandage on my internal wound, the kind that doesn't help but still makes you feel as if you tried.

"Oh, paper from Leondell!" she squeals, running her fingers over a few of the pages.

"Brennan gave it to me."

Her eyes flash my way, but quickly return to the journal as she flips through its pages. "It really is just questions about descendants," she mumbles, perusing my notes. "Aww, August, look at you doing homework for your new job." She looks up at me like I'm a baby bird she's watching hatch, her tone reminding me of one that Nova's mother would use when I told her about a new crush at school. "But just ask if we bring up something you don't know. Bianca couldn't get back to Neb because she passed through to the other side of the Capital

Shield that all capitals have around them. It's why you have to have a Sovereign permit to enter a capital city. Once you're in, you're in."

I get the sense that she knows I'm embarrassed by the interaction, because she doesn't even look up while she tells me this. I watch her grab a quill from my bag next. I let her—watching as she reads through the rest of the questions and adds a few notes of her own to the pages. At least I haven't included anything she could trace back to the Resistance—a rule I still follow from my Quinthold days. "There. Your next tutoring session can be during our next wine night."

"Well, you three look like you're having fun." Zalya stands in the doorway, leaning against the frame, arms crossed.

"Zalya! Come join us!" Mia practically begs, patting the pillow to her left. I don't know how she does it, but I imagine she could make anyone feel comfortable, regardless of whether she knows them or not. A trait that healers must innately utilize.

"Please," I throw in, a little less enthusiastically, as I swallow against the guilt in my stomach. I did not consider Zalya just popping in on us tonight. Even though I thought about inviting her so she wouldn't be jealous, when I didn't, I just assumed she would never know that a gathering happened without her. But then again, the last, and only other, occasion that I spent time with her was at the bar, and I left in tears.

Is that sadness on her face?

She straightens, blinks her eyes twice, and tosses her hair over her shoulder, wearing a saccharine smile that doesn't quite meet her eyes—putting on the mask she's determined fits her needs currently. "No, thank you. I wanted to see if August was ready to plan for the Constellation Ball, but it looks as if she has prioritized other things for now." Her voice is unbearably cheery given the tone she used when she originally greeted us. This interaction feels just like the night we met, when she offered me my job. When she went from alleviating my panic attack by putting out the fire, to perky courier, to straight venomous.

How does she do that—change demeanors so fast you second-guess yourself?

"Come find me this week when you're done socializing." She gestures her hand broadly in our general direction. "You three have fun." Tossing us one last smile, she turns and leaves the way she came.

We sit in silence, staring at the door, listening to the tapping of her steps on the stone stairs, waiting until we hear the door click at the bottom of my stairwell before we speak. "Did Zalya seem—upset?"

Mia is still frowning in Zalya's direction. "Maybe? I can never quite tell what that girl is thinking, but she seemed different somehow than the times we've met before."

"So no one is going to point out how bitchy that was?" Bianca finally asks, still staring at the door under lowered brows.

Mia and I burst out laughing at the offhand comment. Bianca reminds me more and more of my lost friend with every word that exits her mouth, and Mia constantly reminds me of my inner edge—the piece of me I've felt disconnected from since Vincenzo died. Tonight, though, I don't think about the Resistance or Nova or even Blaine—I hadn't realized how much I missed just being with friends, or whatever these girls are or could be to me.

The girls finally decide it's time to leave, and when I remind them they are welcome to stay in my room if they don't want to walk back in the night, Bianca reminds *me* she can teleport. Swaying back and forth, Mia joins arms with Bianca and waits for her to use her gifts to get them back home. Only, they teleport approximately ten feet to the left and crumple into a giggling fit on the floor. By the third try, I watch them from the window as they make it to the entry steps of the castle, and then teleport about twenty feet at a time until they make it back into town.

Piatt returned from collecting the journals most excited by the revelation of an undocumented war mentioned in a couple of them. He didn't have many details, but told his confidants that he believed the conflict centered around a balance of power.

—An excerpt from *Recovered Journals of the Fallen*

By mid-November, I've developed a routine to balance my time in the kitchen. I spend Mondays and Tuesdays all day there, planning and prepping for the week. Distribution day is Wednesday, and ever since Rowan freaked out about having to deliver a message to me, I've agreed to handle delivery days on my own. It's only a couple hours of ensuring inventory is as expected and then, of course, handing off or receiving any *correspondence.* Thursday through Sunday is then mine to use as I wish, unless there is a big event.

For smaller events and day-to-day management, Rowan now leads Wednesday through Friday, and we've trained a couple of junior assistants to handle the weekends, which are the slowest if no events are planned.

Hazel helps me find books I may need, and I've even loaned her a couple of romance tales from my collection. It turns out that quiet little Hazel can devour an adventurous romance novel, and we bond over reminiscent daydreams about trading places with our favorite characters from our books. Bianca, Mia, and I have continued our Friday wine nights, which are still filled with gossip and "tutoring," as Mia calls their time answering questions. Mia even started to bring Snitch with her, who clings to me like the mother she no longer has—it's one of my favorite things about wine night.

Even Zalya and I have seemed to find a good groove with spending time together planning for the Constellation Ball, a short three months away. I still haven't been able to predict which version of Zalya I'll get on any given day, but she hasn't been outright cruel again, and I've been able to pretend I don't hear when she makes certain underhanded comments. Though I don't miss that we haven't talked about Rivian since that night at the bar.

I still haven't received anything from the Resistance that's actionable for me inside the palace. To my knowledge, Blaine is no longer looking for me, and it isn't strange for months to go by with no major updates for our movement. Information tends to come in waves. Bigger waves usually after the quarterly Advisory updates, which I could expect in another six weeks or so.

I do slip out details I learn about the Fallen's journals. That particular tome from Brennan has proven to be full of information I wasn't aware of. The dominant theme being that it seems there was a war across the lands prior to their entombment that I don't recall learning about in school. Even Hazel isn't aware of it when I mention it to her in passing. I don't tell her I found that information in a book from Brennan—rather, that I thought I saw it somewhere—but she's been spending the past week looking for herself.

I also send a message informing units of the Constellation Ball, and to let me know if there's information I can try to glean from the extensive Sovereign invitation list for the event. Unlike the Convergence dinner my first night in the palace, I can be prepared for this event, to ask the right questions.

But it's Rivian my mind keeps turning to when it wanders away from the people I'm with or the places I'm in. A few weeks ago, I asked Cliff what Rivian's favorite breakfast was—cinnamon toast. So I made a fresh loaf of brioche bread, churned some honey butter, and ordered in Terrlyssian cinnamon for the next week's breakfast. I checked his calendar with Zalya, pretending I thought there was a business meal I needed to be aware of, and hand delivered the special meal to his office unannounced.

He opened the door to see me, and the sun from his windows poured around his silhouette like a bird against the morning sun in the sky. He had slightly disheveled hair, and he'd left the top buttons of his shirt undone, showing a peek of hair across his toned chest. This space wasn't just where he worked; it was where he didn't have to be the perfect face of Auralia—it was how I viewed my studio in Quinthold. That wide grin that I fell in love with the first day pulled me in, like an asteroid pulled into orbit, before he could even gesture for me to come into the room.

I'm not sure what I expected Rivian's office to look like. Possibly small and dark, with a tone of mystery, or gilded from wall to wall like the ceilings throughout the palace. But his office closely resembled the feeling of the library—quaint and relaxing. The bookshelves were arranged according to topic. Not a single item littered his desk, and a peaceful indoor fountain could be heard near the door to drown out any noise from the outside. Currently, the walls and ceiling were light blue, speckled with white to simulate clouds. When combined with bright sunlight streaming through the tall windows, it created an illusion of being outdoors. He told me the room was enchanted to lighten and darken automatically with the path of the sun, so the light blue would soon turn to dark, the fireplace would alight, and the sound of crackling embers would replace that of the fountain.

We spent all morning next to each other on a plush golden couch by his fountain, trading childhood dreams between bites of toast and sips of coffee. My hand brushed his shoulder a time or two when he mentioned nonsense, like wanting to grow up to become an Advisory dragon trainer, or join the traveling theater, giggling at the thoughts. And his hand may have rested on the skin just above my knees—right below my miniskirt, which was methodically chosen that day.

On my turn, I told him of dreams of making love in the rain, after dancing to a symphony, of course—because string quartets often performed in rain. It was a romanticized idea I read about one time in a book, where the couple came together after a ruined evening.

In that moment, as he looked into my eyes, I thought he might lean in, seek more, and a warm feeling settled over me like a fur cloak. But Cliff interrupted, throwing open the office door to barge in and ask a question. I cringe thinking about how I drew doodles of dragons in my journal that night, like a schoolgirl writing notes to a crush that she'll never send. But the next day I returned from the kitchen to find a small figurine of a dragon waiting for me on my bed—another gift that pulled the type of smile to my lips that I hadn't smiled since my early days with Blaine.

Two weeks ago, Rivian popped into the kitchen while I was prepping for the week with an urgent errand for Rowan in town—conveniently leaving us alone for the day. He found the batter I was making for the week's pastries fascinating, and I spent the afternoon teaching him how to make scones. I then spent that evening telling myself that the shivers down my spine from each touch he snuck, or from when he wiped batter from my chin, was because the kitchen was cold, and not because I was excited to see him. That I was strategically seducing him so well that even my mind was playing into the role. But that didn't stop the dreams about him on top of me, his hands on my skin, just like they were that first dinner when I wore my low-back silk gown.

I've been eager to re-create a moment like that ever since, but I wake up this morning to find out that he is going to be gone for three weeks on business. The handwritten card on my nightstand greets me like the sun after a month of storms, and my heart flutters at the words "Love, Rivian" scrawled across the bottom. So now I'll have to focus on other Resistance intel strategies.

It was a Thursday, so I could go to the library, but I decide to spend the day out in the vineyard instead. It's a warm day for November, and I know there's a pit to build a fire in for warmth should the breeze become too strong, plus there's a service station nearby to snag a glass of wine, which is always a necessity when conspiring or celebrating.

By the time I lazily bathe, plait my hair, and match my outfit to my new favorite accessory—the gold-chain obsidian necklace from Zalya—the sun is high in the sky. I make it out the back doors of the palace and walk down the cobblestone path to a stone circular patio in front of the arched entryway, marking the center row of the grapevines. I can hear birds flying overhead, or singing from their perches atop the wooden stakes that hold the vines upright throughout the shrubbery.

It's about time you left the walls of this palace, my other voice echoes through my mind as I let the strong late-autumn rays soak through my thick sweater and into my skin, warming me from the inside out.

When I make it to the patio, I throw my bag down next to a lounge chair facing the sun and plop down, continuing to gaze high in the sky. The chairs here all have thick cushions and side tables, meant for leaning back in comfort. I know I'll wake up in the morning with my freckles three shades darker, but that can be a tomorrow problem for August.

"You look happy." Cliff's voice makes me jump, and I look to my right and see him in a chair next to me. The high backs of the chairs, especially when reclined, make it so I couldn't see his head from behind.

"I think I am." His skin has a touch of warmth to it I haven't seen there in the past couple weeks, which makes sense if he's been out here all morning. "You don't look too grumpy yourself, Cliffy."

He takes a slow sip of a viscous red he's poured himself. The intricate goblet he holds reflects the sun with the motion, and his face is momentarily a scattering of sparkles from the reflection. "I've got a good drink, the sun is out, and now company. What should I grump about?" His words are drawn out, like his tongue feels thick, and I wonder just how much wine he's indulged in this morning.

"Celebrating?"

"You could say that." The grin that spreads through his beard and crinkles his eyes tells me this must indeed be a special day, but I don't think I've ever gotten more than six words at a time from this man, so I don't ask him to elaborate, knowing I only have a few more before he'll leave.

I walk to the service station, wanting to experience a semblance of the weightlessness I see in Cliff right now, hoping the liquid courage brings me "the right questions," as Brennan would say. I go for an open red, a bright blend if I can read the color correctly against the light, and watch Cliff continue to gaze at the sky with a cheeky smile on his face.

"Well, if you won't tell me what we're celebrating, what will you share?" I ask the open-ended question, awaiting what wine-drunk Cliff will come up with on his own.

He sits there, and I wonder if he's fallen asleep as I watch his chest rise and fall, his eyes still closed. But he opens them and turns to meet mine when he says, "You and I aren't so different, and one day I'll finally be able to show you."

Not what I was expecting.

My brain spins, trying to see any meaning behind his words. As far as I know, Cliff and I share an indifferent attitude toward idiocy and a love for a good drink, but I can't place what else he could be talking about.

"Take yourself to bed, drunk," Zalya interrupts, sneaking up from between the chairs we sit in. She looks at Cliff like something she found stuck to her shoe, making me want to step in to defend him.

"Gladly." Cliff stands, nodding once to Zalya, then turns to me and pauses, smile fading from his face quickly—but not in sadness, more like contemplation. "Don't give yourself away, A." And then he turns on his heel and walks off. I assume he didn't want to remain here with her any more than she wanted to spend time with him, and I watch him stumble back up the path to the palace.

Zalya watches him leave, then pivots, asking, "What in our Celestial Mother's realm was that about?"

Once he's out of earshot, I turn to Zalya and say, "I honestly have no clue, but I know that there were probably kinder ways to suggest that he leave."

"Since when do you care about being kind? I see the way you talk to the kitchen staff, notice how you avoid me, except during our planning sessions."

Well, that hurts.

"Did you need something?"

"I wanted to talk about where to host the party again." She steps fully into the space, crossing one leg over the other as she places herself in the chair that Cliff just left. "I know you think it will be too cold to host the ball outside, and I know we looked into enchanting the ballroom to give an outdoor illusion, but I can't get over my vision of having the ball on the vineyard patio."

I open my mouth to respond, but she cuts me off, raising her voice so I can't speak over her.

"And I know you don't want your food to get cold! But I found us a solution. There's a descendant in town who has a trace of fire magic in his blood, and he's agreed to help us enchant the trays to stay warm for the entire evening! We'll just have to get him kindling to place under the trays, and he'll do the rest." She looks at me the same way I used to look at Vincenzo when I would ask to take on a task he hadn't allowed me to do before.

"But what about the people? Warm dinner doesn't make having a ball outside in January any less cold." She can't argue that one; surely I'm not the only person who wouldn't want anything to do with dancing in the snow.

"I'm working on it, but I have to order decor and hire planning staff, so I need to solidify the venue now. I swear I'll figure out the rest." Her voice is pleading, and I look to her chest where she fingers her matching gold obsidian necklace. I know I can't say no without bringing out the wrath of a version of Zalya I have no interest in seeing again.

"Fine."

"Thank you, thank you, thank you!" She jumps out of her chair, coming over to give me a hug. When she releases me, she opens her mouth, as if wanting to ask more, but clamps it shut and turns back around.

I glare her direction as she slowly walks away, and though I might regret it, my curiosity once again wins. "Was there something else?"

She stands next to her chair now, fingers knotted together. I can see it on her face, the urge to say something. She stares at the ground before finally taking a deep breath, spilling out lines I assume she's rehearsed on her own several times. "Listen, I know I haven't been the easiest person to be around."

I open my mouth to respond, but she again cuts me off. "Can I come to your next wine night?" She doesn't look up. In fact, her eyes clamp shut, as if she can't fathom even seeing my reaction. I'm learning that when Zalya has something to say, she has to get it out, and I wonder where in her past she felt so muted that she needs to control every conversation now.

My stomach drops, remembering the few other vulnerable times that she's mentioned being excited I was here, or even telling me how she needed a friend. And just like when I realized how selfish I'd been by not being honest with Blaine, I hate myself for not meeting her in the middle. "Of course."

Her eyes light up, but I know she hates being vulnerable as much as I do, so I don't blame her for running off as quickly as she can. "See you Saturday," she throws over her shoulder as she returns to the palace.

Scholars have attempted to re-create Linea's techniques of imbuing power from the land into another—be it sentient or not—to no avail. Not only does the imbuing technique require intense focus and strength, but its limits and longevity are yet unknown. Additional research is needed for this scholar to recommend normalization and increased usage of this advanced magical sourcing.

—An excerpt from *Celestera: The Beginning*

"If you don't quit cutting the tomatoes like a common street whore with the opium shakes, I am going to teach you proper technique using something of yours that I have a *feeling* you wouldn't want close to a blade!" I scream at Rowan from across the kitchen, staring down at decimated fruits I am supposed to be using in a salad later this evening.

The clickety-taps of Rowan's kitchen loafers stamp their way from the pantry to beside me as he stares down at the bowl I'm looking into. "I refuse to take responsibility for what happened to these poor innocent babes." He picks one up and holds it to the light, as if assessing it for life.

"Well, then, find out who did and ensure they don't get anywhere near a knife in my kitchen ever again," I grate through clenched teeth. I've been on edge the past couple weeks, impatiently waiting for any Resistance correspondence to come in while I spend my nights staring into historical accounts of events that make no sense, each chapter feeling farther and farther away from relevant to the Break at all. I have never felt so stuck and hopeless. And though he's been as gracious as I believe he's capable of, I've been unfair to him the entire time. "And get new shoes! Yours are too loud!"

"You need laid." He glares at me with an audacious look that tells me I won't get away with another threat of demotion, and then he scans me from head to toe, as if he's sensing sexual tension radiating from my skin. In all actuality, he might be. His gifts at sensing auras can intuit the morality of my soul, but I don't know if he can sense other *needs*. It wouldn't surprise me.

"Do you have any suggestions that might be plausible?" I ask, attempting to smile, but aware the look is likely closer to a baring of teeth.

I don't know how Vinny did it back in Quinthold: kept us motivated even when there were no updates for us to work with. In fact, I always knew my purpose—never had to question it. I didn't come to Liravel assuming it would be easy to establish a line of communication from my new home, but I also didn't think I would go over a month with nothing to report.

Rivian's meetings are all closed-door, and even the couple of times now that I've snuck myself into his office to look at them, his correspondence are all locked away. I keep up my late nights reading, taking messy notes in my journal and cross-referencing them with Mia on wine nights, but even that's on hold since she's been out of town. I don't know where else to look, or what else to listen for—but I need something soon, something that can keep the thoughts that I made a big mistake by coming here at bay.

On nights when the moon is bright and I can't keep its glow from lighting my entire room with its wonder, I lie awake trying to convince myself of this. That I didn't throw away everything that I had, that one day I'll look back and consider leaving Blaine, and Teliquis, and Norris all worth it—that they'll look back at me not with loathing or pity, but pride. It's on these nights that I feel Teliquis's strength, the kind I would feel while sitting with her on the beach, the kind that would radiate through her scales and into my soul, recharging a piece of me that I wasn't aware needed her.

Maybe the Obsidian Witches were onto something by worshiping the moon, I think to myself.

I'll support you worshiping anything if it puts you in a nicer mood. Apparently even my subconscious is sick of me.

"Well, I was going to wait until the Constellation Ball to give this to you, but you need a pick-me-up before you give yourself and everyone in this kitchen an attack of the heart."

I wonder what he's talking about, regarding the gift—I know what he means about my attitude. But I watch as he struts over to the pantry and comes back out with a gift box, wrapped in gold with an indigo bow. I hold the gift in my hands, running my palms across the thick gilded paper.

"Rowan, did you wrap this?"

"Of course I wrapped it! Do you think anyone else in this castle can make a crease that perfect?" He scoffs, offended that I would suggest he outsourced his gift wrapping.

"Is this paper standardly available in the palace, or is it yours?" I ask quickly, holding the box in my hands like the proof it is. I knew Rivian had been leaving the gifts the past month, I could feel it, but he had never labeled them, never admitted to them. Assuming he wanted them to be small surprises, I never asked. But now…

His eyes grow in understanding—a man caught.

"Just open the gift, or give it back, but no more questions."

"You've wrapped all the gifts I've received. Have you also been delivering them? Do you know who they're from?" I need to hear it out loud. If Rivian has been giving me these gifts, it's another example of his flirting, proof that I haven't been making up the affection in my twisted mind. It may just be the validation I need to stop worrying about upsetting Zalya by pursuing him.

For the Resistance, of course.

Of course. Okay, slamming the wall on my other voice.

"Please just open the box. You're really taking all the joy out of trying to reduce your bitchiness with material gifts." He sulks, stomping one foot in resemblance to a toddler's tantrum, his fists balling at his sides.

"Just tell me one thing. I'm begging you. Why is he sending them?" This is my chance to see if my attempts at flirting have been successful too, to discover if Rivian is falling for me. If so, I may get laid *and* have some Resistance intel when he returns. An admittance that I would never tell Rowan. He'll just suggest I go to bed with a man every time I boss him around.

"Swear you'll never tell him you know. He wanted to be anonymous, and I don't want to get in trouble." He looks at me with weary eyes, face angling to the side slightly, as if I can't be trusted with the knowledge of my admirer. "Honestly, I don't know why he would be so secretive about it. You aren't going to fall in love with him if you don't know the gifts are from him."

"So he *does* like me?" I ask excitedly, a smile widening across my cheeks that I can't help. Finally, something is going my way.

"Like you? I've never seen the man like any woman before—I don't know what that would even look like. No, the man is in love with you. Now. Open."

"You haven't? What about Zalya?" Rowan has been here in the palace for nearly a hundred years. He's seen many versions of Rivian, and he's telling me he never once had a relationship? Not even a crush?

Rowan gives me a look I can't read, but suggests the question seems odd, before running a hand down his exasperated face, his chin hanging in defeat. "Listen, I've known the man since he was young. I was friends with his father, in fact, not that you'd be able to tell from how well I've aged. No. The man has kept to himself since he was young." Something emotional fills the final statement, like it's hard for Rowan to say, hard for him to remember those days himself. I set the gift on the worktop as I gaze toward a version of Rowan I have yet to know.

"Rowan—"

"No. I won't talk to you about that. That's not my story to tell." He straightens, and in the blink of an eye, he adjusts himself back into my sassy assistant.

Regret sinks in as I watch his demeanor flash back so abruptly. Not over inflicting the grief I saw in his face, or the many questions that led him there—but that I've not gotten to know that side of him before now. I've spent my entire career working in kitchens, and the latter half leading them, all the while treating each assistant that crosses my path as temporary—a tool for the evening. But that will never be Rowan. I don't know how he's become different, but I know with certainty that my role here would not be the same without him.

I sit with that thought for a moment while I stare at the gift, given by a man who so quickly accepted me into his kitchen where he has spent the prior hundred years, all because he can tell I'm frustrated. And I have never felt so small.

"Open the gift, or I will fill your coffee pots with vinegar." And like the blessing he is, he lifts the mood back to where we function best.

"Try me," I retort back, giving him a thankful smirk that I can only hope relays my appreciation for him.

I rip through the paper, watching him cringe in discomfort at my barbaric methods, and open the box to reveal an oddly familiar blade. The black matte steel reflects nothing, and it's icy to the touch as I run my fingers across the curve of the spine. "Rowan, why am I looking at my own knife, and how did you get it?"

"I thought you could use an upgrade."

I look up, confused. The knife is the same as the one I received from Zalya as a welcome gift for accepting the job, but there is something that feels different about it now.

"I know you like to practice throwing with your blades, and I figured you needed one that would actually protect you if you ever needed it. I imbued this one with a bit of my power. It will now call to your targets' auras."

My hand pauses a few inches above the box I just lifted the knife from, my breath hitching. The hilt seems to sing to me, its energy vibrating up my wrist and forearm from where I grip its hilt. My skin pebbles, as if the icy chill of the steel sinks straight to my bones. I may not understand what he means, or how this magic works, but I cannot deny its existence.

"How?" I ask, in awe of the knife in my hands, holding it close to my eyes to examine faint indigo waves floating through the wood grain of the black hilt.

He gives me a kind smile, his face softening with the naivety in my question. "If you ever need to wield this blade, it will defend anyone it or yourself deems good."

"And what about those that aren't good?"

"It's a knife, it can't do more than your intent for it—but I have a feeling the day you need to pull this one out, you'll have already made your intentions clear."

24

THE ADVISORY IS AN INDEPENDENT AND UNBIASED AGENCY WHOSE MISSION IS TO PROTECT ALL THOSE WITHIN CELESTERA. HOWEVER, IF AN ALTERCATION ARISES AGAINST A SOVEREIGN GUARD UNIT OR OTHER UNMARKED MILITARY GROUP, YOU'RE TO DO ANYTHING WITHIN YOUR POWER TO ASSERT STRENGTH AND INDEPENDENCE ON BEHALF OF THE ADVISORY AND CITIZENS OF CELESTERA.

CONFIDENTIAL: REGULATORY CODES OF THE ADVISORY, ARTICLE 39, SECTION 10, INTERACTIONS WITH DESCENDANTS OF VARIOUS MAGICAL LINEAGES

I find myself with an open afternoon and a strong late-autumn sun sitting in the sky a week later when Rowan kicks me out of the kitchen for scaring an assistant in training.

I scolded her placement of the ricotta in my lasagna. Honestly, I don't know why Rowan would train anyone on my signature dish, but I wasn't able to stand there and watch my precious recipe be annihilated like that.

"Morgan, how do you feel about finally showing me the throwing targets?" I ask, needing to take out the frustration on somebody or something.

"Tonight?" he asks, and I can tell by his tone that he's searching his mind for an excuse to say no.

"Yes, and if your job is to guard my rooms, but I'm not in there, wouldn't a better use of your time be actually guarding me, while I'm out there throwing big, scary, dangerous knives through the air?" I ask, stepping into his space.

He looks uneasy, glancing down the hall in both directions, as if someone may turn a corner and relieve him of this moment, when I remember his weakness.

"What if I bring Bianca?"

Heat rising in his cheeks is all the response I need before I sprint up my stairs to send a message into town for Bianca. An hour later, she teleports straight into my room and launches herself onto me in a hug. I suppose that means she's excited for the evening.

We follow Morgan through the palace, passing through the guards' wing, which isn't nearly as ornate as the rest. Rather than the colorful rugs and tile, the floors here are plain stone, often stained from water damage through the years, and the walls hold portraits of previous captains of the guards. Just like the portraits of the Sovereign from the underground, no one portrait is the same size or style as another.

There is a large painting of a portly man atop a gryphon, two swords raised to the sky, his mouth open in a roar. Another smaller painting depicts a thin man behind a desk, no weapons on him but staring intently down at a map with various colored pins placed throughout. My favorite, though, might be a smaller painting toward the end of the hall. A man sits atop a mountain, staring out toward open fields displaying the brutal aftermath of a battle, holding a tattered leather jacket in his arms. Only his side profile shows in the art, but the weight of the scene weighs across his solemn face.

Most of the doors remain closed as we pass them, but I slow down as I walk past a room full of younger guards all gathered around a table. They're playing a game with paper cards and laughing raucously. It takes me back to meeting up with Blaine after his shifts during his early days in the Advisory.

I freeze when I pass another door open to a dark room, mesmerized by a table casting a glowing map onto the ceiling above—a projection made of light. I stand mesmerized, watching the map rotate slowly in a circle, audibly gasping when it stops and zooms in to a section of detailed mountains. Various marks display across the terrain, a few "X's," another few "O's," occasionally a line connecting two marks. Morgan must feel my pause—he turns and tries to pull me along, but I don't budge, instead entering the room with my mouth agape in awe, stopping completely when I see Cliff reclined in an armchair, staring at the map above.

He jumps from his chair at the shock of seeing me enter and waves his hand in a swiping motion, making the map disappear altogether.

"A?"

It's funny to see him so flustered by my arrival, as he gazes toward me with his head slightly cocked to the side. "What were you doing that's so secretive?" I ask, staring at the ceiling where the map once was.

"Sorry, Captain," Morgan sounds from the doorway, face scrunching in embarrassment when he realizes Cliff was in the room I entered, but standing at attention all the same. "I was just escorting these ladies to the range."

Cliff's neck pivots, turning from Morgan to me and back. I obviously caught him looking at something I wasn't supposed to see, and now I have to know what.

"Up for a good time, Cliffy?" I had intended to drill Morgan about Cliff, but with Bianca present, that was going to be difficult anyway. Only an idiot would miss their hands brushing past each other every ten steps on the way here. "We can make it fun and wager with whiskey." I up-tilt my voice, hoping to excite him. Blade throwing, Rivian liking me, Rowan's gifted dagger, and now possibly drunken questioning with Cliff—this past week was turning out to be a delightful change in pace for my plans.

I know I have him when his shoulders slump and he rolls his eyes. *My friend and his whiskey.*

The four of us now stand in a row, staring down our own lanes of the palace's range. The ground between where we stand and the targets is littered with divots and broken bits of arrows that haven't made it to their intended spots. Morgan stands at the end, followed by Bianca, then me, and Cliff. We each have a small wooden post to set our blades down on, and anything else we may have brought with us.

I have to intentionally stop myself from gawking at the two to my left, from begging them to go find some privacy, every time they look at or speak to each other. Cliff catches me staring when they simultaneously reach for a knife lying between them, and fall into a cycle of giggling when they both pull their hands back. They repeat this a few times, neither ever coming back with the knife. It's like I'm watching a calf attempt walking for the first time, awkward and clumsy, worried its tiny little legs are going to break with one wrong move.

Cliff must feel the same—he takes the glass decanter he brought out with him, sets down two small glasses in front of him, and pours us each an ounce of the amber liquid. "Gonna need a few of these if I have to endure *that.*" He nods once in their direction and throws back his whiskey, offering my glass with his other hand.

I would worry about them hearing us, but the two are so caught up in their own world that I'm sure we could leave altogether and they wouldn't notice. I take the drink, needing its warmth against the chilly December air anyway, and set the glass back down next to his.

"Let's set ground rules," I say, and reach down to my bag and unsheathe five blades, inserting them into my bandolier for easy access and turning to face Cliff. I don't grab the black steel today, not sure how it may react when used, though I can feel it, humming from the sharpener holster across the bottom panel of my bag.

He stares at the hilts now sticking out diagonally across my chest, like I've grown scales down my front. After a too-long moment, he seems to remember where my eyes are and lifts his gaze to mine. Something between shock and respect sits on his face, and I wish more than ever that I could read his mind.

"What?" I ask, innocently batting my eyes for him, which I have deemed an important form of communication for our friendship.

"Just didn't expect you to—" He pauses, lips pursing while he searches for words.

"To what? Own knives? I do work in a kitchen, you know."

He hums to himself as I wait for him to figure out how to say what he means—that he didn't know I was a badass.

But the words never come, and I take pity on his scrambling mind, wanting to get to the part with the bullseyes and more whiskey. "Well, you let me know when you figure that out. Until then, best out of five?"

He agrees with a tentative nod of his chin, and I watch as he turns back toward his lane, stretching out his shoulders and chest muscles, and reaching up to smooth his wavy hair back away from his face.

He has no idea what he just agreed to, and I'm going to enjoy every moment. I haven't had true fun, outside of the past few wine nights, in longer than I can remember. A junior guard walks by behind us, and I ask him to grab bread from the kitchen for our group, feeling like we'll need snacks for when we're done here.

Cliff raises an arm, ready to throw, when I interject, "Wait, I have one last stipulation."

He lowers it, grunting once—which means "go on" in Cliffy.

"Winner gets to ask the other a question, and since I know you're gifted with truth, you'll know if I answer honestly. So you have to agree to grant me the same."

He gives me an affirmative nod, and even through his beard I see a small grin bloom on his face, his eyes narrowing at the corners in subtle glee.

I glance at the other two once more, just to make sure they aren't waiting for the rules as well, but Morgan is currently behind Bianca, guiding her wrist to the correct holding position and moving her arms in throwing form. He leans in, whispering something in her ear, and her resulting giggle has me happy for my friend.

Yeah, they aren't going to play.

Cliff and I go back-to-back, and I let him win this first round, not ready to show him just how much I've practiced this in my past, enjoying the face he makes when he thinks he went easy on me. The cocky sway in his movements as he pours my losing shot of whiskey is comical.

"Why did you take the job?" he asks, hushed so only we can hear.

I have to think about how to answer that. He'll know whether I'm telling the truth. "I lost an old friend, realized I had grown apart from my boyfriend, and needed a change," I say, raising the glass to my lips and taking the drink in one shot, hoping the words came out with enough conviction.

Another nod from him and we line up for round two. I let him best me again, watching him nail the first two, ensuring I got the second two, and giving him the win on the fifth throw. His shoulders actually shimmy this time when he reaches for the bottle, a little happy dance as he internally congratulates himself. I take the fresh glass from his outstretched hand and await my next truth.

"Where did you get those scars?" He stares at the double lines at the top of my left shoulder, his words soft but pointed.

I look down at the thick, raised scars myself, lifting my right hand to graze my thumb across their ridges. "I gave them to myself." I need an extra moment to mentally reset after that one, taking my time to return my gaze to Cliff—whose eyes haven't left my shoulder. A muscle tics in his jaw, the edges of his mustache twitch downward, and at the risk of falling apart, I face the target again.

Okay, time to step up.

I expected Cliff to come out and ask lighthearted questions to begin with. I thought we could start off light, and then the more targeted questions would feel more natural. My strategy might need adjustment, as I'd hoped to ply him with whiskey for admissions.

I start off *barely* beating him, hitting my target true on the last throw and over-celebrating when I win—feigning shock at my accomplishment. Bianca snaps out of her lusty haze long enough to clap my hand and show her support.

I pour Cliff the whiskey. "Is it hard living away from Brennan? Do you miss Leondell?"

"That's two."

I shrug, giving him a sly smile and watching as he rolls his eyes back at me.

"Brennan is an ass, but yes, I miss both him and Leondell."

We go a few more rounds like this. I learn Brennan was married at one point and lost his love to an incurable illness. Cliff heard about how I came to live in Quinthold after the Break and how my guilty pleasure is my obsession with romance books about fairies.

I decide he's loose enough to press when he slips and tells me he's looking forward to the traveling theater coming to town. His face gets so red that he turns away from me, pretending to cough from the whiskey. As if choking on it is less embarrassing for him than enjoying the theater.

Before we start the next round, Bianca taps my shoulder to give me her farewell before she leaves and make sure we're still on for wine night next weekend when Mia gets back. I ask Morgan if he is going to stay with me and Cliff, but he declines, saying he needs to make sure Bianca gets home all right. I know it's a lie—they're unwilling to say outright that they're leaving together, so I pretend not to notice.

They make it inside, and before Cliff can say another word, I rapid fire all five of my blades, each hilt sliding through my palm in precise movements. At the other end of my lane, all five now branch out from each other, fighting for the same spot on the surface, marking the center.

Cliff's eyes, now slightly glazed over, are glued to where I just guaranteed this round without him even taking one turn. "Fucking Fallen," he whispers under his breath in disbelief.

Finally, the "badass" confirmation I was waiting on.

I pour his whiskey, hand it over, and watch as the realization hits his eyes—the questions are about to get a bit more difficult.

"What was that map of?"

I watch his jaw clench as he stares down at the glass in front of him, determining how to play this out. A man from Leondell would have a hard time lying, especially when he promised he wouldn't, and I doubt Cliff is the type of man not to finish his end of a challenge. Slowly this time, he tips his glass to his lips, then sets it down, blinking a few more times than natural.

"It was a map of locations with reported rebel units that the Advisory has captured, crossed with known Advisory missions of unknown intent and the death tolls in those locations." His eyes ask me if that answer was adequate enough, but his grip on the table in front of us, white knuckles threatening to tear through his skin, and his flexed forearms, veins working hard to keep his blood flowing, tell me he did not want to answer that one.

All the whiskey in the world didn't prepare me for that.

When I don't answer, he turns toward the palace and walks away.

Part Four
Main Sequence

I have called on Linea herself for aide; however, my calls remain unanswered, and my lands remain unsettled. The latest travelers to cross through Thessarlan spoke of a plague that forced them from their homes. They spoke of desolate fields, dry lakes, and crops without yields. They told me the plague moved fast, and I saw the truth in their eyes as they recalled it.

—An excerpt from Fallen Reginald's journal

"Please." Biding his time, Reginald pled with Titania for his life. Tears streamed down his face as he gripped the quill until it snapped in half, leaving a smear of ink across the parchment in its path.

"Reginald." Her voice came out like the song of a mourning dove, bright and youthful, while she gently laid her hand across his shoulder. "You are stronger than this."

"How would you know? How do you know who and what we are?" He kept his voice sure, letting the tears fall while the anger swelled within him. Each moment he kept her talking, kept himself from writing, was another moment he could contemplate his words, another moment he could devise a plan.

She momentarily turned to face the others, meeting the gaze of each of them with not an ounce of regret or remorse. She examined them as if they were nothing more than a litter of harmless vermin she found in her garden, nuisances in need of extermination. Reginald knew the group had committed atrocious crimes deserving of judgment, but were her methods any more humane than the worst of their transgressions?

She blinked once as she turned from Gabriel, her final examinee, back to Reginald, as if resetting her mask. "I am aware of every being that enters my lands, aware of their actions, their desires, their motivations. Just as I am aware of yours right now."

"What would those be?" An edge entered Reginald's voice with this statement; he was unable to hide behind the solemn shadow he had created for himself any longer, and he hoped she assumed the tremor in his voice to be fear.

"Statues aren't constructed of those who sat behind desks. Battles aren't won by the scholars who were too scared to fight. Love doesn't land in the hand that can't defend its honor." The words came out of her mouth as if she were musing over tea while watching the sunrise.

Reginald had already felt a range of emotions in this one day that most wouldn't feel over an entire month. Anger was not a typical reaction for him. And when he did allow himself to feel anger, it rarely owned him, drove him, consumed him. In that moment, though, Reginald ground his teeth to halt himself from releasing venom on the serpentine woman before him. "Why would you give a quill to a man whose only legacy will be earned with his words?"

His gifts weren't those of a warrior, but those of knowledge. He could not defend himself with strength or force. If there was ever a time to hold pride in his mind—it was now.

A small smile tipped up the corners of her lips; her eyes narrowed in delight. "Because I pity you, Reginald. I pity your heart and your mind for romanticizing the truth, for thinking integrity can be worn like a badge. But I am not without empathy for your plight. If getting to write your own history will have you following me with your head held high, then I shall allow it. After all, I need you complacent for our future endeavors."

Reginald seethed. A visceral knot formed inside him, twisting his insides until his muscles surrounding his core spasmed in need of release. If he could move, if his feet weren't frozen to the stone by her mists of magic surrounding them, he would launch himself on this woman.

Titania dipped her chin toward the parchment, her cue for him to continue, and so Reginald did.

"At the second annual occurrence of the Convergence of Aeons, Linea executed her long-contemplated plan. A plan to remove the Fallen from power and give the lands to their bloodlines until peace could be found once more. The battles breaking out across Celestera were too much for her to continue to watch—this was not the world she sought for them.

She called on her Fallen. Their unwavering loyalty and fierce dedication to her would be the cornerstones of her plan. Just as she convinced each of them to believe in her vision of a world built on peace, she would convince them of her plan to abolish their current court. Their kin would each take over rule of their lands and houses as Sovereign, effective immediately.

While the Fallen had been populating the lands, Linea had been busy practicing magic of her own. She had uncovered deep powers, forged from centuries of knowledge and practice, and accessed the strength of the land to cleave a hidden kingdom into existence. An entire civilization hidden behind a veil of her strength, never to be found except by those who knew of its existence and needed to access it for good. She told them of her plan to send them all to this new kingdom, where they could live out the rest of their lives, entrusting the continuation of their legacies to their offspring.

Linea watched as aggravated chaos erupted amongst the council. Knowing she had to act quickly to avoid war breaking out all across Celestera, she sacrificed herself for the greater good. She didn't have time to get them to her newfound kingdom, reserved for their immortal leisure. She prayed Micah would understand, prayed he would go on without her, that he would raise their kin to continue her legacy.

Reaching deep into her soul's reserve, she called upon her gifts and entrapped the members of the council within the pillars of her temple. Light and wind and shadow and sound erupted from all directions. Each pillar transformed from a cylinder of stone support to carved statues of the Fallen. Each entombed forevermore. Only her own direct descendants would know how to call on her from her own statue on the temple throne, and only in a time of dire need."

25

You are cordially invited to the Annual Constellation Ball, a moonlit masquerade, hosted by the Auralian Sovereign Court this February 11 at sundown.

Please join us for an enchanting evening under the stars, where elegance and mystery converge to create a night filled with magic and revelry. The Constellation Ball promises to be a celebration like no other, with music, dancing, and entertainment fit for royalty.

A week later, Cliff's face still replays through my mind—the way he stormed off, the sound of his voice as he gritted his teeth through the words when he told me about the map. I stayed on the range until the sun had completely left the sky, and I was sure he wouldn't come back out to interrogate me—to stop me from what I would do with that information.

I went straight to my rooms, drafted the Resistance memo, and took it immediately to the delivery gate for the next day's truck. The sooner I got the message out of my hands, the less I would debate with myself about whether it was worth betraying Cliff's trust to do so.

Intel can't wait for my conscience to catch up, I told myself as I handed the scroll to the courier.

Your conscience shouldn't have any issues if you're doing nothing wrong, my other voice responded, as if its sole purpose is to make me a good person.

Betrayal. That's what it was, though. I made a man who holds the value of truth above all else answer questions I knew he wouldn't want to answer. And I'm an idiot if I think he didn't leave that range wondering why I would care, why I would push him for it.

Who is Cliff to me anyway, though? Just someone who has the same boss I do for a few short years? In contrast to his long life, the few years I spend here are but the blink of an eye. The bigger question is why I can't seem to get him out of my mind, why I care so much. I finally have something tangible to share with the Resistance, and all I can think about is Cliff's grumpy face.

I push all those thoughts away, though, while I gather wine and snacks for the girls to come over tonight. Mia and Rivian just got back today from their trip to Curatia. Since Rivian had work there, Mia accompanied him to see friends and family. So I doubt she will want to stay long tonight, but I brew some coffee just in case.

I rearrange the spread across my dining table several times before agreeing with myself that it doesn't matter, then I start a fire, alternate opening and closing the balcony door when I can't decide what the temperature should be, and change my outfit four times out of consideration for my future comfort.

Why can't I sit still?

Guilt is a powerful emotion, my other voice says back. I mockingly mimic its words to myself while I finally settle onto my couch to calm down before the girls arrive.

The knock of sweet, promised distraction finally sounds against my door. But it's not the girls. A palace messenger stands on the top step with a box in his hand, extending it toward me with both arms.

"Have a good night, ma'am," he calls before I can ask what it is.

The large box is wrapped in plain butcher paper, and when I open it, I find a note waiting for me.

Love,

While the indigo dress is one that will forever remain stained in my memory, just one vision will not do. I found this during my travels in Curatia, and couldn't leave without it. It was made for you—and yes, Mia approved.

Will you do me the favor of gracing me with it at the Constellation Ball?

P.S. Open your door.

Rivan

The gauzy magenta gown is weightless as I lift it in front of me—formfitting, with a sheer overlay ruched back and forth across the shimmering bottom layer, like wispy clouds casting a thin veil on a starry night. The front and back plunge in deep V's from the straps to the waistline, and there are even small sheaths built into the fabric, hidden in the overlapping layers of gauze, for blades.

I stand there momentarily, wondering what that conversation looked like between him and Mia, what all he said—already planning the interrogation I am going to put her through when I see her next.

I gently take the delicate fabric to my closet before wandering to the door, curious about his note in the card. A peony sits on the landing, on top of another note, with handwriting I couldn't miss.

Love,

I wanted to respect your "wine night," which Mia tells me is your new tradition, but I couldn't stop thinking about you the entire length of my trip. So, your friends allowed me to be selfish this one night. Would you join me for an evening in the courtyard?

– R

The peony is fresh. Its soft petals remind my senses of a garden after rain, fragrant and alive.

Rivian convinced Mia to stay home so he could have me to himself.

Clutching the flower to my chest, I stare down the stairs toward the courtyard where Rivian waits, when another colorful item catches my eye—every third step has a stemmed flower on it, waiting for me to pick it up.

One by one, I follow the flowers. First a rose, then a tulip, a white carnation, then a calla lily, collecting them on a path leading me to the courtyard. My heart flutters in my chest as I make my way through the palace. I try to tell myself that I can use this time to get answers, that I need to make a list of questions, anything I might connect to why Cliff has that map in his office. I can start by thanking him for the dress, and then ask about his trip.

But that's as far as my thoughts take me. The door to the courtyard opens at my arrival, and my heart sinks. There must be a thousand candles, all twinkling in the various colors of the world. Ruby-red rose petals scatter on the stones from the door to the fountain in the center, where Rivian stands, hands behind his back and a roguish grin on his face that has me forgetting every question I'd lined up in my mind.

"What is all this?" I ask, frozen to the stones beneath me as he slowly closes the distance between us.

"Do you remember when you asked me about 'my girlfriend' and I told you that there had never been a woman who would have been able to handle a permanent role in my life?"

I look up at him, my collection of flowers in one fist and my other arm now hooked through his as he leads me toward the fountain.

How did we get here? There is no way that this man has fallen in love with me this hard—this quickly. I think back on the past several weeks here, the immediate connection with him I felt. Not just a physical attraction, but something deeper, something I haven't been able to explain, something I've been trying to justify.

What about you—are you in love? My other voice counters my doubt.

"I do. The night you came and saved me from Zalya at the bar."

"Well, I have a confession." He looks down at me, the moonlight catching on the waves of his hair, perfectly mussed in that effortless way that he prefers to wear it.

A bottle of wine rests in an ice bucket on the ledge of the fountain, and we pause while he stops to pour two glasses.

"And what is that?" I ask while he takes my bouquet and sets it to rest in the ice bucket with the open bottle of wine.

"I've also never gone three weeks unable to shake a woman from my mind," he says, his words like velvet against my skin.

Something ignites within me at those words, and I hate myself for it—but I also know that there is no way I can stop myself where he is concerned. I can't stop the way my cheeks ache from the grin I can't hold back. I can't stop the way my heart races the moment my eyes meet his or the way my skin tingles at his touch. I can't stop the way my mind settles when he walks toward me. I want to—but I can't.

"August, love, will you do me the pleasure of joining me for an evening of watching the stars?"

I nod, my words lost in lust as he takes my hand and leads me to the bed.

I don't think this is love, but it feels a lot like it.

Can you love someone you've conspired against?

Several inches still separate us as we lie on our backs, gazing upon the stars above, the multicolored flames of the candles casting a rainbow of shadows on every surface of the courtyard.

"How was Curatia?" I ask, hoping to gain control of the conversation early, avoiding the wine so I don't do anything stupid.

"Curatia is wonderful this time of year."

Normal, nothing strange or intimate about that.

You also know that he couldn't stop thinking about you while he was there, my other voice chimes in.

Not helping.

We lie there, gazing at the night sky, listening to the sounds of the evening echo through the courtyard. Each moment that passes allows another layer of calm to settle over me, and I begin to wonder if he truly did just want to watch the stars in silence.

Good, maybe I misread the evening, I try to convince myself.

But then, a few drops of rain fall from the sky.

"We should go back inside." I say the words, but make no effort to leave the bed, closing my eyes against the sprinkles of rain and letting them soak into my warm skin.

"Do we?" Rivian turns his neck to face me, and when I meet his gaze, my eyes betray me for a split second by moving to his lips. The glow from a nearby candle twinkles against his irises, and that boyish smile that attracted me the first day I met him is back— and contagious. "You know, someone once told me they've always wanted to dance in the rain."

"Did they? Well, surely they told you it would be to a string quartet," I counter, knowing he's referring to me.

On cue, instrumental music begins playing faintly from somewhere nearby. Rivian sits up halfway as if he's heard something in the distance, leaning on one elbow and furrowing his brow, while he cups his other hand to his ear. "Can you hear that?"

I follow his gaze to the fountain, where the stone figures have come to life, forming a string quartet. The quartet was solid stone just a moment ago. Yet now, their bows flow against the strings in a symphonic delight. I've always considered what I create in the kitchen to be my form of art to present to the world, but music is really a gift that this world has given back to us. The stars must endear those blessed enough to deliver it—an art so pure that even humans are worthy of listening.

A small laugh escapes me. Fountains come to life, string quartets, and dancing in the rain—these are the plots of fairy tales and children's books. Not my life.

Entranced by the magic, I don't feel the bed move or see Rivian cross my path, but suddenly he's standing to my side with his hand out. "Care to dance?"

I take his hand, letting him lead me to the stone quartet playing a romantic ballad.

"Wait, I—" But my vision whirls as one of his arms wraps around my midsection, and I'm dipped low, one foot off the ground, breathless.

"You don't think I'd ask you to dance and not lead, do you?" He holds me there, his face only inches from mine. The only warning that we're about to move is another core-melting wink before he tightens his grip on my hand, pulling me up and spinning me out to his side and back in.

My palms find purchase on his chest while I recover from the loss of steady ground, but he doesn't miss a beat, spending the next couple songs leading me through every dance move I wasn't aware I could do, not once breaking our physical contact. And I lose myself in the moment, becoming one with the music and dancing. I'm not sure how long we spend twirling and spinning to the beat, laughing when one of us misses a step, but I lose count at song number ten.

Lightning cracks in the distance, finally breaking our focus. Only in our pause do I realize just how sore my feet will be from this evening. We both stare at each other while we catch our breath. The rain has picked up, and clouds now cover the stars and moon.

"Well, a true gentleman would end the evening by walking you back to your room," he says, taking a small step closer, freeing his hand from mine to palm the nape of my neck. His fingers tangle in my wet locks, but I'm too focused on his lips to notice.

Forgive me, Fallen. I'm only human.

"Yeah, he would," I respond breathily, positive I would fall if Rivian didn't have both of his hands in a commanding hold on me, keeping me upright.

"You have about three seconds to ask me to be a gentleman."

Rivian and the Resistance—I can have both, right?

IN AN EFFORT TO MAINTAIN A COHESIVE RELATIONSHIP WITH THE SOVEREIGN DESCENDANTS OF THE PROVINCES OF CELESTERA, THE ADVISORY REQUIRES QUARTERLY ATTENDANCE OF THE COUNCIL AND GRAND GENERAL TO ADDRESS THE STATE OF THE LANDS. FAILURE TO DO SO WILL BE CONSIDERED TREASON AND PUNISHED ACCORDINGLY.

CONFIDENTIAL: REGULATORY CODES OF THE ADVISORY, ARTICLE 26, SECTION 1, RELATIONS BETWEEN THE ADVISORY AND SOVEREIGN COURTS

"Three." His warm breath is a cloud between us as he walks us backward. "Two." His grip on my waist tightens, and his hand moves from the nape of my neck to the back of my head. His fingers knit through my hair to protect my head as my back hits the limestone wall—the space completely closing between us. "One." He leans his forehead on mine, his eyes close, and I'm positive he can feel my racing heart through our touch. "Zero."

His mouth is on mine, and he uses his tongue to part my lips. My hands find the front of his shirt, and I grab on to the fabric to pull him closer, my body already pressed firm between his chest and the wall. The moan that escapes my throat is less than subtle, as I take the kiss as deep as he'll give it. This is the culmination and release of many weeks of wanting. I'm past the point of making the decision that my brain tells me I should. I want him. It may have started as a game, a tactic, but there is nothing imaginary between us right now.

Reaching up, I wrap my arms around his neck for leverage, standing as tall as possible to reach him. I mourn the loss of his hands for a split second as they release my head to reach down and grip the backs of my thighs. He lifts me, his fingers digging into my skin, pinning me to the wall in one smooth movement.

He wants this as much as I do. I feel it as his hips press into me when I lock my ankles around him. My hands move to his scalp, threading through his wet hair, pulling him closer. His mouth moves to a sensitive spot behind my ear, then he runs his tongue down my neck to my shoulder, his teeth lightly scraping along the way, igniting me from inside. My wet clothes suddenly feel suffocating, and he's my oxygen.

He pins me against the wall, creating friction from the pressure, and allows his hands to roam. His right hand finds the curve of my breast, while his left reaches to press against the stone above me, caging me here while we devour each other.

His mouth finds that spot on my neck again, his warm breath vibrating my skin, sending chills straight down my spine and coaxing another involuntary moan from me. I feel him grin against me while his lips ghost over every inch of my collarbone. The stubble of his beard increases my sensitivity everywhere he goes. There is nothing romantic about the way we're now conjoined, teeth clashing and lungs fighting for air, but we both continue to hold each other like the realm may end if we break this.

A door slams from the other side of the courtyard, and both of us snap our attention in its direction.

As quickly as the moment came, it's gone. An immediate sense of shame slams over me, my stomach sinking.

Have I lost all self-control? What is wrong with me?

I push against him, and he lowers me back to the ground, though his hand never leaves my waist.

He turns back to me, leaning his forehead against mine again, both of us still catching our breath. "Please don't bite that beautiful lip of yours." He lowers his hand to cup my cheek, gently tilting my chin until our lips meet again.

But I push him away.

This was a mistake.

"I'm sorry, I—" I don't finish that statement, instead taking off toward the door to the palace, needing to get as far away from Rivian as I can to think straight again.

"August—" he calls after me, but I ignore him. I can't stop now, I can't risk turning back.

By the time I'm halfway to my rooms, the high from my arousal has settled as a churning in my stomach, like I may be sick.

How did I let myself get there?

No. Not *may be* sick—will be. I stop next to a large potted plant off to the side, and heave.

I don't even realize that I've been mumbling self-assurances to myself through my chattering teeth until I reach the staircase to my rooms—and see Zalya leaning there, eyes glued to the floor.

"Zalya, hi."

"It was wine night, so I came to find you."

"I'm so sorry, I—"

She raises her gaze from the floor to meet mine, and the sadness radiating from her eyes makes the churning in my stomach intensify. "He doesn't love you, you know." Her lip wobbles as she says it, and somehow I wish she was angry, I wish she would yell at me over the pain in her voice.

Betrayal.

I open my mouth to respond, but no words come out.

She nods once, biting her lip, before pivoting off the wall and walking away. But she turns after a few steps. "I made this for tonight." She sets a tray of cookies down on a sideboard next to where she stands.

It's possible that my rain-soaked clothing causes the heavy weight that seems to have settled on my shoulders, but I rarely feel the weight of wet clothing like a slap to the face.

It's possible there's some flaw in my genetic makeup that has made it impossible to form healthy relationships with others. I sure have fucked up my fair share in the past few months.

I pursued Rivian, all while *knowing* that Zalya loved him and had been with him before. Was that alone sufficient to make me feel this way? If that wasn't bad enough, I sure as hell made things worse by abandoning Zalya for him on her first wine night.

I make my way into my rooms, peeling off my clothes as I go, leaving them where they land on the path I take to the bathing chamber to draw myself a scalding bath—little breadcrumbs of water and drenched linen. The air is cold against my wet skin; I can feel the hairs along my arms prickle up in the evening breeze drawn into the room through the cracked window. I don't deserve to use any of the scented oils this evening, I hardly deserve the plush robe I'll wear afterward, but I knew I shouldn't have kissed Rivian and still did it. So why draw the line at a nourishing bath?

On that note, I pull down my favorite oil, lemongrass, and drizzle an excessive amount of it into the rising bathwater.

What's gluttony when added to an already lengthy list of flaws? After all, if I'm going to soak in my own self-pity, it might as well smell of lemongrass.

The tub is about halfway filled by the time I finish adding my various salts and oils to the basin. The steam rolling off the water warms my face, and the hints of lemon I receive remind me of a lemon cheesecake bar I made a few years ago.

I wonder if I could source quality lemons here. They would be a great addition to the dessert spread at the ball.

You're thinking about lemons, right now? My other voice breaks through my self-loathing.

I ignore it for a moment, stepping into the scalding-hot water—so hot I think I may have heard a sizzle when my skin first touched the water.

Good, I deserve pain. Pain is real.

Before sitting all the way down into the tub, I grab a pin from the shelf above to pin my hair up. I run a rag through the hazy spirals of the bath oils clinging to the top of the water, then sprinkle a couple pinches of the bath salt directly onto the cloth before squishing the rag in my fist, ensuring the salts have worked their way into the fibers.

You can scrub at your sensitive skin all day, scrub until your freckles come right off, but the pain and irritation you'll experience won't erase your actions from today.

"Still worth a try," I respond out loud as I palm the rag into my skin with a firm hand, rubbing it against my arms, shoulders, chest, lingering as I swipe over the two raised scars on my shoulder. I stare at them both for a moment, wondering what Nova and Vincenzo would think if they saw me now.

Nova would probably ask me all about the friends and the life I've built since the Break. She'd ask if I was happy, if I'd found love, or possibly where my favorite bookstore was. She'd talk so fast that she would probably start telling me about her own life before I could even open my mouth to respond. She would have loved Blaine as much as I do—*did.*

Vincenzo would simply stare at me with an interrogating glare until I caved and confessed to having a mental breakdown over his death and the Resistance bust in the same week. He'd pinch his nose and ask if Blaine had gotten a fair transfer with the Advisory at least, or if I had found a respectable restaurant in my new town to lead. And when I told him I had left Blaine and was now working for a Sovereign Descendant, he would take one of my good knives away and give me the silent treatment until I came to my senses and fixed this mess.

"I wonder if they think of me," I contemplate—Nova from across the sea or wherever she ended up, and Vincenzo from the aether. I fold the rag over the side of the tub and hug my knees to my chest in the water.

Of course they do, and they aren't the only ones. For instance, the hot and bothered Sovereign you just left in the courtyard, the heartbroken beau you blindsided in Quinthold, and even the jealous friends on the other side of the castle.

"Blaine should not have been blindsided by that decision."

You impulsively broke up with him in the middle of him begging you to put the relationship over a cause.

"For a voice in *my* head, you don't seem to be on my side."

Just giving you the same tough love you would give anyone else.

"You act like you know me. *Are* you me? Am I just talking to myself right now to justify my actions? Or are you someone—something else?" I say straight into my knees while resting my forehead above them.

Would one answer mean more to you than another?

I sit there silently for a few moments, just absorbing the cooling water, deciding I don't really want to know. "Did I actually do anything wrong tonight?"

Do you think you did anything wrong?

"I don't think there's anything wrong with falling in love or dancing in the rain."

I stare down at the water, my reflection contorting on the surface from the oils. The vision matches how I feel—broken.

27

Purity Celebrations were largely celebrated amongst the provinces east of the Liravel River, where pureblooded magical lines were considered an elitist status symbol. After the first Descent occurred in the year 4263 in The Runda Isle, the concept seemed to dwindle in popularity, as magical strength was renewed and a new family resumed power.

Over the following century, the remaining provinces each experienced their own Descents, except for Linea's line, bringing to question if Linea exempted herself from a Descent like her Fallen.

—An excerpt from *Celestera: The Beginning*

The final two weeks between that night in the courtyard and the Constellation Ball felt like an eternity. I avoided everyone I could, unwilling to show my face to half the palace, using direct routes from my rooms to the kitchen when I did leave just so I could do my job.

Mia came and found me after a few days, worried that she hadn't seen me. I told her everything—crying over a plate of cheese between pulls from a bottle of wine. After all, it wasn't as if I could get any more embarrassed by my actions. She even stayed the night with me one night. It was nice to share a bed again—feel weight and warmth a few feet away, even if it wasn't from that of a lover.

I went years without a single tear shed back in Quinthold, years without an emotion hitting me so hard I would get sick with its weight. I've lain in bed every night for the past two weeks wondering why I came here, why I thought I could get people to trust me, why I care that I've upset people along the way.

In three short months, I've accomplished nothing. Just made a palace full of people resent me.

Are you done feeling bad for yourself? my other voice asks for what feels like the hundredth time.

I wish I could be. I would do just about anything to shut off the wave of emotions that have felt like an onslaught of weakness since coming here.

Today, though, I can no longer ignore the rest of the palace. Tomorrow is the Constellation Ball, and with many guests in town already, a purity celebration was planned for this evening—a formal ceremony celebrating the birth of a pureblood Auralian. I imagine the uproar that a human would get for the same celebration.

Descendants would burn us in the town squares for simply suggesting it.

Rowan told me last week, though, that it's actually rare for a pureblood infant from any magical line to come along, due to centuries of magical lines mating with each other. This infant will be able to trace its bloodline on both the maternal and paternal branches all the way back to its Fallen, Niall.

A bit incestuous, I think to myself as I chop various vegetables for a winter salad, but then it occurs to me—it *is* incestuous.

I drop my knife on the worktop, haphazardly wiping my hands of the juices and water from the produce on my apron as I find my bag from the corner of the room and pull out my notebook and a quill. I snap off the string to get it open and scratch out a reminder to myself to ask Mia next time I see her, jotting the words "Who did the Fallen originally mate with??" in it.

I hear the door swing open behind me, so I quickly toss the notebook back in my bag and turn around—confused when I see Rowan strut around the corner.

"Miss me so much that you came in on your day off…" My words drift when I see a stern look across his face—twin lines set deep between his eyes.

I had told Rowan to take the day off. After all, there is no use in my continuing to take my inadequacies out on him, not when I will need his full support tomorrow.

Is making out with your boss a personal inadequacy, or just a poor decision?

"Making poor decisions is my inadequacy," I retort back to my other voice.

"What?" Rowan looks at me over a crinkled nose and squinted eyes, like I'm a rotten piece of meat in his supply that he's afraid to touch in case it holds maggots that will spread.

"What, what?"

"What poor decision did you make this time?" He emphasizes *this*, as if I make a new mistake every day. In his defense, I've opened up to him about a few of my regrets from my time here—nothing incriminating, nothing about make-out sessions in the rain—but enough to get it out of my system.

"I didn't realize I said that one out loud—" I shake my head at myself before continuing. "Just choosing apples over pears for the salad." I try to resume chopping the salad, but I'm thrown off my rhythm by his entrance. Dropping the knife, I give him my attention again. "You're here why?" I knew I would have to see everyone later, had prepared myself for it, but I was hoping for some time alone in the kitchen during the day.

He's striking today—wearing dress slacks and a dinner jacket, unlike his usual nicer but still kitchen-appropriate clothing, and I wonder how he'll possibly top this look for the actual ball. He spoils it, naturally, by glancing over his shoulder before looking at my salad on the worktop and scrunching up his nose.

How in Celestera his nose isn't stuck like that is beyond me.

His pretentious shoes stamp across the shiny tiles toward the pantry, where he hangs his jacket and pulls down his apron, clean and pressed just like everything else he wears. The clacking of his shoes hammers annoyance into me with each step that he still hasn't answered yet why he's here.

"Rowan, why do your shoes seem to clack louder than any other shoes that have ever existed?"

I need more coffee, I think to myself, pushing my palm into my forehead, attempting to force a good mood into my social energy for a bit. But if I feel like this just seeing Rowan, it is going to be a long day.

"You know, I really don't need help today, Rowan. In fact, I'd prefer if you and anyone else in this *Fallen-forsaken* palace would just let me be for a bit," I yell toward the pantry while I resume slicing an apple to shreds with a resolve it doesn't deserve.

"Oh, you need help." In a slightly more brusque tone than normal, for him.

He carries a bowl of flour in my direction, and I watch as he drops it right in front of me, flour scattering onto the fresh-cut apples, the sound of the stone bowl on the thick wood counter echoing through the kitchen. Something about him is off today. Like we're both one wrong action away from attacking each other.

"Please do something that will convince me I'm dreaming, because this is the opposite of help in all ways," I whisper incredulously, holding myself back from wringing his neck while staring at the flour coating the worktop and fresh apples. Pointing to the bowl, I add, "Not to mention, I already made the rolls."

"I like them a certain way, and if I have to sit through a purity celebration, I better have good bread." He looks over his shoulder again, then turns his head to look out the window, as if he has all the time in the world to stand here and ruin my day.

My eyes are dry from how wide open they've been for this entire interaction, or maybe it's the stress that causes them to twitch—I get even more frustrated that I can't rub them with my fingertips thanks to the flour that now coats them. But I notice again his brows furrowing while he stares out into the distance—something is off about him.

"Plan to make rolls with—"

Rowan cuts me off with a silent whip of his gaze back in my

direction, his eyes flaring as he holds one finger to his lips, and I see it this time. I've never caught it before, but his eyes glow for a split second. If I weren't so perturbed by the entire interaction, I would ask him to do it again—the indigo flash of light was gorgeous against his silver dress shirt. His eyes dart down to the bowl of flour and back to mine, though, calling me to follow his line of sight.

"Please tell me you stocked that good oil? The kind from the coconuts of The Ivory Hills?" He asks me louder than necessary for only being a couple feet away, still looking from me to the bowl of flour. Either he has lost his mind, or there is something I'm supposed to see in the bowl.

"Are you asking if I ordered everything off last week's list, Rowan? If so, then yes?" I repeat just as loudly.

I've played this game before. It's a tactic we would use in Quinthold at the market—have a normal conversation with your words, and a completely different one with your actions. Sometimes it would be following the person's eyes, like with Rowan right now—other times, it might be making an overt movement to hide their sleight of hand.

"Thank the Fallen. I'm going to go grab it. Do me a favor and sift that flour while I fetch it. I don't have much time before the ceremony, and if I miss the welcome march I will freak out."

I stare at his retreating back as he heads through the door into the old stairwell that will take him to the wine cellar, where we also keep the gallons of oils. I should have questioned what just happened before impulsively running my fingers through the powdery distraction lying in front of me, but what's one more mistake on my hands? The least I can do is keep the man I have to share a kitchen with on my good side. Not to mention, it would eat at me not to know what he wants to tell me at this point.

The flour is cool to the touch, soothing even. It takes me back to playing on the bank of the river as a child with Nova, hiding different gems and rocks in the sand from each other and seeing how long it takes the other to find them all. I lift my hands, cupped full of flour, letting the granules run through my fingers back into the bowl. Each time watching as if my own thoughts are dispersing into the floury haze now floating in front of me—until my hand brushes something. A small scroll barely sticks up out of the surface of the flour.

Bless the Celestial Mother, Rowan knows how to be sneaky.

I continue the motions, mindlessly looking around the kitchen— now hyperaware that Rowan had been checking for the presence of other people. The flour above the counter expands outward with each sift, like a cloud vaporizing in the breeze on a warm day.

In one swift—albeit unfortunate for whoever has to clean my kitchen later—movement, I accidentally breathe in flour when I yawn mid-sift. A sneeze rips out of me, flour flying from my hands when I instinctively turn my face into the crook of my elbow to shield the food. I blink flour out of my eyes, staring at the surrounding mess, as if I stand in a halo of grain.

This will take forever to clean, I confirm to myself, leaning back against the wall and stuffing my hands into my apron's deep pockets— allowing the scroll I'd snuck into my cuff to fall into one for later.

"You really *do* need help," Rowan calls out as he crosses back toward me with two gallons of oil in his hands. "Good thing the juniors work the weekends. I'll go find one." He skips off, leaving me to stand amid the flour coating the kitchen and the ruined winter salad.

He returns with a spindly assistant whom I vaguely remember meeting a couple of weeks ago, but never learned his name. The man's face lights up when he sees mine, eyes widening and smile blooming as he scurries past Rowan to get to me. I bite my lip in order not to laugh overtly at the face Rowan makes toward the back of this man's head as he brushes past him on his path to me.

"Chef, how can I assist? I wasn't aware you were in today. I apologize, I would have been here sooner," he rambles in a shaky voice, head swiveling as he takes in the mess.

I look to Rowan, hoping he can save me the embarrassment of showing the poor man that I don't know his name, but he's already back in the pantry grabbing his evening jacket.

Turning back to the assistant, who still gapes at me as if I'm about to spill the secrets of the Fallen themselves, I improvise. "I need to set up the buffet—would you mind cleaning up this mess that Rowan made?"

"That *you* made!" Rowan's muffled voice yells from the closet.

The assistant's head snaps to the pantry his reaction dripping with disdain. This time I snap my hand across my face, covering my mouth to hide my smirk—this man clearly wants to make a good impression on me.

"August, maybe I'll see you at Connor's after the ceremony." Rowan is gone before I can respond, my mouth hanging agape in the direction he just left.

It doesn't matter, though. My nameless assistant is cleaning up the mess. I was just slipped a covert message—which I'm about to go read in private, and then I'll meet up with friends at the pub.

This is the most normal *day I've had since arriving here.*

28

IN TIMES OF DIRE NEED, A DISTRESS CALL CAN ALERT THE NIGHT FORCE. THE NIGHT FORCE SHOULD BE CALLED UPON WITH CAUTION. WHILE UNDER ADVISORY COMMAND, THIS UNIT IS UNDER STRICT ORDERS TO NOT CEASE ATTACK UNTIL ALL THREATS HAVE BEEN ELIMINATED.

CONFIDENTIAL: REGULATORY CODES OF THE ADVISORY, ARTICLE 16, SECTION 8, LAST RESORT DEFENSE TACTICS

With the time I now have on my hands from abandoning the salad altogether, I'm able to take my time setting up the buffet for the event. The space Zalya set up on the vineyard patio is inspiring. She always excels when she sets up event spaces in the open air versus inside the ballrooms, and this afternoon is no different. Sometimes I wonder if, like the Obsidian Witches she idolizes, she gains her energy from the moon's rays.

A ceremonious bassinet sits under the archway that leads from the patio into the vines—indigo gauze and frills line the basket. Small tables fill the space for people to mingle between formal activities, and there are sections of chairs grouped together in sets of four on the sides for people to congregate in. Vibrant blue and purple cacti line the exterior boundaries of the patio, and a fire pit enchanted with indigo flames burns bright in the center. There is a light breeze today; the pit's flames sway with the energy of the air and the sounds of its crackling embers fill the space.

I keep myself busy, making excuses to go back and forth between the event space and the kitchen for various items, but there are only so many things I can pretend to forget. Zalya seems to do the same, frequently finding reasons to be anywhere but the patio. I watch her now as she walks down the stone path from the palace doors with another plant in her arms. I'm not even sure where she's finding all these cacti.

No sign of Cliff yet, though I'm not sure if he'll even be here since he's not Auralian.

Should I even be here? Maybe I'll use poor decorum as an excuse to leave. I hardly think a human attending a purity celebration is considered customary.

Are you really going to hide forever just because you kissed your boss, upset Zalya, and frustrated Cliff? my other voice asks, reminding me of my professional responsibility here.

I turn back to the table to rearrange the hors d'oeuvres for the tenth time in the past hour, as the violinist begins playing near the staged bassinet. The crowd of attendees all pause their conversations to turn and look up at the palace. The gentle hum of the music weaves in and out of the strings of the violin, filling the space with an air of hope—a palpable energy calling us to celebrate the new life in Rivian's arms.

Or maybe it's just calling to me?

The violin takes me back to the courtyard, pressed against a wall in the evening rain—his hands, now holding the baby with such care, gripping my thighs like they're the only thing keeping him alive.

The distraction from earlier with Rowan in the kitchen is proving to be short-lived as I throw myself back into my reality with this event.

I can want intel, love, or friendship—but I can't have all three.

Maybe the right decision wouldn't force you to choose at all? my other voice pops in, ever the philosophical optimist. Too bad it's not that easy.

I find Zalya staring straight at me from the opposite side of the patio, as if monitoring my reaction to seeing Rivian more than caring about his grand entrance. I lift my hand in a subtle wave, which she doesn't return, but one corner of her full lips tilts up ever so slightly, and a small wave of relief falls over me at the small gesture.

I hold Zalya's stare until she breaks it, the most I can do to show her where I stand, but eventually she returns to meandering through the guests, checking on their drinks, and slightly adjusting the tulle on the bassinet. Rowan shoves an empty glass in her face, and her reaction to him might be even funnier than the one he gave the sycophantic assistant earlier.

Rivian continues to walk down the cobblestone walkway in rhythm to the music, holding the infant with fragile care. The swaddled bundle sits silently in the crook of his arm, swaying back and forth with each step toward the celebration in its name. Two of the palace guards march behind them in synchronicity, their boots on the ground marking time with the violin.

Rivian wears a formal uniform today. Silver buttons adorn the front of the tailored blue wool, and various pins and patches stretch from epaulet to epaulet. His hair sits polished atop his scalp, not the purposeful tussle he wears around the palace, and the late-afternoon glow from the setting sun lights his face in a way that I can only describe as intoxicating.

"Have a minute?"

I jump when I hear Cliff's voice behind me and drop the tongs for the ice bucket I had been holding to prep glasses for fresh drinks. "Um."

That's really all you've got?

My teeth clench at the audacity of my other voice, but I force a pleasant-enough face before I turn to Cliff. "You look—"

Cliff's hair is slicked back, and his beard has been combed and trimmed. His formal captain's uniform is slightly more tailored to his body and fully adorned with several pins and patches, like Rivian's. And he currently stares inquisitively at me while I stumble for the word I'm looking for, hands clasped behind his back and chin dipped so he can look at me under raised brows while keeping his face pointed in Rivian's direction.

"Yes?" He leans in and whispers the word, close enough now to avoid making a scene during Rivian's entrance that I can smell his—is that cologne?

"Good?"

I didn't mean it as a question, but Cliff giving me the same look of incredulity I've seen from both Zalya and Rowan already today finally breaks my streak of composure. His eyes flare in amusement when a laugh bursts out of me, the sound bringing another small ounce of relief to the stress of how I started the day.

Several people turn in my direction, including Rivian, who now stands at the front, gently placing the infant into the bassinet. I feel my skin flush against the cool early-winter air and instinctively raise my hand to cover my chest, hiding the hives I'm sure are blooming. Thankfully, Rivian clears his throat, calling the attention back to him.

"Smooth," Cliff chides, leaning in, his shoulder bumping mine.

"How can I help you today, Cliffy?" I ask under my breath while I resume stocking the bar station. The violinist's tune has picked up the pace from the ceremonious march to a joyful melody, and Rivian kneels on an indigo cushion next to the bassinet with his head hung in prayer.

"Can you step away?"

His tone changes to one more serious, and I look up to read his face, but he stares blankly toward the front—an expression stamped across his face similar to the nonchalance he wore during the first dinner I attended.

The man really takes formal events seriously, doesn't he?

"I'm kind of in the middle of—" I cut myself off when I see Rowan snaking through the crowd toward us, a tight, but polite, smile on his face while he nods to each person he passes until he reaches me. "If you can keep your footsteps quiet against cobblestone, I know you can do so in the kitchen."

Rowan gives me his signature *not going to humor that* stare, then blinks twice and turns to Cliff. "Sir Onnoc?"

"Arrives tonight," Cliff responds under his breath, to which Rowan simply nods. Then he grabs a fresh drink from the table and walks back out into the crowd.

"Who?"

"You don't know him. Come with me."

Cliff drags me to his office in the guards' wing, where, with a wave of his hand, the map I saw him looking at a couple weeks ago appears on the ceiling.

"The map," I gasp, staring in awe at the rotating illusions above me. In the dark room, the images bathe the space in hazy shadows.

"I'm sorry," Cliff apologizes, barely loud enough for me to hear. Cliff took a seat on a black velvet couch against the far wall of his office when we entered, while I stood in the center, craning my neck to see the map lighting up the room like the constellations in the night sky. "You'll hurt your neck if you stand there like that." He scoots himself to the far side of the couch to make room for me to join him.

"Why are you showing me this?" I ask tentatively, slowly backing up to join him.

With another twist of his hand, he angles the image of the map slightly down so that I can see it better, creating a multidimensional image rather than flat lights against the stone.

"Whoa." I have never seen magic like this. Small enchantments were everywhere in Quinthold—torches that lit automatically, small objects moving by themselves, waterproof hats for the rain— but this was no enchantment. An entire map is being cast out of nowhere, rotating in front of me, and it's all being done by Cliff.

"There's no reason you can't see it. I shouldn't have tried to hide it from you a few weeks ago." He shrugs as he states this matter-of-factly, but a smirk pulls at the corners of his lips.

"What are you grinning about over there?"

"You."

Well, that's a new one.

"I'll try to hide my surprise from now on," I mumble, watching the Luneris Lagoon come into focus on the map. "You going to tell me what I'm looking at?"

"A, I know what you're doing." His voice is barely above a whisper now, still clear and steady, but soft enough that he's ensuring only we can hear.

Fuck.

"What do you mean?" I attempt to sound as innocent as possible, painting a look of confusion across my face.

I can do this. It's possible he means something different. How could he possibly know of my involvement with the Resistance?

"I know you were involved with the Resistance in Quinthold, and I know you've sent communications from inside the palace." His voice is so calm, so steady. "I know it's why you've spent so much time researching our history."

My fingers tighten on the arm of the couch, and I sit on my other hand to hide its shaking.

"I don't know what you're talking about."

Cliff still doesn't turn to look at me, but I look at him. His eyes glow—he knows.

"A." He finally turns my direction, his eyes illuminated in the dark room drilling holes into me. "You know you can't lie to me."

"I—" My heart races while I think through my options. I can't lie, and I wouldn't win in a fight. "I can explain."

He blinks his eyes, shifting them back to their normal hue, and uncrosses his legs to lean forward and brace his elbows on his knees—his hands interlocked before him. "Don't."

I am going to die, I think to myself. Every muscle in my body braces for attack. I knew this was a possibility, but I at least thought I would achieve something—anything—before I was caught. I left Blaine, Quinthold, everything to fail within three months.

Celestial Mother, help me, I plead to my fictional goddess.

A low, contemplative growl leaves his throat, like he knows he might regret his next statement. "Let me help you," he grumbles through his wrists, leaning his forehead against his interlocked hands.

There is no way I heard that right, and at the risk of saying something I shouldn't if I open my mouth again, I ask, "What?"

He turns his neck, a look I can't read written across his face, like he's conflicted about what he's about to say. "Let me help."

Well, I wasn't expecting that.

29

The Ritual is a right of passage, a window into the realm of witchhood, a portal to a life one cannot return from. Performing the Ritual alone does not guarantee that the performer will be accepted into the Obsidian Coven; only the Celestial Mother can make that decision. On the evening of a full moon, a sister may offer a piece of her soul—with the blood and hand of her Venatae—and pledge her eternal loyalty for the good of the Coven, the good of the land, and the good of the Celestial Goddess. If the Goddess deems the sister worthy, she will be granted access into the Obsidian Coven, and her life will remain bound to the Coven and her Venatae forevermore.

—*The Tales of the Obsidian Witches* by Tresta McVey

I pace my room; it's only a couple of hours until guests will arrive for the Constellation Ball, but I left my kitchen in the unruly hands of a hungover Rowan because I couldn't stand another moment in the crowded kitchen. Apparently, he and Cliff had quite the after-celebration over at Connor's when the purity ceremony ended, and now he's a little on edge with the junior staff.

Rowan told me that while they were there, he read Bianca's aura for me in a drunken attempt to make sure I was surrounding myself with quality company—and he confirmed she is about as pure-intentioned as a descendant comes, with an extra note of authenticity he couldn't place, which I assumed was too much whiskey fogging his gifts. I knew this, of course; Bianca couldn't feign evil tendencies if she tried. But hearing it said out loud, hearing Rowan tell me he cared enough to scan her simply for being my friend—that felt good.

I attempted to ask Rowan throughout the day about his night with Cliff, mainly what they spoke about. I hoped I could glean whether he knew about my and Cliff's conversation from yesterday afternoon. I had no idea Cliff and Rowan could have even pointed each other out in a crowded room, let alone were close enough to share ales at the local pub. So, it took some quick adjustment on my part to process the conversation with Cliff about the Resistance, just to turn around and immediately learn that he was leaving me to go out with Rowan.

If Rowan knew anything, however, he never gave it away—just complained about his head all day between prepping food stations and bossing around junior staff. So when I accepted that the food was as prepared as it was going to be without me physically carting it all out to the vineyard patio myself, I dismissed myself back here to my rooms—to pace anxiously until the event.

Cliff's words from yesterday keep replaying through my mind. I'm not to tell anyone else about my involvement, or his knowledge of the Resistance, and I'm to come to him if I hear or suspect that someone else may be aware. The suspicion that the entire conversation was a trap occurred to me several times, but I also watched his eyes illuminate turquoise with his truth magic while he told me how he and Brennan have been spending years working toward figuring out where Linea ended up. That was enough for me.

It wasn't as if Cliff was asking me to do anything in that moment, wasn't putting me in direct danger, or threatening my life, so there wasn't anything to actively defend myself against with him. That was the extent of our conversation, and in true Cliff fashion, when I asked about what he knew already about Linea, he told me I would have to earn that level of information. Then he patted me on the shoulder and left me alone in his office to watch his map shimmer and rotate until the lights faded slowly and it disappeared.

Now, the magenta gown that Rivian bought for me in Curatia lies across my bed, along with a matching mask. The mask has a layer of shimmering gauzy fabric stretched across its expanse that somehow still allows the wearer to see through the eyeholes with complete clarity. I pause in front of my bed to run my hand down the fabric, admiring it's unique construction, the fabrics overlapping to create sheaths, the step-in design—whoever created this dress did so with function in mind.

I suppose there's no use in delaying the inevitable, I think to myself while I slip off the robe I'd adorned since my post-kitchen bath.

The dress, while appearing thick and stiff, stretches and flexes easily with my movements as I step into its skirt. Deep V's plunge down the front and back, and the openings on the side dip below my rib cage, tastefully exposing more of my torso than I typically opt for, but making me feel a sense of sensual power all the same.

I may be nothing more than the palace's human chef, but tonight, I'll do so in a dress that makes me feel like I could conquer the world. *Maybe I will.*

"What are you doing?" Mia calls from my doorway. I hadn't heard her come in.

I freeze, hand halfway through an imitated movements of unsheathing a dagger from one of my dress pockets and throwing it at a mystery attacker across my room. "Nothing. Just getting ready." I smile, attempting to clear the embarrassment from my voice, coming through a bit squeaky and suspicious.

"Did you get him at least, whoever you were just pretending to kill?" she asks, walking over to sit on my bed, crossing her long legs when she does.

"Straight to the heart, as always," I affirm, nodding my head as I picture Beryl lying on the ground, me watching him die without the slightest remorse, all because he caused the Break.

I head to my vanity to plait my hair with a ribbon to match my gown. "Hey, are you sure it's okay for me to wear your provincial colors? The Sovereign isn't going to see me and admonish me for some descendant custom I wasn't aware I was breaking?"

Mia rolls her eyes at the question before popping up and joining me at my vanity.

"Stella—the Sovereign's name is Stella—and no, she won't. Like I already told you, she'll have my wrath to answer to if she gives you a hard time." Her eyes narrow in pretend fierceness, as if getting ready for the fight that will never happen.

"Thank goodness, this party could use some excitement."

"I actually came to see if you'd seen Zalya today. Guests are arriving, and she had asked if I would help her welcome them in as a member of the palace staff, but I wasn't sure where she wanted me stationed."

"I haven't actually," I consider out loud. "Which is odd now that I think about it."

Zalya and I don't always see eye to eye, but she takes her events seriously and doesn't let our personal differences interfere where they are concerned. I expected her to be frustratingly obnoxious today in preparation, but Mia's right, I haven't seen her anywhere.

"I'm sure she's fine," she tosses out. "Ready to head down to the vineyard? The Celestial Mother is requesting our presence in her moonlight." Mia holds out her arm, as if beckoning me on a date, her own mask dangling from her other wrist.

"As ready as I will be," I say, grabbing my obsidian necklace from the corner of the mirror and looping it around my neck before following her out the door.

"Surely you knew the health hazard you presented wearing that dress tonight." Rivian's warm breath brushes my ear as he presses in behind me, playfully squeezing my hip. "I had obligations tonight as the host, but you've made the focus on those quite hard."

I sidestep out of his reach, attempting to ignore the blanket of serene warmth that covers me in his presence, and lean over to get myself one of my quiche cups. It's not nearly the temperature it should be to bring out the fresh herbs I was able to get through this week's delivery, but the quality of the eggs comes through in the coloring. "I can promise you, my only intentions were to showcase my delicacies. Getting to wear this dress was just a bonus."

Fallen, he smells amazing. Notes of mint and cedar cling to me from his touch, airy and sweet.

The musicians are playing just loud enough that we need to speak up or lean in to hear each other, making simple conversation a hard task. I haven't seen Zalya yet, but I couldn't miss Cliff. He's been next to a cocktail table toward the edge of the patio, ignoring me all night.

I see Mia with Stella across the patio. She must be so nervous, speaking with the strongest healer of her home province, though if she is, she doesn't show it. They wear matching dress magenta jumpsuits, both with open backs, where the healer's signature tattoos of wings can shimmer in the moonlight. Mia's eyes light up, and I follow her gaze to the bar where Bianca stands with one hand on her drink, and the other playfully pulling at a button on Morgan's dress coat. Good—she deserves to have a little fun.

I move at a leisurely pace down the buffet, keeping busy with analyzing my spread, mostly to cover my nervous hands. A clumsy side of me comes out when I'm nervous—the thought sends me into a flashback from my first dinner here, remembering accidentally slicing Cliff's hand open. I slide my hands across the table linen while doing my round to subtly dry my sweating palms.

A woman in a purple gown places a third cheesecake square onto her plate, and I can't help but feel a sense of pride—I knew lemon would be a hit. Rivian follows me, a few paces behind, the entire way—the dress seducing him as he promised it would in his note. The closer he gets, the more I want to abandon all resolve, find a secluded corner, and jump him.

Maybe Rowan is right, maybe I do need laid.

I may feel better about my friendship with Cliff after yesterday; knowing I can trust him is a relief I didn't know I needed, but I still have no idea where I stand with Rivian, except that I become a spineless lush in his presence.

"Tell me, August, if you were going to monitor the food station all night, why punish your staff to make them stand here doing the same?" Rivian looks pointedly at one of my staff, standing ten yards from the table, looking bored.

"Hmmm. You know, you're right. I've got the food handled out here. He might as well go help clean in the kitchen." I make my way to where the staff member stands when Rivian catches my hand.

"Ah, ah. I have a better idea."

"But—" It's no use. He has a firm hold on my hand and is leading us back to the dance floor. I take once last glance back at my cheesecakes, assuming I won't have another moment with them tonight.

Goodbye, my tart beauties.

Okay, it's one thing that you talk to me, it's another thing to talk to your food, my other voice points out as I trail behind Rivian toward a sea of couples.

"How do you do it?" I ask, looking around the room, attempting to ignore my body's reaction to his hand on my waist when he stops to guide us into a slow waltz with the music.

"What is that, love?" His thumb draws circles along the curve of my waist while we sway and step our way among the dancers on the crowded floor. His steady hand calms my restless nerves.

Make me feel like the we're the only two people in the world, like nothing else matters when I'm with you, is what I want to say, staring into his deep indigo eyes like they're the last piece of art in a world full of ruin, like I could surrender myself to him and be okay.

Instead, I say, "How is it you always have a line ready? I have a hard time believing you've never had a girlfriend with a mouth like yours."

And like the lush I am, my knees nearly buckle at the smile he gives me. An action that results in him needing to catch me and pull me into a tight embrace to cover my falter.

Fallen, not just his mouth—everything this man does makes me swoon.

I leave my face in his chest for a moment, soaking in the time to pretend no one could have possibly seen that—completely aware of the heat creeping up my neck, and I have never been more thankful for the darkness of the night sky.

Thank you, Celestial Goddess.

I feel his breath on my neck before the whisper in my ear: "How does it feel?"

I lift my chin enough so he can hear me, resting it in the crook of his neck. *Like it doesn't matter, because I'm with you,* are the first words I consider, but again, I find enough self-preservation within me not to say what I'm thinking, and instead offer, "Like I shouldn't be allowed anywhere near a dance floor until I can learn to stay on my own two feet."

"I was actually referring to how it felt to be the most beautiful woman here?" He's the one who pulls back this time, just enough to see the reaction of me rolling my eyes at the cheesy line. "Okay, so you don't believe me? Humor me this, then. Why are all eyes on you?" As he says it, he pulls out the same move as he did in the courtyard. I go from dipped down to spun out, and when he spins me back in, he holds me with my back to his chest for an extra moment. Just long enough to tuck his chin to my shoulder and say, "See?"

With my back against his chest, I can feel his words vibrate through me—a sensation that has me closing my eyes, and leaning in farther. Then he spins me back, and I have to take a moment to catch my breath and blink the stars out of my eyes from the quick, dizzying movements. That smug grin hasn't left his face yet.

"They aren't looking at me, they are looking at you, and probably wondering what you are doing dancing with your chef." I look around, seeing if I can find Zalya yet. She should have been here by now, and I really do not want to be dancing with Rivian when she walks in, but one more moment in his arms and I may decide I don't care.

"You're distracted."

"I just—I don't want to lead you on. I-I think it's best if we remain professional," I stammer through my rehearsed words.

Look at you following through, my other voice says, sarcastically congratulating me.

"Follow me. I have something for you." He breaks our dance and starts leading me away.

"Where are we going? We can't just leave, can we?" My neck swivels to look back at the dance floor and all the guests still enjoying themselves among the music and festivities.

"*We* can do whatever we want."

I try to pull my hand from his, create distance any way possible, but he tightens his grasp with each of my feeble attempts. "Rivian, I really feel like my presence will be more valuable here or in the kitchen this evening. What if my staff needs me?" It's not a lie, I'm not usually this far away from the food during an event of this size.

"You can come willingly, or I can carry you. Either way, you are coming with me." He gives me a glance that says *try me*, and I have half a mind to turn around and see if he means it, but I already know he does.

You can handle this, August.

"Just let me say bye to Cliff. I promised him a dance this evening," I offer, but when I turn to where Cliff has been all evening, he's no longer there. There is also no sign of him when I scan the whole area.

"It appears as though Cliff has changed his mind about that dance." His hand still grips mine as I turn back to face him. He gives my fingers a light squeeze. "Come," he says, and he gently tugs me toward the palace.

So much for my plan of simply avoiding being alone with him anymore.

We walk mostly in silence, passing a few couples along our way looking for a cove of privacy of their own. His pace is quicker than normal, or maybe I'm not used to being tugged around in heels, but I wonder what he could possibly need right this moment.

"This way," he says, stopping in front of a door I've never used before, opening it for me and waving me through.

I realize quickly that the door is the back door to his office, though the decor is themed for evening, which I've never seen before. During the day, the walls are a sky blue, and a fountain graces the front corner, but at night the walls are much darker and a fire replaces the fountain. The enchantments that transition the room from day to night make the illuminated map in Cliff's office seem ordinary.

"Rivian, why are we in your office?" I ask, admiring the stars twinkling across the ceiling, meandering along the windowed wall and watching the stars outside battle those inside for a more powerful reflection against the glass.

"For this," he responds from across the room, his voice strained as I look over my shoulder to see him reaching up to the top shelf of his bookcase for a dusty tome.

30

The Recital of Creation is a testament to the power of the scholars to document historical records with a caliber of excellence unachievable by those without the gifts of truth and knowledge. However, the Recital can also be deemed an example of how even the elite can make mistakes. The omission of any details regarding Linea's Descent, her lover Micah, or the future of their lineage proves this.

—An excerpt from Celestera: The Beginning

"I want you to have this." He holds out the book to me with both hands, giving me a look of anticipation I haven't seen him wear before.

"What is it?" I ask, taking it from him and lightly wiping dust from the cover.

"A collection of my mother's recipes."

"Oh, I can't take this." I push the book into his chest, shaking my head—the sentiment behind the gift crushing my resolve to stay away from him. I look around the room, eyeing the exits. I need to get back to where we're surrounded by others.

"It's a gift, and it's yours. My mother was an amazing woman, she would have loved you." His voice is soft, and while I stare into his twinkling eyes, pushing the book to his chest, I fail to notice how close he gets, how his hand now lightly caresses the nape of my neck.

"Why me, Rivian?" I ask when his lips are only a few inches away—trying to find any reason to give in to or run away from this man.

"Does your heart let you choose who it beats for?" He looses a deep breath, and then adds, "Because mine chose you."

We're giving in.

That layer of safety I feel in his presence tightens itself around me, like a sweater buttoning up, with every breath we share, as if my every question is answered in his arms. I told myself it was strategy, but now, I can't remember where the plan ended and the wanting began. I have no control over myself where he is involved, and maybe I don't need to, maybe I'm not supposed to. Maybe this isn't supposed to make sense, maybe I need to let go of what I think I want to find what I need.

His hands slide down my arms—slow, as if he is afraid I might change my mind. My body responds to him of its own volition, and I embrace where it goes: the shivers down my spine, the haze hanging in my mind. Lust clouds any semblance of control I ever thought I had. Pretended to have.

"Ask me to kiss you," he says in a low voice, sending my doubts into flames.

"Rivian—" I attempt one last fight, one more denial, but they're just words. There's no longer any piece of me that wants to leave this moment, this touch, this man.

His eyes close, forehead leaning to mine. He finds the spot along my rib cage, his palm ghosting the fabric of my dress—just enough that my back instinctively arches to feel him, just enough that I feel my skin pebble, the hairs on my body standing and expanding out in all directions from his touch. "I will always give you the chance to say no, but with you in my arms—"

His breath intertwines with mine. I can't think, I just need. "Kiss me."

He smiles. Not the boyish one that breaks me, or the one of a Sovereign he uses to command a room. A genuine one, a softer one that makes me want to re-create it day after day. Then he kisses me.

And Fallen, I let him.

His mouth is soft, coaxing my lips to mold to his. His fingers tangle in the overlapping layers of my gown like they are a puzzle he already knows how to solve. I kiss him back with everything I have—anger, regret, guilt—he can have it all, I don't need it anymore when I'm with him.

His hands slip under the fabrics of the dress he bought me, through the open sides—now too heavy, too thick between us. He splays his hand across my back and pulls me closer.

I grip the front of his shirt, needing to hold on to something. We're but a tangle of silk and desperation. His coat hits the floor, and the ribbon that held my plaited hair follows.

"Tell me you want this," he murmurs against my skin.

"I want this," I whisper between breaths as his mouth ignites sensations on my skin I hadn't remembered I could feel.

I deserve this, I think to myself as my head leans back to rest on the windows behind us.

That affirmation was all it took.

He kisses me deeper—his tongue parting my lips. Then he lifts me, slipping one arm under my knees and scooping me into his arms in one swift motion—our lips never disconnecting. He walks us to his desk, gently setting me down. My legs spread instinctively to make room for him, and his hands slide up my thighs beneath the layers of tulle and silk, pushing farther until he finds bare skin. I put my palms behind me on the desk, resting back on them while he leans over me, one hand holding my lower back, the other testing my physical control across my inner thigh.

He coaxes a whimper out of me when his fingers brush the lace between my legs, already too much pressure for me to handle, and pure arousal shoots through me at his responding groan.

"Are you trying to destroy me?" he growls, a low vibration emitting from him straight into my core as his lips trace the lines of my collarbone.

I don't answer. I can't. My head tips back again as he kisses down my neck, tongue rolling in time to every beat of my pulse, and I jolt when he lightly bites down on the spot behind my ear, his hair brushing my cheeks.

He rips through the lace between my legs, my final layer of defense falling away like snow melting with the afternoon sun. I moan into our kiss with anticipation—his hand so close, yet so incredibly far away under the plentiful layers of my dress. He pauses, hand resting only inches away from where I need it, and his other one finds the nape of my neck again. For what feels like a lifetime, I stare into the eyes of a man who has tested my mental strength with every interaction, who is showing me I *can* have it all, who could ruin me if he wanted. His eyes catch the moonlight, and the shimmer they reflect sends my heart into overdrive.

"Rivian," I breathe out, eyes fluttering when his thumb resumes slow circles across my sensitive skin, lazy strokes that make my thighs tremble around his hips. And just when I think I can't take the distance anymore, his palm closes the final few inches—two fingers glide across me, spreading the physical proof of my need for him across me like the declaration of submission it is.

He teases me with shallow strokes, slowly increasing in pressure and speed, and my hips instinctively rock against him. I don't know when his lips find my skin again, lost in the sublime friction tantalizing my senses, but a chill kisses my breast when he slides the strap off my shoulder, positioning his hand behind me for leverage.

This time my moan is far from subtle, far from the involuntary whimper of before—this is need and want and months of tension releasing from a place deep within me.

His fingers push inside with devastating precision, curling in a spot I wasn't aware existed, sending sparks into my vision and my hips shaking. In and out in a steady rhythm that has my desire winding inside me, preparing for release. I lock my ankles behind him, and my hands clutch his shoulders, nails digging into his linen shirt.

"You have no idea how many nights I've dreamt of watching you come undone"—he kisses me—"of the sounds you would make"—his lips move to my neck—"of the way you would taste." He continues to list out his desires while he works his way across my décolletage.

He drags his fingers up and down, coating me entirely, occasionally drawing a circle at the top of his path that has me praying for more, and when he curls them inside me again, his thumb presses into the top of my slit in irresistible bliss. Another moan escapes me when he pulls his hand from the layers of dress that sit between us.

"Not yet, love," he tells me between continued lavishing strokes of his tongue against my neck and chest while my core still clenches around a touch that is no longer there.

He straightens when I reach for the front of his trousers to undo the buttons with shaking hands, hissing through his teeth when I free him. My heart races as I watch the way his control cracks when I wrap my hand around him, as his eyes darken and he hangs his head, gripping the edges of his desk on either side of my thighs and leaning in close enough for me to drag my lips up his chest, on display through his undone shirt. I spread the evidence of his pleasure down his length, already enough to prove this night isn't one-sided—we both want this.

Stroking him up and down, slowly at first, then quickening when his hips stiffen, I watch his entire demeanor switch from lust-drenched to primal dominance. He clenches my shoulder, a firm hold imitating the focus he uses to absorb the pleasure of this moment, and pushes us all the way down until my back makes contact with the desk. My hips slightly lift from my hold on his waist, and his hand snaps to my wrist.

"Not yet...more," he breathes.

"Please," I whimper, a voice I couldn't imitate if I wanted to coming from somewhere within me, on the edge of surrender.

His hand finds my cheek again, those indigo eyes drilling holes into my resolve and heart, and I wrap my own arms around his neck, ready to pull him into me—ready to follow him wherever he will take me.

"There's something I need to ask you, before—" He cuts off, eyes shifting to my mouth.

"You better ask, then." My chest continues to rise and fall, my breasts grazing the edges of his undone shirt with each heavy breath. My pulse pounds in tandem with my need, and I watch him while he considers his next words.

"Would you come with me—if I asked you to follow me—away, to leave Auralia."

His brow furrows, awaiting my response, and I smile, letting that thought sink in, realizing he's feeling the same sweet escape in this moment that I am.

"I have a feeling I would follow you anywhere," I sigh, giving him a playful grin to accompany his hypothetical question, and raising my head to give him a playful bite on his full bottom lip.

His face lights up, and just when I think he might ask me another lofty question about leaving this place behind, his eyes shift and he asks, "Fast or slow, love?"

"Yes."

He takes the opening, lining up at my entrance, his eyes fluttering when his tip touches my wet core, but I don't have time to think before I scream out when he drives into me.

"That's it, love." His words come out in between rough thrusts, his hands gripped on my hips to keep me from moving farther up the desk. "I've got you."

Yes, he does.

I bite my lip, attempting to hold back the emotion working its way through me, my nails digging into his back, edging dangerously close to oblivion.

He pauses briefly, leaning back and grabbing a small pillow from his desk chair and sliding it under my hips, then dips down, looping his shoulder beneath my left leg and driving forward. He reaches new depths with each of his thrusts. Thrusts that are no longer steady—no, these are deep and unrelenting as he lets himself go. He curses softly against my collarbone, his hips hammering into me in hard, deliberate strokes, each one ripping a cry of pleasure from my throat.

Why did I ever try to avoid this?

"Look at me," he begs.

I do. His eyes burn into mine, dark and deep and full of my potential downfall. His hand slips between us, fingers finding my clit with infuriating skill. I won't last another ten seconds, five seconds.

"I have you."

He has me.

His vow is enough to send me over the edge. I unravel, my body trembling around him, every muscle taut with pressure until it spasms within me, sending my vision into rays of color and stars.

A groan of pleasure rips through his chest—the sound satisfying a heady void within me. His hips stutter as he fills me, and the weight of his limp, sated body, collapses above me.

When he finally lifts his head from my shoulder, he graces the top of mine with a gentle kiss, wrapping his arms around me and carrying me to the chaise. Placing me between his spread legs, with my back to his chest, he wraps his arms around me.

We lie there entwined for what feels like an eternity, not even taking the time to fully remove my dress, still bunched around my middle, tracing the lines of our bodies with our mouths, drawing delusional promises of escape with our fingertips—until we're ready for more. The fire casts our shadows against the wall, and I watch the outlines of his hands on my curves like he's a sentient work of art, watch his hands work their way across me like I'm a map to his freedom.

Just when I gain enough strength to shift myself to straddle him, my body entering an already familiar routine with his, he stops me. His hands brace my hips, fingers splaying across my bottom with one hand, and the other rubbing lines up my thigh, holding me captive while I suffer through him already twitching below me with need.

"Once more?" he asks, a bit more sternly than the moment feels, twin lines forming deep between his brows.

"For tonight?" I ask innocently, running my nails across the curve of his hairline where it meets the back of his neck.

"Yes, tonight, then we can pack, and leave—I have a place for us, love." He leans in to resume, but I push at his chest, needing to clear the air before I can continue.

What does he mean—he has a place?

"Rivian, we're not really leaving, right? You're the Sovereign of Auralia." I stare at him, watching his features tense, teeth clenching in his lower jaw. His eyes close for a long moment, his chin dips down to his chest, and I worry I've said something wrong. "Rivian?"

Something isn't the same. Every muscle in his body seems to tense with an unknown threat. I can feel it against my skin—radiating from his demeanor.

His head lifts, his eyes snapping open to reveal vibrant milky white globes brighter than the full moon, and a devious grin that has me scrambling backward off the couch.

He stands, watching me slowly putting distance between us, his glowing eyes not dimming as they stare down at me from above. "I tried to do this the easy way, love." A tone of determination laces his words.

"Rivian?" I ask, trying to find the man from before somewhere in the predator now before me, as he continues to prowl forward. I stand slowly, never taking my eyes off him, adjusting my dress as best as I can, but I'm limited by its many layers.

"You made this all too easy you know. From the day you arrived here, desperation dripped from your aura." He scans me up and down—I somehow feel more vulnerable now than with him inside of me. "Your need for change, your need for acceptance, your need for love."

My back hits the door to his office, the one we came through, and he stalks closer to me, each step feeling like a countdown of my final moments alive.

My heart races.

Who did I just sleep with?

"Who are you?" I say through trembling lips as my hand searches for the door handle behind me.

He closes the remaining space between us, leaning down and pulling my bottom lip into his mouth in a possessive kiss that has me wishing I could run. "This was never personal, love," he says when he pulls a couple of inches away, but remaining close enough to continue sharing a breath. "We both want to save the world. You just happen to be part of my plan, while I was the destruction of yours."

There's nowhere else for me to go, to run; he has me pinned against the door.

Will anyone even hear me if I scream?

"What is it you want?" I ask through my teeth, turning my face as far as I can in his proximity.

Then he places one hand on my waist, not in a loving embrace, but rather a possessive hold, one of leverage to guide our next move. He leans into my ear to whisper, "But that was a fuck I'll never forget." Then he lightly grazes my earlobe with his teeth while he angles his hip into me, digging his stiff cock into my lower stomach to prove his point.

My stomach roils, sending the taste of acid and fury up my throat.

I'm going to be sick.

You need to focus on living, my other voice assures me.

"I hate you," I seethe, right before I spit straight into his mouth.

He turns his neck to the side and wipes the remnants of my saliva off his bottom lip with his thumb. Then he sucks it into his mouth. "That's right, love. I like my women with a little bite."

And in a flash of purple smoke, his arms wrap around me and the world goes black.

31

TAMORRA, SOVEREIGN DESCENDANT OF TERRLYSSIA, HAS FAILED TO APPEAR BEFORE THE ADVISORY COUNCIL FOR TWO CONSECUTIVE QUARTERLY SESSIONS. BORDER ACCESS HASN'T BEEN GRANTED TO OUR AGENCY, AND THEREFORE WE ARE UNABLE TO VERIFY HER WHEREABOUTS. IN AN ATTEMPT TO PRESERVE THE SAFETY AND WELL-BEING OF THOSE RESIDING WITHIN HER BORDERS, ONE MORE FAILED APPEARANCE WILL RESULT IN THE ADVISORY ASSUMING POSSESSION OF THE LANDS.

CONFIDENTIAL EXCERPT FROM AN ADVISORY BULLETIN DATED 8608 A.L.

He releases me when we land on one of the cobblestone paths that twine through the vineyard. I see the palace in the distance, can faintly hear the festivities still in full swing across the rows of grapes. Rivian paces a small line back and forth on the stones, his hands raised ahead of him as if feeling along an invisible wall, his candescent eyes illuminating the space around him.

"Shield," he seethes under his breath, releasing a growl in frustration before cursing the responsible party. "Damn, Vellas."

We teleported.

And you were saved by a shield, so now do something, my other voice urges me.

With his back to me, examining the impermeable wall I can't see, I take off running down the stone path toward the palace. I don't know why I think I can outrun him, but it's my only chance. I throw off my heels, hopping on one foot for a few paces each time as I reach down to unhook my ankle from the liabilities, tossing the shoes off into the vines. It doesn't matter at this point. Whoever saw me now would know immediately what I'd spent my evening doing just by taking one look at my disheveled hair and swollen lips.

It doesn't matter what you look like because you need to live, not because of what they'll think, my other voice stresses.

I don't make it far, though, before the air abandons my lungs, like I've been punched in the gut, and I collapse to my knees. Jolts of pain shoot up my extremities, and pressure builds around me, as if a wet blanket has been thrown over me, weighing me down and dampening my consciousness. A ringing sounds in my ears, and my vision spins— my senses so heightened that I can't hear my own yell of pain.

How is he doing this?

I can't hear, I can't see. I attempt to blink my eyes back into focus, but when my vision clears, I'm no longer in the vineyard.

Before me, the dining area of The Goblet is aflame, smoke filling the room. My skin and lungs remember the scene far too well as my forearms sting with burns that aren't yet attacking them. The scent of the incinerating building surrounds me, but it's as if a makeshift rag is once more tied to my face, inadequately filtering ash-filled air. I hear a cacophony of the distant screams of Quinthold's streets as the market clears and passersby avoid the flames. Ten feet ahead of me lies Vincenzo, lifeless on the floor of the kitchen. I close my eyes, unwilling to put myself through this memory again. But I can't turn the visions off. They're all I can see.

This isn't real, I tell myself. *It's a memory. You survived it once, you can survive it again.*

"I really didn't want to have to do this." Rivian's voice cuts through the visions like a warm blade against taut skin. I look up and see him with his hands folded behind his back in a casual stance, watching me gasp for air below him. He's here too, in The Goblet, as my heart takes the beating of one of the worst moments of my life. "Memories can be debilitating, can't they?"

"How?" I risk a breath to ask, the words grating up my throat like gravel, though I can't even hear my voice through the crackling flames surrounding me, the continued chaos of the streets outside. My lungs burn and my eyes sting.

"Want me to stop?"

Think, August, think, I tell myself. *Maybe the others can hear me.*

I scream in agony, both emotional and physical, a visceral reaction bursting from me, the culmination of the day.

"They can't hear you, love," he muses, as if explaining a simple custom to a young child, patronizing me over my lack of knowledge of his powers. These are deeper than the magic of Quintessence, though: aura readers can't force one to relive memories. No, this is Mind Work.

I don't respond, hoping that the less I engage him, the sooner this will end. Every muscle in my body tenses with the heat of the flames still surrounding me in my mind and vision. My heart threatens to beat straight out of my chest, the intensity of it shaking my rib cage.

Birds scatter from the vines surrounding us, as if they can feel the panic rolling off me—doing exactly what I would if I had wings. I hope they get away, that they never take for granted the ability to ride the winds.

"This isn't real," I grate through my braced jaw, the taste of blood filling my mouth from the memory of biting through my tongue that day in The Goblet. I want to raise my hands to cover my ears, hoping it helps drown out the sounds of my past streaming through my mind, but I lock my joints with the effort to continue to hold myself up, arching my back in pain when a phantom flame licks my cheek.

Rivian hums above me as a loud crack, like lightning striking rock, sounds through the flames. My visions spin, dizzying me until I feel like I might fall over with the unease, until I'm submerged in murky water and crashing debris, being thrown backward in an undertow. My head hits the back wall of the port station in Quinthold, knocking me out of consciousness for a moment.

Water fills my lungs, my eyes—I move to swim to the surface, but I'm jerked backward. No longer am I breathing ash, but water. I'm somehow able to breathe in, but each gasp feels like taking a drink—water rushes down my throat, filling my lungs. Each time I open my mouth, more water floods in.

I am going to drown.

Blaine reaches out his hand, straining his arms to get to me, but my bag holds me hostage, the strap stuck on the port station bench. Citizens swim for the small rays of light shining through the cracks and openings in the port station, making their way to the surface, the few rays of sun acting as beacons for dry air and land.

The scene continues to play through me as I sit back on my ankles, curling in on myself. My sensitive forearms are sore from burns that weren't real; they now sting with the cold salt water rushing over them. I'm twenty-one years old, and I'm scared.

Rivian has even renewed my emotions from that day, as I relive the Break, every fiber of my being viciously repelling his mind games, and failing. Blaine still reaches for me, straight ahead, wearing his Advisory wetsuit and looking toward me with the heroic resolve I admire and a body I could devour. Just a handsome boy who offered his bench and jacket to me, now risking his life to save me.

I reach back for him. His muscles strain against the current swelling around us, but I can't get to him, and my vision fades with the remaining oxygen in my lungs—just like that day in the river.

Why is he doing this?

"You won't break me! I don't know what you want, but you won't win," I yell into the surrounding void, wondering what I did to deserve this. I still can't hear myself through the haze, can't hear anything but the whoosh of water tugging me deeper into the Liravel River. Blaine's face is determined to save me, but I can't leave Nova's bag, the bag that continues to pull me down. He defies the tides to remain underwater, unwilling to leave me.

August, get up. My other voice echoes through me.

I can't.

"I'm not sure which scene I get more satisfaction from. Getting to relive the Break through your eyes does add a bit of flavor to the memory," he considers out loud, his voice contemplative in my head. "But does it top the sensation of your cunt clenching around me in devastating need?"

"STOP!" I roar, looking down at the palms of my hands, blood streaming into the flowing waters from the crescent-moon gashes scattered across them.

"The others will come to find you soon. It will be much easier if you play agreeable, ask them nicely to remove the shield so that no one has to die today."

I don't miss his admission to the Break.

He hums to himself again, crouching next to me, his face now inches from mine. He grasps my chin between his forefinger and thumb, pulling my face up to meet his eyes. "You know, I really did fall for you, in some sense of the term. If you hadn't been so set on tearing me down—on finding answers—we could have had it all. Together."

Another loud snap sounds in my mind, vision blurring, and this time my body can't withstand the pressure. As if the Liravel rolled me to shore in a tidal wave, I fall to my side. My head cracks when it hits the stone, and I feel the warmth of my blood drip from my temple into my hair.

"Pathetic," Rivian says, standing again beside me while I am forced to endure another vivid memory.

I would recognize the intricate design of these ceilings anywhere. The blues were meant to look like a sky, fading to greens as the paints reached the walls to mimic the forests. My childhood home.

I stare straight up at the ceiling, yelling coming from somewhere I can't see. Is that—*my father?*

His voice, along with a woman's I don't recognize, yells incomprehensibly from the distance, mumbled disagreements fading in and out of my hearing. Clearly a passionate argument from the tone of their shouts, though I can't understand them through the sounds of a child's cry nearby.

I turn my head in search of the cries and find an infant about a foot away, flailing his tiny arms and reaching straight up toward the sky in jerky motions. His face is speckled pink from the screams, and he clenches his little fists. Tiny freckles sprinkle over his entire body.

Why did he bring me here?

I look back up when a woman reaches down to pick up the screaming infant—a woman with long, wavy chestnut hair and enough freckles to share. Her orange eyes shimmer with her emotions, and tears stream in rivers down her face. A much younger version of my father stands next to her, wearing a terrified look. His lip wobbles, and his eyes are wide.

Is that fear?

He reaches to pull the infant from her grip, but she clutches the baby in a grip like a vise, raw determination in her expression despite her tears. I don't understand what he says, as if he's speaking another language, but I can tell he's angry. I know this tone and expression well, the way his hands erratically conduct his feelings in the air with his words, the clenched muscles in his jaw.

Shaking her head, she clenches the infant as tight as she can to her chest, one hand behind his tiny neck, another held below his diapered bottom. Incomprehensible words come from her, but she gazes at me, mouthing something I can't understand, before turning back to my father, saying one last word, and leaving.

He stares in the direction she left for a long time, his expression blank. The crying starts again, first small coos for help, then loud screams, sobbing, choking, fighting for breath.

It's me.

My air comes in small gasps as I choke through my screams. Still, my father doesn't look my way. He walks away, leaving me free-falling into panicked suffocation.

I shake back and forth, convulsing with the intensity of the sobs ripping through me, though they are slowly fading from my hearing. My hair, lightly matted to my forehead from the blood, catches on the stone as I rock against the ground. My vision returns, blurry shapes first, then angles and colors—my breathing settles with it.

Vomit retches up my throat, my stomach releasing anything that was still in it from the ball. I'm numb in the aftermath of Rivian's mental attack, feeling nothing but the warm blood in my hair and the vomit spreading beneath my cheek and shoulder—every muscle shaking in fatigue.

Cliff crouches in front of me. Not in my childhood home, not in the Liravel River, or in The Goblet, but on the cobblestone path of the vineyard. His mouth forms my name over and over, but I still only hear muffled silence while he grips my shoulder. I'm not trembling, I wasn't rocking back and forth against the stone—he is shaking me. His eyes hold a lethal message, a pointedness I've never seen before shining through them.

Cliff is here.

"Cliff?" I ask, my voice sounding so far away, though I can hear it now, can feel connected to my own voice.

Make it stop, please make it stop, I plead to my other voice, to the aether, to the Fallen themselves at this point.

Hold on a little longer, my other voice answers.

Vines sway in the wind behind Cliff, and ravens continue to scatter the fields in droves, many circling above the vineyard now. Black wraiths flitting about the sky, silhouettes soaring against the light of the full moon.

"When did you figure it out?" Rivian asks Cliff, his voice still loud and clear in my head.

Cliff responds to Rivian, his response muffled in my trance. Still, he doesn't take his eyes off me.

The sky shatters into a purple rain, illuminating the vineyard for a split second in a hazy glow.

Vellas.

As if the channel from Rivian's mind to mine has finally fractured, I heave my first real breath, my body spasming with relief. I try to rise, calling on any strength left in my body, using one arm to prop myself up, but I crumble back into my own fluids. Strong hands come underneath me, and Cliff raises me to his chest. I cave in on myself in his arms while he takes slow steps, walking us backward.

When he stops, he leans down and whispers, "I've got you, A."

Rivian told me the same thing, I think to myself. But I couldn't fight Cliff right now if I wanted to; I don't have the strength to stand, let alone fight. I close my eyes, and time pauses while his lips rest on my forehead and I subconsciously lean into the touch. His words continue to process through me, somehow the same words Rivian gave me, but settling in with a layer of trust I didn't feel before.

Blaine would have committed any crime to keep me safe, his chivalry being one of the traits that made him perfect for the Advisory. Vincenzo all but adopted me after the Break, giving me a feeling of home, a purpose, and a sense of inclusion I had never felt before. My father self-proclaimed himself a savior for simply raising me when my mother wouldn't. The concept of a man stepping in to save me isn't foreign to me. And maybe my exhaustion has me reading too much into Cliff's words. Or *maybe* there's something intimate in knowing that not only is Cliff *saying* he would fight for me—would risk himself to save me—but he's also *showing* me.

Over Cliff's shoulder, I watch Vellas walk toward us through the grapevines, the bottom of his purple robes stained dark from the fallen fruit, their juices dampening the land and sweetening the air with each step he takes. He takes a moment to remove a loose thorn lodged near his thigh with a level of nonchalance that doesn't match the panic tormenting my nerves.

"I was hoping Cliff made a mistake, but here we are." Vellas's booming voice naturally carries across the entire space. He gives me one nod before directing his full attention to Rivian and standing to the left of Cliff.

"Eyes here, love," Rivian calls to me, snapping his fingers as if trying to capture the attention of an animal. Cliff's arm stiffens at my back, and I turn my neck just enough to meet Rivian's gaze.

A shiver runs up my spine in repulsion as those solid white eyes glare my direction, giving me a chance to take him in without imminent fear distracting me. Thin black lines surrounding milky irises look back at me in that predatory gaze I ran from earlier. In response to my reaction or the sight itself, Cliff tightens his grip on me, turning me away, and shifts slowly to place me down. He wraps one arm around me to steady my weak knees while he draws his sword from the sheath across his back with his other arm, angling it toward Rivian.

Rivian smirks at the gesture, eyes crinkling in amusement while they scan Cliff from head to toe. "Don't worry, Cliff, you'll have your sad attempt to save her, but let's wait for the others, shall we? I would hate for everyone to miss the show." Then Rivian unfolds his hands from behind him, raising one arm to reveal a tendril of white light emitting from his fingertip. He draws the wisp through the air, snaking it toward Cliff, wrapping the magic around his raised sword and, in one swift flick, ripping it from Cliff's hands. The sword hovers just ahead of us before it drops to the ground with a loud clang as the metal hits stone.

My damn face betrays me as usual. I gawk at the scene, my jaw unhinging from a combination of shock and fear.

How is Rivian doing any of this?

The sky flashes turquoise, as if several shooting stars are on their way to their next realm, and the ground rattles. My knees buckle, but Cliff's grip tightens on my ribs, preventing my fall.

A large, soft hand reaches down and grasps me under my elbow to steady me further. I flinch at the surprise of the tickle of another beard against my ear, as a low voice sounds, "Sorry to scare you."

Brennan.

He lifts the mask off his face that he had adorned for the ball, tossing it to the ground, and gives me a wink. I don't see a weapon on his body, though relief floods through me just seeing him.

"Rivian—or should I say 'Shahar'? Get on with it," Vellas

commands, not even acknowledging Brennan's entrance, and clearly losing patience.

Shahar? Linea's heir?

Part Five

SUPERNOVA

Should I ever go missing, ever leave this world too soon, you should know to trust the lines of Niall and Gabriel; their bloodlines will remain good, and their lands will always remain open for a Leondite in need. Should any of the six provinces west of the Liravel fall, one should seek solace amongst the Evergroot Mountains.

—An excerpt from Fallen Reginald's journal

Reginald laid down his quill while the tips of his fingers shook and the sounds of his pulse echoed through his ears. He had completed his assignment, had falsely accounted for the day's events and solidified them on parchment to be referenced for the rest of time.

With a steady hand, Titania hovered her hand above the document, and the parchment radiated with a light of preservation. His words were officially documented, sealed forever in a written state for all to see, his tears still visible amongst them. She rolled up the parchment into a scroll and placed it in a pocket of her dress before she stepped forward to address the Fallen.

"Thank you for your cooperation during this daunting time." Her voice was commanding yet lyrical, as if the words came out on the freshly strung strings of a violin's bow. "I hope that one day, when you're ready, you'll look back at this day in understanding."

"You can't do this!" Quincy bellowed from his spot in the pews, anger lacing his tone and etching deep lines across his forehead.

With preternatural speed, Titania's eyes flashed into malicious slits, canine teeth elongated from her gums, and claws snapped from her manicured hands as she turned to Quincy in rebuke. She snarled toward the Fallen blessed with the powers of the air around us, as if he was nothing more than a rat being handed to a serpent to play with.

Quincy withdrew, cowering at the image of the ethereal woman turned monster. The rest of the group remained silent, no longer yelling out in anguish, or releasing sobs of fear—their fate was apparent. They would leave with this woman, or they wouldn't be leaving at all. As quick as Titania had transformed into the monster, she flashed back to her beautiful form, rubbing once at her jaw when her teeth shrank back within her lips.

"How can we help to right our wrongs?" Reginald asked in an attempt to move the day forward, terror now filling him at the act he just witnessed.

Titania beamed at him. His question loomed in the air like an unanswered prayer—she turned to the room with a tone of excitement as she responded, "We have roles for each of you past Linea's walls."

The others exchanged looks of confusion, and murmurs sounded as they confirmed with each other that they had heard Titania correctly. But Reginald knew the truth when he heard it, and while he wasn't sure what walls Titania was referring to, he knew they must exist.

"All of you will join us. I have convinced my Advisory to enter your continent as a security measure and to allow your communities to remain on their lands. We hope to hide the truth of today from them, so that they may continue to live in peace. Once every ten generations, we will allow your return to Celestera for a fortnight, to mate and rejuvenate your bloodlines, during a time we'll call your 'Descents.' We hope under this plan that we can avoid painting a war from this world amongst the constellations. And before any of you think you'll come back and resume your spot here as a Sovereign Leader, you'll be watched, and you'll be unable to speak. Our entire plan only works if we keep the truth locked within us." Her words were succinct, thorough, as if she read off a script. Then she added, "Callie, Alloria, Quincy, Reyna, Willow, Tomas, please rise and join me upon the dais."

Those called didn't argue as they stood. Callie appeared the most solemn of the group, while Alloria didn't hold any visible sign of regret in her stature. In fact, Callie was the only member of the group that appeared ashamed—her peers each held their chins high as they walked to the dais. Pride exuded from their group, and Reginald couldn't help but feel as if it was for all the wrong reasons.

Reginald looked to the five members of their council still sitting amongst the pews, then back to the six who now stood beside him while he attempted to decipher any distinguishable difference, anything that stood out as to why they were split in half this way—when it occurred to him.

These are the six Fallen Leaders east of the Liravel River, where Aetherion also sits.

"Thank you. You six have been responsible for the mass execution of innocent lives for decades now. While our council holds no blame for blindly following Linea to these lands, we cannot excuse the inhumane actions you have committed since arriving." Titania paused, as if to give any of the standing Fallen a chance to refute their actions, and when they didn't, Valerie let out a held sob in realization from her pew. Quincy tilted his chin an inch higher, Reyna glared down at Titania, but it was Tomas who dared to speak.

"And I would do it again to protect my lands."

Titania didn't gawk at the comment, or raise her voice in reaction; she knew the responses she would likely receive. "Is that what Linea communicated to you, that the original inhabitants of our lands were threats to you? You, who arrived centuries later to drain the lands and take ownership overnight?" She took two slow strides toward Tomas, whose only physical response was a narrowing of his eyes. Whether this was news to him or not, Reginald never found out.

"Linea is gone. She will only return if her current lineage dies out, so I hope you left behind the type of legacies that will ensure these lands remain peaceful."

Reality sank into Reginald like a blow to the face. Each moment that passed felt like a lifetime while he awaited his fate.

"I've been urged to end your civilizations. To wipe you away like the plague you've been to our lands since you fell here. However, I am the *actual* originator of these lands, and I believe in retribution. So while I may make a mistake by allowing your kin to live on and continue benefiting from these lands, I will not disconnect myself from my soul to the extent that you six have over these past decades. I will not curse children for the sins of their ancestors." The final line was directed at those standing atop the dais.

"You six will come with me, to live forevermore rehabilitating the grounds from which your communities have been stealing their powers."

Callie's eyes clamped shut, and a tear broke through her lashes. Callie had always had a quiet strength. Her power to lead the beasts of the lands could never be conveyed in their language, anyway. Reginald looked to her now like she was a sinking ship, soon to be gone, but never forgotten.

Titania then turned to the others still sitting in the pews. "You five will have the chance to start new lives within our Advisory. Each of you possesses unique skills that we hope you'll share for the greater good. Should you cross us, you'll join the others in the wastes." A weight lifted off Reginald's shoulders, one that he had been wearing since the moment Titania entered the temple. He unfortunately wouldn't return to Loree, but at least he wouldn't die today.

But then Titania turned to him directly. "And Reginald, we have a special assignment for you."

The Celestial Goddess, your Mother Moon, will protect you. If you find yourself in danger, it is through her that you will survive.

—*The Tales of the Obsidian Witches* by Tresta McVey

Rivian dips his chin in a poor attempt to hide a sly smirk. The dimple in it catches the moonlight above, accentuating the angles of his face, and I stare at him with a loathing so intense it will destroy me from the inside if I don't let it out. "Well, since you asked so kindly." He snaps his fingers to the side and he's gone, in a colorful whirl of wind so strong that the cut at my temple reopens when it rips my matted hair away. I'm forced to cling to Cliff against the assault.

Cliff's grip on my side is so firm it may bruise my rib cage, but I would fall without him. "You okay?" he asks while I hide my face in the crook of his arm.

"I didn't tell him," I admit to Cliff, praying he doesn't think I betrayed his trust after yesterday.

"I believe you," he tells me while continuing to hold me upright, his grip quickly becoming my only piece of stability this evening.

The wind stops, and I uncover my face to look up at him, silently portraying my appreciation—a short-lived sentiment, I realize when I turn back to where Rivian disappeared.

Shahar now stands where Rivian once did, gleaming in an all-white three-piece suit, almost the exact—no, *the* exact—ensemble Rivian wore to the first dinner I attended here in Liravel. The well-crafted suit, lacking the jacket, blends into his alabaster skin. Skin so thin I can see his veins running underneath it, like a spider's web, or the cracks of shattered glass. His white hair is wiry, showing his age, and he wears it in a slicked-back ponytail at the nape of his neck to disguise the texture. Those iridescent white eyes are now just foggy abysses within the concaves of his strong cheekbones, which, combined with his sharp jawline, give him an intense appearance of malnourishment. He shifts slightly, and a glare catches my eye from where a silver chain wraps twice around his neck, a moonstone dangling from it by his sternum.

Brennan catches me off guard when he steps closer again, interlocking his fingers in mine as the sky flares green.

The mountains behind the vineyard shake, and the sound of rotating and crumbling rock echoes throughout the fields. Straight ahead, the Auralian Mountains split open down the center, and through the crest soars a magnificent golden dragon.

"Show off," Cliff grumbles to himself.

The levity breaks through my panic for a fleeting moment, and I bite my inner cheek to hide my ill-timed grin—I can't help myself. The reaction is just so *Cliff*. I suppose it must be hard to possess powers of the mind, powers hidden from the naked eye. Maybe that's why he works so hard to be physically fit, to have a visible example of his strength. I can't believe I never took the chance to ask *why* he wanted to be Rivian's captain of the guard—can't believe I didn't spend every moment I could getting to know him.

A woman sporting kelly-green leathers walks up from behind us, stopping on the other side of Vellas. Ravens have multiplied in the skies, but they scatter from the path of the dragon as it soars straight for us, landing about fifty feet behind the new woman in green and smashing several rows of grapevines beneath it. The woman wears several daggers sheathed up the sides of her vest, while her hair falls to her shoulders in well-kept curls—she was at the ball. I feel a warm breeze caress my neck—dragon's breath—and look back over my shoulder toward the source. The gorgeous golden dragon turns its neck toward me long enough that I worry I've offended the beast. I mouth "I'm sorry" it's direction. It nods its neck all the way to the ground in response before swiveling back to its owner.

"Gaia, sorry to end our dance early, but as you can see, something came up," Brennan states from my side, addressing the newest member to our line.

Gaia. I wrack my brain for where I know the name.

"Sovereign of The Ivory Hills," Cliff whispers through the corner of his mouth. "And those two are Stella and Kai, Curatia and Eshrador respectively," he adds, noticing two additional Sovereigns joining our flanks on the other side of Brennan.

Thank you, Celestial Goddess, for bringing me Cliff.

I met Stella at the first dinner, after she healed Cliff's hand when I sliced it open, and again tonight when Mia introduced us, but Kai is a new face altogether—ironic considering Eshrador was my home province. To my left and right now stand seven of us. The five Sovereign Descendants from this side of the Break, along with Cliff and me.

Are they all just learning that Rivian wasn't who he said he was? The lack of surprise exuding from this group tells me they came prepared for the possibility. Suddenly the timing of Cliff opening up to me about knowing of the Resistance doesn't feel like such a coincidence.

"Get up to the castle," Cliff whispers in my ear, leaning down to rotate us and push me behind him, putting himself between me and Shahar. But Brennan releases my hand and grabs Cliff's forearm.

"August stays," Brennan commands in an authoritative tone that I haven't heard him use before. This isn't a brother making a suggestion, it's a Sovereign giving an order.

I stand here, helpless, while they argue over where I should be.

Because I'm a helpless human who thought she could save the world. Because if a battle were to break out, I will die, and likely bring others down with me.

Believing you will fail will lead to its truth, my other voice jumps in, providing minimal tangible help, as usual.

"Do me a favor, August. Think about help coming. I've always felt we can will our needs into existence, and what a time to try it," Brennan says to me, eyes not leaving Cliff. Again, not the cheery tone I'm used to hearing from him, but a gritted command. A Sovereign leading his crew.

I look back and forth between the two, not willing to insert myself in the conversation that is wholly about me.

"You want to put her life in danger on a hunch that she can *will* help to arrive?" Cliff asks, a deep red hue beginning to peek over the top of his beard.

"Yes."

Shahar's words draw our attention back to him. "Thank you all for coming, though you didn't have to go to such lengths to give me a warm welcome. I would have accepted a light spread, maybe some champagne." He pauses, his hand floating to the side as if holding the imaginary serving platter he references. Waiting for a reaction from us, he scans his eyes down our line expectantly, and when no one gives him the commentary he's attempting to extract, he continues. "Oh, that's right, my apologies, I was busy fucking the chef. August, love, next time, please keep your clothes on long enough to play host."

If I make it out of here alive, I'm going to have to bathe a hundred times before I feel clean again, I think to myself, eyes closing in disgust as knots form in my stomach again, the scent of my vomit from earlier still fresh on my skin.

Shahar rocks back and forth on his feet, hands in his pockets, still gazing down our line. "Such a quiet crowd today. Brennan, surely you're curious to know where your friend is? You and Rivian have been close since you were just boys, yes?"

Brennan's face doesn't shift in any reaction at all. His stoicism is impressive. "You wouldn't tell me, even if I asked. So I'll start with—why?" Brennan's glowing turquoise eyes drill into Shahar. If a look could kill, Shahar would be dead.

Shahar enjoys this, knows he has a captive audience. I see it in his eyes, wide with anticipation, and the twitch of his fingers in his pockets. "Why? Why what?" he asks, his words quickening and his tone bordering on manic. "Come on, Brennan, you should know better than to ask such an open-ended question." His voice rises an octave in excitement, as if we failed his first riddle, as if this is all one big game for him.

This was never about escape or deceit. No, if he wanted to escape or kill us all right now, he would have tried already. He wants notoriety—he wants to know he gave us a fair shot and could still defeat us.

Whatever us *is.* I still don't know what he's fighting for, or we're fighting against—except that it all seems to revolve around *me.*

The corner of Shahar's mouth continues to defy the muscles of his face, curving higher and higher, until he speaks again. "I'll tell you what—" He turns on his heel, pointing one waving finger at Brennan and scratching his chin with his other hand as he paces the length of our line, back and forth, his feet crunching on the occasional stone or the squish of a rogue grape the only sounds between words. "I'll give you three questions before I gather what I came here for and leave. Everyone is welcome to stay, of course. Maybe one of you can even get August to actually throw together that spread I mentioned." He gestures up to the palace, casually indicating his invitation.

As if on cue, an explosion sounds from that direction, and we all turn to see smoke billowing from the center of the palace, presumably the courtyard.

What in the aether?

In response, the others all hold their palms open out to the sides, chins raised slightly toward the sky, eyes all locked on Shahar.

I guess we're all just going to ignore the explosion?

Cliff releases my ribs, and I take a step out of his embrace. Brennan nudges me, and I turn to see him nod once at his own raised palms, then once toward my hands, and once more when I copy the others—affirming that I've followed his silent directions correctly. My hands shake, but I muster all my strength to do what he asked.

I'm willing to try anything at this point to survive, I think to myself as I imitate the Sovereign Descendants to my left and right. The pose becomes more difficult than it seems when I realize just how weak I am without Cliff's arm to hold me up—the place where his hand grasped me now stings with the December chill in the air.

What is wrong with me, yearning for the touch of a man not hours since I slept with another? I ask myself pathetically.

You're yearning for support, and learning where you can find it, my other voice tells me, distracting me from spiraling through my own self-loathing—for now at least.

Brennan straightens in my periphery. "Where is the other half of Celestera?"

Right to the point, then. Shahar showed me earlier that he was behind the Break, but Brennan wouldn't know that yet, at least not from me. This means Brennan already knew, or at the very least suspected something was going on. I tuck this information away in order to continue focusing on the moment.

Shahar's brows shoot up, giving emphasis to a brief, pulsing glow in his eyes. "Ah, a fun one to start." He touches his fingertips together in front of him, contemplating how to respond. "Linea kept many secrets when she fell to Celestera. Most of the Fallen never thought to question the gracious leader who granted them power, land, and a new world full of hope—didn't think to question whether or not the gifts were hers to give, or if she truly gave them all she could offer. If the constellations found her here, she'd need to get away fast, and knowing this, she kept a fair share of resources hidden for herself—I used them."

Brennan's chest rises and falls, processing Shahar's words. His glowing eyes cast turquoise shadows against his cheeks while he assesses Shahar's statements for truth.

He must determine them good enough, because he continues with his next question. "How long do we have until all the Descents overlap?"

I can't control myself this time as my neck snaps to Brennan. As far as I know, two Descents have never overlapped, let alone all of them. It would take thousands of years of strategically aligned generational births and deaths.

Something much bigger than I thought is happening.

"If I knew the answer to that, I wouldn't have bothered with *her.*" Shahar jerks his head toward what I believe is my direction, though I can't be sure as he doesn't look my way. His brows furrow as if he himself is frustrated by this question, while he continues his pacing.

Brennan's voice is determined now, closer to Cliff's growl, though clear and commanding all the same. "Where is the twin?"

Shahar stops, turning to face Brennan—no longer frustrated, no longer manic. "Only August can lead us there."

What? Confusion seeps in. Did he say twin? I feel the blood drain from my face, a validating wave of existential dread coming over me as I weigh the information I've received in the past few hours—dread at the amount that I actually understand, and the amount I don't.

"Enough." Vellas's deep voice rips me from a sinking panic, and when I look over, his purple robes are billowing around him in a wind I can't feel.

On a silent cue, the six others grasp hands, and I instinctively do the same with Cliff and Brennan. The instant I do, my insides melt to liquid, like lightning flows through my veins. The burning returns; only, unlike Shahar's invisible flames that engulfed me earlier, these are internal, begging for release. My stomach heaves, but there is nothing left in me to vacate. Cliff and Brennan both clench my hands hard enough I worry they'll crack under the pressure, holding me up with their strength while my knees buckle and I bend at the waist in agony.

"*Make it stop,*" I scream to myself, only realizing I've said the words out loud when Cliff turns and yells back, "It's almost over, A."

"NOW!" Brennan bellows, breaking through the ringing in my ears.

The searing pain doesn't fade, even as Cliff and Brennan drop my hands. Colorful tendrils of their power weave in and out of the Sovereign Leaders before me, forming an iridescent glow around us—a protective shield. They shake from holding the shield before us, all while I stand and watch.

I'm nothing more than a liability. What could I possibly contribute beside six of the most powerful descendants of my time? I stare at the shield before me, shame and amazement clouding any rational thought.

Cliff turns to check on me, and his eyes flash in surprise when they meet mine. Something akin to fear or shock looks back at me. A bead of sweat drips down his temple and onto his shoulder, despite the temperature dropping as we approach the midnight hour.

"I'm. Fine." Each word needs its own breath as I emphasize them, the pressure of being inside the protective shield similar to Rivian's earlier barrage of mental warfare.

I look to Brennan, and his eyes widen slightly too. But rather than showing any fear, he gives me a small grin, something closer to approval shining through him. I nod back, the momentary surge of heat that flooded my veins already subsiding, leaving my skin tingling with the energy of the shield.

Shahar stops his pacing to imitate the stance the others just abandoned, palms out, gazing toward the sky, when his eyes flare open, and if possible, pulse even brighter in the darkening sky. I follow, staring in disbelief at the movement above.

Ravens. Thousands of ravens.

Ravens have now blanketed the sky. Even the moon and stars are hidden behind their layer of wings. The only remaining light comes from the incandescent glow of the shield surrounding us, and a faint orange shadow flickering off the shadows of the vineyard from the flames in the castle behind us.

Brennan speaks first. "Wound, but do not kill. We cannot allow a Linea Descent." He has to yell for us to hear him through the energetic hum of the protective shield.

"August, I need you to stay within one of our shields. Do you understand?" Brennan asks at my side, still focusing his energy on keeping our shield intact. His arm muscles strain with the effort he puts into keeping his flow of magic coursing through his palms, and I can see his beard shift as he grinds his teeth in painful determination.

"Tell me how to help," I beg, needing to do anything but stand guarded while those around me fight. A fight I don't understand, but I know involves me. The irony of them fighting for me, when I came here to fight against them, hits me with a level of guilt I would never wish on anyone. I've killed before with less emotional toll than this.

"You can help by remaining with one of the Sovereigns until this is over." He turns to the woman in green, bellowing, "Gaia!"

Gaia takes her hands away from our protective shield, and a stream of green flows from her fingers straight into the ground. With her other hand, she leads the green light through the ground, glowing vibrantly from beneath it into the vineyard surrounding us. The vines pulse as her magic brushes their roots, and slowly they knit themselves together. I watch as the vines grow, shift, and form walls in various paths across the field. She has turned the vineyard into a maze, and I stare through an archway standing beside us, showing a fork in the path.

"Stella, Vellas, take her." Brennan continues in the role of general as he gives his orders. I don't have time to understand what he just meant—one moment I'm on the cobblestone path, the next, Stella, Vellas, and I are in the middle of the vineyard, surrounded by grapevines and pitch-black skies. I'm barely able to see either of them in the night.

33

Many scholars have attempted to dive into magical theory, particularly around the topics of limitations and capabilities. Some scholars believe that magic could be infinite, if one only knew how to source the power themselves. Others believe that there are limitations set innately in a being from their birth—determined by factors such as bloodline and environment. This scholar believes, however, that the truth is somewhere between these two theories—that magic creates its own laws, and we would be wise not to test them.

—An excerpt from *Recovered Journals of the Fallen*

"What did you do?" I roar at Vellas. Flashes of light and distant clangs of metal suggest fighting in the distance, though I can no longer see the others. "We can't leave them!" I scream, pleading, grasping his robes in my fists.

"Listen to me, August. You would die in a battle right now. You have no weapons, no training. We need to hold Shahar long enough to deplete his energy—that way he can't get away, or worse, follow us when we do." Vellas's face appears apprehensive when his purple eyes meet mine; they shrink as he cranes his neck back to get a better view of my face.

Stella's magenta irises glow on the other side of me, and her apologetic gaze lets me know I won't get any further trying to fight with her.

I have never stopped to consider the strain that emotion holds on a body, nor the number of emotions a being is capable of experiencing. I used to shut emotion out. *No room for feelings in the kitchen*, Vinny would tell me. In the past twenty-four hours, I have gone from panicked over being caught in the Resistance, to falsely believing I had found love, to willing to throw myself in rage onto one of the Sovereign Leaders of my world. A more intelligent version of myself would consider where my hands are right now, would consider my place in society—but logical thinking doesn't seem to be where my mind wants to go right now.

Remember New August, the one you were excited to be when you came here, the one that was going to stand up for herself and lead a Resistance from the inside? Maybe it's time for her to make an appearance, my other voice suggests.

It's right. New August was going to do things her way, not Vincenzo or Blaine's way—but just when I think to run, a voice sounds behind me.

"August, another gathering you didn't invite me to? And here I was, thinking we had talked this out." The unmistakable coo of

Zalya's voice slices through my final stretch of patience. I release Vellas's robes from my fists to spin around.

Zalya hovers over the ground, tendrils of shimmering black magic looming below her. And in her outstretched arms is Mia, lifeless.

"MIA!" Stella shrieks, her magenta eyes glued to the unconscious citizen of her province.

No.

I stumble backward into Vellas, who catches me beneath my arms before I fall. Any strength that had returned to my tired joints is gone with one sight of my friend lying limp in Zalya's clutch. Zalya's washed-out skin starkly contrasts against her sheer, long-sleeved black lace gown, which plunges all the way to her navel and flows freely from the waist. The bodice is a similar cut to mine, though the lace creates an illusion across the neckline that suits her, as if the lace is tattooed to her skin rather than resting upon it. Her skin, so pale in the moonlight it appears almost iridescent, shimmers beneath the gold-chain necklace she wears with the obsidian charm on the end. Stopping several feet away, she gently places Mia on the ground.

I finger my own charm, still hanging from my neck, warm from the evening of dangling between my breasts. Zalya and I have come a long way from when we first met, from the friendship she hoped she was creating by giving me this jewel.

With a wave of Vellas's hand, another protective shield forms in front of us, and Stella raises her own trembling hands to help keep it steady, her gaze never leaving Mia. Her magenta tendrils, knitting themselves before us to form the shield, hiss as they move, as if filled with the grief consuming their owner, as if holding back from attacking the pale aggressor smirking at us through the shimmering shield.

I was wrong each time I thought someone looked at me today with fear, with apprehension. The way Stella looks at Mia right now is fear. The pain in her gaze cuts through the moment, time seeming to slow with each passing second that she doesn't even allow herself to blink her eyes away from Mia. Her emotions radiate off her, her magenta tendrils now sizzling when contacting Vellas's matching purple wisps, as if the pain is boiling through them. I catch Vellas flinching a couple times, as if he can feel the sting each time their magics react.

Was everything earlier just part of Shahar's plan? Are he and Zalya working together?

Zalya struts over to us and, with one poke of her long black nails, shatters our shield into thousands of shards of color and light. "It seems our August has been keeping a secret this whole time. Care to show us any new tricks?"

"What have you done?" I seethe through my teeth, bitter tears brimming in my eyes—not in preparation of sobs, or devastation, but in rage. I stare at Mia's chest, praying it continues to rise and fall with breath, not capable of being aware of what I may do if she stops.

I can't do this anymore, I think to myself while the reality of my situation continues to sink in, continues to wind itself within me, preparing for my revengeful release.

My other voice comes through.

You must.

Zalya doesn't immediately respond to my question, her gaze oddly absent, so I ask again. "Zalya? What have you done to Mia?" Standing before me is no longer the girl who desperately wanted a friend. Matte black irises look back at me, leaving not even a reflection of humanity. "What have you done?" This time the question leaves me as a plea instead of a command—a final search within her to answer whether she has a soul to save.

Zalya takes another step toward us, then pauses, eyes narrowing at a spot behind me, and flicks the air in front of her as if a gnat were too close to her face. Vellas yelps and I turn to see him on the ground several feet away. He must have tried to step in.

Celestial Mother, save us all.

Focus, August. My other voice reminds me to stay in the moment. A feat that is becoming harder and harder with every minute of my dwindling energy, with each new turn in the day bringing on another emotion, another visceral reaction that I'm not sure I have the strength to handle. It takes everything in me not to collapse to the ground and surrender to whatever may come. If it was just me out here, I probably would. I'm angry, and I'm grieving, and I'm scared.

With the shield gone, and Zalya distracted, Stella races to Mia, leaving me alone with—who is this? Is Zalya a witch?

The witches aren't real, my other voice reminds me. But I'm not sure I believe anything I ever knew as real anymore. I'm not sure I know what matters anymore. My entire decade of Resistance work feels like a joke after this evening, my entire relationship with Blaine, my search for Nova—

Zalya closes our distance, lace dress silently flowing on a breeze around her, until she's embracing me with cold arms, her fingers gripping like icicles behind my back. I stiffen at her touch, from unease or chill, I'm not sure, but she leans in and whispers, so close and soft that I can barely hear, "I'm going to distract Shahar so you can get out. I just need one last thing from you first."

What? She wants to help me?

"Zalya, what—" I go to pull away, but she catches my wrist in her frigid hands. "Ahhh." I hiss a sharp breath in through clenched teeth and look down to see blood dripping out of a gash the size of a dagger tip in the center of my palm—a long slice to go with the crescent-moon gashes littering my lower palms.

At least if a friend dies today, I'll already have the scar to prove it.

She drops my wrist long enough to give herself a matching wound before joining our hands together, bowing her head, and kneeling to the ground to lean over a book I didn't see on her before, our hands with the matching wounds now interlaced together through her icy fingers.

"What are you doing?" I ask tentatively through the corner of my mouth, confusion consuming the part of my brain responsible for decision-making. I can't pull my hand from hers; the frigid chill of her bones, mixed with the warm joining of our wounds, sends a stinging chill up my arm each time I try.

Vellas stands behind us, braced for defense, staring at Zalya with a look of pure revolt. Stella leans over Mia, still on the ground, her magenta eyes shining in the night and matching tendrils of magic flowing from her fingertips to my friend. Without their eyes or powers, I wouldn't be able to see a thing—except. The longer I stare down at Zalya, reciting indecipherable chants under her breath, the more her skin seems to sparkle, seems to illuminate, almost the same shade as the—no, a human can't shine like the moon.

I don't recognize her chants at first, but I catch it as she repeats a second verse—the final stage of the Obsidian Witch Initiation Ritual. She's reading from a copy of the Obsidian Witch tales. Not a copy, *my* copy. Zalya was the one who stole my book.

The custom-bound book on the ground was the one Nova made for me—I hate this woman so much. "You stole my book?"

She ignores me, her attention homed in on the ritual she believes she's performing. A vine snaps nearby. My neck whips in that direction, but still Zalya doesn't stray. A subtle breeze in the air has turned into erratic gusts of wind caused by the wingbeats of the ravens above us, circling in one unit as if imitating a vortex in the sky.

Twice more, she repeats the chant, her grip on my hand so tight that I'm forced to stand there, unable to pull away while she finishes a fool's mission. She can't honestly believe she can bring this fable to life—that she can transform into a witch. She looks back at me when she's completed her fourth verse, her dark eyes studying me comprehensively as our hands unlatch, scanning me up and down as if searching for signs that her ritual worked.

I feel no different, still in pain, still covered in blood, still angry and bitter and a million other emotions battling for the primary spot in my motivation. Blood clots on my head, hands, and knees, and vomit solidifies on my skin in a visual representation of the chaos running through my mind.

"I hope it did work. You don't deserve a soul, anyway," I state loudly enough so the others can hear. Then I lean in and whisper, "The Obsidian Coven isn't real." Something cold and stiff shifts along my hip, and the cool steel point of a blade threatens to break the skin of my upper thigh.

How did I get a knife? My hands rub the outline of one of the sheaths sewn into my dress, and I finger the tip of a hilt beneath the top layer of gauze.

"It's not real," I tell myself this time, under my breath, staring down at my hip where the outline of a blade can be seen through the fabric of my gown.

A smile twists the corners of her mouth through her cold mask. "Isn't it, though?"

"Okay, so you say you're a witch, and you say you're here to help, so why Mia?" I ask, now staring toward my lifeless friend, the piece of this puzzle that still makes no sense.

"Oh, August, the way to get your attention *is to hurt* those around you." Zalya looks Mia's direction, nose crinkled in disgust. Apparently, her jealousy of that friendship hasn't completely subsided. "Your loyalty, while scarcely given, is the doorway to your heart."

"Why did you need to hurt me, though? If you're here to help me, why hurt me at all?" I demand after hearing her admit to that callous reasoning for Mia lying on the ground.

"You're my friend." She shrugs, also gazing toward Mia and Stella.

Her face slackens in a brief show of remorse, and I know—Zalya truly thought she did the right thing. She considered her options and hurt Mia thinking she was saving me in the process—or thought hurting Mia would increase her chances of being able to save me. We don't have time to talk about it right now, even if I thought she could be reasoned with, so I accept this interaction for what it was—Zalya tried to help.

"I won't forgive you if she's hurt."

"I know."

Stella holds Mia in her lap, her palms continuing to emit her magenta powers as they hover over Mia's heart, forehead, core. They look so much like each other, both in their matching healing suits.

They could be mother and daughter if it weren't for Mia's platinum hair being so opposite of Stella's.

But then, Mia stirs, restoring a small amount of hope in me that I hadn't thought was possible. I sprint to her and throw myself to the ground to embrace her, forgetting how sore my knees are from the stones earlier.

My heart threatens to pound through my chest. I can hear it in my ears. I can feel it in my core—like a drum rhythmically beating to the song of my panic and relief, trapped only by my rib cage. But it gets louder, and stronger, till even the vines are swaying with the beats.

That's not just my heart.

I gaze at the sky—a black mass with a small, shimmering spot of white, defying the night, soars our direction. I would know that underbelly anywhere.

Teliquis.

"No, they can't be here."

Blaine.

A guttural screech sounds through the air, loud and vicious. I look up to see Gaia's dragon streaming straight toward them, poised for attack. Teliquis doesn't see her in time, and I'm forced to watch as the two dragons latch on to each other mid-flight.

"NO!" I'm standing, running through the maze of vines, screaming toward the dragons. "STOP! We know them!" I continue to wail into the night, waving my arms through the air as if he'll stop to consider a human's wishes while mid-battle. Willing each of them to realize I'm talking about the other, I plead, "They're on our side."

I'm just about to call again when two long necks swivel my way. Teliquis's eyes are narrowed in rage, and the gold body of the other dragon thrashes in frustration, whipping her neck away from Teliquis in a snarl.

Did I do this? Did I actually stop the dragons from fighting?

My other voice validates my efforts.

See, you can help.

They now fly parallel to each other toward where we stand, both occasionally chancing a glance at the other while they soar, both giving each other wide berths, but no longer showing any signs of imminent attack. I look around, trying to see where they'll land, where they can go, but there's not enough open space in the vineyard's new maze design.

A loud squawk tears my attention away. An orange streak flashes through the sky to my right, spiraling my direction, narrowing in on the spot where I stand. And when it's maybe twenty feet away, a black mass releases from its talons.

You too? I think to myself, watching another familiar body hurtle my direction, another friendly face I wish wasn't around to see what is happening today.

Snitch skids across the dirt, stopping next to me, and directly at my feet now sits my dragon-hide bag. Without hesitation, I throw the straps over my shoulder and lock the waist buckles so it can't slip off.

"What is wrong with you, friend? You shouldn't be here!" I tell the tiny filaminx, wondering how it knew where I was, or where it found my bag. But with my knives at my back, I'm no longer completely defenseless. It may not be magic, but it's all I have.

The vines behind me begin to unknit, thorns crunching as they break down and twist, untangling themselves to open a small doorway to another turn in the maze. "Now that you're ready—" Zalya grabs my bicep and hauls me through the gap.

She drags me along as I pivot my neck to watch the vines grow back, the wall reappearing after we pass through. We run, and I see Snitch fly into the distance and I wave to her, hoping she finds safety somewhere.

I can't see the ground through the dark of night and trip twice before I plant my feet. But I'm ready for answers. "Where are we going?" I ask between pants, my hands clutched on my knees.

But then Shahar's wicked laugh sounds through a wall of vines nearby, and both our eyes flare toward it.

"Just run," she pants out. We take off again, away from the direction of his laugh, pausing only when we come to another fork in the path.

Three aisles branch off. Zalya hums to herself in contemplation, holding up her hand and staring at it for a moment before pointing a finger down one of the rows. A black ray of power shoots from her fingertip, and I hear the firm base of a vine crack as it slams to the ground.

34

It is said that Micah didn't possess the ability to speak, and scholars have debated over the years about whether this occurred as a result of natural phenomena, or whether his mutism was inflicted upon him by another. His historical accounts remain the most mysterious and vague. There are perhaps many answers that could be discovered upon finding his journal specifically.

—An excerpt from *Celestera: The Beginning*

"Good to know I can create obstructions!" she excitedly states under her breath as we take off down another row.

The thought occurs to me I could be making as grave a mistake with Zalya as I did by following Rivian earlier. That logical version of myself that seems to have excused her presence tonight encourages me to at least consider what we will do when we find our way out of this maze. Or whether there will ever come a time I feel safe enough to stop running from this place at all—but for now, I do. I run as fast as I can, as fast as this gown will allow and my bare feet can manage through the fallen grapes.

We continue weaving through the aisles, choosing directions at random. A stitch forms in my side, but I tune it out. We begin to turn a corner but stop when we run into Brennan, barreling toward us from the opposite direction.

His glowing eyes have dimmed since I last saw him, and with better light, I assume I would say the same about his skin. A thick gash wraps around his forearm, extending from his wrist to nearly his elbow, and he flinches when he reaches out that arm to grasp my shoulder. His eyes stare into Zalya in warning.

She lunges, simultaneously interlocking my opposite hand with hers. "Mine," she chides Brennan, as if she's claiming her favorite chair at the dinner table.

I cough in surprise. "Yours?" But Zalya won't meet my eyes, locked into a silent battle with Brennan over possession of me. "Zalya, I don't belong to you—" I say, then turn to Brennan. "Or anyone."

The levity in this moment reminds me of how I felt watching Cliff and Brennan fight over me earlier.

I'm done being the reason for this battle, with no say in how we fight, in where I stand.

Brennan squints at Zalya through agitated eyes, his lips pursed with the words he wants to say. I rip my hand and shoulder away from both of them. "Enough. Neither of you gets to call my actions any longer."

They both look at me for a split second before turning back to each other, resuming their childish fight over responsibility for me. Zalya juts her chin up at him, as if to say, *Try to take her and see what happens.*

This is why I don't make friends, I think to myself.

Speaking of friends—my other voice cuts in.

A blast of fire consumes the area to our side, and all three of us pause our standoff, shielding our eyes from the flames. Dozens of rows of the vineyard now lie charred on the ground, revealing a large, barren oval of space. Teliquis stands to the side, huffing smoke out of her flared nostrils. Her agitated neck swings violently from side to side, communicating her anger to me with the erratic motions. I see the bite mark from Gaia's dragon slashed down her neck. And Blaine is there, mounted on her back. Blood drips, slowly but steadily, from his boot. He's hurt, but he's alive. Our eyes meet, and his face softens. I know him, though, know that while relief floods him right now, there is deep pain still burning within him.

"Teliquis, I'm okay," I call to the dragon I've missed more than I realized, attempting to hide the enraged terror in my voice while I stare at her wounds.

Smoke clears, and the embers left on the burning vines shed some light around us. The breeze occasionally blows past a burning branch, enough to bring it to life, and small flames flicker up in the wind's path. Straight ahead, Stella still holds Mia, who appears to be awake, though still weak. Vellas must have taken off after Zalya and me, as he's now by himself several rows away—conveying a silent message to Brennan when their eyes meet. I feel Brennan's hold tighten on my arm. Kai and Gaia come running down a row that Teliquis's flames didn't reach and stop abruptly when they take in their surroundings, only feet behind Stella and Mia.

Cliff.

Cliff is the only one missing. I count us again, making sure I haven't missed him, sweat forming on my palms, across my brow as I count and count.

Stella, Mia, Kai.

"Brennan?" Panic rises in my tone as I count our group over and over, convincing myself I've made a mistake.

Vellas, Zalya, Brennan.

I go to move, but both Zalya and Brennan grab a shoulder and hold me back, feet planted.

Me, Stella, Mia. Where is he?

A flash of white light pulses like lightning around us, its strike cracking through the air, littering my vision with stars. Shahar appears across the opening, and with him is Cliff.

No.

Cliff kneels to the ground, head hung to his chest, bound by the wrists and gagged with white tendrils of magic.

"Cliff!" I wail, jerking forward, but Zalya grips a strap of my bag with her other hand, holding me back.

I have to do something.

"DON'T! You need to play along," she responds as she releases me and begins slowly strutting toward Shahar.

The rest of the group rushes to each other, meeting in the middle. I don't miss Brennan's limp with each step he takes. The ground beneath us rattles as Gaia's golden dragon lands behind us, smashing several more rows of vines beneath her again, near where Stella still holds Mia on the ground.

"Would you like to claim defeat now? You don't exactly have the powers of warriors amongst you," Shahar presses with a cocky undertone. But then he pales when he sees Zalya approaching him, his last few words dissipating on his breath.

He's scared of her.

I still can't trust either of them; after all, neither are who they said they were—but for today, Zalya hasn't lied. And when it comes to life or death, choosing between two evils, I'll choose the evil who was honest every time.

A flash of Shahar's magic hits Zalya in the chest, and she falls back to the ground, much like how she knocked Vellas back earlier. Cliff groans in pain, a macabre sound that echoes through the charred debris and into my heart. Energy explodes within me—rage.

Shahar must die, I think to myself as I watch him focus on the witch before him.

"Shahar, baby, it's me," Zalya purrs as she stands back up, dusting off the front of her dress as if the blast had been nothing but a strong wind—a careless trip over a loose vine. Her voice reminds me of the one you would use with a scared toddler, light and tentative. "You're just in time, actually. I was telling August here about how she could've been a part of *our* plan all along. About how she could have joined us—how good we could have all been together." She emphasizes the sway in her hips with her long, slow strides across the charred ground—ever the sensual goddess she enjoys playing.

Shahar said those same words earlier to me, that we would be "good together." I can taste the deceit hanging in them now, in hearing them used against him rather than on me. Can feel the manipulative intentions twisting within me as I think back to everything he said to me, the feeling of his lips and hands all over me—all manipulation tactics.

I can't read his eyes; they're barely visible through the hazy orange smoke drifting off the glowing embers encrusting the vines and ground around us. The glowing milky globes give nothing away, but he doesn't take his eyes off her while she speaks. Black tendrils of magic stream from her pointer finger. She draws shapes in the air while she talks to Shahar as if he simply needs to be reminded that he is in love with her. Her powerful wisps of power somehow shimmer in the night as she casts them from a source I still deny to be true.

Zalya is human. She doesn't have powers.

She doesn't have to look my way for me to know her next words are for me. "I just thought we could be friends—show Celestera that two humans didn't need magical gifts to be powerful."

"I never wanted power. I wanted justice," I yell toward her back.

That orange glow from the vines burning around us gets stronger and stronger, as if—despite the ravens blanketing us above—the sky has mimicked the fiery hue of the field's flames. Or maybe my anger has altered my vision, consumed my senses until I allow its release.

I stand in a line with Brennan, Kai, and Gaia. To our left are Teliquis and Blaine. Behind us now stands the other dragon, and just ahead lie Stella and Mia. Everyone is focused on Shahar. If it's power I seek—here it is.

The tendrils Zalya draws out as she walks to Shahar all come together to form a serpent swimming through the air, and with another flick of her fingers, she sends it shooting toward him, fangs out—only for it to redirect when it gets about three feet away, evaporating in the breeze.

She hums to herself, pursing her lips in thought, then breaks into a playful grin and a ghost of a laugh. "Moonstone. Clever. When did you figure it out?"

"I found your book."

"Oh, you can thank August for that." She looks back in my direction briefly. "I knew our destinies were intertwined. Though I'm just a little upset you didn't think you could trust me with this plan of yours," she says, gesturing broadly.

Another manipulation tactic, pretending to want to join his plan, to want to be with him.

Once she stands before Shahar, she runs one of her long black nails down the buttons of his shirt, whispering something the rest of us can't hear.

I look to Cliff. Just moments ago, it was me lying on the stone while he waited for me to gather the strength to rise.

It's my turn now.

I flinch, tensing when Brennan bellows from beside me, "SHIELD."

All at once, Vellas, Brennan, Gaia, and Kai throw up their hands, knitting a protective shield before us. I do the same, as if my human strength can add anything to their magical cast, remembering how Brennan asked me to imitate them earlier.

In the same moment, Gaia's dragon swivels her neck above us, breathing in and blasting fire across the already burning vineyard. My eyes slam shut at the intruding light.

The glowing force pulses once under my raised hands, and I shake with the fatigue of holding myself there, with the rage building in me, with the magic stinging my palms and flowing through my veins, with the dragon fire licking the ghosts of burns I was forced to relive earlier this evening.

"Roddrerre! A little more warning next time," Gaia calls sternly over her shoulder, glaring up at her dragon, but it's a soul-piercing scream that pulls my attention. If pain was a sound, this is it, sentient, resonating like an eighth member of our group.

Mia crouches above Stella, shaking, screaming, her hands roaming for enough space to hold on to her Sovereign—for a spot of skin that hasn't been incinerated, that isn't smoking with the aftermath of burning flesh.

No.

A whimper expels from my tired lungs. Stella is but a smoking husk of the woman who once stood here with us. Mia's screams carry across the fields and echo through the splits in the mountains.

Kai, being closest, grabs Mia from behind, pulling her away. She fights him, but he wraps his arms around my frantic friend. There is nothing that can be done.

Stella is gone.

No.

I stare up at Roddrerre. Deep remorse shines in her eyes as she swings her neck back toward the spot where Stella lies, and then straight toward the sky. She lets out a powerful roar, a tear falling from her eye and down her neck as it extends to the atmosphere above.

But it won't bring Stella back.

"She was protecting her rider and providing you light," Zalya calls empathetically from next to Shahar, and I turn to see her drilling her black eyes into me, seeing if I heard.

But all I know is Mia is screaming, Cliff isn't moving, Blaine is bleeding—and it's all because of me.

No one was supposed to die today, but now one more will.

I step forward. "If it's me you want, here I am."

35

Obsidian connects the sisters of the Coven in a similar manner to many other magical bonds in existence. Use the bonds wisely, and the Celestial Mother will bless you. Should you need to imbue additional crystals, contact the Ceress.

—*The Tales of the Obsidian Witches* by Tresta McVey

A breeze drifts through the charred vines, bringing with it the smell of burning flesh—sour and thick. It takes me back to a too-familiar kitchen, and a mentor I couldn't save.

I'm fucking sick of this smell.

The hilt of my blade is cool in the palm of my hand despite the scalding smoke dancing throughout the vineyard. The steel hums with an energy floating in the air, and I circle my wrist several times in preparation to throw it.

The breeze from the wingbeats of the ravens above

fans the flames farther outward across the field with each beat—they're almost to the mountains now, and a smoky haze, glowing vibrantly orange, sits thick in the air. I faintly hear those behind me, yelling my name, but I tune them out. No one else will die for me today.

Shahar's greedy eyes twinkle at what he thinks is the sight of me surrendering myself to him. I watch as the corner of his lip curves a bit more with each step I take, as the tendrils of his power glow brighter, dancing around his palms.

"So, it is possible to persuade her," he calls in my direction, eager to make a move against me.

What he doesn't understand is that I don't need persuasion to defend my friends, that I won't stand aside and watch as he uses those around me as manipulation, like they are nothing more than bait for his prize.

His eyes scan me, up and down, as if he is calculating in his mind how he can get the most pleasure from my demise. He won't kill me. No, he wants to own me. He wants control. It helps that he no longer holds the form of Rivian, no longer looks like the man I had inside me only hours ago—an image I'm not sure I could stand against as confidently.

"Let Cliff go." I utter it no louder than if he were a few feet in front of me.

I risk one glance at the sky—still a midnight-black blanket of ravens atop an orange, hazy cloud of smoke. Another glance to Zalya, still inches from Shahar. But I don't miss that she stands with her legs staggered beneath her dress, braced for the moment she must move, or that while she stares at me, her obsidian tendrils of magic drift pointedly toward Shahar.

"August?" She tentatively calls my name, as if checking for proof of a soul still within me—a question I'm not sure I can answer, at least not one I want to hear the answer to.

Will I have a soul after what I'm about to do?

"So the love goes both ways," Shahar states contemplatively, gazing down toward Cliff's hunched form beside him.

I raise my arm slowly, rolling my shoulders as I flex my grip on the hilt of my blade and angle it into throwing position. My strides are slow, but I don't stop, not when my bare feet slice open on another branch, or when they step on a burning ember, not even at the continued shouts from those I left behind me. No, I won't stop until I reach my target. Proximity will be my key to accuracy…and power. I need this shot to be lethal.

Shahar's eyes narrow in amusement as he huffs a laugh toward the ground. "Do you really think you can defeat me with a blade?"

Yes is what I want to say. Instead, I repeat, "Let Cliff go."

He holds out his bare hand. No magic glowing in his palm—a simple gesture. An offering to join him willingly, to reconsider the offer he made me in his office earlier.

"Let Cliff go."

"August, what are you doing?" Zalya asks tentatively, somehow breaking through the current of rage sounding through my head, the continued beating of the ravens' wings above, the crackling of the burning vineyard surrounding us, and the shouts of those behind me.

I'm not the young woman about to drown in the Liravel River. I'm not the terrified apprentice crawling through the flames at The Goblet, suffocating under the weight of her dying mentor. I'm not the heartbroken girlfriend who accepted a job to be anywhere but Quinthold surrounded by desolate memories and clinging to hope that she could find a way to carry on the Resistance. I'm not even the woman I was earlier tonight, caving under the weight of my worst memories while Cliff carried me to safety. My anger vibrates through me in wave after wave of power.

The sky shifts in a torrent of wind as one by one, ravens dive toward us, toward the ground surrounding us. I take the opening of Shahar's instinctive switch in attention—hurling my blade as hard as I can in his direction. My aim is true. Though he responds just in time to deflect it with a wave of his hand and a flash of his power.

Zalya's screams pierce the air, and I chance a short glance directly at her to see blood streaming from under her palm, which she clutches to her cheek—where Shahar must have deflected my knife into her.

She seethes as she slowly removes her hand to gaze at the blood, then up at me, then back to him. A look settles in her eyes that tells me we're done with deceit, done pretending or distracting, this man has taken enough from us both, and it's time to end him or die trying. Taking a large step away from him, she raises her hands in front of her so that her shimmering obsidian magic glows at her fingertips.

His eyes flash, that same weary look as when he first saw her earlier. Good, let him feel cornered. Let him feel betrayed. I may have been under his thumb for a few months, but she has a decade of transgressions for him to answer for.

His gaze swivels between us, and he takes one step away from Zalya, angling himself to better see us both. Suddenly, Cliff is rising from where he was kneeling. Shahar must have released him to focus his energy on us.

The ravens continue their onslaught from the sky, slowly sending another wave down from above and thickening the smoke as they fly through its clouds. Shahar swats at each one as they come too close, but they give me a wide berth, circling around me instead, as if providing me a protective shield from the chaos around me.

Remembering that I now stand weaponless, I reach into the side holster of my bag and pull out the knife Zalya originally brought me—the cleaver Rowan imbued for me.

My final chance.

"Are you hurt?" I call out to Cliff, watching as he continues to slowly stand. Blood drips down his jaw from the magical gag, and his wrists are raw from the bindings, but he moves gingerly my way.

He's alive.

Shahar cleaved the lands in two, tearing me forevermore from my best friend. He sparked a Resistance that has killed innocents on both sides, ultimately leading to the death of Vincenzo. He used my time in mourning to manipulate me into leaving Blaine and joining him here, and to trick me into falling in love with him. All for what? How could a hopeless human like me possibly be that integral to the plans of Linea's heir?

The rest of the sky falls at once, and the wings of thousands of ravens swarm us. But not me. Still, the birds leave a few feet between themselves and me, even as I continue slow strides toward my target. They block my vision from anything outside of where I stand.

"August!" Zalya screams through the chaos, fear dripping from the word, from her tone.

Strong arms wrap around my middle from behind, and my breath rushes out of me as Cliff tries to tug me backward. "We will find another way, A, but first you have to live." His voice cracks, and with it, so does my heart. He keeps his arm around me as I spin to face him—both of us now together in a hazy orange dome created by an aura of ravens.

We. He said we.

His eyes ask silent questions I can't give him the answers to, pleading for me to go with him. His beard is stained red from the blood dripping from his skin where the magical gag wrapped around his head, singed straight through his hairline. His fingers shake, and I look down to see the raw burns and skin around his wrists from the bindings. His voice trembles with a level of fear I never could have dreamed he could possess.

I want to stay, I want to stay in his arms, and follow him to where he says its safe, and never leave… and I almost do, but there's still a friend in danger, and I cannot leave her.

I can't stand here forever, and words aren't going to change his mind right now. But I can make sure Cliff knows how I feel—where I stand. I wrap my arms around his neck, rising up on my toes to reach him, and when his mouth meets mine, I relay what I want to say in the tender brush of our lips. It's not a long kiss, or one of passion, but it's one that shows I heard him when he said *we*. A kiss that I hope says *I'm sorry*, and *thank you*, and a dozen other things I will say out loud after today—if there is an after today. A kiss that feels real.

He squeezes my waist once, before loosening his grip, and I know he understands.

I pull away and take a large step backward into the sea of ravens, mouthing the words "I'm sorry" as I watch his form get swallowed into the wings of my protectors.

"AUGUST!" Zalya's painful cry breaks through the wingbeats again.

I turn back around and storm forward, toward where I know Shahar stands, raising my blade, ready to strike again, allowing its imbued powers to radiate up the hilt and into my veins.

My other voice tells me it's time.

Now.

The birds scatter like a dandelion being blown apart in the wind, giving me a path to hurl my blade.

My cue.

I release the hilt and dive to the ground, narrowly missing my own knife flipping through the air back in my direction—but not the one I just released. The one I threw earlier—my cleaver.

Then, silence.

I raise my neck enough from the dirt to see Shahar lying on the ground, red soaking his white suit in steady streams from the middle of his core where the hilt of my blade stands tall, his pale hands shaking as he clutches it. The expanding river of blood across the seams of his suit takes me momentarily back to watching the spilled wine soak through my packages in Quinthold during my fight with Blaine, and I recognize something symbolic in the way that both of these events have coincided with my decisions to fight for myself.

"What. Kind of. Blade. Is this?" His fights for his final words, and they come in spurts, not unlike the continued gushes of his blood around my knife in his stomach. His eyes don't leave mine, widening with the first awareness of impending death, a version of terror I'm proud of instilling in him.

No longer covered by the blanket of ravens, the moonlight and stars shower us in an evening glow. The ravens have scattered in all directions, back to their homes and nests for the night, and I can hear the rest of the group rushing this way. Standing, I grab my cleaver from the ground a few feet behind me, and close the final gap between us.

"See. A blade is a powerful tool. One most people don't respect enough to deserve its grace." I pause a few feet away, kneeling where I know he can't quite reach me. "You probably would have killed me if this had been a dagger you had hurled at me," I muse, looking down at the cleaver he initially threw. "But kitchen blades differ from daggers. They're weighted and only angled sharp on one side, so if you're not trained in throwing one, it's bound to spin erratically from your grip. You'll miss your target every time with a misthrow like that."

A wet cough sputters blood out the corner of his mouth, a bit spraying across his chapped lips at me when he hisses, "Bitch," through labored breaths.

"You gave me that blade, you know." I nod at the hilt clutched in his dying grasp. At the blade Zalya gifted me the evening she offered me the job here in the palace. "A friend helped make it powerful, but it still feels right that I got to end you with a tool that brought me here."

A small whimper sounds from where Zalya kneels, wide-eyed, staring at Shahar's blood pooling at his sides. She looks up at me when I close the few feet between us, something close to relief hinting through her tired eyes. "He's really gone?" she asks apprehensively, as if jinxing reality by saying it out loud.

"He's gone," I confirm, collapsing to the ground next to her and wrapping my arms around her shivering frame, small sobs already coming out. "We're safe. He can't hurt us anymore."

But I barely get the words out before she stiffens in my hold, gasping a thick breath in.

"No!" she screams, kicking her legs under us in an attempt to propel us backward.

Pain sears through my core straight to my extremities before my whole body goes numb; white-hot lightning flashes through my vision.

Zalya frantically rotates us to the side, laying me on the ground. My head shifts to the side, and the last thing I see is Shahar, face down with his arm extended toward me as the others appear above me—Mia's face inches above mine while her eyes glow with her healing power.

Shahar may have used his dying breath to kill me, but my friends will live.

36

Rays of sun stream through the windows, warming the plentiful pillows at the head of my bed and stinging my tired eyes while I listen to the rhythmic snores from across the room, from a tiny chair under the far window.

I could never miss the familiar form, scrunched

uncomfortably into the chair—Cliff. His legs hang over the arm, and his head leans against the windowsill. White lines extend from the corners of his mouth, around his head, through his beard—scars given by the binds of Shahar's magic.

It wasn't a dream.

I'm hesitant to wake him, perhaps because I don't want to. I doubt my heart can return to the Cliff it knew before yesterday—or whenever that was. I'm not sure if I want to go back, if I'm capable of going back to a different Cliff. Even now, I gaze at his sleeping form, wondering what it would be like to curl into the chair with him.

But I'm also not positive I'll ever love another like that ever again.

My body aches from lack of movement, or possibly still-open wounds, so without moving any part but my neck, I orient myself to the space. Trees stand tall and plentiful through the windows, and if I'm seeing correctly, I'm on an upper floor. Light green paint covers the walls, and a fire burns in the corner. Only the four-poster bed, where I currently lie, breaks up the monotony of the room. Even the dresser, desk, and nightstand are simple and average sized, made of matching Leondite cherry.

We must be in the north.

I glance down at my side, remembering the pain from the stab through my core—how quickly the world went dark after. Remembering Zalya's frantic eyes as she watched Shahar lunge from his deathbed to stab me with his dying breath, breath we had shared, intertwined in each other, only hours before he attempted to kidnap me.

A light tap sounds on the door before it slowly swings open. Mia peeks her head in, and the sight of her has me forgetting everything else. I go to lean myself up on my elbow to talk, but collapse.

"Don't do that. You need to heal." She rushes to my side to place an additional pillow behind me, propping me up to a half-seated position.

I hold my finger to my lips before pointing to Cliff in the corner, but it's no use. The brute stirs to life at our conversation, and when he sees that I'm awake, he's out of his chair as quickly as his size allows him to be. "Never mind, too late," I comment when we make eye contact.

He's standing, but now frozen in place, like a scared animal, and I stare back, wishing I had thought about what I'd say before now.

Mia leans in, whispering, "He's refused to leave your side. Go easy on him. Four nights in that chair can't make for good sleep."

"I've been out for four days?" I ask louder, raspier, than I expected.

She frowns for a moment, wringing her hands in front of her. "We didn't have the ingredients here for a pain tonic, and I needed to heal you, so instead, Cliff gave you his sleeping powder during each healing session to help you manage." She looks back at Cliff with an expression that signals a plea for help, as if she hopes he'll verify her story.

Cliff gives her an exasperated look before plopping back down in the chair, bracing one arm on his knee while the other reaches to rub the back of his neck. "Dammit, Mia." His voice comes out in his usual growl, but I can tell he's also tired, and I wonder how long it's been since he's had anything to eat or drink.

"I just wanted to check on you and bring you some water," she says, resuming her fussing over me, lifting the blanket from my shoulder and shifting my shirt so that she can place her palm on my side. I watch as bits of red and blue lighten under her touch—relief coming with each second her hand remains there. I watch her eyes as she works, watch her signature healing glow, and I can't define what's different today, but something has changed about Mia.

Maybe we've all changed.

She grabs the pitcher of water from the desk and fills a glass, bringing it to me.

I look over to Cliff to offer the water. "Cliffy, need some?" I ask, hoping the use of his nickname will lighten the mood.

He doesn't look up from the floor, and Mia makes herself busy tidying up my nightstand, which has all of three items on it. I hand the cup to Mia and close my eyes when I'm done, attempting to hold back tears I can feel coming. I'm just not sure if the pain is physical or emotional.

"You'll rip your stitches. Just give him time," she whispers to me.

Cliff clears his throat, and Mia straightens, suddenly moving toward the door again, her voice trailing behind her. "You know, I just remembered that I said I'd help in the kitchen. August, you're very missed. Can't wait for you to be back on your feet."

"Mia, wait," I call before she can leave.

She pauses in the doorframe, turning back in my direction, eyes wide in anticipation of my need, ready to help with whatever I ask her.

"I'm sorry." I wipe the stray tear away before it can escape my eye.

She nods in understanding, her face falling with the gesture, while she closes the door behind her.

Cliff's eyes stare me down in my periphery, though I keep my head leaned back against the pillow, gaze focused on the ceiling. If I move my neck, the welling tears will fall.

Damn my emotions when my blood sugar is low. I need food.

"I—" he starts, but I cut him off.

"Where are we?" I ask, trying to keep my voice light, even through my wobbling lips, taking a deep breath through my nose to steady myself. *It's a lot harder to cry when you're breathing deeply,* Nova would always tell me.

He doesn't respond for several breaths, creating an unbearable silence as I imitate all the ways this conversation could wind up hurting me by the end—but then he says, "You're in Leondell, on Brennan's grounds."

"How did we get here? And if you tell me you used your sleeping powder again, I'll never forgive you." I grin in hopes that my joke brought some levity into the air and then finally muster the courage to turn his way.

"You don't remember?" His chin dips, eyes scrunching while he tries to read me.

"I remember—I remember you—"

Am I scared to speak to Cliff?

The man I kissed in the middle of battle. The man who carried me away, covered in my own blood and vomit after Rivian had spent hours attempting to destroy me. Am I scared to see if he has any intention of talking about it? Do I even want to talk about it with him? Is this just a delayed reaction to Stella's death? I try to bend my knees to curl in on myself, but the pain in my side shoots up my spine, and I cry out in agony.

The bed shifts with his weight, and his hand finds mine, resting on top of the blankets. And just when I think to say something, the door swings open, and in it this time is Blaine.

"Blaine?"

My hand goes cold. Cliff now stands several feet from the bed.

"I'll leave you two to catch up," Cliff stammers before scurrying out of my room.

That whole interaction was painful, I think to myself, wishing I hadn't woken up.

"Can I come in?" Blaine asks when I don't directly address him—my next emotional opponent for today.

"Since when do you ask?"

"It's been less than four months, August. This isn't our home that we've shared for ten years—I'm doing the best I can." His voice cracks, and the resignation in it cuts deep.

I nod to the chair by the desk, wincing through the pain of my stitches stretching. I don't feel like offering the space Cliff just abandoned to Blaine, the bed feeling too intimate for the conversation we're likely to have. "You were in Auralia."

"Yeah, well, Teliquis has always had a soft spot for you." Blaine wears a hopeful look on his face, and he grips the arms of the large chair that he easily moved to my side. "She'd love to see you, preferably not in the middle of battle. She really missed you."

I think of the dragon I've been on countless times before. "I miss her too."

"When I arrived and saw you"—he pauses, shaking his head—"I was terrified." Now he hangs it. "I had told myself to let you go, but I never did. It was the most scared I've been in my entire life. I couldn't think, I couldn't breathe. All I knew was that I needed to do whatever was possible to get to you."

I swallow the lump in my throat while I gaze toward his leg, where

I know he must have a wound still from Roddrerre.

"I should have never forced you to choose between us and the Resistance. If I hadn't pushed, you would have never left Quinthold, you, you would still be with me, you wouldn't have almost died." His voice breaks on the last line. "I snuck into the Advisory main office that day and overheard that there was an urgent matter in Auralia. Something to do with a woman named August." His hands interlock behind his neck as he struggles to get out the words.

"You continued sneaking around the Advisory?" I don't mean to sound so accusatory, to sound so blunt.

"I'm rambling, but I don't know what to do, what to say, how I can get you to come home to me again." His hands knot through his hair, and I'm sure he's going to rip some out. He reminds me of how I woke up to find him after the fire at The Goblet, that day feeling like a lifetime ago. "Please come home, give me another chance, give *us* another chance. We'll do it your way. We can do whatever you want. You know so much more, we can reform the Quinthold Resistance. We—"

"Blaine, I'm not going back to Quinthold."

Seeing him, hearing his voice, I realize that I never stopped loving him either. I've loved him for the past ten years, for saving me from Beryl's attack. I love that he loved me and supported my cooking, or the way he knew just what I needed after a stressful day. I love his cocky swagger and his ability to create a conversation with anyone. I love how driven to leadership he was in the Advisory. I love that he's here, because I would show up to save him too.

"I left Quinthold for more reasons than our breakup, Blaine." Fresh tears warm my cheeks, tears of closure, of the conversation

I refused to have that day back in Quinthold. "I loved you, and will always love you, but I needed more. I'm not twenty anymore, not the ambitious girl you met soaking wet in a port station. I was reckless taking this job, and yes, it nearly got me killed, but it validated all those years in the Resistance. I need to see this through. There are issues far bigger than we ever thought. Blaine, I've finally made friends."

"Like Cliff?" he asks quietly, staring down at his lap.

"Yes, like Cliff, but others too."

His palms fist, and he releases a held breath through flaring nostrils. I know this look. I've memorized them all. He's trying to hold back from yelling. "You had friends in Quinthold, you just didn't let them in. You know, Mel found me the night you left. She was so worried about you after the Resistance meeting that she wanted to work on finding you and ensuring you were safe. I went to the apartment. Our neighbor left a note that they missed you. They knew you had left, not because you said goodbye but because they could no longer smell your cooking. And did you know Verna passed away? Yeah, she gave me a jar of her best jam to give you when I went to the market last. She was saving it for you and didn't know why she hadn't seen you in weeks."

Every time I feel like I make a stride toward becoming a better person, I'm reminded how fucking selfish I've been along the way.

The pained weight of his words hits me harder than the look in his eyes ever could. "I'm sorry." It's all that I can offer. "I can't go back and love them better, but I can do right by those around me now."

"And what about doing right by those you left behind? You have people at home, in Quinthold. You can come home. Please just come home."

"I'm afraid that's not really an option," Brennan states from the doorway.

Another one?

I'm not sure how many more visitors I can take.

"She's a grown woman. She can come back to Quinthold if she wishes," Blaine says, standing up straight and assuming his general-in-the-Advisory demeanor.

Brave soul, standing up to a Sovereign Descendant, general or not.

"She can, to a certain extent. She carries a protection. She's proven her loyalty, we've all grown quite fond of her. However, you are now privy to information on our locations, our wars—" This is Sovereign Descendant Brennan. His voice takes me back to his commands in the vineyard.

"What do you mean? I'm on your side. I showed up to fight with you. Information or not, I've proven my loyalty," Blaine says, folding his arms across his chest.

"Yes, you've shown that you care for August, but you have yet to prove that you understand this war. Just how extensive it may get. I won't let you leave and return to Quinthold, to your Advisory position, though you are not my prisoner and will receive the same rights and privileges as anyone else in my home. The Advisory will know by now about your efforts in this battle. You'll be in grave danger. They'll either kill you immediately or torture you for information."

Blaine simply stares at Brennan, unblinking. He's not fighting the accusations, trying to compromise or find another way. He knows Brennan is right, that this could be a possibility all along. "The Advisory is the only reason humans have any semblance of safety in a world run by Fallen."

Shut up, Blaine.

Brennan takes another step into the room, head held high. "The Advisory has many purposes, but I can ensure you, the safety of humans is hardly one of them. You'll leave August to her rest now. I believe she's made her point clear, and continuing to cause her more stress will only delay her healing."

I watch Blaine nod in acceptance of defeat, before giving me one last solemn glance, laced with frustration, and leaving.

"Humans really are so fun to boss around," Brennan muses, giving me a wink—his demeanor quickly changing back to the carefree friend I know. "You need to sleep. Mia told me you shouldn't be out of bed yet. Would you like a small dose of the sleeping solution? I don't make it as strong as Cliff, but it should get you through tonight."

"I want to know what happened, see everyone, know what we're doing next. I want—" I pause.

Is it something that I want, or someone?

"Please," I beg, past caring if I sound pathetic.

Brennan gives me a sympathetic look, one that pisses me off. I don't need sympathy, I need answers. But he clears his throat while moving to pour a glass of water. He pulls a vial from his pocket and sprinkles a dash of powder into the glass, then passes it to me. "I'll only continue speaking if you drink this and promise to rest."

I gladly take the glass anyway, fatigue weighing behind my eyes.

He gives me the short version of events. "Shahar met his demise at your hands. Your blade, though, was enchanted, so his retaliatory stab, we were certain, was going to cost us your life as well as it was coated in his blood. Cliff carried you on Roddrerre, alongside Mia and Gaia. During the flight, Mia dedicated herself to reviving you, working without rest throughout the entire journey. And Teliquis was gracious enough to allow me to ride back with Blaine. Now rest, August. We'll still need you when you're healed."

Witches aren't born, they are made. Witches don't defend, they protect. Witches don't wait, they act.

—*The Tales of the Obsidian Witches* by Tresta McVey

The wooden floors of my room creak as I pad across them, slowly willing movement back into my sore muscles and stiff joints. A change of clothes waits for me on the desk across the room, and I gladly peel off the layers I've been wearing for Fallen knows how long. The thought of finding coffee and getting some fresh air sounds amazing, but I need to bathe first.

There's a bathing chamber connected to my room, so I tend to my needs and finger comb my hair as best I can, smoothing it down with a splash of water. My skin is wan, and I stare at my reflection for a long moment, trying to find myself in the glass. My freckles are dull, my hair is dry—I hardly recognize myself.

I suppose I should just be happy to be alive.

Starting with food seems like a good idea, so I leave my room and follow the hallway until I reach a grand staircase—voices come from somewhere down the stairs, and I use them to guide me to where I need to go.

Brennan's place is much smaller than the palace in Auralia. Natural wood flows from the floor to the walls, fireplaces are available around every corner for warmth, and a hint of pine tree hangs in the air. The rugs aren't as soft, instead thin and worn with age.

The closer I get, the more voices I detect. A couple I know—more that I don't. So I stand around the corner, trying to see if I should make myself known. Or avoid whatever is happening—sounds of disagreement echo around me.

"I don't care how many times I have to repeat myself, I don't agree with this plan." I would never miss Mia's direct voice, nor do I care to be on the other side of the table from her right now.

"You can repeat yourself until you run out of breath, my dear, but you aren't the only deciding vote in this room," says a deep woman's voice that I don't recognize.

"But I do seem to be the only one advocating for her and considering her in any decision we make," Mia responds. "Cliff, Brennan, care to pipe in?"

Are they talking about me?

"What I think Vega is trying to say here, is that we need to lay out some reasonable options for how to proceed and each of us cast our vote for whichever decision we feel is least detrimental to the group as a whole." A younger man's voice, another I don't recognize.

"And how are we to trust her, hmm? You're telling me that Auralia is in turmoil, Linea's Descent is upon us, the Advisory is moving in—all events that were triggered by her actions—and I'm just supposed to trust the opinions of a few descendants and blindly follow?" an elderly man's voice asks, and the room breaks out in a cacophony of response.

Okay, now I'm positive they're talking about me.

The sound of a fist pounds the table, making me jump even from the hall.

"You are in my home, and we will treat this quorum with the decorum my home deserves. August is staying"—Brennan answers the question still floating in my mind—"that is final. We need her on our side. And I would remind any of you still questioning the sequence of events to look back ten years, and then ten thousand more. August is not the cause of this war, but she might be the solution."

"What?" Impulse takes over, and I find myself standing in the entrance of a large room, staring toward an oval table in the center. About a dozen individuals are sitting at it, and they all now stare at me.

A woman with a shrill voice finally speaks up, gesturing toward me standing in the doorway—speaking about me as if I'm not here, or can't understand. "Well, is someone going to tell her to leave? She cannot be here. These meetings are confidential to the Guild."

"Why was the door left open if the meeting was so confidential?" I prod, over feeling as if those around me are making choices about me without my consent, flashbacks to Liravel streaming through my mind.

"If Cliff can be here, then there is no reason August shouldn't be here too." It's Mia who speaks up in my defense, before turning to me and rising from her chair. "Come, take this seat. I'll grab another."

No one says a word as I slowly enter the room, yet twelve sets of eyes watch as I make my way to the table and sit down in the seat where Mia once was. She already has a new chair a few spots down.

Cliff was seated next to Mia, and he leans over to whisper in my ear, "Welcome back."

I am back, I think to myself and nod in acknowledgment.

"Mia has a point, and since these are my grounds, August stays," Brennan announces from the head of the table.

"Mia has only been eligible to be in this room for a little over a week. She is hardly in a place to demand decisions that affect the entire Guild," a tall man says, his voice airy, with a touch of nonchalance. His pale skin almost glows in the torchlight's reflection, and he wears his billowing black coat even at the table.

Where in Celestera would he be from?

I try to wrack my brain to guess his province based on his appearance, but decide to ask instead, "Sorry, can someone let me know what the Guild is?"

"Well, since you're here anyway—" A thin woman with long black hair leans across the table toward me, her shimmering skin reminding me of someone that I can't quite place. "We are a collection of leaders from across the world of Aleidos." She gazes down the table of her peers, ensuring that no one else intends to step in and stop her from continuing. "And, regardless of fault, what happened in Liravel last week triggered the imminent return of Linea, an act this organization has sought to prevent for centuries."

I stare blankly at this woman as my mind tries to put the pieces together.

Aleidos?

"Sorry, I'm a little confused. Did you say Aleidos?"

"Yes, dear. The ground beneath your feet is much larger than Celestera, and unfortunately the descendants are about to learn the truth."

"So there are more lands than just Celestera?" My mind is spinning trying to take in all this information. I turn to Cliff, then Mia, hoping one of them will confirm or deny what I'm hearing, but no one stops the conversation now happening between me and— "Sorry, I just realized I don't have your name."

"You can call me Ceress," she says as she fingers a long golden chain with an obsidian charm hanging around her neck, giving me a devious smirk.

Acknowledgments

No one prepares a debut author for the feeling they will have when their book is finished—the overwhelming sense of accomplishment for the story just existing, regardless of sales or accolades from external sources. But I would be remiss not to acknowledgement and thank those who made this journey possible.

Nate… you cheered me on and never hesitated to bring up my book when I was too shy to talk about it myself. You made my coffee and refilled my wine. You even held me accountable when I was procrastinating my deadlines. But most of all you've loved me in the safest way I've ever known and reminded me that love doesn't have to be hard. I'm not sure what I did in a past life to earn a happily ever after with you, but I thank the goddesses that I did and leading me to you.

To ALL my friends… you made the Found Family trope the easiest subplot to ever write. Thank you for showing me every day what it means to love and support without bounds.

Britt… you may be responsible for this book altogether, your insistence that I pick up reading again and our book club nights renewed a love I forgot I had and took me back to a place of healing—I'll never be able to thank you enough.

Unhinged Belles… y'all are crazy—promise to never change. Our book exchange group entered my life at the best possible time and brought me the most incredible humans in each and every one of you. At the risk of needing to add additional trigger warnings to my book, I'll save the rest of my thoughts for our group chat.

My fellow Writer's Conservatory classmates from 2024… our critique circle and monthly writing feedback were instrumental in forming who I am as a writer and in helping me to mold and form this story and my craft. To you I send many thanks, my sincere gratitude, and the biggest IOU that could ever be granted. I look forward to the day that I have an entire bookshelf dedicated to our published works.

Feral and Turtle… you two were my biggest hype girls, super fans and internet megaphones. Even on the days that I didn't believe in myself, you did, and the praise, feedback, and energy never once went unnoticed.

To the artists who have spent hours drawing and illustrating my characters… you are the real MVP's. You've brought my characters to life and given them personality in a way that I never could with words. Seeing my characters on screen will forever be a cherished memory. May your coffee remain warm, and your pillows remain cool.

To my followers… Thank you for believing in me, following my journey, sharing my content, cheering me on, and engaging with me in any and every way. Your support has led more and more readers to find my work which is the ultimate win as an author.

And finally, to you, my readers… Thank you for being here, picking up my book, and giving this debut author a shot. I hope you enjoyed reading *Auras of the Fallen Stars* as much as I enjoyed writing it. Support like yours fills my soul with so much warmth, and I will never find words grand enough to express my gratitude, so for now I'm hoping these are enough. Thank you!

And Chris… get ready for that tattoo. Auras of the Fallen Stars will be a best seller before we know it.

ABOUT THE AUTHOR

Mara van Nacht spends her days dreaming up stories of dragons, secrets, and magical worlds, and her nights insisting that coffee and wine are food groups in their own right. An avid traveler at heart, Mara prefers to be in motion whenever possible, and has likely drafted more words on airplanes than in any office or café.

When she isn't writing, she can usually be found with her husband and two cats, caught up in a board game at a local trivia night, or yelling at the TV during a sporting event—anything competitive tends to win over her heart.

Auras of the Fallen Stars is her debut novel, though she's eager to share all the tales her inner child dreams in her free time.